DOwN iN ONe

Simon Breen

First published in 2000
by REVIEW

An imprint of Headline Book Publishing

10 9 8 7 6 5 4 3 2 1

ISBN 0 7472 6446 5

Typeset by Palimpsest Book Production Limited,
Polmont, Stirlingshire

Printed and bound in Great Britain by
Clays Ltd, St Ives plc.

HEADLINE BOOK PUBLISHING
A division of Hodder Headline
338 Euston Road
London NW1 3BH

www.reviewbooks.co.uk
www.hodderheadline.com

for eve

'Nobody told me there'd be days like these, strange days indeed.'

John Lennon

GREEN

'My dog ran into a parked car.' I started sincere.

'It didn't.'

'No, it did.'

'Well, if you say so.'

'Of course,' I smiled. 'It's not as simple as that.'

'Why don't you tell me all about it?'

Her mill-town accent kissed me on the ear. She really was very pretty, and her name was Janis and she seemed lost and left alone in a corner.

'I was eleven,' I continued. 'Dog's name was Amber.'

'Foreign?' she asked.

'No, female.'

But I could tell by the lack of light in her eyes that it was only early. Janis was young enough to learn, pretty enough to last, northern on a Friday. I stood my ground.

'Babe, it's a colour.' Made my point. 'You know, like traffic lights. Between red and green there's amber, the halfway place, limbo land, not here, not quite there yet, imperfect amber in the middle of nowhere.'

'You mean orange,' she frowned.

'Christ, you're right, I should've called my dog Orange, that would've been a much better name for a dog. Orange didn't stop or go, she just stayed in between.'

'You're not actually making any sense.'

'You want to know what happened to my dog or not?' I snapped.

3

'Yes.' Her browline creased a smile. 'I would love to hear about your dog.'

She wasn't even twenty. I was twenty-seven. Thinking about teenagers. Talking about dead dogs. All right for a Friday night.

'It was a normal day, I took Amber for a walk in the park.'

Bumpy grass landscaped around an old people's home. By day it was full of toddlers gone ancient and their do-nothing dogs. I pictured Councillor Duxbury flatten his cap, fuck a whippet behind a bush.

'The park,' Janis prompted.

'They put plays on there in the summer time,' I told her.

'Interesting.'

'They always get rained off.'

'Shame,' she levelled.

'Maybe.' I reached for a smoke.

'But,' Janis frowned, 'why did it happen?'

'Well, I think it had to do with the inherent naivety of the Arts Council's summer-season plan, plus the general lack of effective climate control in the north of England.'

'Amber?'

'Outside, in the open, asking for trouble.'

'Your dog?'

'They should've built a bubble.'

'Why did Amber run into a parked car?'

'She was tied to the chicken.'

'I'm serious.' Pretty girl, bad choice of bottled beer, wide mouth, loads of make-up, focus. 'What happened to your dog?' she asked. 'What happened to Amber?'

I'm tweezed if I didn't ask the same thing as I ran towards my downsized twitch of a dog, breathing its last on the dusky road home. 'Amber! What the fuck just happened to you? You're a smart, personable dog with a pleasing canine demeanour. Why the fuck did you run into a parked car?'

'Amber died chasing a bouncing ball,' I told her.

'But you said—'

'I'd let her off the lead.'

'You shouldn't have done that.'

I wasn't about to explain that I grew up in a ghost town where dogs without leads were as common as goals without nets, bikers without bikes and dogs without leads.

'Tell me,' Janis hissed.

'Amber set off after that ball at top speed,' I explained. 'She chased its mad, bouncy path faster and faster. She actually outran the fucking ball, went right past it. I was having a giggle till I clocked that Amber was heading straight for this parked car.'

'No!'

'I shouted her name, but it was no good, pup didn't respond, badly trained, y'see. In-between Amber charged right into the back bumper of some bastard's second-hand Sierra. At full fucking pelt.' My eyes went wide. 'My dog went WHACK!'

'Christ!' Janis gasped.

'Exactly!'

'But why?'

'Excitement, happiness, the pump in the blood.' Checked to see if Janis knew what I was on about, probably not, so what. 'The doggy thrill of the chase, it made Amber's brain go pop!' Janis flinched. Thought I might want to watch Janis flinch again, maybe later. 'Amber got hit from the grassy knoll of dog consciousness with the canine magic bullet.' I raised the volume, laughing. 'Don't turn left in Dallas, dear doggy!'

I turned my girl into a corner.

'Amber wanted that ball too much,' I rolled along. 'She was mad for its bouncy bounce. She got caught in the animal magic of the moment. All that instant sheer desire, it made her brain explode!'

'*Animal Magic*?'

'Look,' I carried on regardless, 'Amber went off after that ball in the full bloom of youth and four-legged joy, but somewhere along the way something went wrong. Somewhere in the madness of pursuit, somewhere in the brilliant moment of switched-on excitement, somewhere between her fucking ears, my unfortunate pooch suffered an enormous, instantaneous, freak brain haemorrhage.'

'No!' Ringed finger hit full lip.

'And the first effect on Amber – can you guess?'

'Tell me!'

'Sudden and complete blindness,' I announced.

Janis's mouth hung open. Her fingernail touched her tongue. Saucy. I felt a sudden desire to change the subject. The dead dog routine had gone too far. It'd strayed beyond touching, was on the way to disturbing. It was time to lighten the tone, brighten it up, hit a more appropriate mode. Almost anything would do. Young love, the pop charts, the mundane career choices of her parents, the price of fish fingers, Johnny Moore's penguin impressions, floral bra straps, frogspawn, basically anything, just not more morbid canine drawl. I dropped my fag to the floor, stamped it out.

'Vet said the dog was dead before she even hit the car,' I told her.

'Vet?'

'Dead dog running!' There was no vet. 'Show me the fucking film rights!'

Janis flinched. I didn't like it this time. I quick-flicked internal channels to find a course of action that might make things better. Not too sure, I reached out my hand and touched the girl for the first time in my long, her short, life. Squeezing the small fabric shoulder, I came up with an idea and I asked an easy question.

'Is that blue eyeshadow?'

'Yes', she fluttered. 'Do you like it?'

But I knew it wouldn't work. It wasn't the eyeshadow, it was her, no, it was me, well, it was us, no, it was the world we lived in, nothing more.

'It matches your eyes,' I said, flat.

I was trying, but my mind was absent elsewhere. It fumbled a familiar partnership with my hand in a search of a back pocket. It shunned eyeshadow, blue or otherwise, in favour of finding a good reason to go on. It prioritised. But it didn't work. I couldn't fucking find it. I breathed sharp, hit another pocket. The close edge of panic crawled across the pub's cluttered floor. Must've left it in my coat. Where was my coat?

'It's not actually blue,' Janis said. 'The proper shop name is "Magenta Pearl".'

I stepped around and reached behind Janis, came up with my crumple from the corner. Hit the parka's inside pockets. Result. I'd got my fingers on one, two, three and a half, fantastic reasons to go for ever on. I sensed the girl's attention when it leant in.

'Charlie, or just whiz?' Miss Magenta Pearl herself asked.

'The word is cocaine,' I snapped back.

'Sssshhh!' finger and lip, too much.

'Why can't you just say cocaine?' I lifted. 'The proper shop name is COCAINE!'

Swift faces turned to sniff the traces of their favourite word. It might've got nasty, obvious, almost unseemly, but I was on my way and moving fast. Forever a step ahead of sad attention, I cut through the bar's swing doors, heading for the toilets. The cool air of the corridor caught me, held me, helped me out.

Breathing deep, I tried not to get upset. I told myself that

Janis couldn't possibly know the significance of Charlie. It wasn't intentional on her part, it had to be circumstantial. I blanked Charlie Charles's dangerous face from my mind. It had been unfortunate, but understandable. I removed his repeated threats from my ear. I managed to remain calm. I booted the bog's heavy door. It didn't budge. I flicked the door handle, smiled, walked in.

I love toilets. When I was young and still ambitious, I badly wanted to be a toilet attendant. My uncle used to clean public conveniences in Blackpool and, though I listened to my family bad-mouth him for his chosen lot in life, I would still sit on Uncle Jack's fragrant lap and listen to his tall tales from the night shift. Uncle Jack once took me to see this *Carry On* film where a toilet attendant got horribly murdered in a head-down-the-toilet incident. And, while all around me the cinema audience laughed, all I could think of was Jack and his proud mop, mop, mop. I don't go to the cinema these days. I go to the toilet all the time.

The door closed hard behind me. The well-lit collection of amenities was bright, clean and free. I passed by the lengthy wall mirror and turned a sharp squeak into my favourite cubicle. It was closest to the far wall and furthest from the door. Perfect for my purposes. More than merely convenient. Happier, I bubbled down a breath of lemon-fresh and slid the lock into its time-worn slot.

The lock. I love the lock. It's the mechanical reason for all the extra time spent in the stall. The lock, to a secretive lad, is the answer to many silent prayers. And the toilet, the public lavatory, is the only room in our common experience with a lock on every door. Locks. Toilets and locks. Locks all over the place. All different kinds of lovely locks. Even locks that let the outside world know that the lock is, in fact, locked. I love the authority of it. Privacy in public. A secure stall, where the world can just fuck off and wait for a while. Champion.

'Fuck!' I said to myself, but anyone could've heard.

My hand was in my pocket, but there was nothing in my hand. So many pockets, so little patience. Why are there matching pairs of pockets on almost every item of clothing? Desperation for symmetry, perhaps? The need for balance in an unbalanced world? Bilateral. An obsession with all things functional? Whatever the weather, I recently threw out any shirt with more than one pocket.

The struggle goes on.

I located the cause of my search and got down to business. It was early yet, so my fingers were accurate, my nails precise, gums fresh, nose and throat clear, brain focused. And it went something like: unwrap, whack, lick, rub, whack, swallow, snort, whack, lick, whack, whack, swallow and one more whack. Whites went whiter, almost blue. The little bit left looked lonely, so I whacked that back as well. I fumbled for the toilet seat and crouched down as my stomach, my head and everything in between turned absolutely inside out.

'Calm down, son.'

The voice was distorted and deep like an echo without origin. It might've come from the other side of the door, it might've not. It sounded like me, but different. Not that, not now, please, not now. I stared fierce eyes at the shifting floor, slapped a hand over my mouth, tried not to vomit, bleed or scream.

'You all right in there, lad?'

'No, I'm not!' I cried.

'Let's have a look at you.'

'Fuck off!'

Involuntary knee-jerk lifted. I slammed a steel-capped and -backed boot into my side of the divide. The defensive snap made my body slide back, my face, face up. I sucked down a gulp of empty air. My eyes scrambled to find a focal point.

Dog-claw noise scratched the outside of the stall door. A familiar face appeared, creening over the cubicle wall.

'Not now, Dad,' I begged. 'Please, not now.'

'You eating right, son?'

'Fuck off!'

'That girl out there,' he nodded. 'She's a bit on the young side, no?'

He was always turning up. His favourite place to appear was in the broken bathroom mirror. He'd start up in the black of a fixed stare, then spread through my face. I'd try smiling at him. The sort of smile that said 'fuck off and leave me alone', with a hint of 'please' thrown in. It rarely did any good. His worn out features would extend into my practice wrinkles. My just-started shadows would darken with real age. Before it got worse, before the agonies of wasted years had my hair out, I'd pull away from the reflection and pray it didn't have the strength to follow me. Sometimes it did; this time it had. All the way to the pub. All the way to the toilet.

'You're not looking your best, son.'

'I've taken too much,' I head-down dribbled.

'Could do with smartening yourself up a bit,' he chipped.

The air tasted half-breathed already. I fully inhaled, let the exhale happen. My heart hurt. My head went down. Stray dribble on the tiles caught my eye, set me off. My guts wrenched. A thick mix of muck spewed on to the tiled expanse of floor. The sheen on the surface was reflective. I watched my face appear and disappear in the details of my father's face. Too much, too early, too young, too much. A follow-up bolt from the deep sprayed my father's face away. I took my chance, triple-blinked, neck-wrenched, banged my hands over my eyes, tried to talk myself out of it.

'Steady.' Spittle dripped. 'Steady now.'

The outer door to the toilets swung open. I snapped my eyes wide, checked up and under the door. Clocked that it was someone coming in, not no one going out. The ankle-owner coughed, spluttered and wore socks like a student, so I calmed it. Breathing easier, I lit up a ciggy and sighed. Dad always came when I was unsure, overdosed or just not ready. Perhaps a pattern was developing, but I'd have had to step back to see it proper and there was no time. It was Friday night, after all. Possessions repacked, I covered an ocean of puke with a mountain range of bog roll and fast flicked the lock.

Southern Excuse was over in the corner having a piss. He avoided my eyes, which was fine, probably wise. I twisted on the hot tap, only the hot, and had myself a splash. It could've burnt, but felt fine to me. My eyes tracked busy aqua patterns in the basin below. I superimposed some scenery purely to pass the time. A country lane opened and I could see corners, coffins and traffic lights, all liquid in the ripples. The sink turned slow motion and orange. I was neither here nor there. I was somewhere in between.

The ball gathered speed.

Hot water fell from my face. The scald felt good. I gripped the thick part of my hair and tugged myself into a smile. Drips in the sink sank down the plughole, scenery and memory went the same way. Felt I had the power to make tides change. Maybe I could conjure the rise of friendly moons. It was definitely too early for torture, and anyway I was too buzzed to care. The water dried on my face, I headed out the door.

Growling in the echoes, gritting my teeth.

The place had become more popular since I'd left; it did that. I looked around, but couldn't see her anywhere. Recalled her expression when I left. Shrugged. Looked around again. The place was horrible busy. I put weight on a person in my path.

'What day is it?' I asked no one in particular.

'Friday,' no one in particular replied.

'Of course,' I laughed. 'Of course it is.'

It was Friday. The overcrowding suddenly made sense. Everyone in the northern hemisphere fancied a pint on a Friday night. The bar had got darker, it did that too. The dimmer switch had been turned up, or was it down? Either way, it was too dark, and it had become almost impossible to place the vague shapes of the dim, swilling and yakking, yakking and swilling. I bobbed and craned for what it was worth, but Janis was a goner. My Magenta Pearl girl had vamoosed. The only comfort I could think of was to cut through the crowd and towards the bar itself. I needed a drink and a mate to go with it.

Stepping into the harsh wash of overhead light, I saw her smile a nod in my direction. She signalled that she'd just have a spit in some stupid cow's spritzer and then come right over. Fucking priceless. I loved our Mags.

Me and Maggie lived together, but not like that. She was like the fast, floating glamour to my deep, shifting dirt. Maggie made up for a lot of the gaps I left empty. She held down a job behind the bar. She cooked macaroni cheese at least three times a week. She poured a good pint. She kept her room clean. She didn't charge me for booze. She was from Birkenhead. She laughed at my jokes. She loaded the spliffs. She rarely walked away. She smiled when I screamed. She, Maggie that is, was my best mate.

'Oi!' I whispered in a really loud voice.

'What?' Mags yelled back.

'The girl I was talking to before, I can't find her.'

'She was gorgeous,' she pouted. 'I was jealous, I killed her, ate her tasty body.'

'Uncanny,' I sniffed.

'Maybe you left her in the toilet with your brain.'

'I don't think so.'

'But you're not sure,' Mags razored. 'It's possible, right?'

Across the way some plain punter wanted serving. Maggie

half checked him, frowned, looked back at me. And my mad eyes.

'Well,' I shrugged, 'I'm sure she'll turn up.'

'You might be right,' Mags grinned. 'She's a fucker to digest.'

'Oi! Service!'

Cunt from before cut in on our chat with a crispy tenner in his outstretched hand. Maggie pouted, sort of naughty-posed, winked for the general effect and reached out for the money. I decided to breathe, shrug and have a cigarette. Managed the lot, no bother.

Feeling a bit stranded beside the bar, I flashed a glance about. My attention skated visible skin, bad teeth, severe haircuts, fag brands. I got a light in my eyes, realised the danger, decided to play it safe. Settled my stare on a fella in the bouncer spot next to the rear door. Couldn't fathom how a small, fat old man was supposed to provide worthwhile security in a busy place like this. I mean, it almost made me want to give him a smack to find out his self-defence secrets. Poor robot really was sort of frail-looking, he had glasses on, for fuck sake. Even looked like he'd brought his ancient missus along for back-up. Crinkle-cut Bonnie and Clyde kept flitting watery eyes in my direction. They looked nervous. They looked sick. On top of that, I scoped that old blind-as-a-batman had come on duty without his uniform, or his bouncer-issue walkie-talkie. All in all, it didn't look right.

'Billy!' Mags tapped my back. 'What're you staring at?'

'That new bouncer,' I shook my head. 'Haven't seen him before.'

'You feeling all right, babe?'

'I feel myself,' I muttered absently, no smile.

'Isn't this all a bit much for you?' Maggie's eyes did a circuit of the fizzy crowd, settled softly on mine. 'You've been in that bathtub all week, you should take it easy.'

'Maybe you're right.' I scratched my jaw. 'It's on the busy side.' We both knew that I hated crowded pubs. Popular places over-packed with unpopular people. I smiled across at the paused scouser behind the bar. 'Think I'll get myself down the road.'

'Will I see you later?' she asked.

'Yeah, I'll be there, don't fuss.'

We both knew where and when and all that. It was Friday night, after all. The bath hadn't completely blown my world apart. I'd solo a few frames of the old time-killer while she finished her shift. I'd pot around in peace, she'd change at home, we'd reconvene at the Haç, where the real nonsense kicked off. I usually beat her down, she almost always beat me back.

'Take care,' I said.

'Precautions.' Maggie winked back, then turned away from me to face the drunks, the shite and the misplaced anglepoise that got her in the eye every time she poured a sweet cider. We'd said our goodbyes, but I held on for a second just to watch her. Poor love. Two more hours of a heavy shift to play for the greatest actress of her generation, and her current audience clearly didn't give a fuck.

Stepping away, I caught sight of Maggie's blonde reflection in black glass. The bar faced a vast, uninterrupted window. It was almost a mirror at night. The staff were forced to watch themselves serve. Plus, the pub was on the town's busiest bus route. Kiddies and biddies rumbled by in low gear, beadying down at the overstuffed fish tank. Our Mags didn't like to be looked down on.

When it rained on Oxford Road, Maggie Shipley's reflection slid and dripped with the eyes and the heads and the rain and the night and the in-between orange of the non-stop buses.

On the move.

Past the noticeboard and the subsidised smiles. The post-card and alternative magazine shop had closed down for the night. A pretty girl waited for her boyfriend on the steps of the cinema across the street. She'd got herself a load of *Big Issues* and was selling them to pass the time.

'Get the *Big Issue*!' she shouted, pure Geordie.

'Got one!' I lied.

'All right, love.'

'Take care.'

'You 'n' all,' she waved.

It was raining, but the snooker hall was only down the road and I wasn't bothered. It wasn't like I hadn't walked this way a million times before. Pub to snooker hall, snooker hall to pub. It all made sense. The rain was nothing new. The right mix in my blood.

Hot-dog-and-curry-sauce stand smelt set up for the late-night short skirts and tight-trousered troubadours that'd descend upon it soon enough. 'D'ya fancy fried onions on your disaster of a night, darling?' 'No way, pal, they make m' breath stink, and I'm up for a shag.' Greasy vendor chanced me a nod, but there was no way.

It wasn't sentimental TV soaps with chimney pots. There were no ginger kittens curled to sleep on sunny rooftops. Most of the corner shops had closed down. Nobody knew or even cared about anyone else's business. The theme tune was more fierce than it was ever friendly. So many things it wasn't, but it was Manchester. And it was Friday. And I thanked the northern lord for giving me my Rainbow Snooker Room.

I arrived at the pick-up-and-pay-for-it counter before I was completely sure that I'd left the bar. Took a quick flash about to get my bearings. The entire enterprise was built on an Indian takeaway's ancient burial ground. The atmosphere was loaded with disgrace.

'Is Charlie in tonight?' I asked late-shift Alf.

'No, it's quiet, Billy,' he creaked back. 'I reckon Charlie'll be off out somewhere, he's more of a day player, mucks about a bit at night 'n' all, if you catch my drift, God knows where with that one, got a nice forty-seven last week, you looking for him?'

'No, I'm not.' Late-shift Alf was unbearable.

And more to the point, he was wrong. It was the other way round. Charlie was looking for me. He'd been turning up in all my favourite places. Lucky no one told him about the bath-tub, or he'd have ruined that for me 'n' all. So, I'd avoided him this far. But the week was easy. I couldn't stay in the bathroom for the weekend, that'd be shameful. It was only a matter of time. Charlie'd said it was a matter of life and death, but that was typical nonsense, and the spastic had to find me first. And for now, at least, I was safely underground.

'Just flash my table light if he comes in,' I told Alf.

'Where'll you be?' he asked.

'Sixteen,' I said.

'It's like that, is it?' came back Alfie. Table sixteen was over in the corner, as far from the front entrance as you could get and bang on for the fire exit. It was a table with a reputation.

'Ask no questions,' I muttered.

'Well, you just look after yourself,' he doddered. 'You're liked round here.'

'Nice one, Alf. I'll watch me. You watch the door.' Point.

'Be still, lad,' he winked. 'Enjoy your game. I'll be here.'

Alf was playing a blinder, but a bit of consideration was what I'd come to expect. After all, I kept the owner and his straggle in cheap sweeties on a full-time basis. Served up the goodies at his all-night meets. Kept the competition lively, that did. It was always hard to tell who was winning and who was getting stuck, there were that many breakdowns. So, up till last week and my lay-off in the soapsuds, I reckon I'd make it down the Rainbow most days. Potting a few, sipping a few in the slow afternoons. I'd always keep half an eye on the comings and goings, helped out where needed and all that. Put simple, the Rainbow was part of my turf. I wouldn't go asking for favours in Moss Side, and Charlie wouldn't get any round here.

I stepped away from the counter light into the dark.

I loved this part the best. The walk in the stale-smelling dark towards the table light, my solitary light. The place was a tomb and table sixteen was the only glow. I felt myself in a safe place with something to do. It took some time to walk the distance and, by the time I arrived, the outside world and its pressing complications were a faded memory.

The ceiling of the Rainbow was low. My pool of light held a green altar to the darkness all around it. If Charlie came calling now he would be faced by my sanctuary. Plus, he'd have to duck his head to avoid an angled cue, or dodge for cover beneath a shower of multicoloured ivory projectiles. And the last resort, one Alfie light-flash and I'd be gone through the fire exit. All in all, back there amid the silent dark, I'd found myself some small peace.

Tilted the tray and let the balls roll. Their hollow tap-tapping sound was as familiar to me as the emptiness interrupted. A random pattern registered. I began a cueless move around the table's perimeter, placing the balls on their ancient spots. And this was how it started. Everything in its proper place. The horses in the gate. The feet behind the line. The racers in their blocks. Always the pause before action. A moment of contemplation before activity. A set of rules dictated by years of tired wisdom, practised by generations of tired conformists.

So be it.

I took the time to take a long sniff, with purpose, and slammed the blue into the bottom left. Had perfect position on the black, the reds remained huddled and dull. Palmed and replaced the five-ball, potted the black. I nodded appreciation at the invisible crowd, found my pitch, started to play.

Snooker, pool, billiards and that one with the funny mushrooms in ye olde English taverns, they're all friends of mine. Once you've worked out the principle the process becomes easy. And the principle is, wait for it, pot the ball. Safety, positioning and hair dye might matter on TV, but I spy no cameras. Keep it simple, stupid, put the ball in the hole, don't miss, don't fuck up. Steady the nerves with speedy powder and make the blues straight. I don't lose. I never lose. And why should I? I've hit more snooker balls than I've smoked cigarettes and I never miss my mouth.

I was on forty-eight. Played a nice sequence of pinks, couple of low balls, even threw in a few reds to keep the tradition alive. While colours came back, reds always stayed dead. I think that was part of their attraction. I was on forty-eight, still had eleven one-balls to play with, was sweet on the brown, looking good for a ton. The lights flashed on two tables to my left.

I almost fell over. Didn't. Craned round quick to check the counter. Nothing had changed. Late Shift was out of sight, probably at the bar. I triple-checked the door, matched it with my memory, decided that no one had come in, calmed down a bit. It was possible that a couple of regulars had come down from the taxi office upstairs. The two enterprises benefited from the same customers and a back door into each other's business. I satisfied myself that Charlie wouldn't know this, and that all I had to worry about was a couple of fat old cabbies buying beer and blowing a few frames. But why had Alf put them so close? Cabbies were committed shit-chatters, and it was common knowledge that I didn't like distractions. Irritated, but not bothered, I looked back at the waiting shot.

Words came out of the balls.

'Had this right cracker in the back today,' crowed the cue ball.

'When you say *had*?' manked back the brown.

A red said something pointless, I giggled a bit and stumbled back to where I'd left three cigarettes burning, one drink waiting, had a bit of both – or was it all four?

My mind was off the game. A week, a day, an hour, or maybe just a few minutes passed. The boys at the bar still hadn't made their unpopular appearance. From where I sat, the snooker table looked like a majestic bed with planets strewn across it. I blinked and it was a snooker table again. Shame. But so what, the whisky didn't stop swallowing, cigarettes were easy any time and what about the drugs? What *about* the drugs? Feeling keen, I eased out and unfolded a fully bulged wrap. It was of the dab-dab variety, so I did that for a while. Took to putting it on my thumb and sucking off the fizzy comfort.

Two men walked through the dark.

I didn't like this. The pair didn't look like cabbies on the slide. I whacked back what was left of the wrap, snapped up to see the lopsided and painful approach of my dad. He appeared to have been beaten up, or maybe it was just my eyes. I flicked my focus to the wide silhouette of a big fella coming along behind. It could only be my grandad Joe. His huge presence was bent in shadow, but I knew Joe Brady whenever I saw him. It didn't make sense. Grandad and Dad had played snooker when I was a child, but in Belfast, not Manchester. Plus, they weren't members. Plus, they were dead.

My grandad Brady stepped from luminous dark into harsh electric light.

The enormous ancient appeared to be pale green and bleeding bright orange from a wound on his head. I lost sight of my father, the Rainbow, the lot. Almost lost my guts 'n' all, but held on tight.

'Fucking hell, Grandad,' I winced. 'You look terrible.'

'Watch that mouth,' he growled.

'But Christ, Grandad,' I shook my head. 'You're a mess.'

'The Lord is with me,' he replied. 'I care not for appearances and watch your blasphemy.'

'Funny,' I levelled.

We were twenty feet, two generations and one cemetery apart, but we breathed together like grandfather and grandson. The pictures went soft, my eyes spazzed. I put my head down, said a soft prayer.

Inside myself.

Grandad Joe made me feel closer to God. Whenever I saw him, it always helped me to believe in an Almighty, but essentially merciful, motherfucker. Fear begets prayer, prayer begets boredom, boredom begets despair, despair begets belief, belief begets a void, a void begets God. It all started with the fear. Old Joe begot an enormous amount of fear in me. The head case had killed people.

Joe didn't turn up as often as my dad, but his timing was better. He would save his visits for special occasions. The word had clearly got round. Maybe the old fella just knew when I needed them the least, or the most.

Joseph Patrick Brady had killed for me. He killed Germans, then turned round and killed English with equal measure. He'd aided fat Winston with his Nazi problem, then told Jack

Flag to go 'n' fuck himself from a nasty hole in Belfast's Falls Road. The forties, inevitably, became the seventies and all my grandad did was change sides with the times. All he ever claimed was that he fought on the side of himself and his own. From the poorest streets of two islands, Joe smelt a fight and jumped up to get the first punch in. Not that my grandad was a man who chased troubles – he was far happier on peaceful grounds, but once he'd found them and grown attached, he wouldn't give up without a good fight. And, more than all that, Grandad Joe had personally told me that he'd done it all to protect the life of his grandchild, his only grandchild, me.

Joseph Patrick Brady had rumbled with the voice of a mountain trapped inside a man. He died in West Belfast in 1976. Head blown off by a British soldier. But he was back now, and his only grandchild was trying really hard to be pleased to see him.

The tricoloured ghoul of my long-gone grandad stepped into the light.

'Jesus fucking Christ,' I couldn't help shouting. 'This is mad!'

'Jesus had no middle name,' Grandad scorned.

'So what does the "H" stand for?' I reached for my drink, swallowed it whole.

'Billy, you know that I will always be there for you,' he whispered.

Nowt good to say, say nowt, smoke.

'In a manner of speaking, I'm inside you.'

Jesus Christ, but he was a big fella, my grandad Joe. Stood this close, I could see the me that had come out of him. Not like with my dad. Joe didn't sneak in through the blacks of my whacked-out eyes. He strode in large, with a weight of purpose and style that suited us both.

'I've killed for you, Billy.'

'I know that, Grandad.'

'Murdered!' His fury rolled off the ceiling, the floor, the walls, and it converged in my heart. His body arched back. The dramatic motion cast light on to the side of his head. Except it wasn't there.

I looked at the big, painful shape, the great man, before me. I saw Kurtz, I saw Bull, I saw the final cut, I saw the ball roll and my hand shake as ash dropped to the carpet and vanished. Joe lowered his head. He stepped in. Everything about him felt so much closer.

'I'd kill for you again, Billy Brady.' His deep voice thumped the air unconscious.

'I know that, Grandad.'

'But you might have to do it yourself this time.'

And I laughed, despite it all. I spluttered naughty-child-in-church giggles and let my face drop down. My blunt fingers dug deep into the soft pulp of my eye sockets. I couldn't look any more. It was only Grandad, only me, only early. But it made no difference. Even in the privacy of my own darkness, I saw the grand man. He was in pain and everywhere around me. I started to weep. I saw my grandad. Heard him, too.

'Never miss the chance to get the first punch in.'

I wept in the beer fumes of Friday night.

'Mind what I say and love your mother.'

Without opening my eyes, I saw him reach out for me. Thought Joe was aiming to lay an epic hand on my destiny-laden shoulder, but shifting focus I saw a brand-new fifty-pound note in his outstretched fist. I snapped forward in my seat, toppled the ashtray, spilt my drink, opened my eyes. The man and his fifty were gone.

Typical.

I slumped back in my seat. I smelt the whisky in my memory and wiped the tears from my face. I decided that it was a good fucking time to leave table sixteen and its dodgy reputation behind. There were much better places to be on a Friday night than the darkest corner of the Rainbow Snooker Room. Charlie could take his chances.

I was more than ready to take mine.

SATURDAY 12.37AM

Halfway there and halfway back, I beamed into the sonic and flash of the arcade games that lined the far wall of the Rainbow. They were the only sound in the place, and the strongest source of light. Nobody was on hand for the machines to defeat, but the flat line of electricity would play with itself all night, regardless. The constant demo mode looped over and over. I dropped into a velvet seat and lit up a smoke. A Galaxian fighter squad swept in a diagonal attack formation. I watched as their bombs hit the target. Nobody was destroyed. Nobody cared. The Galaxians never learnt not to fight. Sort of reminded me of a dead relative I knew.

The steady rhythm of the machine's meaningless repetition helped make my thoughts mundane. I wondered if I might, one day, embrace a routine, take an interest, become an enthusiast, get a job, grow up. Maybe, I smiled, maybe I could be an entire football team for unrealistic three-minute matches. Or I could fly stealth bomber missions over Middle Eastern war zones. Better still, I might clean up with Mrs Pacman on my arm, or be a maverick bounty hunter, blasting the shit out of anything that moved. I wasn't sure what else these games had prepared me for. Office work, perhaps.

I looked away from the games. My mind dragged like a razor back over the days.

It had all started simply enough. With an idea. An idea to make us rich, and Manchester as mental as fuck.

Manchester. The streets hummed. The bars and clubs were built brick by high-speed brick. All around our dreary pint walk, the attention of a nation and the night-time twist of furious life exploded on wet streets. Public toilets, car parks, abandoned factories, phone boxes, pubs and clubs became standing-room-only meccas for the slick mechanics of a new and improved generation. The demand spewed suppliers, and we were the sickest of them all.

Martin, Mark and me came on stage on time, we knew our lines were appropriately attired, we looked good in the light, never missed a beat and we never, ever blew a deal. We'd been in business for almost three years. Started out with the small stuff, worked our way up the old monkey ladder. The game had recently got significantly richer. A couple of car-loads to Coventry had got us wadded and instantly ambitious. We decided to pursue a monopoly. Not on customers – we would've been dead inside a week – but on a product.

It had all started with an idea, my idea.

I came up with a concoction called the Traffic Light. It was to be the smartest drug of all. It combined the finest flavours available. It guaranteed full satisfaction in one easy swallow. The almighty chemical cocktail, the unbeatable Traffic Light, totally my idea.

The Traffic Light. One powder trowel of purest MDMA, two of pink champagne, half a Strawberry tab, one drop of Clarity, cover with half a crumbled dove, add a powdered quarter of an industrial-strength valium, place inside a capsule, half orange, half green, take it outside, charge ten quid a pill. Eureka. The first batch of two thousand mighty Traffic Lights were set to speed our success through the inner city of the human system. We would be laughing all the way to the Leeds.

It was the big deal that everybody always talked about.

Martin. Martin ran the show. He was the expert, the

artist. He was the chemical professional. He talked the talk, always on a mobile phone. He had an Audi, a genius touch for measurements, a picture-perfect girlfriend and a lasting fascination with furniture design. Marty left the easy glare behind without a thought. Bright lights missed him, he didn't miss them. He didn't get involved, he got things done. He loved my idea. He was the sleeper of the Traffic Light dream.

Mark. Mark was the dodger, artful in the extreme. He sensed meaning, had instincts, came through in every clinch. He took blind corners at incredible speed with responsibility nailed to his back. Mark was an elusive and dangerous dark alley. He carried subtle silverware, floated kilos in the drug canal and kept the world's secrets safe. Plus, the amazing fucker could beat me in an arm-wrestle any time.

I was Oliver on the make. In the open, selling, selling, selling and always wanting more, more, more. I fronted up the soon-to-be-coming down. I gave passengers tickets to the night. I handed outs, I got backs. My line flew me around the world, making people happy in all the strangest places. It steered me through trouble, talk, music, toilets, daughters and doors. I was strapped on the bumper, the road was straight and ferociously fast. It was speed I liked best, but I'd take anything.

Charlie put up some cash for the powder, pills and paper that made up the Traffic Light. He'd extended us a tab. He was a drug dealer and a southerner and that was all.

Coming back, I opened my eyes to the half-light of the Rainbow. I absently recalled saying bye-bye to Martin and Mark almost a week ago. I set off inland with three well-packed bags of the fresh-made superdrug, the Traffic Light, stuffed safe in my pocket. It was time to make money. It was a point of no return. The rubber ball bounced and I set off, charging after it.

But what a night, day, night, day, night, day. By the bottom of the first bag, the whole of my Manchester was holding each other up, pointing at traffic lights and laugh, laugh, laughing out loud. I straddled the top of the highest set in the city and called the colours as they changed, changed back. The simple sequence sent me into orbit.

Cars hit hard shoulders to overturn, I ran into fields, was wary of the bulls, ate the grass, spat it out. Hills in the distance weren't so far, looked hardly high. I door-bashed breakfast tables with my open bag before me. Cups of tea and daylight weren't the only answers. I lay on my back and read semaphore messages in a cloud-written sky. I replaced God's floorboards with cheap, electric light. I saw the sun and it could've burnt for ever.

Maxine, Rita, Angelique, Rosalee and legless Brenda all wrote down their numbers. All lost, all found, all lost for ever. Stairs went up frosted balconies, arrived at important tables. I leant over the pinheads in wide-eyed wonder. And stairs went down, dark and liquid, into corners where fingers, hands, arms, even entire lives couldn't be seen. I touched on. We left off.

The bags, easy opened, slowly dwindled. The lights blazed. The music played thunderous soft. Soft local soccer star put his arm on my shoulder, told me 'bout the goal in the corner. I couldn't see it, but smiled blind, happy, regardless. The entire city came up a carnival. Priests were the people, we became the priests. My holy sacrament turned orange, green, upside down, skin-side out. Hungry hounds carrion-clawed at feeding time. Evil burnt screaming.

Free drinks got paid for later.

Speeches, jokes, announcements, narration, loose fucks, plastic bags. The streets were cushioned with dry-throated choruses of just joy. My head shook. My eyes kept up. I spied car rides, poster paint, countrysides, traffic wardens, traffic lights. I was naked, fried, fused, edged and centred.

I was never home alone. I scrambled days, nights, early dawns, halfway houses, sunsets, moonrises. Tic-toc-tic-toc. I was the bag man, I was the rag man, we were the beg men. Tic-toc-tic-toc. I came in clothed and unfed, not lost, not found, just berserk in the creamy milk float of my mind. I was at the happy back of the parade with one bag left, waving a banner that screamed bye-bye.

Spent other people's money, earned it.

Manchester went from grey to green to orange to red at the flick of my twitch. Three televisions joined hands, two phones sprang into action, one Traffic Light worked, but five worked better. I ran laughing at every light from every light to every light and always in the light. I put my arm round an angelic, forbidden celebrity. A taxi stopped, we hopped in. Had no idea why, where or what for. Heard laughter and cigarette noise in the city. The broken angel leant her midnight voice against my ear and whispered it's all over now, baby blue. And somewhere a car ran out of petrol, a father fell down, a drop of rain hit my cheek. My spine crumpled, my bag emptied. I was on the supersonic slide straight down. I tried to hide, but momentum and her fat sister beat me home.

The Traffic Lights were gone, all gone, all of them and all free of charge.

Fuck.

The broad notion struck me at an intersection of a long, wandered-home dawn. I was leant against a cement luxury looking at the flick-flick-flick of the three-stage mundane miracle. The lights went from green, to green and orange, to red, utterly ambivalent to the absence of cars. The beauty of action when nobody else was around. Stimuli absent, lights active. They behaved separate and detached for whole half-minutes, then they did it, they changed. The traffic lights changed to entertain themselves. They did it because they could.

SATURDAY 1.17AM

I walked down the road and deliberately through a deep puddle of engine oil and rainfall. Waves of cold air blew in from the sea. They swept away the stains within. The length of Whitworth Street sloped safely orange all the way down to the Haçienda. I could see people gathered around the entrance as faint traces of extreme volume drew me in. Come on, from every street to a single door. Come on, from any day to all the nights. Get ready, unsteady, lose it. The motion around me slowed, I sped up. Nowhere near there was nothing like it. The outside of the club didn't look like much, but inside left no outsides to see. The bass dragged my heart through the wall. I head-downed past them that waited, turned up when a break in the brick meant the door.

'Trisha,' I said softly.

'We're packed out! You'll have to wait!'

'Trisha!' Louder, better.

'Billy!'

Trisha, the guest-list hag, turned away from the batch of eager upturns that headed the substantial queue and wide-eyed away at me. I leant in and planted a kiss on the sticky rouge of her cheek. Her arm came around. Someone behind me said something snide, but sod 'em. I was the fully fucked-up member, after all. I'd paid my subs a million times before. That lot could wait, like I once had. They could wait, wait and learn, on their own time, not mine.

'So, how's it been, Trish?'

'Christ, Billy, you know.'

'Yes, I think I probably do.'

'You on your own?' Trish checked behind me and fidgeted, a well-bit biro tap-tapped between her bad teeth. I followed her sharp eyes, thought about doing the tasty midget in a placcy mac a favour, but couldn't be bothered.

'Yes, just me.'

'What a little loner.' She released me. 'All right, Bill, have a good one.'

Stepped past. 'Oi, Trish!' Quick flash back. 'Is Charlie in?'

But Trisha's amphetamined attention span had snapped back to her one-dimensional door-bitch discipline. I decided that she had enough to be going on with without my worries. I clocked the midget in the mac smile a perfect midget smile. But not for me.

I ducked through detectors, bypassed the busy cash counter, paused for thought. All that currency changing hands. Knew I could use a night's takings very well. The cash flow that went on in here would sort Charlie out straight away. It would leave a good stack to spare. But forget it, I decided, rich fuckers got nowt for free and I rarely paid for anything. A smile at the door. A bit of muscle for an endless blast. A mumble for a drink. A favour for a favour. A fast hand for a piece of vinyl. And the peanuts! The fucking peanuts came on regular and regardless. This city had me on happy coupons. I lived in the free world. It was the only one I could afford.

I stepped round the corner and came up with a decent grin for the sweaty, but busty, cloakroom girl. The little bubbler reached for my coat, fussed about a bit, then handed back a pale blue raffle ticket with the number 207 on it.

Hoped I'd win, never did.

'How are you Billy?'

'Tip-top.'

'I haven't seen you in a while.'

Fuck. This was horrible. Cloakroom attendants terrified me. Trapped and responsible in places of public chaos. The briefest encounter with a fabric snatcher always had me feeling guilty.

I'd been traumatised by experiences in my youth.

I used to go to a club called The State, where a pink-haired senior citizen was employed, part-time, in the cloakroom. The full-time granny gave and received coats from 10pm to 8am three nights a week. It was easy to see that she hated it. I sometimes thought of her slicing a Battenberg, or some other fondant fancy, and telling her granny gaggle about the horrors she'd been forced to see. Made me feel terrible. Keeping her up like that, all night, all weekend, sending her back and forth, back and forth, for cigarettes, drugs, ballpoint pens, money, second packs of cigarettes, Wrigley's gum, poppers, all the essential forgettables and all left in the pockets of dirty, usually wet, coats. I always made a point of apologising, probably overdid it. Granny just smiled as arthritis, migraines, alopecia and lung cancer probably killed her with more grace than we surely did.

The State closed down, thank God. The vibrant mix of locals and queers finally ended in wide-scale violence. Cuts a rare combo when you're filled with the bliss of supreme intelligence and you turn your happy head to see some part-time security guard beating the living shit out of a puff with an excellent pair of pants on. As the all-round battery heightened, I saw the poor old girl actually abandon her post for the first time since for ever. A policeman found her later, under a pile of fake fur, jabbering on about the Blitz.

'Don't lose your ticket.'

'Got it! No! Right! I'll definitely do my best.'

I forced the blue scrap of future irritation into my back

pocket and realised I'd left my cigarettes in my coat. Fuck it, the club sold something similar inside and the disgusting mark-up would have to be my penance.

'Have a good one, Billy!'

'Right.'

I was stepping away when I caught myself. Despite the aversion, I needed information. Virtually everyone in the place had to've checked a coat, it was December, it was Manchester.

I cut back, leant myself across.

'Have you seen Charlie?'

'I was going to ask you the same thing.'

'What?'

'You know, Charlie.'

'No,' Christ Almighty. 'Have you seen Charlie, the person?'

'Charlie?'

'You know, Moss Side Charlie. Big, nasty, ugly bloke.'

'Moss Side Charlie! He's not ugly, he's gorgeous. I fancy him, actually.'

'Right, fine. Have you seen him tonight?'

'No, I don't think so, why?'

'No reason.' Stepping away.

'If I see him, do you want me to say you're looking for him?'

'No, absolutely not!'

'All right, take it easy! Hang about, that reminds me. Martin came in about an hour ago, asked if I'd seen you.'

'Martin?'

'Yes, it was a while back, but he hasn't left yet.'

'Great!' The devil and the deep blue sea. 'Fucking fantastic.'

Why did I bother? All I wanted was some good news, all I got was this. I was well on my way to tanked, somewhat snookered behind my grandad's tricky words, the dog was definitely dead, belly always empty, I was a certified speed freak trying to live the larger life on a Friday night. But I was being tracked from two angles. The two opposite ends of the equation were ganging up on me, on me in the middle. But who really cared? Fuck them and their noisy drama. It was all so predictable. Fuck them and fuck their precious drug deals. I was all right. I was alive and well and regardless. Positive snot hit the brain. I absently conjured toilet tops, doors with locks, piles of powder, a millionaire's smile, the anonymous underwear takeaway, frozen smoke and the night's bliss-filled vista. So what if I'd fucked it up? So fucking what. Now was not the time and definitely not the place. They could wait. It could all wait. I was occupied. I was utterly engaged.

I turned myself into a club.

And there it was. The place always looked amazing on first take in. Religion, addiction and plenty of additionals layered thick over transparent sliding surfaces. The permanent need in my permanently unsatisfied system became transfixed by the easy, rolling thrills. The sensation grew to pure joy. The answers, all the answers were in here. And I'd walk down teasing hallways to find them. I'd push through beautiful crowds towards personal space. I'd walk floors of light through corridors of sound in search of answers. My senses were primed for double overtime with no tea break in sight. Power powder clicked the five locks on the five doors fronting the four and a half corridors of perception and the fucking crowds rushed in.

A girl standing in front of me had decided to wear a tiny bra over bulbous, vibrating breasts. The well-framed centrepieces pulled my head straight.

'You look fantastic!'

'What?' she manked back.

'You look fantastic!' I amplified, simplified. The girl was in her underwear, it looked fresh on today. I couldn't help but bounce off the dirt in her brown eyes.

'I can't hear you!' she screamed.

'I said, you look fantastic!'

I was bent down at half-height, beginning to be ridiculous. I took a breath and directed my words straight at her visible ear. I chopped every edge of the once-casual remark.

'Fantastic!' I dribble-screamed.

'WHAT?'

It must've looked like I'd somehow happened upon the meaning of life, hand-picked the appropriate recipient of the late-breaking news and was in the act of handing down the elusive secrets all at once and all to her.

'FANTASTIC!'

'WHAT?'

Fuck. My head span. I took a step backwards as the Marks & Spencer's sampler turned towards her nearby friend. She spoke something, they both smiled, started to laugh. I couldn't fucking believe it! Either her friend had a City & Guilds in Pretending to Know What Daft Birds Outside in Their Underwear are Saying, or she'd heard every word. Fuck, I'd become impossible to understand. It was time to retreat, recharge.

'Got to go,' I said, back at normal volume.

I accompanied my parting line with some amateurish BBC2-style sign language. I was well on my way. I waved goodbye to her and faked hello to a place exactly away from where she stood. I missed her breasts for a blurred moment, clocked another girl wearing a smaller bra over bigger tits and forgot about them both for ever.

'Billy.' Left side.

'Oi! Billy!' Right side.

'Right, Bill.' Inside.

'Billy!'

My name jumped out from the rows of vocal cords that walled the fleshy corridor leading to the flooded bathroom. I couldn't know whether these words sprang from genuine outsiders or were just a single shout that triple-bounced off the inside of my reflective skull. Thinking hard, I put it down to the carnival night and all those bastard Traffic Lights I'd shelled around. It'd only been a week, and some people still remembered that far back. My stupidity had, clearly, won me a few hundred new friends. I was wonderfully confused. Kept smiling, kept moving.

Half stumbling, full-smiling. I knew that no one in the place would take offence at my state, only notice. I'd probably suffer one or two of the regulars later in the week, while they added their boredom to my boredom in the middle of an already dull day, telling me they'd seen me 't'other night', they'd say that I looked 'well fucking out of it, mate', and they'd casually ask if I'd 'got any of the goods in?'. And I would sink back in my chair, not change the channel from kids' TV, pray that the sky would get dark, that the clubs would reopen and that they might all finally fuck off and give me some peace. That's partly what the bath had been about. Isolation therapy. Thing was, I'd lived in Manchester for too long. I'd become too easy to find for almost anyone who wanted to. Door knocks in harsh daylight had made time stretch out still longer. The proximity of nights out and days in had made me the master of changing the subject to silence or, failing that, absence.

There was a queue stretching from out the toilets; it almost reached the edge of the bar more than twenty feet away. Sorry lads, but there was no way. I walked right past it. Smiled to reassure the students. Dropped in ahead of them. I raised my game when some cunt came out of my favourite, far cubicle. Distracted the predators, avoided the mirrors, swung the door open, slammed it hard behind.

And it went lock, breathe, pocket, fumble, place, shake,

check, not bad, tap-tap, eyes down for a good whack. The split in the fresh gram bag had sweat itself shut. Plastic bastard. I had to take a breath, focus my attention, master the package. I needed to get down to business. I dug out a tenner, rolled it, bit the bag between my teeth, worked on the note. The bag sealed up again from being pressed in my mouth. So, I switched. I put the tenner between my teeth and set about reopening the bag with my twitchy fingers. I began to feel that the end of the tenner was getting soggy, but I'd got the bag open. Next thing was to coordinate the placing of my soggy currency into the shifting slit of the bag. I swore to myself, took a big breath.

'C'mon in there!'

'FUCK OFF!'

I finally managed to sneak the rolled tenner into the open bag. I breathed out long. Checked the full submersion of the note in the coke, tapped a nostril, placed the entire operation on the outer edge of my system, closed my eyes and sucked with all the effort of a desperate man.

Too strong, too much, too late.

I managed to shake the dose down. Had a dodgy moment when I thought my dad was watching. Checked fast around, accounted for all the sounds. Abandoned ghosts in favour of all the good stuff my monster hit would mean. First, I wouldn't have to fight my way into the toilet for a while. Second, it saved me the bother of re-clipping the bastard fucking bag, since it was empty. And, third, last, best, it sent me completely off my noggin at about the right time of night.

On my way out of the bogs, I considered cutting a lecture on clubland's limited toilet facilities in direct relation to its limitless eager parties. It could've included allusions to Woodstock, the early days of the Raj, the contraflow system of the human heart, the ongoing 'hairspray/mousse' debate, the emergence of family stands, unwanted pregnancies, the long-running failure of UB40 to be any good, supermarket checkouts, the internal combustion engine, equal rights for penguins and so much more. But the sweaty bastards all looked too desperate to appreciate.

I just got the fuck out and fast.

SATURDAY 2.33AM

'Bilbo!'

The call came well loud. It could only be one man. I span round to see my good friend Luke leant easy against the long bar to my left. He foot-to-footed, rubbed his hands together, let out a follow-up blast.

'Bilbo! Bilbo! *Bilbo!*'

I took a quick-step away, as if to leg it, doubled back sharp, pulled my head into line, grinned lunatic Cheshire and walked straight into an embrace that would've saved darker days.

'Oh! Oh! Oh! You out on your Yoko Ono, Bilbo?'

'Not any more, matey!' My arms wrapped round.

'You got that right, boyo!'

Luke loved the letter 'o'. And if the letter was his passion, the sound was his life's work. He was a rare and brilliant chanter of the round vowel and would add it to almost everything he said. I once spent a long night with Luke and a fat, family-size tin of Alphabetti Spaghetti. As it got light outside, we came to the conclusion that brother Heinz was similarly in love with the letter 'o' by a ratio of around two to one. We had a bit of a barney when I accused Luko of dropping a rogue tin of spaghetti hoops into the count while I was chucking up in the bog, but we'd put that behind us and remained friends.

'You look a bit Serge Blanco, our Bilbo.'

'I've dropped all my cabbages.'

'Dropped someone else's cabbages is how I heard it, boyo.'

'What's done is done, happen.'

'Happeno!'

'Aye, happeno.' My hand went after a cigarette. 'Fuck!'

'Come here, boyo.'

Luke flipped the lid on his gold packet, pulled out a tab, even lit it for me and passed the essential dose over. I sucked down half the length in three furious blasts, put my hand on Luke's shoulder and breathed.

'I'm well fucking buzzed, matey.'

'You want to get in the left lane once in a while.' Luke nodded to the right, I cracked up. 'I mean it, Bilbo. You're looking a little psycho.'

'Hard travelling, Master Luke.'

'From what I've heard, you've been doing no travelling at all.'

'Who the fuck have you been talking to?'

'Look, laddo, it's common knowledge that you've been locked in your bathroom, sat in that tubbo, for an entire week. So, no one is very pleased with you at the mo, but that's no reason to be sleeping with the rubber duckos.'

I knew what was coming next, tried to distract the flow.

'I need a booze.' Stepping away. 'What'll it be, noble Jedi?'

'Keep your money, sounds like you'll need it.'

There were no extended 'o's in Luke's last remark. It was sign enough that the milk was about to sour. There was a girl behind the bar, but I couldn't reach her. Felt Luke step close, his grip turned my shoulder.

'Not now, Luke, for fuck sake, not now!'

'But we're worried.'

'Who's worried?' I snapped back, jolting my shoulder, throwing him off. 'Come on, then!' Free to move, I cut in fast. 'Who's so fucking worried? Who's losing sleep?'

Luke didn't back down.

'All right then.' He called my bluff. 'Martin, for starters. His reputation is fucked on this deal, and if you blow the payback, he's done for good. Mark can't make a move since the Traffic Lights fell through, and you know full well that he put most of his roll into them pills. Then there's Maggie. She had a word with me before. Told me she had to go round gay Derek's to brush her teeth.'

'So?'

'So, we're worried!'

'We! We! What's it to you all of a sudden?'

'Billy, I live in Moss Side.'

One gram before, plus the stuff in the pub, Dad in the toilet, Grandad in the Rainbow, Charlie on my trail, Luke in my face. The drugs weren't doing it, I already felt completely exhausted. The smooth lip of the bath, where I had rested my head for six whole days, called from an impossible distance. I knew it was time for a walk, or time to stand my ground.

'Listen, Luke!' Stood my ground. 'I'm sorting it, this weekend, for certain. It'll all be sorted this weekend, you'll see. Martin and Mark, they'll be straight by Sunday, I've got it all worked out, few side deals, few favours, you'll see. Maggie's got a sink in her room, she fancies gay Derek and I'm not in the toilet now, am I? She can have the bathroom all she wants. Look, you can see me. I'm here. I'm not there. The toilet's vacant. It's free. And I'm not hiding any more. I'm out. I'm sorting it out. All of it. So drop it. Please, just drop it. It's been a long week. Let me have a bit of a night out. Everything is going to be fine.'

Luke still looked unsure. I must've left something out. Fuck.

'And as for living in Moss Side,' I'd left Luke out. 'That's a risk at the best of times, and nothing I do is going to make that better or worse.' I pulled a grin from somewhere remarkable.

'I'm right, you know I am. Come on, admit it, you know I'm right!'

Luke looked away. I closed my eyes. I watched Grandad sink the last black before walking back into the dark. Didn't know if I'd convinced the old man. Or myself. Or even Luke, for that matter. My intentions were good, but my reputation was flaky. The pitch needed a sweetener. I placed a matey hand on Luke's shoulder, waited for his full attention, fumbled a hand in and out of my loaded pocket, nodded. Our palms joined halfway in the for ever strange formality of a dealer's shake. The emotion behind the motion was unclear. Luke knew the powder was a short-term gag order, not a good answer, but the fucker took the drugs all the same.

'Nice one, Bilbo.'

'Nice one yourself.'

Luke tapped 'see ya' on my shoulder, turned away and headed for the bogs. He walked straight past the queue, we all did. Sometimes I wondered how a queue formed in the first place. Sometimes I remembered the existence of students. Leant myself against the bar, looked at my feet.

I loved Luke. Soft thing to say, but his straight talk had cleared up a fair share of shit over the years. Most of what he'd just told me was the first I'd heard. The debt to Charlie was in danger of wrecking my small world. And not everyone would be persuaded by fast words and a wrap or two of average whiz. One thing for sure, it was going to be a long weekend. I patted my pocket and thought, fuck it. I had chemicals, I was stood beside a bar, it was Friday night, fuck it.

I told myself 'not now' between breaths, waited to be served.

There was only a couple of bar staff and they were right down the far end. No fucker bothered with the bar in here. Not surprising, really. By this time of night, all the bag-eyed barmaids had on offer was a ridiculous range of Lucozades, mineral waters, variety packs of Wrigley's Spearmint Cum, all served with sober misery. It was well after two, so all the alcohol enthusiasts had long since crashed into senseless walls of wasted money and funny curry. Consequently, the dry bar in here was left wide open for a thousand drug-riddled Daly Thompsons to neck performance-enhancing fluids to their heart's content.

I vaguely tried to recall which of the blue, green and yellow cans of sports pop were meant to hinder and which were sent to help. I knew it had something to do with citrus, more to do with morons. I couldn't believe the number of times some day tripper had droned on about drinking a can of fizzy orange only to find themselves crashing down like a Chinese 747. I mean, when I'm up and afloat in the high altitude of Chemical Airlines, it'd take the serious attention of several skilled doctors to pull me off the ceiling. These lame fuckers worried about a can of fizzy fluid that could be bought in most paper shops for less than thirty pence. Grow up, children, it's past time you did. And the next night you see someone having a bad one, don't force-feed them more fizzy pop than a hyperactive eight-year-old on a spending spree in the chip shop could handle. Just give them some friendly but firm advice and, if that doesn't work, show them the nearest door. Out there, back in the grey, they'll soon reclaim their anchor in the humdrum and find out for themselves that most problems will eventually get solved by the soft touches of sleep and selective amnesia.

'Water!' I shouted at the anthropology student behind the bar.

'Which kind?' she yelled back.

'Tap, please.'

'We don't have tap. It's bottles only.' She sounded annoyed.

'Bottles?' I'd give her a reason to be.

'Yes, bottles. Which kind would you like?'

'Milk, please.'

'But I thought you said you wanted water.'

'Tap water, that's right.'

'We only serve water in bottles.'

'Yes, milk bottles.'

'There is no milk.'

'Look. I don't want milk, I want water in a milk bottle, please.'

'We have no tap,' the barmaid blurted.

'So, what's that, then?' I grinned at the mysteriously shaped silver thing to the right of my left hand. 'It looks like a tap.'

'It's for the cleaning.'

'But it's a fucking tap.'

'It's not for drinking, it's for washing.'

'Let's have a bit of that, then. I need a good wash.' Put my face up to the light. 'Look, I'm all sweaty.' Instantly clocked my mistake.

'You're Billy Brady!' Barmaid pointed with a flourish that made her *Fuck the Poll Tax* T-shirt wobble. 'You got any of them pills from last week?'

'Look,' I ducked down, sharpish. 'I don't want any of your fucking water.'

Her bad spirit had slid itself across the surface of fake marble between us and punched my good spirit in its invisible face. I became annoyed, she noticed, I reached for a cigarette, she smiled, I didn't have any, she folded her arms across her large breasts, I lost it.

'Look, you silly cow! I don't need a drink! I don't drink bottled water! Or milk! Or Irn Bru! Or Tango! Or fucking Evian! Or Perrier! Or Volvo water!'

'Volvic,' she corrected.

'Christ! You sell French, German and Jap tap water, but you don't sell the local brew. What the fuck is wrong with you people?'

I reached out fast, barmaid jumped back. I turned on the nearby tap and felt cool water run over my fingertips. The horror in her eyes. She looked like she might call security on me. The horror in her open mouth. She wobbled furious. The horror in her tiny defeat.

I smiled at the marginally less feminine barkeep. He looked as if he was about to make a play for the NUS Gold Star of Courage (Posthumous Award). I gave him a wink, put a handful of water to my lips, spat it out, set off for a wander.

I ploughed through high crowds towards the far side of the dance floor, where a set of narrow stairs led down to the basement. Along the way, I lost and found myself on several fantastic occasions. Eventually I managed to find the right gap in the wall and began to stumble down the busy stairs. Halfway to the underground a dark recess with a balcony came to my rescue. I decided to take a break in my epic, aimed for the overhang.

An emaciated smackhead with bulbous, all-black eyes and spiked hair greeted my lean against the low rail with a catchphrase *du jour*.

'It's totally mega down here, matey!'

'Game of two halves,' I snapped back.

'Totally, totally, mega!'

'Mega, yes.'

'Mega! Mega! Mega! Mega!'

The kid's lightweight skull bounced back and frothed. I tried to get past him, but his frame shivered in the way. I leant back against the wall and breathed. Now, I don't mind commentary for the football, and I hate those cunts who turn their telly down just because Brian Moore did a deal with Sky, but I've never been flush for obviousness and the kid was playing in spades. I reached for a cigarette, still didn't have one.

'Totally fucking mega!' Nod, nod, nod.

'The horses are in the gate.'

People seem to love these straightforward statements of nowt. My new friend had, unintentionally, taken me back to my living room on any random weekday afternoon. Unwanted visitors crowding around with their 'wicked buzz', their 'dark at three o'clock', their 'it's cold out', their 'have you seen that rain', or, the number one best-seller, 'have you got any of the good stuff, Billy boy?' So many voices without presumption, imagination, perception, or even much opinion. So many voices, all the same.

'Look at her!'

I followed the smackhead's bulbous fix over the edge, down the wall and to the raised platform a few feet beneath us. A cartoon's dream date danced around in graceful and fulsome flow.

'Would ya take a look at her, MAN!'

'I'm looking.'

'She's the fucking best, man! She's ma perfect fucking woman!'

'Really?'

'I'm up for talking to her tonight!'

'Is that right?'

'Well, no, probably not, not just yet, anyhow. I need a bit more courage for that, and I need a bit more money for courage, like. But I'll definitely give it a go, like, later maybe, you know what I mean, man?'

Smack Lad had me sparked with that little lot.

'So, do you know her?' I had to ask.

'She lives down our street in Chorlton! Well, it's not our street. Our street is nowhere near Chorlton, but hers is. Her street is in fucking Chorlton! D'ya know what I'm sayin', MAN!'

His head followed his eyes, his body followed his head, his words sprayed.

'That girl there! That magic fucking girl right there! She

lives down a street in Chorlton! Chorlton's in Manchester! I'm from Manchester! Always fucking have been! She lives by us! She's practically my fucking neighbour, MAN!'

Poor lad couldn't take his eyes off her. I watched him.

'But do you know her?' I tried a second time.

'Of course I fucking know her, right enough I know her! Well, no, not actually her, but I know a friend of hers! Well, they're not really a friend of hers, they're more a friend of mine! And they don't really know her, but they've known me for fucking years! We've been best mates for FUCKING YEARS, MAN!'

And I had to laugh, to myself, despite myself.

'Look at her! Look at her! Right there on the podium! I've known her for fucking years, man! Look at her! Look at her! I know where she lives! A street! A street in Chorlton! Mega! Mega! Mega! I'm going to talk to her tonight! I'm definitely up for it tonight!'

Noticed that he was leaning right over the low-edged balcony.

'Watch you don't fall over, pal!'

He clocked what was happening, leant further still.

'I'm gonna fucking fall, help, HELP ME, PLEASE!'

I turned fast to grab him, but instead of doing what he said he was going to do and falling head first over the balcony, Smack Lad went for the exact opposite. He pulled back from the demon drop way too fast and was on his way down, but in the other direction. To his everlasting credit, the kid screamed 'MEGA!' on his way down, but the damage was done.

I didn't look round, couldn't. Sights like that could send me into a premature tailspinner of moron giggles for a while to come. Either that, or I'd pity the poor fucker to death and make an unwanted friend for life. From the angry sounds behind, I guessed that a round of imported waters would kill Smack Lad's quest for courage. Shame, I felt he needed it.

I took a few sharp steps away, didn't look back, looked down.

Christ, but she did look good. Smack Lad might be fucked, but he'd been right. I took deep, involuntary breaths and felt warm, pleasant tension churn tasty mashed potatoes of the body and mind. Sensations circulated to the heart of all that mattered. Thunderous bass beat. She looked excellent. Beat. Christ Almighty. Beat. I needed a cigarette. Beat. She looked up. Beat. I forgot about the cigarette. Beat. She smiled. Beat. At me. Beat! Beat! Beat!

The DJ hit a long, dangerous curve that mixed fast tracks with our world. I felt my heart go slow and my blood forget its repetitive slide through a million veins. I felt the cells cool down. The lazy sensation drifted round corners that were used to being buzzed. I watched an action replay of something that hadn't happened yet. My body iced. I felt my eyes shift out of the blue and freeze on her motion below. This was Bella.

This was my girlfriend.

SATURDAY 3.28AM

'Wake up you dopey bastard and get down here!'

I focused on her lips, picked up on her hand motion. She pointed at me, descended the stairs, did a sexy finger walk across the busy dance floor and pressed two fingers to herself. Bella touched her breast and laughed out big and loud. Her dumbshow told me what she wanted, but I got 'dopey bastard' solely from the clear perfection of her thick, moving lips.

Chugging down the stairs, I noticed that as ever and for ever, Bella had come out with her nocturnal selection of trust-till-death-with-your-life friends. She had this 'p' word that she'd cooked up to describe them. It came out of the Wild West, made a home in the south-west, wasn't welcome in the north-west. I tried to block it out. I knew they secretly referred to themselves as 'The Coolest Southeners in the North', but I'd never been aware of an official competition. Always pictured some spastic edition of *It's a Knockout* where the winners were the first to fall down and shit themselves.

Despite all her eager pointing, waving and finger-walking, Bella continued to do exactly what she'd been doing fairly regardless of my arrival. She danced on the podium, beautifully shielding those beneath her from the merest suggestion of another grey dawn. I watched for a while, knew the way it worked, wanted a cigarette, looked around for the nearest soft touch.

'Wotcha, Oscar. Give us a fag.'

'Wotcha,' Oscar nodded back, but didn't take his red-rimmed eyes from the hands and hips of the female DJ currently sweating it out on a set of rented decks that she'd never be able to afford. Thing was, Oscar came to the club solely for the music, the mix, 'the sounds, man!'. The entire social aspect was irrelevant to Oscar. And you fast found out why when you got stuck talking to the daft bastard.

'Fucking great mix!' I shouted, strictly for laughs.

'Little light on the loop groove.'

'Is it really?' Fuck the loop groove, I was gasping.

'She should build up a stronger bass rhythm before bringing in the vocal sample for the hook.' Oscar took a pack of Marlboro Lights, of course, from his top pocket, flipped one into his slack gob and lit up.

'Oscar!'

'It's all about timing.' His frail hands epied back and forth over imaginary turntables and non-existent imports. He blew smoke from a deep nicotine blast.

'Oscar!'

'Sounds like she's a little soft on the top end.'

'Sounds to me like your brain has hit a loop groove with your mouth, you daft cunt. Come on, Oscar, give me a fucking tab!'

'Timing.'

'Takes a cigarette.'

I reached out and just lifted the pack from his pocket. I pulled a filter into my mouth, lit it up and inhaled. A surge of fantastic relief put my instincts back in place. I looked at Oscar, slipped the box into my pocket.

'Bowie,' Oscar muttered, not noticing, not anything.

'Bowie,' I corrected.

'It's essential that you know your high-level limit before you set the mix.' Oscar's spastic stride was gaining speed. 'Pre-set all your levels, know where they are, avoid distortion and, above all, surprises.'

'What about thieves?'

'You must practise your set the day before and mark all levels with colour-coded sticky tape for each individual mix.' Began to think that Oscar might be clinical. 'I use blue, green, red and purple circles. I've been doing it for years.'

'That and talking complete shite, you stupid cunt!'

Determined to get a reaction from this wired-up subhuman entity, I'd maybe taken it too far. For the first time since I'd pulled alongside, Oscar turned to face me. The fully looped look of shock and horror on his pitiful face almost had me feeling sorry.

'What did you say, Billy?'

'Fucking great mix, mate.'

'Well, it's not bad.'

Poor lad didn't look too comfortable. He was out of his element, being dragged deeper into mine. I laid an arm across his weak, hunched back and leant closer to Oscar's blinking eyes.

'You having a good night, matey?'

'It's the bizness.'

But he really had no idea. Oscar smiled one of the saddest smiles I'd ever seen. His pained and empty twist of face made me think of all those trust-fund kids, forever sat in formless clumps in front of foreign stations, chasing the ultimate party, lost in foreign nights.

'Oscar, your train will come.'

'Man, I hope so.'

Fuck! That's what I lived for, just that. The briefest of encounters, despite the odds. Clarity in the chaos. Me and Oscar looked at each other. A moment's connection made precious by its rarity. The mix kicked in. Oscar flinched, shrugged and was gone again. That's the way it came and went, quickly. Oscar flipped back to his lonely world with no visible sign of enthusiasm and no cigarettes.

I looked at him, looked away.

'Billy! Darling! You appear to be utterly, utterly fucked!'

And, thank Christ, it was Lisa. A well made-up memory from the glass-bowl pizzeria where she worked and where I sometimes ate the occasional bottle of fine wine. Whenever I saw Lisa, it made me want to look at the specials. Yucca plants beamed from her eyes. Complimentary lighting followed her everywhere. Lisa had delicate dreds and a cheese-sauce smile. She made me think of my mother's fridge. She was gorgeous. She was Bella's best mate.

I slipped an arm round her slow-dancing waist.

'So, what's on the menu for tonight, Lise?'

'Drugs! Drugs! Drugs! And more lovely, lovely drugs!'

'Does that come with or without the drugs?'

I looked up at Bella, not long now, the games we play. I glanced over at Oscar, lit up, turned back to my waitress. She'd been giggling at my chuck-away enquiry for far too long. It struck me that Lisa was as fucked as she ever was. I exhaled, leant in, caught some of that rare atmosphere.

And I never could resist smooth curves on cheap amphetamine. It's the giddy movement of casual twirls and the all-round naughty night-time of it. It's the ease of mumbling some lightweight nonsense and getting a reaction that was never deserved or expected. Distortion in the right direction. Sweet Lisa gestured that I should bring my ear closer to her mouth. So, I did.

'Would you like to sit down in the corner with me, Billy?'

'That depends.'

'On what?'

'All sorts of things, I imagine.'

Lisa took the lead. She pulled me through a few easy steps towards the dark and not too distant angle. An involuntary tensing of my arm made Lisa turn and take a look back. Her brown eyes twinkerbelled. Her soft, warm breath blew heat on the chemical ice pack within me. Her wink had me going, but I caught myself in time. I stopped myself from falling, made sense of standing up. One determined tug brought Lisa back to where I stood.

'You've done something with your hair,' I attempted.

'Went shopping!'

Lisa was busted. The girl was the colour of fresh cherry trifle and had the eye control of my granny after five sherries on Grand National day. I consolidated my resolve.

'Let's give the corner a miss, Lisa.'

'I was planning on it!' More wild laughter, she stumbled.

'Watch yourself!'

'I'd rather you watched me, Billy.'

She straightened up and moved right into me. Her features began to glow. The space between her lips widened somewhat. Me and Lisa looked at each other for a time that anyone who wasn't right there would've measured all wrong. The clock ticked over. Bella busted in.

'Finally made it then, did you?'

'I've been here for hours. I've been looking for you.'

'Billy Liar, back in town.'

'Bella, it's true. I've been looking for you ages. I've been all over upstairs.'

'Me-*mer*!'

'How was I to know you'd be down here?'

'Me-*mer*!'

Bella's perfect impression of the wrong-answer klaxon from *Family Fortunes* had me wishing for an easy escape. I turned my head and watched Bob Monkhouse crawl into the girls' toilets as the much-loved quiz show made the crossover into club culture.

I felt Bella's arms come around me. She was soft in places, but well fucking strong when she wanted to be. I looked down, she looked up. I sensed her eyes sending out invisible tracers that grabbed at the sides of my shifty retinas and pulled my attention on top of her. I felt taken in. And from where my perspective floated, the shape of Bella's head in the pretend moonlight made the mountains of Manchester prepare for permanent sunset. My girl laughed out loud. It was funny. I smiled. Bella kissed me high on the lips.

'You should lay off the drugs, Billy.'

'Bit late for that, babe.'

'They'll make me impossible to leave.'

'I've only just arrived.'

'You should say no to drugs.'

'I don't talk to drugs.'

'But you converse with bad pushers on a regular bass beat.'

'God damn that pusher man,' I edged back.

'You got that right, honey.'

Bella had been brought up in north London by a mother who put Billie Holiday in the hip-hop milk. This jargon was standard sweet stuff, and it pretty much annoyed me every time.

'To tell you the truth, babe, I've very few drugs to say no to, right now. Maybe I should go get some, have a nice long chat. It'd have to be better than this.'

'What's wrong with you?' Bella frowned.

'Have you seen Martin? I've been looking for him for hours.'

'But I thought you were looking for me.'

'That was last week.'

'Stop it!'

'I need to find Martin. Have you seen him, or not?'

'No, Billy! I haven't!'

'You're sure?'

'Yes, I'm sure!' She snapped.

'Fucking brilliant!' I bit back.

'What the hell is wrong with you? Why are you being like this?'

Bella didn't know about Charlie. She knew Charlie. In fact, she knew Charlie a little too well for my liking. But she didn't know about me and Charlie and the money. Least, I didn't think she did, not yet, any road. I hadn't told her, and she would've mentioned it by now. She wasn't shy. One thing for certain, in this town it was a matter of not much time before she found out. I was determined to take care of business before the bad word went any further. I wanted to make it better. Or, maybe, just no worse.

I shifted my attention from somewhere above Bella's head and looked at her face. Beautiful. The edge of her hair was like a borderline to perfection. Down in the country of her features everything made sense. The dark shades, the darker shades, the rage of centuries, the belief in better days. She was far too beautiful. I reached out a hand to touch her cheek. Even in the electric light of speed-freak night, my hand looked sickly pale in comparison to her rich tones. Bella pawed my advance away, her voice came in well fucking cross.

'You're a disaster!'

'Where can I get a suntan, babe?' I asked her gently.

'What did you say?'

'I need a fucking suntan!'

'How about Boots, they sell suntans.'

'That's funny, I like that.' Remembered to smile.

'Is there anything else I can help you with?'

'No,' I muttered. 'It'll be fine.'

'What will?'

'It will. It all will.' I opened my arms. 'Come here, please.'

And I found myself balancing everything I had left on the low head of my dredded loved one. I scratched my lack of a memorable shave against the rough texture of her hair. My laziness, her origins, a good match. I became beautifully aware of her lips pressed against the hollow of my chest. She was nearer to my heart than anyone, still on the outside, but close. She smelt like the earth, all of it.

'You're sweating.' She pulled back. 'And you don't look well.'

'I'm off to Boots, right now.'

'It's closed.'

'Fine, I'll try the toilet.'

'All right, Billy. I'll be right here.'

And I stood utterly silent in her diminishing presence. I felt myself fading, but not for ever. I stepped away, Bella's harsh attention stayed strong. I let her take me in. I let her see me from a more sensible distance. She expressed her opinion with a sound made sharp between extremely white teeth. Fuck it, a familiar sense of disappointment and compromise floated in the flat air between us. I nodded a weary goodbye and pushed towards the sanctuary of a nearby toilet.

SATURDAY 4.21AM

Martin was in the toilet, dealing drugs to schoolkids.

'Marty, baby!' I boomed. 'What the fuck are you doing down here?'

'Sod off, Billy.'

'I was just talking about you.'

'Yeah, who to?'

'The police, they're outside.'

'Funny.'

A southerner in the far corner actually pissed down his leg. Martin didn't even look. Martin remained Martin. His eyes fixed down and focused on business, no visible sign of stress. Come to think of it, the bizzies could've been in there with us and it wouldn't have mattered much to Marty. Years of study had made him a grand master of concealment and illegal calm.

Martin and me had been mates, till I fucked it up.

The classy bastard had worked some rare magic on me over the years. It was almost always Marty who got the short straw when I was on the crack-up. It'd be after a three- or four-day binge. The place was always a pub, and I'd be one more desperate pubee on the verge before noon. Marty'd start slow and work his sanity in. It'd likely last all day, him muttering close, sound responses, me hitting double after double, chewing my own head off. He'd seen this boy stand on the burning deck more than once. In the end, he'd usually get me so drunk that I couldn't speak and slip me a pair of industrial-strength sleepers. I'd wake up sometime in the week, gagging for a curry.

We'd worked together, we'd been mates 'n' all.

I loved watching Martin practising the ancient art downstairs in the club's toilet. Can't imagine he'd done it in years, hadn't needed to. The on-site lay-offs had always been my job, and even I avoided the bogs when it came to business. A little on the sad side of the industry. I leant back against the sweating toilet tiles and looked down at Martin's half-hidden hands just in time to catch the elegance of the pass-over. That was my trick. My limited area of excellence. My senses had learnt to sense action and, these days, almost only action. Details were my downfall. I skipped so many details. I'd always known there'd be a price to pay.

Marty nodded good riddance to another drop in the ocean. I clocked an excess of powder, in plastic, return to his pocket. Knew what I needed and what I needed to do. I stepped next to Martin, our backs against the wall.

'My precious,' I smiled.

'What the fuck do you want?'

'Pleasant company would make a nice start, Marty.'

'You blew pleasant company about the same time you ruined my life.' He stepped and pointed. 'Or have you forgotten giving away two thousand pills that we hadn't paid for?'

'This was last week, right?'

'Right! Right! Last week! You clever cunt!' Martin smacked the wall.

I didn't blink, too wired.

'Why the *fuck* do you think I'm down here doing these pigeon-shit deals? I can't buy in bulk from anyone, even if I had the cash, which I don't!' He lowered his tone, moved closer to me. 'While this debt to Charlie stands, nobody can come near us. The word's out that we're not good for it. Until he's paid back, we're underground. So, here I am. Here I am in the downstairs toilet of the fucking Haçienda selling scraps to students!'

'Them last two were never students.'

'Leave it, Billy!'

'At least it's nice and quiet for you.'

'Quiet! Quiet!' He was raging. 'I've been in here for three hours! It stinks! It's full of queers! And all anyone wants is one of this! A tenner of that! And not everybody loves the fucking toilet like you do! I just had a smackhead with dodgy eyes ask me for half an E, for fuck sake!'

'Didn't know you did halves, give us one.'

'The whole operation has gone to shit and you're joking about it!'

'Look, Marty, I'm going to sort it, I've got it all worked out.'

'I feel so much better!'

'No, be serious, mate. I'm definitely going to fix it, this weekend, no sweat.'

'Fix it! Fix it! How the fuck are you going to fix it, Jim? Charlie wants his money back! I want my pills back! What the fuck are you going to do? You're broke, you're out of credit, anyone who ever helped you is about to vanish and Charlie Charles is on your trail. Billy, the drugs are gone! The Traffic Lights are dead! How the fuck are you ever going to fix that?'

A pair of giggling homos crashed through the door. They took a gay shufty at me and Martin. Eyebrowed it a bit, then turned and walked out. Still giggling, still homos.

'Leave it with me.'

'Leave it with you! Leave it with you!'

'That's right, Marty. You leave it with me.'

'Well, you fucking lunatic, at least you're right about that! 'Cos that's exactly what I'm going to do. I'm going to leave this whole fucking mess with you.' He was on his way, he came back. 'And forget the pills. Forget trying to fucking fix it with me, 'cos I don't want anything from you and I don't want anything to do with you. I'm getting as far away from you and this mess as I can!' He turned his back, was definitely leaving.

'One thing, Marty.'

'What?'

'I hate to ask.'

'NO!'

'Come on, now.'

'FUCK OFF!'

'Look, Marty baby, if I'm going to sort this all out in the space of one weekend, I'm going to be busy. I've said I'll do it and I will. I have a plan, but it doesn't work if I sleep. If I sleep, it'll ruin everything. If I sleep, I'm fucked!'

'Billy, you're already fucked. I will do nothing to help you.'

'Martin!'

'Billy,' the sly bastard smiled. 'All the speed in the world will not help you outrun Charlie. So I think I'll say goodbye now.' He started walking. 'Goodbye now, Billy.'

'Now that's funny.'

But Martin had left.

I slid down the wall, closed my eyes, scrunched up tight in frustrated pain. It wasn't worth it. Hadn't been worth it. Would never be worth it. One action, or many repetitions of one action, had ruined everything. Each and every Traffic Light that I'd given away had pushed me further into trouble. The connections that kept me in were cutting me out. The supply was being yanked clean. The easy nobility of a constant supply was drying up. And it was all because of one fabulous fling, all because I'd wanted too much, given too much and gone too far. The excitement, the happiness, the pump in the blood. I'd been running too fast, found it impossible to slow down. I went blind chasing a mad bouncing ball and WHACK!

There were so many different kinds of death.

I reached into my pocket and took out my last bag. It was half done, but good enough to get me home, where the emergency stash would come to my rescue. I unclipped the corners and emptied the contents down my throat. My last, dead bag dropped to the floor, where it found a million dead plastic friends. I retched dry and harsh in the toilet light. My eyes were closed, but a tear still made it down my face.

'What a waste of life.'

'Fuck off!'

'Watch that mouth.'

'Grandad?'

'There's no need for swearing to make a point.'

'Sorry, Grandad.'

'You'll have to fight your way out of this one, lad.'

'Yes, I know, Grandad. Please, I know.'

'The toilets aren't safe any more.'

'Don't say that.'

'Get a fucking grip, Billy!'

'Grandad!'

I whacked open my eyes, but old Joe wasn't there. A young lad with bad haircut, dog collar and ridiculous flares stood inside the door. I focused on his face, saw that he was smiling, almost laughing. From where I was, crouched in the corner, I suddenly saw what he saw. Some older than average scally muttering through his tears on the wet floor of the downstairs bogs. The shame of it. Realised it was possible the kid knew who I was. It was a desperate situation, no mistake. Get a fucking grip, right enough. I watched the kid step closer, he was about to say something. I mad-scrambled up, pushed the juvenile aside, cut hard out the toilets.

I sprawled through caves of my own creation. Couples were walls before the walls became walls. Shoulders and hair were interference at eye level. People and plastic and cement and sound switched properties on me. A set of soft purple strip lights played in the corridor; I pushed for the stairs. My eyes frenzied at a world gone beyond. Skirts, skin, fake tans and endless details. I looked above my head and saw nothing, which was what I wanted to see. I looked beneath my feet and saw nothing, which was what I wanted to see. I fell forward, held on. I feared the presence of security that only brought danger. I turned away from the audience that only brought laughter and the next day closer. I found myself unravelled, on the hinge of a scream, steadied myself instead, switched to automatic, stood up straight. I reached inside for a cigarette, lit the fucker up, got the hell out of the downstairs part of the club. It always freaked me out.

'Where are your fucking clothes?' I shouted at a passer-by.

'Fuck off, weirdo!' The nearly naked girl screamed back.

'Your knickers aren't even clean!'

'Fuck off, weirdo!'

'I know where we can get some Ariel.'

'I bet you fucking do.'

'Let's go to the all-night laundry and do a service wash.'

'You got any drugs?' Marks & Spencer touched my stomach.

'No, but thanks for asking.'

'What?'

'I don't talk to drugs.' I was on my way.

'Oi!' she blared. 'Come here, you!'

'Go home.' I whispered, kept moving.

But the simple phrase got stuck in my head. *Go home, go home, go home*, repeated itself on the inside loop. I tried to outpace it down a dark, touching corridor, but the words were within me. The homegoing chorus hooked in. *Go home,*

Billy! Billy, go home! sang inside my skull. When I opened my eyes a wall of strangers' mouths shaped the words over and over. Thought I might be imagining it, till a fat bloke blasted it, right in my ear.

'What?' I screamed back.

'TOPONE!'

'What did you say?'

'TOPONE!'

'You said I should go home!'

'WHAT'S THAT, MATE?'

'Answer the fucking question, you fat cunt!'

'I HAVEN'T GOT ANY!'

'You're looking for Charlie?'

'TOPONE!'

'No!' I grabbed his flabby arm. 'Listen to me! I'm asking you a question!'

Fat Lad's face was jumbled confusion. He tried to pull his arm free, but lacked the necessary vertebrae. He looked around for his girlfriend, but would never have one. His brain checked notes from previous experiences, came back blank. An empty state possessed his face. The fat fucker shrugged, didn't stop dancing.

'SHOULD I GO HOME?' Loud as I could.

'TOP ONE! YES! TOP ONE!'

Willy Wonka came up with a fresh gold ticket. The Charge of the Light Brigade ate curry sauce behind enemy lines. City won the cup. A smart shark came out of the wide shot and swallowed the self-righteous paddlers whole. I had an answer, fatty said 'yes' and enough was enough. I wasn't about to be told what to do by a fat cunt with no girlfriend, no backbone, that couldn't and didn't know me. I clenched him steady with one hand and smacked him hard with the fisted other. Sloppy bastard hit the ground before he even knew that Ecstasy wore off. Walls screamed and clutched half-naked breasts. A gap appeared in the human undergrowth. I cut my losses, headed for the exit.

'Oi!' came the obvious shout.

'Fuck off!' I wired my words into the sound system. 'GO HOME! GO HOME!'

My loud sound bounced with the breakneck backbeats that drove the whole world crazy. A tall, dark-suited and bow-tied muscle-man with fake hair and a Mercury moustache came stumbling out of nowhere. He reached for my arm and snarled.

'Come here, you!'

'GO HOME!'

The virtually hairless chimp flinched when my right hand blasted real firepower. The bouncer didn't bounce, he fell and stayed down. I knew his paid-for mates would be closing fast. So, I focused and fled. I kicked open the emergency exit, laughed a little, did one.

And all the grey lights switched on. And the forgotten rain charged in. The freeze in the wind sobered me straight. I stopped sharp to check my valuables. Pat-dig-pat-pat-what-valuables! I saw the rented penguin get himself up. I sensed revenge was on its way to hold his hand and do me in. I banged my head down, remembered my dog and sprinted hard across the deserted grey shades of Whitworth Street.

SATURDAY 5.18AM

I kept a pace, crossed lights, charged past shut-down shops and soon-to-be-built bars.

The car park was on fire. The blaze raged angry out of street-level gratings. I passed them by, speeding up. The stench of boiling oil, fried fish and stale rainfall blew through the dawning air. I sped up. I began to melt. I reached a hand to hold my heart and missed. The rare morning orange turned deep, dark red. The world felt less friendly than when I'd last left it. Sweat boiled and froze on my face. Multiple gunshots blasted around crumbling walls.

A man screamed. It sounded like me.

My brain yelled that all the blue Ford Fiestas were about to explode. That the kid on the battered tricycle had crossed into the line of fire. That a beautiful, out-of-work, African actress had parked her history on top of the bomb. That there was no good reason to run. That if I slowed, down, to, a, stop, then dull streets would return, that the fire would suck up, that normal life would return. So, I did. And it did.

I slow-grumbled further up the street with no particular thought for nothing, except the fantastic cigarette moving towards my mouth. I lit it, inhaled and instantly wanted a drink. I knew that at this time of the morning alcohol sales were beyond illegal. But that only meant that the drinks were forced to be free, and I had a good idea where they went when the cuffs came off.

I pushed upstream towards where me and Maggie lived.

India House. An unusual, but not inappropriate, name for the collection of irregular-shaped spaces that made up Manchester's most ludicrous housing initiative. The idea behind the venture was to allow people of low, or no, income to live in the city centre. Some midweek time-waster had told me that India House started life as an abstract tourism idea aimed at making Manchester look like outsiders expected it to look. Story went that some southern yuppie had superimposed his vision of wild and crazy Madchester on an old insurance building, India House. Whatever the initial plan had been, it'd backfired all the way up its own arse. Freaks and junkies, puffs and slags, clubbers, dealers and all the subsequent casualties paraded in and out of the city's most privileged address. Outsiders were not only confused, but also terrified. It was a remarkable catastrophe. An underground horror movie released into the heart of the delicate mainstream.

It was central, perfect for clubbing.

I guessed that Maggie would be guzzling cheap vodka with some local small-talker and small-talking. I had no idea what time it was, but felt certain that Mags would inform me the minute I started banging the fuck out of her deadlocked bedroom door.

Flick. I appeared on spy-cam for a brief episode. Flick. My character was black, white and blurred. Flick. I fumbled behind reinforced glass at the building's magnetic door. Flick. I stepped into the gaudy atrium. Flick. I struggled across the confused carpet. Flick. I appeared to be well lit and focused. Flick. But too fast to see. Flick. Fire doors wide, no smile. Flick. A parting hand gesture to the security station. Flick. Knew all along that the cameras didn't work. Flick. Turned the key in my lock. Flick. Walked into the flat.

My foot caught on something. A skeleton had fallen down. I lifted the loose limbs back on to the vacant hook above my head. There were nine skeletons in our corridor. They were the descendants of a respected Czechoslovakian artist who lived in a shithole squat somewhere in Hulme. She had a name, but it didn't come easy.

The skeletons were quite good, actually. Maggie had used them as stand-ins for her family in a one-off performance of a one-woman show she'd put on in the local free-for-all theatre. I hadn't actually made it to the big night, but I heard the skeletons stole the show. We had nine home-sewn skeletons in our corridor. The Arts Council paid for them. It was a good deal. Arts Council covered the decor, City Council paid for the rest.

Our corridor was in perpetual dark, due to the national bulb shortage.

I stepped into the grey light of my room and was vaguely surprised to find Maggie upside down on my foam mattress. Soft girl hid a giggle with a fast hand. I went and stood over her, feet either side of her wrigglesome hips and looked down. Her good humour made me uneasy, almost edgy, but I wasn't about to show it.

'What's the matter with you?' she snapped.

'I need a drink.'

'Surprise, surprise!'

I chose to ignore her easy sarcasm, focused on business instead.

I stepped away from the bed, got up on an empty bookshelf. Almost tumbled, but steadied a hand against the wall and edged along. The operation was intentionally precarious; it was the only way to reach my emergency stash. The goody bag rested in a gap between a fake Tibetan reed curtain and a genuine Mancunian hardboard wall. I was up on my tiptoes when Maggie's laughter broke out behind. I stretched further into the empty space, but still couldn't find the fucking bag.

'Watch you don't fall!'

'Fuck!' Lost my balance, never really had it. 'FUCK!'

My foot slipped, hand grabbed. I managed to catch the clip that carried the joist that ran through the reed that held the whole mercy purchase to the wall. The entire structure collapsed, right on top of my brown-bottle collection.

'FUCK!'

'At the third fuck the time will be . . .'

'Maggie, you cunt!'

'That's a naughty word.' Maggie carelessly jiggled and stretched. I was hobbled, close to tears. She was upright and grinning. 'What have we said about naughty words, Billy Brady?'

'Where the fuck is it, Maggie?'

'Where's what?' She looked lovely and smiled.

'Come on, Maggie, you know the story.'

'A story!' Mags leant in, kiddy keen. 'Is the fucked-up dirty stop-out going to tell sweet little Maggie a tale or two?'

'For fuck sake! Not now!'

'You never tell me stories any more.'

'Fucking hell!' It was the only way. 'Once upon a time, in a land far away, there lived a strangely deformed evil young tart called Maggot.'

'That's me!' she squealed.

'And with Maggot lived a poor browbeaten lad called Bilbo!'

'That's you!' She pointed with infant perfection.

'And every time Bilbo left Maggot at home alone, do you know what the little tart did?'

'No,' Mags's head shook in mock innocence, her finger twisted curly hair. 'I do not.'

'She'd break into his room and steal his fucking drugs!'

'Never!'

'All the time!' My patience snapped. 'The end!'

'That's a very short story, Billy.'

'No, Mags, it's a very old story. Now, give them to me.'

'But is this a genuine emergency?'

'Yes, it fucking is!'

'Because you said,' her hand moved towards the pillow. 'You said that if it wasn't a genuine emergency, I had to keep them from you.' Definitely the pillow.

My rare-fried brain sped ahead of Maggie's slow hand. It was an obvious hiding place and I wasn't taking any more games. I took action instead. I hit the edge of the penalty box at high speed, checked the crowd for kids and launched myself, full length, towards the prize. Maggie screamed, the ref blew, but I was under the headrest with my hand on the bag before any fucker could think to sing 'That's What Friends Are For'.

I pulled myself upright, propped my back against the wall and silently thanked the toothless fairy for her latest delivery.

'Happy now?' Maggie asked.

'You have no idea.'

'You have everything you need?'

'What about some vodka to wash this down with?'

'Yes, my lord.' Mags bounced to her feet. 'One thing though, sir.'

'What?'

'We have no glasses!'

'Tragic.'

'We have no ice!' Maggie was in the corridor, moving through the skeletons. 'We have no slices of lemon!' She echoed in the faraway kitchen. 'No, nor lime neither!' Loud scouse sound. 'No mixers! No fruit juice! No little placcy brollies! No curly-wurly straws!' A door slammed. 'We have no fizzy pop!' She was on her way back. 'No milk!' Her body hit the joining wall that my head was leant against.

'Fuck!' I spilt a bit.

'Our supplies are not good!' Closer. 'Our lives are not good!' Closer. 'We're not fucking good!' Closer. 'But we do have loads and loads,' the bedroom door exploded, 'of lovely,' Maggie was beaming, 'LOVELY!' a big plastic bottle came from behind her back, 'VODDEEEEE!' Maggie laughed, spun the screw top from the bottle and whacked the big glugger back. The two-litre container was about three-quarters full. Fantastic. We had all we needed most. Drugs, drink, a rare strain of conversation. Life, indeed, was sweet. I passed Maggie a freshly capped mixture of uppers, smoothers and shakers. She handed me the bottle. I hit it without thinking. She popped it without asking.

Through the haze of satisfaction, Maggie's words drifted in.

'I've got Jim, the vegetarian chef, tied to my bed. He's taken the weekend off work and says he wants to spend the entire time in my bed. But he's said that before and he's usually gone by Saturday morning. I think he's a puff who does too much speed and wishes he was straight. I feel sorry for him, but he annoys me. He's completely useless in bed. He talks about all the mad stuff, but he can't even get a hard-on. So I tied him up good and proper and walked out. I'm sorry I came into your room, but please don't make me leave, let me stay in here for a while. If Jim wants to be in my bed the whole weekend then I think he should be. It'll probably do him good to stick to what he says, for once.'

There was an edge in her voice by the end, a sad tightness. I put my arm out; Mags fidgeted closer. Her head came down and in, I gave her a squeeze. She breathed a beautiful sound into my neck and her body went loose. I reached for the vodka and fags, took my time with both.

'All right,' I said, eventually.

'All right, what?'

'All right, we can leave Jim tied to the bed, but we're not staying in here.'

'What do you mean?'

'Get up, we're taking a trip.'

In the instant I thought it, the idea became the remedy to all immediate problems. Why the fuck was I hiding in a bath, haunted in a snooker hall, threatened in a nightclub, when I could just roll out of the city and let it all cool down for a while. Me and Maggie agreed in an instant of eye contact and jumped fast to our feet. I felt a positive current run through my body. Drugs and drink played their part, but new-found direction did the rest. All in all, clarity of vision, chemical energy and absolute belief came together to make escape seem simple.

'Train?' Maggie fizzed.

'I'm not taking a fucking bus.'

'We could fly.'

'Think I already am.'

'Train it is, then.'

'Yes, but where to?' I asked her while looking out the window and wishing I had a car. It was Christmas in a week. I wasn't holding my breath.

'Scotland,' Mags suggested.

'Too far.'

'Leeds.'

'Too depressing.'

'Liverpool.'

'Your family.' Maggie's family was insane.

'But it'd be nice to feel at home, somewhere.'

'That's it!'

'What?'

'Go home. We should go home. I should go home, for fuck sake!'

'You mean?'

'Yes!'

Wanted to pick that visionary fat bastard up off the deck, dust him off, give him a peachy smacker. They'd all been right all along. Or maybe I'd been right all along. Didn't matter, I was going home, me and Maggie were going to my home.

'First Glasgow train departs Piccadilly at seven-twenty-five, arrives in Lancaster at eight-fifty-three. No changes! And no fucking problem, matey!'

'Perfect!' Mags pitched and jumped in the air three or four times.

Maggie grabbed and kissed me. Close human contact joined forces with massive relief and powerful morning cocktails. The fusion warmed the room. It fed our frenzy.

'Lung-cancer!' I shouted. 'This is Lung-cancer!'

'You're a Lung-cancer lad born and bred, Billy Brady!'

The allegedly historic city of Lancaster was waiting for us sixty miles up the train tracks. My mum lived there, alone in the house where I grew up. It was on a hill, near a park, with a fridge. All we had to do was get there. It was suddenly essential to my momentum that we got that seven-twenty-five train. I snapped around for a clock, didn't have one.

'What's the fucking time?' I snapped.

'Whatever we want it to be.'

'Be serious, Maggie.'

'How should I know the time, my clock's in the bedroom with Jim.'

I needed to know the time. I needed to be in control of my immediate destiny. I needed this plan to work. We had to hit platform 12a perfectly on the mark and roll the fuck out of grim with a degree of style and ease. Obviously, I didn't want to miss the train due to tardy arrival at the station. But, equally, I didn't want to be early and have to wait like a dickhead. I couldn't stand the idea of being stuck on a sorry platform, watching the porters and peasants dribble disdain in my direction. At this point, any obstacle, however small, would probably finish me off.

I needed to know the time, but how?

My rapid eyes met the telephone in an ugly stand-off. We'd reached such an advanced stage of non-payment that we could only use the everyday piece of technology to call to beg BT for the privilege of paying the bill. I pushed the phrase 'long-term repayment plan' to the back of my mind and picked up the phone.

'You'll never do it,' Maggie hissed.

'Mouth shut, ears open.'

The dialling tone sounded, beep-click-rush.

'Telecom, this is Sandra, how can I help you?'

'Say something, you moron!' Hissed like a scouse snake.

'Hello, this is British Telecom, Sandra speaking, how can I help you?'

'What's the time?' I flapped.

'Brilliant!' Maggie cracked up.

'I'm sorry, but is this call in regard to the payment of an overdue amount?'

'Yes, absolutely yes.' I replied. 'That's exactly what this is.'

'Thank you.' The frosty voice of British Telecom iced down the line. 'Now, could you tell me your caller ID code? You will find it in the top left-hand corner of your latest reminder.'

Christ, you'd have to get up pretty fucking early to put one past Sandra. And that was it. I'd got it. With that random thought, with that involuntary and utterly clichéd response to resistance, a plan was hatched. I took a deep breath, reached for a cigarette, dropped into character.

'This is all so fantastic, Sandra,' I hoorayed. 'Really, it is.'

'I'm sorry?'

'The wife told me it would be far too early to call regarding our unfortunate billing situation, and on a weekend as well. I say, Telecom really are getting there. I can't wait to tell Nelly when she returns from the abattoir.'

'Thank you, sir. We do our best.'

And I'd become 'sir'. My plan had not only hatched, it was clucking around the room pecking for gold. And from suicide station zero, in the dark recesses of BT's vast empire, I sensed Sandra's corporate pride glow like a friendly beacon leading me home. Another cliché, pride before a fall, occurred to me, and my confidence had a growth spurt. I moved in for the kill.

'Nelly said I wouldn't get through till after seven.'

'Well, sir,' came back Sandra. 'That used to be the case. Your wife would've been right up till about three weeks ago. This is, in fact, the newly introduced, seven days a week BT NightWorks Initiative.'

'NightWorks, well I never.'

'Yes, sir. A few weeks ago and you'd be talking to a machine.'

'Hardly, Sandra.'

'No, sir. You would.'

'I'd hardly waste my time talking to a fucking machine, now would I, Sandra?'

'I'm sorry, sir?'

The proverbial penny had long since floated over the precipice of genius and dropped into my lap. Granted, our Sandy here had a terrible job, which I was, no doubt, making worse. But what the poorly paid communicator didn't know was that she doubled as a sundial. She was a subtle form of the speaking clock. Sandra was part of the night shift, she finished work at seven, she was still there, so it couldn't be seven yet. I should've been able to tell by the dark. It was after six, I could, definitely, tell by the light.

'Sir?'

The perfect light.

My personal shade of soft bright orange bled from the car-park balconies across the street. It washed the filthy, hidden corners of my room in its all-forgiving glow. It made me feel blessed and safe. The clouds would come again, of course, but for the time being it was safe and good outside. The Lancaster train would be on paradise track waiting for us at seven-twenty-five in the brilliant am. We had, at least, twenty-five minutes to walk the half-mile to Piccadilly. We were going to fucking make it.

'Sir, are you there?'

It was over and it hadn't even happened yet. I placed the receiver back in its empty space and turned to look at Maggie. Her face shed details of joy in the room's translucent light.

'You are such a clever boy when you try,' she beamed.

'I'm bright, me.'

'You're a light bulb.'

'And you're a toaster,' I smiled. 'Now, get your stuff – we're going.'

'Can we go to the Tower?'

'Of course we can, but hurry.'

I closed my eyes and conjured the distant sea. I stood myself up on top of the Jubilee Tower. It was an ancient lookout for defending forces of years gone by. Over the years it had turned into a good place to do hallucinogenics and maybe the occasional bright-cheeked girl. It had a certain isolated quality that suited passion. Plus, it helped the locals keep an eye out for any daft fuckers trying to move north from Blackpool. I felt a weight press against my chest. Thought it might be a heart attack, but it was only Maggie, resting her head.

The contact snapped me back.

'Come on, Mags,' I urged. 'We don't have much time.'

'But I've got nothing to wear.'

'Get something out of that lot.' I pointed at a sizeable but various pile of women's clothes that were in the corner of my room. Various women had left them there to depress me. But that didn't bother Mags. She jumped into the fabric confusion like a fiery granny at the annual jumble sale.

I laughed out loud, lit up and looked out the window.

SATURDAY 7.03AM

'Christ, it's cold!' I was forced to stop. 'Maggie, I'm so cold.'
  'Come on.'
  'Wait! I can't! It's too fucking cold!'
  When I'd reached for a cigarette my arm had fallen from
Maggie's half-breasted elbow. I'd needed a smoke due to the
maddening cold, now I was stranded. My hands were too cold
to light up, anyway. So I just gave up, I called it a day. Halfway
to the train station, halfway from home, all the way cold.
  Maggie'd put on every single item of random clothing from
my floor. The bras and knickers were in her pocket, but the
rest were put to use. Soft lass looked ridiculous, but warm. I
couldn't fully grasp why I felt so cold.
  Grasped.
  'No.'
  I'd left my coat in the club.
  'No.'
  I'd left my dog, dead on the road.
  'No!'
  I'd left the one girlfriend who hadn't given me a hard time
about drugs.
  'NO!'
  I'd ruined Martin's life.
  'NO!
  Charlie was going to kill me.
  'NO!!'

From where I stood screaming, I saw Maggie cross the second of three roads between us and Piccadilly station. She hadn't broken her stride. Hard, but clever, girl. She knew full well that I'd fallen into some random funk, that I was crawling into a hole of my own creation. She knew that at any point I could blow it, that I could jeopardize our entire escape. She kept walking. It was her only way.

But I had a choice to make. I could turn round and head back to the club. Still open, amazingly still open, no wonder we had a reputation. My mind approached the cloakroom, the busty cloakroom. It was too cold to check if I still had the ticket, knew I probably didn't, but knew my coat was still there. My brilliant cold-proof coat, tagged, warm and waiting for me. My other option was to accept the loss, the agony, the utter defeat and catch that train before I caught something permanent.

Maggie was getting smaller in the sub-zero distance.

The losses piled up. Late equalizers, missed penalties. Front teeth, nose bones. A Harley-Davidson limited-edition T-shirt, my favourite felt pen, clarity of vision, clear memory. Charlie's fucking money, Martin's friendship. Bella's mother-earth earrings from Ethiopia. The photograph of all of us together, a game of snooker, my grandfather, my dad, my dog. Home and so far away, all the places in between, the bastard losses piled up.

It was now or never. It was both.

I carefully placed my parka in a respectable fifth place on my all-time list of all-time losses and leant forward. I almost forced myself to fall. My leg came involuntarily out to save my chin; I set off running after it.

'I left my coat in the club!' I panted, coming alongside.

'I left Jim tied to the bed.'

'I left Luke at the bar!'

'I left school at sixteen.'

'I left.' I couldn't think, too cold.

'I left my heart in San Francisco,' Maggie laughed. 'I left my long-lost lover from Liverpool. I left my foot. Left is the colour of my true love's hair. Left at the lights, straight on till night. Left my heart at Wounded Knee! Left is the new black! Lefty, get off the fucking phone!'

Maggie was too good at times like this. The rhythm of her chanting pulled me along. Mags strode up that cold road with enough purpose and belief for both of us. I put my hand back through her arm. I didn't feel much warmer, but was beginning to feel a bit better.

Thank Christ for decent company.

'Maggie,' I clenched.

'What?'

'I love you.'

'Shut up, you soft bastard.' But she pushed out her chest. 'Let's just get on that train and leave this all behind for a while.'

'I might never come back,' I muttered.

'Billy, all you need is a break.'

The warmth of Maggie's easy optimism made me nod along in time to our mutual foot-drops. Nodding and walking, walking and nodding, nodding and walking, walking, nodding and freezing. An involuntary shake began to build into my nods. It made me feel less cold, I chose not to resist it.

'Keep your head still,' Maggie snapped. 'You look like Muhammad Ali.'

'Thank you.'

'You've got all his latest moves.'

'I'm floating like a flutter-by, shaking like,' my brain froze. 'Fuck!'

'You're shaking like a Stevens.'

Maggie's laughter buzzed with energy and heat. It kept me moving along. I switched attention from my body to my brain.

I imagined wobbling into some bar, shouting out a shaky order for a breakfast of champions, overhearing some bottle blonde at a nearby table coo to her friends, 'Look at him by the bar, he moves like Muhammad Ali.'

'Shit!' Maggie yelped.

'And piss,' I observed. The stairs to the station were a disgrace.

'No,' Mags, suddenly serious. 'I mean shit, have we got any money?'

'Well, I thought we could exchange a few spare pills for a couple of second-class returns to Dottingham.' My howler got no response. 'Either that, or we could just nick on.'

'Be serious,' Maggie glared. 'This is fucking serious!'

I matched Maggie's intense stare with a pretend one of my own. Hit my pockets. Pat-tap-tap-pat-dig-pat. Leaving my coat in the club had cut the pocket possibilities down to four. Small fucking mercy. After a couple of failed attempts I began to feel nervous. It was time to go Zen. I began to fiercely visualise the blissful existence of large quantities of cash on my divine person. Taking the next descent into my subconscious state, I conjured folded wads sliding out of the metal slots of mythical Midland. Sinking deeper, I spirited cashpoints across the land reaming themselves in joyful counting frenzies all for the greater glory of me. As my visions reached the core, snowstorms of tenners and fivers blew in the sunshine of my eternal soul. Brigitte Bardot came naked and calling with a fifty-pound note stapled to her forehead. My frozen hand entered the last pocket left on earth. Brigitte set on fire as my iced fist came back full of cash. I didn't care how it got there, I just got to counting it. Fantastic, seventy quid. I counted it twice, one hundred and forty quid. Even better, loads more than enough. Fuck Buddha, we was liquid.

The man who sold me the tickets was an elegant blank.

We were on time and, miraculously, so was the train. I

quick picked up a few packs of fags and a glossy for Mags without even looking at the cover. We scurried through the pedestrian tunnels playing the proverbial echo game. Maggie was better, but I was louder. Some early-morning old cunt gave us the crinkle, but who cared, the train was visible, death was irrelevant. And, at long last, my feet departed the cold cement that covered our dawning world.

A whistle blew shrill and life moved on again.

'I think we have a carriage to ourselves!' Maggie blasted, happy.

'We've got the fucking train to ourselves.'

'Don't be a spoilsport.'

'Well, for Christ sake!' I shouted. It was the third empty car Maggie had paraded us through. She'd come up with that 'carriage to ourselves' line fresh each time. She showed no signs of flagging, or settling for a seat. It was beginning to piss me off.

'All right! All right!' she squawked. 'This one will do, where shall we sit?'

'One thing,' I muttered, looking at, not out, the windows.

'What is it?'

'Is this a smoking compartment?' I asked.

Couldn't see any of those obnoxious red stickers on the filthy windows, but I hadn't been keeping up with British Rail policy of late. For all I knew they'd shut smoking down completely.

'It's two hundred quid if they nab you!' I cried.

'Calm down.'

'But I want a cigarette!' My new pack looked brilliant.

'So, have one.'

'But what if the guard comes and asks me for two hundred quid?'

'Tell him you haven't got it,' she laughed.

'That's my point, you stupid cow!'

'Keep going, Billy.'

'Fuck this!'

No signs nowhere.

'I said, fuck this!'

Why couldn't they just let me know, one way or the other, be clear.

'What am I doing on a train?'

I punched the stupid, stickerless window hard.

'I want to go back to the club!'

Fuck, I'd hurt my hand.

'Maggie! I want to go home!' I screamed.

The train hadn't even moved yet.

'I want to see Bella. She'd look after me. I want to sleep in her nice semi in Chorlton. I want to be woken with eggs benediction served on generous cleavage. I want to smoke a fucking cigarette. I want my coat. Give me back my fucking parka!'

My shakes were going nuts, the train lurched.

'Fuck! Fuck! What am I doing on this miserable fucking train?'

'That's right,' Maggie blasted. 'That's right. Keep going, Billy.'

'What?' I screamed. 'What the fuck did you say?'

'Keep going. Go on. Go mad, you selfish bastard.' Maggie sounded angry. 'Go on. Talk complete shite. Shake like a spastic. Go on about Bella and her big tits. Don't worry about me. Don't spare me a second thought. Why would I care? It's only my holiday, too!'

'Stop it, Maggie!'

'No!' she spat back. '*You* fucking stop it!'

'I'M FINE!' I screamed, completely losing it.

And something about reaching the pinnacle of absolute fury made 'smoking' or 'non-smoking' seem somewhat less crucial. Call it perspective, call it survival, call it over and smack it in the chops, call it what you like, whenever you want. I told myself that things would only get worse if I didn't make them better. I realised that, in the scheme of things, freaking out about cigarettes was like nudging the tip of a dangerous iceberg. I had to remain calm, or the whole world would come chewing for my brains.

I focused hard on Maggie's angry eyes, ripped the top off my brand-new pack and grabbed at the visible filters. A few fell to the floor, but who cared? There was no law against dropping fags on the floor, was there? I saw no stickers about it. I saw no stickers at all. So, I lit up. I just lit up and breathed in. And, after the glory of the longest time, I breathed out again.

'Better?' Maggie asked gently.

'Better,' I nodded.

My head was definitely on the slow-down. I noticed that the train was a good way out of the station, away from the centre. I heard Ringo whisper, 'Calm down, lad. Thomas'll take care of you. And, by the by, have you got any of the good stuff?' I smiled, began to feel far less troubled, began to feel not bad at all. I leant across a set of seats and blew thick smoke against the uninterrupted window pane.

The outskirts of Manchester opened up within the plume of my dirty exhalation.

I looked over at Maggie. She was gracefully window-seated. I saw her shift her body to make room for me. I looked at all the emptiness around us and laughed. She pat-patted the complimentary cushion beside her as I rolled down the fast-accelerating corridor. After a few wobbles, I dropped myself into the seat next to Maggie, rested my head on her easy shoulder and looked out the window.

The early-morning landscape unruffled before us.

Expanses of green split with grey made great shapes. Subtle divisions of incarnations of poverty and wealth. Pubs I'd never get pissed in. Churches I'd never be forced in. Distant houses on halfway hills where glow-faced girls with perfect breasts lived. All the parts of the whole, irresistible, north. My medication mixed with country air and the whole scene went soft. Me and Maggie moved to hold hands. Together we looked at pictures from our own private exhibition. It was that good to be going home.

'Jim?' I muttered, recalling the strapped ponce.

'Jim will be fine.'

'No, I think he might die.'

'So,' Maggie smiled. 'We all die.'

'That's deep.'

'He'll be fine,' she waved, nonchalant. 'He's probably enjoying it.'

Don't know why I cared, I didn't even like Jim very much. First off, he was a vegetarian chef and, second, he was Maggie's 'on-again, off-again' boyfriend. I didn't need any more reasons, didn't need to go any deeper, didn't like him. But the thing was, we'd already had problems with the Housing Association, and I felt sure that an unregistered stiff, not paying rent, occupying our place while we were away, might mean homelessness, or Hulme.

'Maggie,' I blurted. 'He'll starve to death.'

'He won't.'

'He'll stink out the whole fucking flat.' The more I thought about it the worse it got. 'Jim will die and he'll go off and he'll stink out the entire flat! Don't laugh, I'm serious!'

'Sorry,' she smirked.

'Well, I won't be the one who has to clean him up.'

'Do you think he might shit himself?' she asked.

'That's not funny!'

'He'd only enjoy it, the dirty bastard.'

'Stop it!' I was becoming agitated. 'I especially don't like the idea of someone that I only vaguely know being alone in our flat while we're not around. It's not safe.'

'He's tied up,' she giggled. 'What's he going to do?'

'Die!'

Maggie laughed out loud while I tried hard to remain calm. I forced myself to look out the window in the vague hope that the landscape might sort me out, calm me down. The graft streets and unemployed industrial estates of Bolton did absolutely sod all to improve my mood.

'It's all so messed up, Mags.'

'What is?' she said, soft. 'Come on, you can tell me.'

'I'm not sure if I should tell you.'

'Billy,' her hand, my arm. 'Tell me, now.'

'It's this business,' my voice cracked. 'This business with Charlie and the money.'

'Billy, I know all about it.'

'You know about the debt, but it's getting worse. Martin and Luke both laid into me last night. Ever since I got out of the bath I've had nothing but trouble. I decked a fat bloke and slapped a bouncer for no reason at all. I've been chatting with dead relatives. My coat's probably the last one left and no one even wants it!' I breathed, concentrated, continued. 'It's all just getting me that wound up, Mags. And I know I'm fucking it up for everyone. I'm sick of being told how much trouble I've caused for all of them. Basically, I have to get Charlie his money back before Monday, but how?' My hand banged my head. 'I don't know what to do! I have absolutely no idea what I'm going to do!'

'Billy, quiet down.'

'This could be serious,' I levelled. 'This could be proper trouble.'

'Quiet down.'

'Charlie is not a nice man,' I said, softer.

'Quiet, babe.'

'I don't know,' whispering, 'what the fuck I'm going to do.'

Watched Maggie's hands move to touch the outside of my scarred fingers. She moved my battered bones aside and uncovered the face beneath. I felt her breath on the surface of my skin. I let my hands drop. I saw her smiling there. I leant forward. And our faces became so close that I could see the speeding landscape in the blacks of Maggie's eyes. Looking closer, I saw the country I'd been born to. A church, a pub, a sky. And slowly but surely, I let go of whatever had gone before. I forgot the names, the faces and the random places that would still be there when I returned to them. I let Maggie kiss me on the cheek, whisper 'not now', smiled and kissed her back.

SATURDAY 8.28AM

The gentle, rolling silence worked wonders.

I lifted myself up from the comfy two-person seat by the window and walked the length of the shifting corridor. The high-speed bathroom with its colour-coded lock made me smile. I swung the door closed and operated the simple action of the lock. The click gave me the confidence to undress. Smoked glass on one side, mechanical steel on the other, I was having a wash. The miserable dribble of water made me think of the ticket price, but the soap was lemon-scented, the toilet didn't get in the way and the door was definitely locked. I relaxed and got on with a leisurely wash.

It wasn't quite the bath-tub, but it had its moments.

Completely clean and feeling comfortable in my underwear, I turned to the count. Did a final check on the lock, it was utterly occupied, emptied my pockets on the toilet top and knelt down to sort out my stuff. The things I fucking carried. Forty-three quid and change, four cellophane Strawbs, at least three grams of coke in a sealed bag, eight wraps of whiz, six quality Es plus crumble, some slaty black, an anonymous phone number on a beer mat, king-size skins, a box of matches and two packs of strong cigarettes. These canvas shoplifter pants had the best pockets. Looking down, I decided that it didn't feel much like an emergency any more, but that, I suppose, was the point of the stash.

They say you can have too much of a good thing, but who the fuck are they?

I tried to decide if Maggie had sneaked any of my supplies when I was out, but I couldn't afford to think like that. Reckoned I was fine with what I'd got, and if Mags had popped a bit behind my back then the girl had more than earned it. I quickly put together a morning refresher involving a three-skinned spliff, a pink champagne gum rub, half a pill, a quick lick of a Strawb, all chased down by a decent line. I recalled my grandad's recent proximity and cut it short with the chemicals before the old fella chose to come calling. I finished the job by flushing the hopeful coaster down the toilet. Leant my back against the wall, decided the job was a good one and exhaled thick, clean, soothing smoke.

My survival kit went carefully rewrapped and packed back into my deep-pocket system. I sealed the miracle Velcro and set about getting dressed. After that, I had a spit and a scratch and was about to unlock the door when I clocked that I'd almost forgotten to have a piss. Toilets had become so multi-purpose to me that their original function was beginning to get lost. I drained off a bit of the poison, told the mirror to stop smoking and flipped the lock into reverse.

I strolled down the double-sided rural cinema.

'What do you look so pleased about?' Maggie asked.

'Just another morning,' I dropped in opposite her, 'taken care of.' I glanced at the familiar hillside and touched my nose against the cool window glass.

'It's beautiful,' Maggie murmured.

'It's the fast-moving world.'

I began to trace myself on a superhuman charge. I watched as I steamed in and out of trees, jumped walls, took verges at high speed. I came in unbelievably fast from the wide-open spaces and crashed crazy into sleepy villages. I automatically clocked the variations on the themes that marked human habitation. Pubs, churches, garages, farm houses, road signs, stray cars. They all had their unique details. They all had purpose. They all went bye-bye so fast.

I couldn't help shouting 'how do' to a bent farmer on a bright green tractor. I yelled 'be seeing ya' before he even had a chance to notice. Up in a house on a hill, I pointed out the signs of damp showing through a war widow's pink wallpaper. She wanted to thank me with a slice of sponge cake, but I told her no and slipped myself next door. I lay face down and gazed upon the worn-out carpet of a mile-a-day country girl. She asked if I'd be wanting fish and chips for my tea, but I wasn't hungry, I was on the move again.

I spotted an incredible racing-green Jaguar and couldn't help but nip myself inside. I tuned the radio from Four to foreign and picked up the pace. Country roads with suicide rights and hairgrip lefts made me marvel. I bumped over funny humpbacks and sent dribbles of fucking fell walkers flying. I finally topped the o-meter on a ninety-degree blind man's bend, the wheels buckled, slid, skidded and swerved. I left the collector's edition steaming and in a wreck inside a local politician's greenhouse and set off on my feet again.

And my feet fell in time with the industrial bass beat of the train. I easy matched the locomotive and kept its steady pace. I started to search the outside of the train's windows for stickers. I didn't have much luck until three carriages from the front, outstanding and brilliant, an entire car was painted and shaped like one enormous cigarette. I pulled my speeding path in closer and there I was. My nose against the glass, a bright light in my eyes and a happy smile on my face.

I didn't look tired, lost, beaten, soft, stupid or insane. I looked clean and content. Not bad, I thought to myself, not bad at all, Billy Brady. My relaxed self on the double seat inside the speeding train looked too inviting to pass up. I effortlessly bled through the reinforced window and rejoined my life back on the track. Blinked.

Reached for a cigarette, lit up, smiled at Maggie.

'You've stopped shaking,' she said.

'Yes.'

'You've passed through.'

I nodded, of my own accord, and considered the curse of the bastard shakes.

The shakes were the visible crack in my public armour. The shakes, to me, were like baldness or acne to a handsome man or dirty knickers on a first date to a woman. Annoying, no doubt, but no more or less than what they sounded. I had the shakes. A tremor of the head that began in the neck, wobbled up to the bonce and spazzed out to the witnessing world. They only occurred in situations of stress, which meant they were pretty much ever present.

They'd first taken hold under a canal bridge. I'd gone there to hear my fucked-up babble, babble back at me. I'd needed someone to talk to and bricks and ancient mortar weren't that choosy. First, I'd thought it was just me talking, but after a while strangers' voices began to bounce about the brickwork that curved above my head. Looking down, I noticed that the confusion of sound was matching time with the ever-changing electric orange of street lights reflected on the surface of the water. The street lamps entered the canal ripples and went straight into my scrambled brain. The sharp edge of each and every aquatic peak appeared to have adopted an alternating current.

I began to nod my head in time to the water light, switching on, flicking off, switching on, flicking off. I wanted to discern a pattern. I tried to convince myself that there was a pattern, and that it had become my destiny to understand and communicate the phenomenon to the ignorant world. I came close to epiphany time and time again, but just as a theory began to form the pattern would let me down. It was, of course, a random action of irregular reflection and what I was attempting was utterly impossible, but drugs'll do that and so be it. Eventually, the lights went out, grey daylight returned, but the shakes remained.

A mad anarchic gay quackster, who was well known for donating Prozac to nosebleeders, told me that the proper name for my condition was St Vitus's dance. It was a signpost on the way to Parkinson's, and it tended to affect long-term residents of old people's homes, snooker players and overenthusiastic club kids. The doc predictably offered me a van-load of Prozac, but after a week of downing pill after pill the only effect I could discern was an irrational craving to wear dungarees and listen to chipper folk music. The prescribed medicine didn't make the shakes any better, it just stopped me worrying about them. Not the cure I sought. One thing though, saintly Mister Vitus two-stepped into a strange auditorium when he elected to use my head for his impromptu swing nights. These days, I shake when things get bad, and it bothers me, which is fine: it should.

I turned away from the window and looked at Maggie. Her eyes were closed and her delicate head lollipopped against the blue-green check of the high-backed seat. I reached across and lifted the *Smash Hits* magazine I'd absently bought her. For want of something significantly better to do, I started to scan through it.

'My God, it's full of stars,' I smiled.

'Hal?' Maggie shifted awake. 'Hal, is that you?'

'Yes, Dave, it is me.' I loved this game. 'Good morning, Dave.'

'Good morning, Hal.' So did Mags. 'Can I ask you a question, Hal?'

'What is it, Dave?' My accent was perfect.

'Could I have a bacon, lettuce and tomato sandwich?'

'I'll work on it, Dave.' I looked out the window at a particularly ugly cow in a pretty field doing about eighty miles an hour. 'Yes, Dave, that would be fine, but I'm not going to get it for you.'

'Fucking typical!' But the prospect of food had Maggie up fast and beaming. 'Which way is the buffet car, Hal?'

'I don't think I can tell you that, Dave.'

'Hal,' she snapped. 'You are completely useless.'

'I think that's the point, Dave.'

'Tell me, please! I'm starving!'

'Actually, Dave, I think it might be that way.' I carelessly pointed over the nearest hill to where I imagined a lonely buffet car in an empty field with a demented steward chatting to a flock of black sheep about the virtues of sandwich spread. 'Yes, Dave. I'm convinced that what you seek is over there.'

'Brilliant!' Maggie wasn't sincere. 'Look, do you want anything?'

'A drink would be nice.'

'No, really.'

And off she went to find her food. So, I didn't want a sandwich, I wanted a drink, just a small one, and there was nothing wrong with that. A jolt of Irish to freshen the morning breath, to sharpen my senses for the day ahead, to make my ciggies taste better. Damn, that's what I wanted, a cigarette, it'd been ages. I hurried one out, sparked it up and flicked the match.

Flick.

Bella was alone on her bed. She gazed out the window at a gaggle of kids mucking about in the community playground across the way. Her music was playing at a sophisticated volume. Some good ol' girl was moaning along about her no-good, drinking man. Bella sang along and sounded better. She made the melody less sad, more mean. She took those ancient, out-of-date tunes and sang them right at you, about you. I'd become the villain of so many scratchy recordings that I'd begun to find it funny. I even enjoyed it sometimes. When Bella wanted to treat me special she'd murmur 'Midnight Rambler' in my ear, real slow. The bit about the kitchen door always got me going.

Flick.

Luke was perched in the bright morning corner of his Moss Side kitchenette. The for ever hero was laughing his sleepless head off. An NUS prototype had just tried to make beans on toast 'southern-style'. Luke had destroyed her confidence to such an extent that she'd scurried away to the deadlocked toilet to cry her sad eyes out. Carrying on regardless, Luke used the kitchen's smooth Formica surfaces to his endless advantage. Chop-snort-chop-snort-laugh-laugh-laugh.

Flick.

Martin was hitting downers and looking at a book about restoring eighteenth-century furniture. He'd got it from a speed freak as down payment on permanent trust. Marty's girlfriend, Samantha, was changing her underwear for the fiftieth time in the last ten minutes. She looked at her figure in the bathroom mirror and frowned. In the bedroom, Martin noted the similarity of his current situation to the challenges faced by woodworkers of the late seventeen-hundreds and promptly passed out. Samantha came sniffing out of the bathroom in a sheer red one-piece and asked, 'How do I look, babe?'

Flick.

Charlie oiled a handgun and stared at a picture of me on holiday in Blackpool.

Flick.

Jim wept on a shit-covered bed.

Flick.

Maggie came back with a sandwich.

Flick.

I stubbed out my cigarette and waited for Lancaster to arrive.

Flick.

SATURDAY 8.55AM

I stepped off the train and took in some pure northern air.

'By heck, you can't beat the restorative powers of that.'

'You've changed your tune, Billy.'

'I love a little of the fresh stuff at the right time.' I sucked down deep in the ice-cold air and blew a smoke ring into the morning light. Maggie handed me a pair of Jackie 'O' sunglasses. I put them on and felt like some effeminate terminator, soppy blade runner, fashion victim. I laughed at my reflection in the station café window.

'Nexus six,' I giggled.

'City nil,' Mags laughed back.

A rust-patched private hire car with tell-tale dints and stolen wheels pulled alongside. I didn't think twice about the indulgence and ducked into the warmth of the shabby back seat.

'Mornin' t' y' both,' came from in front.

'Morning,' I replied flatly.

'Where's it you pair've hailed from today?'

I closed my eyes. The interior smelt of farts, and the misshaped blob in the front seat was obviously a talker. He appeared determined to offer an experience when all I needed was a service. I sometimes thought that was why you had to pay more for a taxi ride than a bus fare. It was the personal touch, the one-to-one element, the inescapable conversation. Well, you could stuff it. All I wanted was the 'a' to 'b' – you could keep the irrelevant rest. Maggie was laughing away at the obvious stench and the potential ruckus. I opened my eyes just as Wobbly turned to bug me some more.

'Did I say something funny, like?'

'Listen, pal,' I sharped at him. 'We're from Manchester, not sixty miles up the road. You might've heard of it, more shops, couple of football teams, black cabs, orange buses, chinese takeaways, public lavatories,' I breathed myself calm. 'But forget all that. Today we would like to go to Grasmere Road.' Pulled up the old accent. 'Up on t' Freehold by t' park, like.'

'I know it well, son.'

'And no.'

'No what?'

'You didn't say anything funny.'

With a local huff sound, fella turned around and, amazingly enough, started to drive. He'd made the two turns out of the station before non-essential shit chat kicked in again.

'Would you young folks mind if I put on my wireless?'

'No,' I conciliated. 'We'd be happy to have a tune.'

Maggie banged her head against the window in mid-fit. The atmosphere might've improved somewhat, but the smell was getting worse. I sat back, sucked hard on a nicotine air-freshener and resigned myself to the punishment of local radio. Up front, Fatty tapped a tape into the deck and altered our entire existence. As far as I could remember, the drunken last-dance classic, 'Total Eclipse Of The Heart' had always started with a gentle piano intro. That being the case, Stinky was about to treat us to the loudest version of the epic ever aired in the civilised world.

In a way, Bonnie Tyler made more sense played at a thousand decibels. She was no better, just made more sense. No fight left in me, I took the Jim Steinman part and played the pretend piano. Maggie was Bonnie, of course, doing the hair throws and belting out the infamous melody. Not to be outdone, Wiffa farted along in the front. I might've cried at the sheer enormity and sentimental beauty of the power-chord chorus, but didn't. We somehow made it to the instrumental break, Maggie took her chance, leant close.

'You can get a gin and tonic for ninety-five pence in Birkenhead!'

'What?'

'You can go out with five quid and a sawn-off shotgun, come back with a road sign and change for the meter. I wish we'd gone to Liverpool!'

'Can't hear you!' I lied.

'I wish we'd gone to Liverpool!'

'Too late!' I yelled back. 'We're here!'

The taxi turned down my mum's sleepy street, blasted the fucking peace and quiet to kingdom come. My window was wound down and I could hear the sound bouncing back and forth between the tight rows of terraced houses. Old grannies trapped inside their halfway houses probably thought that the end of the world was no longer nigh. I banged on our pilot's headrest, he lurched to a diagonal stop.

'That'll be three-fifty!' he barked.

'Turn the radio off!' I yelled back.

'What?'

'Turn it off!' I gestured frantically. 'RADIO OFF!'

'No need to shout, son!' He hit stop. 'Great tune, don't you think?'

'I try not to.' Dropped a crumpled fiver on the front passenger seat, got out.

I turned to see the stupid bastard wink and tap his booze-swollen snout. Maggie laughed, but the silly fucker was beginning to wind me up. I glared down into his insane, stinking cabin. Fucker winked again, flashed me a peace sign.

'Well, kids.' He reached for the 'play' button. 'I'll be offsky.'

'Don't you fucking dare!'

He shrugged, wobbled and hit it. Bonnie struck back up for the benefit of her fans all over town. Deaf, determined to prove a point, or simply Bonnie Tyler's fattest fan, I didn't fucking care, the cunt was in trouble. I lunged for the door handle, missed. The shitheap pulled away fast, blasting my mum's pretty street with its obnoxious soft-rock alarm. I could hear the demented chorus rolling all the way down to town. I wanted to chase the bastard back to the station, rip him from his glorified wheelchair and beat the crap out of his personality. But all I could do was stand there, shaking wild, screaming vicious obscenities inside my head. All this noise in front of my mum's peaceful house. It wasn't right. And it was as if I'd brought it with me. I caught sight of a curtain twitch. The cat-thief pensioner from across the street was predictably peaking. I imagined her snitch, 'I saw your Billy this morning, Mrs Brady. He's certainly a strange one, no mistake. And no, Mrs Brady, I haven't seen your cats.'

I spat blood in the gutter, turned to face my mum's front door.

To be honest, I didn't want my mum to be home. Of course, I wanted to see her, it'd been a while and catching up would be nice, but not quite yet, not in this state. First, I needed to calm down a bit, get myself settled, have a few drinks, close the curtains, generally acclimatise to the sentimental environment, remember who I was, where I was and all that. Then I'd be ready, then bring her on, then would be better, but not now, please, not just yet. I reached for the key in my pocket, muttering quiet prayers.

Hand outstretched, keyed up. I caught a reflection of myself in the glass of the front door. My features were familiar, so familiar, but older. I realised that this simple door had stood before me my whole life. It'd reflected my changes through all the stages. It, like my mother, had always been there, always let me back in, however far and wild I'd been and gone. I hadn't always had a key, hadn't always been able to reach the lock. Now I had a key and could more than reach. It was all significant and precious. On a more mundane level, it was so much simpler to sneak inside the refuge whether my mum was in or out. I moved to unlock the door like a lifetime's well-learnt tune. Easy insert, shake, rattle, rusty bolt, subtle boot, strain, tweak handle, turn, release, serious boot, push, open, enter.

'Mum!' I called and waited.

'She's out!' Maggie ran past.

I dropped my keys on the hall table. The atmosphere of the place hit me hard in a soft place. The smell and the light and the exact replication of how it used to look, how it'd always looked. I hung back in the hallway, leant my head against the cold stone wall. I wasn't sure if coming home had been such a good idea, after all. The last thing I wanted to do was bring this business anywhere near my mum. I'd walked through that familiar door with a few crackers in my time, but this felt different. I lit up, wanting to replace my sensations with smoke, wanting to get the fuck out of that house.

'Oi, Maggie!' I called. 'What time do the pubs open round here?'

'How the hell should I know?' Heard my mother's fridge door open.

'Fuck!'

'Relax, Billy.' Maggie shouted. 'We're on holiday.'

'So, where are the brochures?' I yelled back. 'Did you bring the phrase book? When do I get to ride a donkey? I need change for the slotties! And why the fuck can't I go on the big dipper?' I'd walked to the kitchen. Mock anger had propelled me through the house. I might've had a sentimental reaction to the kitchen, but it was surpassed by the sight of Maggie's fluorescent arse stuck in the air. My guest had clearly taken an advanced position inside my mum's fridge. Her head was invisible; small animal noises came from beyond my sight.

'Any luck?' I asked.

'She's got Marks & Spencer's pork pies.'

'She's got Marks & Spencer's knickers, do you want to eat them?'

'Don't be disgusting, Billy!'

'You ate on the train, how can you be hungry?'

'You had drugs on the train, how can you want more?'

And we were well matched. Maggie came out and stood up, smiling. She'd taken a pork pie from its box and was biting into it with visible relish, no pickle. I shrugged and turned to put the spotless surfaces to good use. Excessive indulgence can be a contagious phenomenon. Maggie chewed her more-than-a-mouthful. I chopped a massive line.

It was all the same to us.

Mags finally stepped away from the fridge and started doing excited little skips around the kitchen. It was probably only to speed her digestion, but it gave me the chance to catch sight of one of those odd boxed-wine affairs. I thought twice; it was the low end of alcohol abuse, but booze all the same. I leant in and pressed out a small handful of loose juice, sniffed it, swilled it, stopped being such a fucking snob and poured myself a pint glass. After a couple of solid swallows for guts, I wandered through to the back room.

Not so bad, I thought. It was where I'd once belonged, after all. I stopped stalling and went to sit down in my grandad's favourite armchair. I breathed in all the incredible atmosphere, took another large pull and closed my eyes.

Yes.

Night park sensation. Cold air clean on my neck. My small hand dragged along by his huge one. Halfway up a local impersonation of Mount Everest in the complete dark. Grandad's gruff and splutter about toughening me up. His gentle talk of my mother and wanting more time. Always the anger of the Troubles and the old war stories. And maybe a dirty joke or a naughty-boy story thrown in to embarrass me. But always the talk. Joe's good and proper talk. Me and my grandad went up those steep hillsides, him and his words pulling us both higher. When we finally reached the top, we'd stand on the steps of the monument. Grandad Joe would fall silent and look at the stars.

He was the best statue I think I've ever seen.

Then the old fucker would growl like a madman and grab for me with scary monster arms. I'd scream and run like fuck. And we'd run, full pelt, all the way back down the hill. Him growling, almost catching. And me, I'd be screaming, crying and laughing out loud. I'd be running with my brain in a frenzy. The happiness, the excitement, the pump in the for ever young blood. And I'd always be safe, he was just behind and home was straight ahead. My mum would always be waiting and she'd be made up to see us both come home, laughing, sweating and still alive. We'd run right past her. Through the hall, through the kitchen and into the back room and my grandad's favourite armchair. I'd get there first, but he'd catch me up, throw me in the air and take me on his lap. And I didn't sleep like that any more. I'd never felt that safe since. I must've been about four or five years old. It was a long time ago.

Fuck it, times change.

I sighed inside, sensed Mags was clearing out the contents of my mum's fridge.

'Leave some scraps for my mother's tea, soft lass,' I shouted.

I heard a wrapper rustle, a scuffle and the hurried slam of the fridge door. Mags came through from the kitchen, cheeks bulging, eyes shifting like a naughty blonde hamster.

'You're a greedy little tyke,' I smiled.

'Sorry, sir.' She sprayed crumbs everywhere.

'Tyke!'

'But, sir?'

'What is it?' I asked.

'Is there any more?'

'No, there fucking isn't!' I necked the last of my pint of wine and sat up sharp. 'And stop eating before it makes us both sick!' A little harsh. 'Look, love, now that we're here, is there anything that you'd like to do?'

'I'd like to . . .' sweet shy pause.

'What is it?'

'Eat!'

'Christ, Mags, isn't there anything else you like to do?'

'Well, now you mention it.' She swallowed something solid. 'I like sex.'

'Really.' My stomach turned.

'We could have sex.'

'No.'

'But we could.'

'No!'

'OK! OK!' She flipped her gaze out the window and grinned. She hair-twisted, half pouted, leant forward a little, flipped back to me. 'Are you sure you wouldn't like to have sex?'

'Yes, Maggie,' I smiled. 'I'm sure.'

'Well, that's it!' she blasted, thrusting up. 'No food, no sights, no buildings of cultural or historical significance, no pubs, no donkeys, no sex, no point, no fucking fun!' Fist-clench, stamp. 'I'm going upstairs to do my make-up.'

Maggie hurtled from the room, snatching her bag as she left. Funny girl. Always had been. Liked to joke about most things. Sometimes even the two of us having sex. We never had, never would. And you can say that when you've been in every situation and every state of mind with the same person without it ever occurring. If it hasn't happened, it's not going to. Plus, I found her thirteen-year-old sister more attractive. Not that Mags wasn't gorgeous, she was. She had that never-look-the-same beauty that couldn't ever be contrived. But Maggie was a mate and I didn't fuck mates. Not until last week, anyhow.

'Oh, my God, Billy!' Maggie hissed, abrupt and back in the room.

'What?'

'Your mum is upstairs!'

'No.'

'Billy, she's sat up in bed smoking cigarettes.' Maggie had hysteria eyes with a mad-mouse squeak. 'I stepped round the corner and there she was, sitting up in bed, big smile, smoking a cigarette. She said "good morning", asked me how I was.'

'Sounds reasonable,' I shrugged, thinking of how it was, how it had been.

The house used to be a sweetshop, back when that was enough for a shop to be. The downstairs was well laid out. Front room, kitchen, storeroom, all in a line, front to back. When the war-years sweet-seller sold up and went to suck sherbets in some retirement home, her hobby became our house. Ground zero effortlessly turned into a lounge, a kitchen and a back room where old relatives could come and die whenever they liked. But upstairs didn't make the transition with quite the same grace. Two bedrooms, one bathroom made sense, but you had to go through the main bedroom to get to the amenities. All through my life, friends had done variations on freaking out, getting bashful, holding it, or, my personal recommendation, taking their business outside. It wasn't that my mum minded, she'd even apologise if some drunken slapper knocked over a pot plant on their way to piss or puke. My mum was fine, nobody else could handle it.

Maggie was frantic, clenched hands in curls.

'Billy,' she hissed. 'It's eight-thirty in the morning on a

Saturday, why didn't you tell me your mum would be in bed? I mean, where else did you think she would be?'

'To be honest, Mags,' I smiled, 'I don't make assumptions.'

'Your mother is upstairs,' the drama reached a peak, 'in bed!'

'Actually,' I listened more closely. 'No, she isn't.'

The old wood planks of upstairs played a subtle accompaniment to my mother's barefoot shuffle. I heard her step around the ceiling, then creak into the bathroom. Hot-water pipes groaned and farted at the demand of her regular tap-turn. Me and Maggie listened. Our eyes melded amid the intent silence. Something started to happen. Delicate at first, but coming in at speed. Our attitudes gradually switched places. Maggie started to smile. I began to sense sharp edges developing in my mood.

'We should leave,' I said, sitting up.

'No,' she giggled. 'We should stay.'

'Maggie, this isn't funny. I'm in no state. I want to leave.'

'Listen, your mum's getting all spruced up to come down and say hello. The least you can do is sit there like the good son you say you are and have a nice chat about normal things, for a change.' Maggie was fizzing, couldn't follow her for all the bubbles. 'I'm putting the kettle on,' she called from the kitchen. 'Does your mum like tea or coffee?'

'Coffee.' I hadn't even noticed her leave the room.

'How does she take it?'

I closed my eyes. I was confused. The sounds from upstairs were becoming more purposeful. Cups and spoons and running water crashed around in the kitchen. Maggie was asking me something, but I had no idea what the question was, let alone the answer. I knew I needed a cigarette, but it didn't seem important enough to hold on to. The word 'spruced' began to loop in my mind and I couldn't stop seeing wind-whacked heather on highland hills. A fist dug into my left eye. It hurt. My other hand made a claw on the worn-out material of the old chair. I saw my grandad in pain. I more than imagined what a heart attack felt like.

'Black, three sugars!' I heard myself shout.

It was my face in the glass of the front door, but more so. It was the utter familiarity of home. It was like a million separate memories ganging up on me, all at once. The mundane came close to unbearable. There was movement in the room. I almost recoiled from its obvious meaning. I almost split atoms. I almost disappeared through the walls into bright, clean air that would carry me anywhere away. But I couldn't, or I didn't. Either way, I opened my eyes.

And smiled at my mother.

'You're looking well,' she said, no sarcasm.

'I'm fine, thanks.'

'There you are, Mrs Brady,' Maggie handed a steaming mug to my mum, walked through into the room, invented a stage, found its centre. 'We got up especially early to come and visit. We're actually on our way to the Lake District for a weekend break, but Billy said we had to stop in and see you.'

'I'm glad you did,' my mum beamed.

'Billy says we're going to go to a place that you took him when he was only a child. He says there are boats there and that maybe we can take a boat out on a lake.' Maggie snapped a sanity check in my direction, I nodded. 'What's it called again, Billy?'

'Windermere,' I replied.

'That's it,' Maggie flourished, 'Windermere. It sounds brilliant. Billy's told me all about the boats and the ducks and the cafés and the beautiful lake, but especially the boats.'

'Yes,' my mum smiled. 'He loved the boats.'

'And the ducks,' I added.

'We're going to have the best time,' Maggie spouted. 'We might stay just tonight, or make a weekend of it. It's like an early Christmas present to ourselves. Billy's paying for it really, but he said he wouldn't enjoy it on his own. He wanted to show it to me.'

'That's nice,' my mum said, turning and stepping into the kitchen.

'Well,' Maggie snaked fast at me. 'How am I doing?'

'Brilliant,' I replied. 'She doesn't believe a word, but brilliant.'

'So,' my mum came back with a lit cigarette. 'Would you two like some breakfast?'

'Oh, that would be lovely, Mrs Brady.' Maggie double-creamed. 'I'm starving.'

'Actually,' I softened my growl. 'I thought I'd treat us to a British Rail breakfast just as soon as we get on that train. You know how you love to eat at high speed, Mags.' I pushed myself out of the chair, took a couple of steps and put my hand on Maggie's shoulder for appearance, emphasis, but mostly balance. 'We should be getting down to the station, love.'

'Well, if we have to,' Mags toned.

'I'm afraid so.'

With my sombre words I led Maggie towards where my mum stood in the doorway. Her head tilted to one side and her eyes narrowed slightly as we approached. She took a thin-lipped pull on her Lambert & Butler, turned and led us through the house. At the front door, Mags and my mum hugged and cheek-pecked with smiles and appropriate sounds. Maggie half skipped into the quiet of the street, I hung back.

'Take care of yourself, Mum.'

'And you, Billy.'

Some rare trick of bouncing sunlight and clean windows put a beam of heaven in the olive of my mother's eyes. I winced and smiled at the same time. My arms came out, her ciggy hit the cement and we hugged. I kissed her bottled, mottled hair and breathed in the for ever scent of nicotine, blue shampoo and safety. As we stepped apart there may have been tears in my mother's eyes, but I couldn't see them for mine.

'You know there's no boats at this time of year,' she said.

'I know.'

'You have money?'

'Yes, do you?'

'Yes, enough.'

'I'll give you a call for Christmas,' I said, walking now.

'Do you have plans?'

'I'm not sure yet, but I'll let you know.'

'That'd be nice.' She had to raise her voice, the distance between us demanded it. 'Take care, stay in touch, lots of love.' Her hand waved, smile returned. 'Bye, now!'

'Bye, Mum!'

No more words, none needed; I was on the move, at speed, up the old street. Maggie giggled as I came alongside. She had a ketchup bottle sticking out of her bag. Together we sprawled ourselves down to the station with the help of a fresh-made herbal remedy that I put together in a bus shelter. And, after what seemed like no time and all time, we boarded the next train out of town, destination not discussed.

Manchester.

SATURDAY 10.47AM

The train was more full this time around.

We slowed to a stop in a satellite town where schoolgirl day trippers giggled aboard in full teenage fever. I could see it in the details. The absolute compulsion to spend the entire weekly tuppence on some mass-produced outfit. The irresistible reek of their cheap perfume made me twitch. I crouched close to the headrest, hoping I wouldn't upset a schoolgirl and, in turn, a schoolgirl wouldn't upset me. Maggie hid, head down, and read her magazine.

So fucked by that point, I only began to consider Lancaster when we were twenty miles done with leaving it. Whenever I even hear the place name it automatically transfers to a rain-soaked motorway sign on a long curve in a low-petrol night. It's like Morecambe to me – will always be – white road paint on a third-gear roundabout. Wigan, a delay. Blackburn, to be avoided. Scotland, a no-score draw. Northern Ireland, newsprint. London, the address of the last job left, where your girlfriend goes home to and a good place to hate. Greece, the musical. Hong Kong, plastic forks. Bangkok, duck. New York, a dream. Australia, where my dad ran, eyes wide, into a heart attack on a beach I'd never see.

Knew I could've saved myself a lot of bother by staying away from Manchester, but the boredom would've killed me in its own sweet way. Plus, the trip hadn't been without purpose. I'd seen my mum. At first, she'd feel a little sad that I hadn't

107

stayed, but as soon as she spotted the spaces in her fridge, she'd glow with maternal pride that her boy might've actually eaten something that she'd carted back from the shops.

'Maggie,' I asked. 'How many pork pies did you eat?'

'Two.' But too quick to be true.

'I'm not going to be angry.'

'Boxes,' Mags giggled from behind her *Smash Hits*. 'Two boxes.'

'So, that's eight pies?'

'No,' she cried. 'It was six.'

'But there's four pies in each box.'

'But both boxes had one missing before I got to them,' she laughed.

'Don't, Maggie. My mum lives on her own. How she eats pies is her business.'

'I'm sorry.'

'Right then,' I continued. 'Did you leave any pies uneaten?'

'Yes,' she chirped. 'A whole box.'

'How many pies were in the box?'

'I didn't look.'

'Tell me,' I demanded.

'Two,' Maggie breathed out, anxious. 'Two pork pies.'

'And,' I lit a smoke, handed it across, 'did you see any baked beans?'

'Beans? Let me think.' Maggie furrowed a moment. 'Yes, beans. Definitely beans, but not Heinz. They were Co-op's own brand and, that's it, they were in the fridge, half a can of Co-op's own-brand baked beans with cellophane wrap covering the top.'

'To keep them fresh,' I thought aloud. 'And did you eat them?'

'No, Billy!' Mags bobbed up and down. 'I swear I didn't eat them. I didn't even touch them. I only like Heinz, and I would've had to heat them up.'

'Good,' I smiled.

'You're not angry?' she asked.

'No, I'm pleased.' I took back the smoke. 'I'm very pleased with you.'

Our smiles became gentle laughter as Maggie rested her head on my chest and closed her eyes. The whole deal was well done. My mum would assume that two people had eaten pies. Plus, she'd seen me sit in my grandad's chair and she knew that made me feel safe. She'd probably guess that I'd graced the wine box, disapprove of the time of day, but you couldn't have it all and it would give us a topic the next time Telecom allowed an incoming call. I watched phone lines keep pace with our speeding train, and sensed the good food digesting in my mother's mind.

The train stopped in Bolton. A girl with big breasts worked her way into one of the four free seats within my immediate field of blurred vision. I waited till she wasn't looking and smiled at her. I pictured nudists playing volleyball, cross-referenced by thick white bra straps in seaside towns and a film I'd once seen about popular deformities in California.

'What are you so happy about?' Maggie quizzed my happy face.

'That girl with large breasts,' I nodded.

'Her,' Maggie spied. 'Billy, she's just fat.'

'No, her breasts are large.'

'She's fat!' Mags snapped, much too loud.

'Whatever the reason,' I hissed. 'Her breasts remain large.'

'Listen, you sad bastard.' Maggie turned and spoke up close into my ear. 'Her breasts remain fat. This poor girl before us probably has tiny, almost no, breasts at all. It is only the layers of fat which surround her tiny body that make her breasts have the appearance of being large.' She leant back, grinned at me. 'And that's all your tiny, but extremely fat, brain can cope with.'

'Give me a minute,' I stalled.

Maybe Maggie was right. I looked more closely, but still couldn't see it. I found it utterly impossible to connect the girl's alleged fatness with her large breasts. It was like school all over again. I had the information, but it didn't make sense. I could accept that the rest of the girl's body might well be described as a little on the fat side, but her breasts still appeared large, huge in fact.

'Well,' Maggie prompted.

'I can't be sure.'

Soft nonsense rolled through my veins. It wasn't a test. It wasn't school. It was funny. I relaxed. Felt myself begin to laugh. I was suddenly, incredibly and irrationally happy. This felt special. It felt everyday and ridiculous. It was the kind of pointless conversation we used to have all the time before the bath, before the debt.

'My God,' I giggled. 'She's a hell of a fat lady.'

'But she's got those lovely big breasts.'

'Lovely.'

And I closed my eyes and saw the whole world naked. Fine for five seconds, but not the sort of thing I could take for too long. Reopened my eyes, reached for a cigarette, looked out the window. I let my gaze shift from the morning sunshine, strong on the fields, to Maggie's perfect yellow features, burning bright beside me.

Her skin glowed. She said something. The speckles in her eyes matched the freckles on her face. Her mouth opened and closed. Her skin flushed. Perfectly.

'What the fuck is wrong with you?' she asked.

'I'm fine, and how are you?' I replied.

'I want you to do the play, will you do the play?'

'What play?' I asked.

'The play, Billy!' Mags had angelic, soft features. 'The play!' she repeated.

'What's all this about a play?' I smiled and closed my eyes.

'For fuck sake!' Mags shouted.

'Quiet.' I shut her out and took her in.

Maggie Shipley was an actress. All she had ever wanted to do was act. It was the single most important thing in her life. She'd told me once that her family had considered selling her spastic brother's body parts to pay for an acting course. I'm sure it was a joke. In the end, they banged a third mortgage on their four walls, came up with the cash and Mags completed the course. But this was all a couple of years back and, sometime last month, Maggie had mentioned that her mum and dad were muttering about payback. Ever since then she'd been working day and night on a play for the city's arts festival. She seemed sure that the production would spark national interest and send her safely, quids in, back to the hearts of her scouse house.

The play's name was *The Cenci*, written by Percy Shelley, a long, long time ago. I'd done a bit of acting and Maggie wanted me to play the lead, Mr Cenci himself. By all accounts, a total wanker who thought he was the devil incarnate.

'BILLY FUCKING BRADY!'

'What is it, Mags?'

'Where the fuck did you just go?' she cried.

'Lancaster.'

'Jesus Christ!' Maggie snapped. 'Will you do the play, you know, THE PLAY!'

'Babe,' I focused on a field, avoided Maggie's face. 'I don't feel that I'm currently up to playing the part of some old Italian cunt who thinks he's Satan and rapes his children.' Grabbed for my fags. 'Not right at the minute, anyhow. It might be a bit of a stretch, if you know what I mean.'

'You know the plot!' she bounced up.

'Hardly.'

'You must've taken it in,' she buzzed.

'Not intentionally.'

'I wouldn't ask, but I haven't got time to get anyone else. Well, I had someone, but they couldn't handle it. Look, I've been doing too many shifts at the bar.' Maggie was all over the place, I gave her a doubtful look. 'All right, you're all I've got, I know it's ridiculous, but I always thought you'd do a really good job and I need to know now.'

'Let me think about it,' I muttered, closing my eyes and thinking about something else entirely. I thought about Charlie. I thought about visibility, I thought about death, but only in a humorous way. No more than three seconds passed before the game was forced to roll on once more.

'The thing is,' Mags razor-coaxed. 'There really isn't any more time to think about it. You've said that before and I've left it alone, but the play's in three weeks and you can't say "not now" for ever. There's a rehearsal on Sunday and you have to be there.' Maggie's eyes weren't pretty any more, they were hard. 'Billy, please, will you be there?'

'Three weeks isn't long enough,' I muttered.

'Billy! We can do it! Everything else is almost ready!' Her tone came down sharp and dangerous. 'The church that I want for the venue has agreed. The Arts Council will give us a grant. The script is edited down to only four hours. Don't laugh, Billy! Please, listen. The production has been listed in the official festival programme. There's a printer who'll do the posters for free.' No breathing, all talking. 'I've cast brilliant actors in almost all the parts. We've had two great rehearsals already. Everybody knows their lines. All I need is for you to say yes and be him. Be the Cenci, Billy! Please, do it!'

While Maggie'd rolled along with her curved ball pitch, I'd travelled inside my heart to take a look around. I saw tins of tuna steak when I'd almost mastered malnutrition. I heard a soft musical voice when I was sure I'd lost my eyes.

I felt hands come and cradle when I could've drowned in the bath. And I heard a thousand midnight doors slam as Maggie came back from midnight scoring for the whipped cripple in the corner. Me and Maggie. Inside my heart. Maggie and me. She was essential to my past, vital to my future, punching the fuck out of my shoulder in the present.

'Stop that!' I snapped hard.

'Will you do it?'

'STOP!'

I glared across, but couldn't even find fake anger to fight with. The simple sound of the word 'yes' floated through my otherwise empty head. I loved Maggie, fucking hated acting. I loved the actress beside me, understood the actor within. Silently praying that some marvellous mishap would crucify the play in preparation, I struggled towards short-term peace. Long-term was a luxury. The weather was irrelevant. I couldn't reach my cigarettes. I leant close to my best mate Maggie and whispered, 'I'll do it.'

The gold-flaked girl went silent and perfectly still. She took me in her arms and cradled my skull. It could've been the good old days of intertwined dependency, but it wasn't. It wasn't the old fucking days. Despite the comfort, the agreement and the temporary calm, I heard myself say a silent bye-bye to fond touches, hello to trouble ahead. I gritted my eyes, buried my head, changed the subject to glorious silence.

Me and Maggie worked our separate ways to isolation. The train crawled south through the north. We were heading back into the sick heart of the city of Manchester. The three-minute release of going home, of escaping, of hiding away and finding what it was to be happy and alive, had all passed by in that one conversation about the size of some fat girl's breasts. I looked up to see that she wasn't there. She'd been my holiday. She'd evaporated when I wasn't looking. She'd departed at some safer stop. Not me, though. I was on my way back in. I looked out the window, saw the city.

Motion-picture postcards. The Tartan Brewing Company. Saturday night at the movies and shipments venturing north through stormy seas. Gaslight memories and damp-smelling streets. Maybe Bella on the bus. Or a canal pint in a brand-new coat. It was the Saturday before Christmas and all the shops were frozen open. Football crowds, racketeers, evening shifts and the great night beyond. Vinyl rooms, electric headphones, dirty cinemas on the cheap chow fan belt. Great waitresses. Occasional cars and easy streets to cross. Stairwells. The mighty flagship of the cruel and unusual North. Tunnels for toddlers. Walls with fists. Home-made hatred and fantastic orange buses. Enormous roundabouts with more exits than worthwhile places to go. Connections. Free tables in the corner and pretend film stars on their backs. Lights on, bets off, it was Manchester, no mistake.

And Charlie was only one man and I was only one man, too.

We rolled deeper and darker in. My fears dissolved. The brave scenery topped my spirits all the way up. My senses grew stronger. I banged my head hard against the window, laughed at determined concrete. I was home, more than ready to fight for it.

I sighed magnificent regret, stood up, aimed for the toilet.

SATURDAY 11.18AM

'Let's go to Neptune's!' Off the train, off my fucking head.

'Perfect!' Maggie bounced pure buzz back at me, gathered up some forgotten girl's skirt and strode ahead. I didn't move, stuck out a fast hand, shouted for Maggie to stop prancing about like a fucking hippie and get in the convenient cab. It definitely wasn't a good time for walking. I could only deal with destinations.

And the destination was Neptune's. It was an all-day, all-night private members' affair that catered to the city's brand-new bastard aristocracy. The place wasn't what you'd call posh, but, at this time of day, it was purely practical, it was the only option. Neptune's was the exclusive recluse for the crazed, insomniac spirit of never-say-sleep Manchester.

The cab ride passed by unnoticed. We ducked through harsh daylight and pushed past an unsigned street door. Relief was reflected down the multi-mirrored staircase. An enormous doorman knew my name from a million times before. The transition from train to hideaway club felt so seamless that I didn't even ask if Charlie was inside. Fuck Charlie. He'd been known to frequent the seedy depths of Neptune's lair, but on Saturday morning he'd probably be cabbaged on some pointless couch watching *Football Focus*, or the weather, or sheepdog trials, or some equally brilliant crap. Charlie was irrelevant, I was alive again. I began to feel much better, back in the city of my choice. I just rode my fat luck down one more flight of mirrored stairs and pushed through one more door. Me and Maggie stepped into the perpetual night-time of the underworld.

And any time was the perfect time to arrive.

Some glorified beggar tart asked me for my coat, but I gave her a look that more than made it clear I wasn't wearing one. The stupid cow retreated while my mind cast back to the oversized, over-friendly cloakroom girl from the night before. She had my fucking coat. I should never have left the club without it. Without my brain, without the blessing of bouncers, without a drink, without provable sanity, without a cluedo, or a better place to be, but never without my fantastic coat.

'Mags, I need a drink, you coming?'

'But I want to go to the toilet,' she whined back.

'That's a much better idea.'

I changed direction without hesitation, sidestepped the usual slappers and swung sharp into the fluorescence. Briefly clocked that I might've misunderstood Maggie, that she might've meant we go to the toilets together. But too late, too early, too much to take in. Neptune's's amenities were crystal-clean, customised for chemicals, completely distracting. No excuses, the girl was on her own and so was I, slipping inside my favourite, furthest from the door, free stall. The purpose-built shelf was smooth and ready, the fantastic door locked solid. I sat down and got about my business. At the crucial moment, loud voices bounced about outside.

'Fucking nuts!'

'Yeah, fucking nuts!'

'It's fucking nuts!'

'Totally fucking nuts, yeah!'

I felt a vague shake. It didn't sound like the sort of conversation my dad and grandad would have, but I closed my eyes, sweating all the same. I muttered 'not now' to parts of me getting ready to give up and forced my lids to lift. Waited for the door-swing sound to be sure that the area was secure, told myself to keep going. Refocused my attention on the three-lined shelf, took what I came for, shook the shit down. I slid the lock in step, passed by the mirrors, wide eyes on the floor, made it safely out of turncoat toilet.

'Billy!' Familiar female voice.

'Hello, Debbie.'

'You all right?' she asked.

'Me,' I grinned. 'Fucking nuts!'

'Looks like it,' she laughed.

'And how've you been, Debbie, my love?'

'Not bad, I'm fine.'

Debbie looked fine, gorgeous in fact, but her gravel-pit voice scratched the underside of weariness. It made me uncomfortable. Reality was other people's weakness, not mine. I shuffled from foot to foot, drugs coming up, wanting to get away. Almost slipped Debbie a left hook, but kissed her on the cheek instead.

'Have you seen Luke?' I asked.

'I saw him over in the corner about half an hour ago.'

'Brilliant.' But I couldn't see a corner.

'God, Billy, I'm that tired, and I've got to be at work in three hours.'

'You'll be all right,' I attempted.

'I'm not sure. It'll be packed tonight. I can't handle it. I might go home.'

'Fucking hell.' Was she trying to piss me off? 'There's no need for that.'

'What's the point of all this, anyhow?' she moaned.

That more than did it. I wasn't up to any more of this crap. I reached inside my pants pocket, isolated a wrap of whiz, couldn't fumble fast enough, palmed it across. The midget-minded solution got me a kiss and a promise of free pints any time, but, to be honest, I was more relieved at the change of pace. Struck me that I was pleased to be playing the old part again. Twigged that I'd just handed out for free, and that was exactly what'd got me in trouble in the first place. But, fuck it, a northern girl went smiling to a northern girl's toilet. Problems obscured and multiplied.

No harm in that.

Feeling an irrational sense of urgency, I pushed off towards the bar. Halfway there I was smacked in the face by the undeniable presence of absolute beauty. It made me stop dead and stare. Fuck, she was here. I hadn't planned on it, but would any day die for it. The girl was off her bonnet and looking lovely. I smiled, missed, moved closer, tried again.

'Billy!'

'Nada,' I shouted back. 'What the fuck are you doing here?'

'Dancing!'

'Shouldn't you be at the takeaway?'

'No!'

'Or home in bed?'

'No!'

'So,' I opened my stance. 'Come here.'

'Yes!'

Christ, Nada was pretty. I could tell she'd spent some time putting it together, but it was well worth the effort. I knew her from the Chinese takeaway that sold me peanut curry for special occasions. If her parents knew she was down here on a Saturday morning, she wouldn't be down here on a Saturday morning. I think it was the strict regime that kept me away. Plus, you could see that Nada would gradually fall apart as the mornings piled up. She was too good to last. Her fragile standards had stretched too high. Nada would, one day, fall into the hard shadows the rest of us called home. But fuck all my sober perspectives, the chemicals were kicking and Nada was only the most beautiful woman in the entire world. It struck me as enough.

I stepped closer, kissed her on the cheek, didn't complain when she kissed me back.

'Dance?' she asked.

'No.'

'Please!'

'No.'

But she began to demonstrate the action right in front of me. I moved to hold Nada, Nada moved away. And there was no easy way to stop her leading me towards the corridor, towards the dark, towards the dance floor, towards perpetual and amazing grace and not another grey midday. Nada, the deep-fried beauty, was probably the only girl in the living, breathing, sweating city that could've got me on the dance floor at a time like this. No more resistance, no more point.

At the end of a short tunnel, the entire world went nuts.

The music blasted in all around, it took me totally over. My thoughts fucked off. I flew all the way into dominant sonic. The levels burnt new bridges into my senses. The late-revival-over-dubbed-digi-processed-rare-imported-remixed-gospel-funk-happy-fusion-house hit me all at once and all over. I saw pictures, improved them. My eyes flicked from shot to shot. I wove a way in and out of stimulated images and perpetual motion. And I smiled wild at all the smiles that had somehow survived. These amazing, moving fuckers. These hard-core devotees of sixteen-hour dance routines. They glowed in the dark. They shone chemical light.

I moved towards them, they moved towards me. And contact. Bomb squads blew up their bombs on purpose. The weather turned tropical. The fucking bastard eagle landed. The beats filled me with unlimited possibilities. The vocal line sent phrases that no one would ever be strong enough to say. They reminded me of love, they reminded me of Nada.

I scoped around, but could only grasp an excess of vague and beautiful shapes. I began to work my way around the tight and scrambled space with only a jumbled sense of searching. And there she was. And I took her hand and tried to thank her for having one. But the girl couldn't hear me, which was no good at all. Immediate conversation was essential. I pulled Nada from the dance floor, led her towards a corner, any corner, where we could sit together. Turned out the random right angle was the one that'd once been known as the VIP area, but too many smashed Manks had crashed it too many times for that daft name to stick. Me and her flopped down, laughing loud, as drinks spilt and deals were undone.

'Oi, Brady!' Heard the voice. 'Watch it!' Fuck the face.

'Piss off!'

'I said, you should fucking watch it, Brady.'

The second speech was more low, more measured. It sounded like someone actually meant something they'd said, for once. I clocked that not too many people called me 'Brady', breathed deep and looked across.

Charlie.

Charles Charlie Charles. Unlikely, unwanted, impossible to deny.

The devil-sent drug dealer and debt collector was too few feet to my left. He had one arm around an almost invisible woman, the other was under the table. In the sharpest of amphetamine blinks, I checked the exits and measured distances in my scrambling mind. Nada had innocently placed herself between me and my immediate escape route. A beautiful woman, it struck again. Much too beautiful to climb over or push. My kind of luck. If the angel hadn't been there, I'd be much better off. I'd be out the door and up the fucking stairs. I'd be giggle-screaming down naughty-boy streets calling for my mother. I'd be long gone. I'd be not coming back.

It was time to make the best of a bad situation.

'How's tricks, Charlie?' I asked, bold.

The pretend movie star acted as if he hadn't heard me. He was staring down a half-pint of Stella. I was tempted to make a comment about Stella being strictly for southern puffs, but thought better of it. There was a general gaggle around the table, I clocked a few faces, no friends. Nada touched my arm, I ignored her, knew I was in this alone. I took a hollow breath, leant towards my tormentor.

'You drinking halves these days, Charlie boy?'

The annoyingly muscular southern starlet still didn't reply. He just moved his second hand to join his first, under the table.

I raised my eyebrows, he made a sound between his teeth. I wanted to say something about hands under tables in public places, but passed on that one as well. Charlie did a half-nod of his head and the woman by his side instinctively got up and walked away. I tried the same trick with Nada, but she was too busy applying fresh make-up to notice. Charlie was clearly winning the early exchanges. I decided to play safe. I put my arm around the oblivious girl at my side. Probably not my bravest action of all time, but it was the exact opposite of Charlie's, so it had a certain charm. On the downside, I'd restricted access to my pockets. I had to reach and pull a cigarette from a pack on the table.

'Don't smoke my fucking cigarettes, Brady!' Charlie growled.

'You smoke these?' I lit up the light embarrassment, inhaled slightly tainted air. 'I'm beginning to wonder why everyone is so scared of you.'

Charlie's silence returned with an extension built on to its intensity. A muscle in his arm twitched. I knew he was up to something. A scroll of options span through my mind, but my sense of humour was wearing thin. I switched back to automatic, considered my environment. Decided that there were too many people around for Charlie to do anything sudden, violent, fatal or final. But the possibility of a knife made it better to back down. I snapped a smile at Nada. She'd finished her cosmetic touch-ups and appeared visibly unsure of the goings-on. Her anxious frown clinched it. Heroics and one-liners could wait, it was time to make a healthy fool of myself.

'Charlie,' I grinned. 'Let's not get into all this now.'

'All what?' It worked, my casual tone snared the fuck. 'I said, all what, Brady?'

'You know what I mean.' Nod, no nod back. 'Look, we should sort this out when there aren't any people around, you know, ladies present and all that.'

Great speech, but I needed something to go with it, I needed a sweetener. I knew that Charlie had all the drugs he could use or I could name, so that wouldn't do. I took a long drag on the tasteless smoke and it instantly came to me. I carefully damped out the half-smoked shit brand and placed it back inside Charlie's pack.

'You're fucking asking for it, Brady!' he snarled.

Subtlety wasn't working. Pride abandoned me. It was time to beg.

'Look, Charlie!' I launched, plaintive. 'I'm a little strung out at the moment. I'm sure you know how that is. Fuck! I didn't meant that! Listen, what I'm trying to say is that I've been up all night. I've had a death in the family. City's home form is depressing me. And I haven't even sorted out my Christmas-card list.' Nice touch, in for the kill. 'So, why don't you and me deal with our problems some other time?' Big smile. 'You know, when there's less distractions.'

'FUCK THE DISTRACTIONS!' he roared. 'WHERE'S MY MONEY?'

I'd been trying so hard to make it nice for everyone. I wanted the crowd around to go on with their morning untroubled. But Charlie's shout had scared the shit out of everyone except him. It was a selfish, typically southern, maladjusted act. It was a red rag to a bull where I came from.

'Your money?' I frowned. 'Your giro late again?'

As soon as I'd said it I knew I'd crossed the line. Might've got away with the crack if Charlie had been whacked away on good smack, surrounded by transparent Pan's People and a million miles from me at the time, but I'd mistimed my punchline and right there and right then, I clocked that the duck and weave would probably be my next dance.

'Can I take that back?' I asked.

'Shut the fuck up.' Charlie razored. 'And listen to me.'

I'd warned my whole body to be ready, listening was easy.

'The only reason I'm not going to deal with this right now, the only reason I'm not going to deal with you right now,' his hand twitched beneath the table, 'is out of respect for Bella.'

'Come again?'

'SHUT THE FUCK UP AND LISTEN TO ME!' Charlie thrust himself forward. The edge of his anger came to within a lazy shave of my face. His southern accent sounded out of place, but completely serious. Had to admit he was good-looking close up. Good- and extremely dangerous-looking. He looked about as serious as a knife attack. Not funny, I thought, slowly leaning back, nodding my silence, reaching for a cigarette. Fuck, only just stopped myself.

'Before I do anything about this,' Charlie knew he was in control, measured his tone. 'Before I do what I know I want to do, I'm going to check it with Bella. I want to know that what I'm planning to do won't upset her too much. She's one of ours, and I have to respect that.'

What? Absolutely unbelievable! Bella. Fucking incredible! How did she get involved? Why was she involved? It was useful, but I didn't like it. I knew Charlie was stuck on Bella, who wasn't, but I didn't have him down as a considerate soul. Maybe it was a weakness on his part, maybe it was posse-related chivalry, maybe he was an out-of-date sexist, maybe he was a pseudo-southern bastard, maybe he thought he could get in bed with Bella. I felt a sudden urge to fuck with the cunt.

Time to dance.

'Is she here?' I asked casually.

'You fucking know she isn't, Brady!'

'That's right,' I smiled. 'I did know that.'

'What's your point?' Charlie snapped.

I looked away from him as if I hadn't heard and leant into silent Nada. I kissed her gently on her perfect cheek.

It could've been the garden of Gethsemane, it could've been the most stupid thing to do at the time, but fuck all that, it was deliberately done to bring Charlie on. Nada didn't react at all. Her almond eyes stared straight at where I'd last seen Charlie. There was a gap in the action. I heard silence ruminate through the walls, take its time travelling, arrive at our dark corner table, clear its throat and scream its fucking brains out.

'KNIFE!' Nada yelped, but I'd known all along.

I span back to see Charlie swipe the drinks off the table. His hand was finally out. I caught sight of the fast-moving metal object. The table emptied fast. My brain cut out, everything else kicked in. I shielded Nada from flying glass, snap-checked back at Charlie, the fake movie star posing away with his sizeable blade. I pushed Nada the fuck away and regardless.

What will be will be, but in Latin.

I threw myself at Charlie. The fucker was too busy catching angles of light on the surface of silver to stab me straight away. We came together heavy across the table. It was a typical tangle of strong arms. Our respective heads went back, the mutual zone shrank. As was almost always the case, one arm each came free at the exact same moment. But Charlie had a knife and, in a fist fight, a weapon is a disadvantage. The kitted-up cunt was fractionally delayed by adjusting and aiming the knife. So, I punched the fucker, hard and clean, in the face. My rings cut into my knuckles, Charlie fell back, I moved to follow, but someone strong and fast grabbed my arm, span me round. The wide-open face of Luke was gritted hard before me. My hands were forced to my sides, my feet left the ground, I was carried fast, back and away.

'Get the fuck out, Billy!' Luke shouted. 'This is mentalo!'

'Mentalo sounds like a mouthwash!'

A full bottle of Heineken skimmed past my face, exploded

in the mirror behind. Broken mirrors, destruction of shit beer, maybe Charlie was on my side after all. I looked across to see him bleeding, snarling, coming towards me.

'Charlie!' I roared.

The DJ mixed the reverb into the ambience.

'Charlie!'

NUS members formed a queue for the toilets.

'Charlie, come on!'

Some girl swallowed an entire scream.

'Not now, Charlie! Not now!'

On the dance floor they still danced.

'Charlie! Charlie! Charlie!'

And with each repetition I identified the man with the knife a little more. Charlie could no longer make an easy cut in a dark corner. The fucker would have to take me on and slice me up in the full view of our morning audience. And each time I said his name, his recognition dawned, his approach slowed. As my voice came slower, sunk deeper, sounded better, Charlie was forced to take inches off his instincts. All the attention wasn't doing him any favours, for once. His closing-in face showed confusion.

The club hadn't stopped still, like in Hollywood where Charlie believed he lived, but there were definitely enough witnesses to cripple a criminal act. Charlie made his play, tried to appear amused by my final-straw show. The well-practised cunt actually came to a stop and smiled. Not for me, but at me. Couldn't help a smile myself, but cut it quick when I remembered the state of the game and the desired result.

The immediate world waited. My sweat went wet. Our eyes mixed and serious hatred, from both sides, met in the middle. Charlie palmed and pocketed the knife, walked towards me. To his unbelievable credit, Luke went to step between us, but I gestured him aside. Charlie was within my reach and I was within his. My tormentor's hand slowly opened and lowered. I didn't think twice. I grasped the universal gesture of survivors.

And we shook. And, for once, it wasn't just me.

'You've got till tomorrow night,' he said, slowly. 'Sunday night, all of it.'

ORANGE

SATURDAY 2.18PM

Tired grannies hit stone-cold streets for a bit of motion and loaves of shite white sliced. Serious shoppers snapped up plastic with plastic. *Big Issue* vendors nodded from notorious corners because I bought one once. Mothers shouted in loud scally at fully mucked-up toddlers. Teenage girls from Bolton, Oldham, Wigwam and beyond looked, laughed and looked away. Bizzies clocked me, recalled the soft council's policy to protect me, reflected on the grief, the paperwork, the big match in Moss Side and let me slide by. Coppers were easy, mothers knew better. 'Specially the single ones with their economy bags, self-inflicted children and awkward walks.

Mothers knew better, yes, mothers knew best.

The pavement turned greyer than the grey it'd been before. My bones turned to dust. True blues dilated to pure black. I spied an incidental tourist off a bus at the wrong stop, snapping an Instamatic. I tried to disappear before anything developed. I tried to hide in the bright winter light. Manchester's meanest streets threw killer punches, hard, fast and unfriendly. I struggled to avoid the quality of the light on the failure of faces. I fought against the invasion of most common knowledge. I was in the open, forced out of the underground. But I hadn't been caught, not quite and not yet. I made it to a new corner, took in a new view. It was hectic as hell and twice as shite.

And roads can turn on you at any time.

I almost ran, stumbled for cover instead. I was desperate to find safety inside. I told myself that the next corner wouldn't be too far away, that the scenery would be brief, that I was almost home. Despite the danger, the distance and the time of day, I didn't give up, I wouldn't let go. Amphetamine roads can stretch for ever, but I held it together and worked my way towards personal rescue.

I thought hard of home. I pieced together blow-by-blow success stories to send me singing in the shower. I focused my mind on gentle bed sheets, reed curtains, favourite tapes paused and waiting in wind-up tape decks. It struck me to sing along to some familiar tune. I pictured a pop star, imagined a movie, kept moving. I blocked out the possibility of any turnaround. There was no way back to the club. There was no way I was going to throw up on the street.

After throwing up, I tried to control movement, inside and out. I kept my eyes tight, hands gripped spastic knees. I didn't slip. I wouldn't fall. Defeat was not allowed. The cold in the air kept me up. I breathed it in, sucked it back, opened wide my eyes. Had to overlook dark visions that crawled inside my lumpy sickness, block out rubbish from the night before, delete the Big Mac from the mouth of the binman across the road. I wouldn't let myself see the bits of grit on the road touched by my fresh vomit. I even ignored the bits that remained untouched. I blocked it all out, indiscriminately out.

I talked only to myself.

'There's a key in your pocket. Cigarettes, yes, plenty of cigarettes. Love the lock, LOVE IT!' The corner was coming closer. 'Coming closer, definitely coming closer.' Packed double-decker. 'WHAT THE FUCK ARE YOU LOOKING AT?'

Wanted to attack the top deck, but tried to stay focused on positive forces. Moved along, I just moved myself mad along. The destination would, eventually, have to stand still. The corner would have to come. And I could wait for it, tic-toc-tic-toc. I could breathe to it, in-out-in-out-in. I could walk round it, one-two-one-two-one-two-three-four-five and contact. I happy-slapped the specially angled cement, swung wide and smiled at every beautiful detail of the brand-new road ahead. My own personal Whitworth Street centred itself into view. I chose a spot on the near left side, called it home, kept it steady.

Ugly NCP passed to my right. Pub's open door dragged me dangerously close, but I ran across the road, laughing, crying, keeping my head down. I bewared of the buses, kept my expressions close, took swift steps up, up and in. I completed the key circuit on my magnetic door, crossed the carpeted entrance hall. Didn't blow it, lose it or even confuse it with anything more important than what it was. It was the long walk home, successfully walked. I slid the conventional key in the lovely lock and breathed all the way out when the click occurred. I pushed the door wide and entered the last safe place left on earth. Couldn't help screaming relief, gratitude and as loud as I could when my thick front door slammed hard behind.

Made it, yes!

SATURDAY 2.47PM

'HELP!'

Fuck. I'd completely forgotten about Jim.

'PLEASE! SOMEBODY! HELP ME!'

'Shut up.'

'UNTIE ME!' he begged through thin walls. 'PLEASE! UNTIE ME!'

'I said shut the fuck up!'

Quicked it to my bedroom, grabbed a magazine, fell on my bed. Tried to shut out Jim's desperate shouts. I needed to focus on big pictures, small words. My eyes made sense out of familiar shapes. 'Betsy was a coal miner's daughter, she comes from Oklahoma.' I propped myself against a pillow, lit a cigarette. 'Betsy,' yes. 'Coal miner's daughter,' possible. 'Oklahoma,' exotic.

'WILL SOMEBODY HELP ME!'

I inhaled deep. 'Betsy.' Deeper. 'Daughter.' Deepest. 'Oklahoma.' My eyes closed, the inevitable skin screen flicked in. Betsy was naked at a coalface. Her pickaxe slipped, a support beam snapped, the mud ceiling crashed down on Betsy's fake blonde head. 'HELP ME! PLEASE, HELP ME!'

I saw mucky tears in her father's eyes as his muscles flexed against the crush. I tried to focus on Betsy's breasts, but they were bent out of shape by the rockfall and I could hardly see them. Scanned back to her eyes. Betsy's expression hadn't changed. Body crushed, eyes inviting.

'PLEEEEEASE! HELP ME!'

My exhausted body spread out, bright sound and light exploded. I skated night-time roads. Skating, running, burning, charging, seeing a parked car as it came closer. I ran faster. The ball bounced in my mind. I opened my jaws to suck it up. Timing was essential. It was going to be close. Some fucker shouted a name.

'Not now,' I whispered.

It was my name.

'I'm asleep.'

'BILLY!'

'Sleep.'

'BILLY!' The voice was closer, lighter. 'ARE YOU IN THERE?'

'Fuck.' Bang on the door, I opened my eyes. 'Maggie, is that you?'

'WILL SOMEBODY PLEASE HELP ME!'

'Betsy?'

'Billy! Get up!' Mags again. 'I need to talk to you!'

'Fuck sake!' I couldn't see my cigarettes, couldn't move my head.

'I have to go to work,' came from the corridor. 'Meet me there.'

'I'll have the usual,' I croaked.

'If you want a drink,' she shouted, 'GET UP!'

'Can't move.' Eyes on the ceiling, still no cigarettes.

'WILL SOMEBODY PLEASE UNTIE ME!'

'Maggie,' I yelled. 'Cigarettes!'

'UNTIE ME! YOU BASTARDS!'

'MAGGIE!' But the door slammed.

'I HATE YOU!' Desperate, loud, next door. 'I HATE YOU BOTH!'

I propped myself up on my solitary pillow and struck out at the open magazine. Betsy went silently screaming into the far wall and my cigarettes, thank fuck, my fantastic cigarettes appeared in her place. I grabbed, shook, thumbnail-flipped and pulled out fast. I lit up and sucked back, managed to breathe again.

'I'M GOING TO DIE!'

'Quiet,' I muttered as sharp edges turned to curves.

I looked through smoke and out my window, took a guess at the time. The in-between light against the naked glaze was dark daytime, not nearly black enough. Too early, I decided, still too early. I couldn't be sure, but thought I'd fallen home around three. Felt certain that no more than an hour had passed since I'd entered the flat.

And before that, I'd been awake for as long as it took most people to repeat the dull conspiracy of tragedies they called their life. The hard-working ones, up bright and early, heartless breakfasts swallowed, commotions strapped, emotions ditched. Bye-bye kisses blown on front doorsteps. Garden paths to waiting worlds grudgingly waddled. Waiting worlds that didn't need, care or even want them very much. All to brush soft shoulders with identikit despair through the clock-watch of single days. To sharpen blunt pencils from the blunt pencils box. To hurry home. To blossom for entire, shared, tragic moments over fat-fried suppers. To sit down in the dark in front of electric light from the tvideogamesoftmachinemonitor. To lose it in the lounging. To drop it in the drooling. To fall at the first fence. To wake up with backache, heartache and endless amounts of bellyache. To creep the frayed staircase back to bed, back to sleep. Then to wake again, a second time, a third time, a thousandth time, alarmed in the early morning. To eat that same breakfast. To walk the same path. Hit repeat, hit fade, hit repeat, hit fade, hit repeat, you're fading fast.

Sleep, the idle bastards loved it.

I turned over on my side and snapped a jealous peg at

the hollow cardboard wall. New hole, sore foot, so what. The pathetic population possessed the secrets of sleep, they wallowed in it. They might die in the meantimes of midday, but when it came to sleep they were superstars. And right there, lying down then, threatened and fairly fearful, a little shaky in the shadow of the knife, whacked from all that'd gone before, I needed it. I needed some hateful waster to tell me how it was they fell asleep. One of them, any of them, all of them, to simply lean across soft and whisper away on the secrets of peaceful sleep.

I tried to imagine hands stroking my head. I half heard delicate words. I conjured the hypnotic rise and calming fall of a good woman's warm lungs and breathed beside her. I placed a pillow between my legs and a protective hand over my head. I sniffed for the sweet smell of sleep, told myself stories filled with soporific magic. I tried so hard to fall asleep. I curled tighter, double-scrunched my eyes, fought the occupational hazard of cranial connections. That was the key. More than anything. More even than the grand prize of gone. I wanted to escape my chemically fuelled train of thought. I needed to leap free as we hurtled past sub-station snooze. I had to fall for ever asleep somewhere near nowhere, just anywhere not here.

But the scenery only sped up.

The sounds in the around only announced themselves clearer, only sounded louder. Every place I stopped became a place to start again and immediately. Every breath that almost soothed was followed by one that sucked up sharp and suggested a shake. I tried to skip every second breath, the disruptive ones, but it wasn't working. Against my arm, within my curl, throughout my exhausted body, a baby shake clawed its bastard way in.

First defeat was in the tiny rustle of the pillow against my ear. The delicate tremor dug a little deeper. My head jolted, sweat dripped into my eye. I bit my lip, tasted blood, tried so hard not to crack. Took a shallow breath. Then another. Almost saw orange. Might've been winning, might've been on my way off when a double-decker, city-councilled, fully diesselled autobus slammed on its air brakes right outside my see-through window.

I snapped straight up, screaming.

Whacked my eyes wide to see an entire upper deck of home-headed shoppers on the return trip from town. Stayed still, screamed, this time silent, hoped to hell they wouldn't see me. Some hope, but not enough. One by one the threatening set of silhouetted heads turned their attention down and in. My entire wreck flinched from its curl. My legs kicked vicious, soft pillow flew and bastard shakes erupted. Right hand reached fast, yanked me towards the handle, towards the door, towards the corridor.

Temporary peace never lasts.

I snapped 'fares please' at the laughing skeletons in our dark passage, ducked fast into the bathroom and hit the electric light switch hard. I decided that my only option was to get back in the bathtub. The week before, within its ceramic walls, had gone beyond boring, but its clean surfaces, constant hot water and inbuilt echo effect had definitely calmed me down. I wasn't committing to a seven-day stretch, but a quick dip was just what I needed. Cleanliness was next to godliness. A change was as good as a rest. A stitch in time saved nine. A bird in the hand was worth a bag of chips in an avalanche. I slapped the side of my head, stopped fucking around, span the taps.

Became rapidly naked in the well-locked room. The water was drawn and the water was warm. Moisture droplets in the surrounding air offered individual promises of peace. I stepped myself into the brilliant bath and let out a long sigh. Began to wash the day ahead into my skin. Possibilities smelt of soap. My future life ran random currents around my shifting body. And the shakes gradually began to subside. The brave glow-worm within returned ready for the night shift. I noticed myself cheering up. Scrubbing, humming, humming, scrubbing, not shaking.

Heard the stash in my bedroom shouting loud for immediate attention. Knew that my craving meant I was in the clear. Ducked the old bonce under the hot tap one last time and got myself out of the bath. Enjoyment of one pleasure, experience of one buzz, almost always sharpened the appetite for the next. Be it bath-stash-beer, or weed-speed-smack, or beer-beer-beer, or birthday-Christmas-death, sequences made life simple and simple was good. I giggled myself dry with a pink towel, glanced in the broken mirror, grabbed up my clothes and pushed back through to my bedroom, fairly certain in the knowledge that I would live at least one more day.

Quick picked up a pack of fags from the floor, grabbed matches and a bit of cash. Threw on the same gear I'd been wearing before, all appropriate. Honed in on my stash, did some smart fingerwork, dropped half a tab of acid, an E, rubbed up the gums with whiz, scratched my head, shivered a bit and headed out the door. Clocked this well-miserable, hung-up skeleton in the corridor, had a crisis of conscience, tapped gently on Maggie's bedroom door.

'Jim?'

Tap-tap.

'Jim?'

Imagined his excited rabbit eyes as Maggie tied him down.

'Jim, can you hear me?'

Wired and smiling wide when she leant over to tug the knot.

'It's Billy.'

Dressed in a thin sheen of delight, not much else.

'Jim, are you all right?'

Poor lad might've been tragic, but he didn't deserve this.

'Would you like me to untie you?'

Equal rights for masochistic chefs.

'Jim!' I tried louder.

'YOU CUNT, BRADY!' Jim blasted. 'I'M GOING TO KILL YOU!'

I decided that one death threat a week was enough, left him to rot.

SATURDAY 3.48PM

The streets outside were on their way to a luminous orange:
I loved it. The wind-chill factor had eased ever so slightly.
Rain was the same. Front door of the regular drinking hole
was already within my sight. I sped up my stride, imagined
a friend.

'Do you think we could move closer to the pub?' I'd
ask her.

'We can bloody well see it from where we live,' she'd reply.

'We can only see the front door, not the actual bar.'

'Maybe you'd like to live in the newsagent's opposite.'

'Maybe I would, Mags, maybe I would.'

'No, Billy,' she'd say, smiling. 'You'd love it! Just think –
to live actually inside your own little newsagent's across the
street from your favourite pub. You'd be set for life.'

'It sounds perfect.' I pictured a camp bed, a crate of toilet
rolls, an inexpensive clock radio and a flightless bird's-eye
view of nearby beer. There'd have to be a hitch.

'Would I have to get up early and deliver the papers?'
I asked.

'No,' she laughed. 'You'd pay some little tyke to carry the
heavy bag while you lay in bed and took first look at all the
exciting magazines.'

'And the chocolate?'

'You don't like chocolate, Billy.'

'Exactly. What would I do with it?'

'Sell it, you moron!'

I reached the corner wondering if I could ever sell enough chocolate to pay Charlie back. I pictured a sugar mountain, a spade, a set of weighing scales and found myself laughing in the rain as Maggie flipped out of my imagination and into my vision. I watched her stretch over the optics towards the creamy cappuccino machine as I waited for the traffic lights to change.

Smart lady, our Maggie. She could follow me round the houses. She took what she wanted, gave me a rest. She'd traced my tracks through to some finally found mornings. She'd always been able to sidestep the shit talk of the all-night nerve-wreckers. Maggie knew how to close down the angles, dismiss all except the essentials, and she even slept less than I did. Plus, I couldn't recall her ever complaining.

But then, I didn't try too hard.

And there she was, working the bar, as smart and efficient and as our Maggie as ever. From where I stood, I saw her turn her head and give a smile that a Russian in a leotard with a hoop in the air would've got a top score for. I reminded myself that she'd probably be expecting me, that the first pint was probably already poured, that I was supposed to be crossing the road. The traffic light changed, the green man flashed, I didn't move.

A noisy double-decker lurched to a standstill between me and the pub. I could still see alcohol light breaking through the bent heads of the slappers on board, but Maggie was obscured. The scouse spell broken, my eyes absently shifted round the options. Cinema, burger stand, train station, taxi rank, phone box, *Big Issues*, personal insurance, phone box. Phone box. Empty, clean and ready for calling. Phone box. I felt the beginnings of a new night push its coins through the slot. I felt the levels lift.

I checked back to the bar, but didn't see myself in there. I couldn't see myself in there. I wasn't fucking in there. Maggie was, but she'd been surrounded by a hoard of middle-aged shoppers. Her central role no longer looked so glamorous, more bollocks. Budget-minded wrinklers had lined the early-evening shadows with their gin-sucking ugliness. The bat brigade had taken temporary command of our oasis. Their greys and purples and pinks buzzed a force field that forced me to pause. Phone box. The decision began to feel much less diffi-cult. Maggie could save herself, I needed someone to save me. I stepped off the pavement, felt in my pocket for change.

I never normally had to call Bella before heading over; she was my fucking girlfriend after all, but the situation with Charlie had taken the legs from even the most simple of steps. Charlie and Bella were what they called friends and, after last night, there was a decent chance he'd gone round hers. I imagined them smoking themselves through to the daylight, Charlie telling muscular tales of a bar-room brawl and a certain unfaithful man. Bella would fold a leg under a leg, Charlie would look, she'd nod her head, he'd breathe out and they'd talk, talk, talk. I imagined soft, dangerous words tripping around a civilised interior. Felt involuntary guilt. After that well-placed but badly timed kiss, Nada's name would be a steady repeat with no fade. Charlie would be working on my faults, dynamiting them wide in Bella's mind. Plus the money, the outstanding money, would, no doubt, be more than mentioned.

Whatever the weather, it was definitely a good idea to make that phone call before heading over. Considered patting myself on the back for being so clever, but crossed the road against the light and swung wide the strangely heavy phone-box door instead.

I touched out the corners of a twenty-pence piece, speed-dialled.

'Hello, Bella speaking.'

'Congratulations.'

'Billy!' she yelped. 'Where are you?'

'Behind the bike sheds,' I smiled. 'Come over.'

'Is your phone back on?'

'No.'

'Are you at somebody's house?'

'Yes,' I lied. 'But it's awfully small.' Her suspicious edge had set me off. 'The walls are transparent and there's a terrible fucking draught. Bitch made me pay to use the phone. It's a fucking disgrace, all round. There's all this stuff to read on the wall, but it's obscured by spray paint. I'm not sure who lives here, but they seem to be obsessed with the emergency services and prostitutes.'

'Billy!' Bella snapped.

'Hang on, I think I see the connection.'

'Billy, shut up, I've got it.'

'Are you sure?'

'You're in a call box, for Christ sake!'

'And the winner of the "Where is He Now Cheapskates" is Bella Avabanna from Chorlton and north London.' I reached for a cigarette, lit it up to pass the silent time. 'Yes, Bella, I'm in a call box, for the sake of our sweet Lord Jesus.'

'Have you slept?' she asked.

'I would, but there's no room to lie down.'

'Come over.'

'Is there anyone home?' I mumbled, shy.

'No,' she replied. 'Just me.'

'No visitors?'

'Now who's playing Sherlock?'

'Fair point.' I laughed, seeing Bella's double-locked Chorlton door surrounded by safety paint. The walk to her bedroom became a gallery opening. I'd comment on a particular image, feel up a new frame, discuss artistic sensibilities with any southerner available. 'I shall be arriving shortly.'

'Good.'

'Bye.' I cracked the receiver down.

The coast had been cleared. The door swung both ways. I was on my way. The clock on top of the tower told me I had time for everything. Streets opened up before me and for me. I walked through history, through the for ever rain, through slow-motion picture postcards, to see my girlfriend, to see Bella.

SATURDAY 4.03PM

I nodded at the fat driver inside his heated hackney cab.

He flipped his paper closed, threw it aside, jowled down at his wristwatch. I was close to the door-handle click when cabbie flashed back, squinted his tiny eyes, shook his wobbly once towards, once away. Bastard put the black cab in gear, got off up the road. I swung my steel cap at the back bumper, missed completely and hit the road with the side of my soft head.

'FUCK!' I screamed.

I'd landed in a bit of a puddle. Felt the cold in the road claw through to my shoulder. Watched the cunt turn left at the Palace. I rolled on my back, closed my eyes, felt raindrops hit my face and imagined the heartless taxi man heading towards the city centre where the somehow more appropriate, less desperate, fares stood beneath the same weather.

Fucking taxi drivers, all they were were bus drivers with shit attendance figures. That's what standards did for you, fuck all. Dress codes for clubs, guest lists for cabs, next you'd have to dig out some fancy slacks just to get on a bus. Perhaps it was the look in my eyes, or the shoes on my feet; maybe it was the scars around my mouth, or Bonnie Tyler backlash. Whatever it was, it was whatever. It was time to send the local fleet of black cabs the way of the royal yacht, down south. What's the logic of hackney cabs in Manchester, anyway? Even the name's a fucking insult.

I heard disembodied voices come from above. Opened my eyes to watch the scurry of students' well-togged feet steeple by. Looked up in time to catch the flow of a particularly natural curl, the elegant glance of a well-made eye, the noticeable speed up in a self-obsessed step away. Fucking students. Fucking students and fucking taxi drivers. The worthless subdivisions of humanity went together so well, suited each other so perfectly. Lying on the road, I realised that was the whole point, and began to feel angry with myself instead. Rolled on my side, but wasn't sure what came next. Saw a granny stumble on the midget steps of the adult cinema across the street. Clocked she was the cleaner, caught a dose of perspective, picked myself up.

On my feet, I took hold of a cigarette. Wobbled a bit as the acid began to bubble under. Checked the immediate architecture just to be sure. The surroundings looked grand, dramatic, almost epic. Clocked that the distortion was undoubtedly kicking in. I lit up luminous, had a harmless spit and a celebratory laugh, blew cigarette smoke into the crystal air and casually began to wander off the way I should've wandered off in the first place. Away from the bastard hackney rank, down the length of Whitworth Street towards Castlefield NCP, level three, and my mate Trevor.

Trevor was an evangelical schizophrenic who lived alone in a red Cortina. He'd be waiting for more than me. Trev had been driving a select bunch of the city's drug suppliers here, there and anywhere we wanted for a good while. He was hooked on the barter system. His meter didn't light up for money. Trev demanded payment he could put to immediate use. His various locations were common knowledge to an uncommon crowd, and weekends found him in Castlefield NCP, always level three.

I'd first come across Trevor halfway home one chuckin'-down night when some see-through star bird suggested I show her exactly how to snort the stuff. We'd somehow woven our stupid way to the back door of an all-night car park. I took one look at the rain outside, the dust inside and pushed her giggling through the gap. Wanting to avoid the interruption of unnecessary security, I started her up the series of internal ramps. I spotted a yellow sign with a printed three, liked the look of it, told her to stop.

The flat concrete canyon low-ceilinged our shadows. She moved towards the brickwork and leant against it. Concrete, gap, concrete, girl. I stood back a sensible distance and did something like smile. She undid her shirt to show me the patterns on her large bra. Orange, light, white and dark, all at the same time. I said nothing special, she became a fantastic topless model in class ads for lubricating oil. I forgot about the car park, the middle of winter, the sheets of rain whipping from the west and smiled across big time. Drugs'll do that for you. I wondered what she'd do for them.

My knees cracked concrete as I opened her up. She giggled again, taking the grains from the back of my fist. Her eyes turned greener than the green they'd been before. My face went between her buttons. It was warm in there, I remember that. But before I could work on any more mashed-potato memories, full-beam headlights flashed on and all over us. I span round angry, standing and swearing. She ran away sharpish, buttoning, leaving.

Trev entered my life and was instantly preaching.

'God told me to turn them on,' he said from his front seat.

'What?' I yelled through the car-window crack.

'God loves light. It banishes darkness, hence it is his godly headlight.'

In the years I'd known him it'd become increasingly clear that Trevor wasn't a normal individual, by any standards. He was indiscriminate forties, said he first found God at a free concert, loved his drugs and went to great lengths to keep himself to himself. It was known around town that Trev had been one of the big dealers in the brown days of late seventies Manchester. Story went that southerners moved up and in, turned Trev off his turf. Trev didn't talk about it. He much preferred to harp on about his Lord, his music and his dream Sundays in the park with four figments of his imagination banging away at the underside of bliss. Soft lad told everyone he had a wife and three kids, but don't kid a kidder, sunshine. With Trevor, I'd learnt to watch the world go by fast enough to ignore.

'Where to tonight, brother Bill?' he asked me.

'Somewhere safe and warm,' I replied.

'Heaven?'

'No, Trev.' I laughed. 'Bella's.'

'Chorlton bound we are, my faithless, ungrateful brother.'

'Here you go, lad.' I separated three tabs, palmed them across.

'Already airborne, matey.'

'How come?' I asked.

'Martin's Audi's in the shop,' he grinned. 'I've been beaming him around town all afternoon.' I caught Trev's eyes, pure black. 'Are these the same?' he bubbled.

'Strawbs.'

'That's them,' he fizzy-smiled. 'Fucking great stuff, I necked four before.'

'Four?'

'Four before, a fine plank.' Trev cried. 'Put them away for us, brother.'

I nodded, popped the glove compartment, dropped the trips inside and got to chopping out a couple of fat one-liners on the Cortina's dashboard. Trev leant low to get a cassette from under his seat. I snorted, he slammed it into the deck. Buttons were pressed and child locks clicked. Trev leant back in his seat, down on the gas, as the long and involved atmosphere of 'LA Woman' rolled in.

We cleared the car park easy.

'Have you ever actually been to Los Angeles, Trevor?' I pitched across.

'No,' he buzzed back. 'But I've been to me.'

'Buy any postcards?'

'Triplicate photocopies double-backed on two-sided Sellotape with vague impressions of beaches, mountains and roller coasters in red, white and blue.' The boy was rolling. 'Practically collected postcards when I was young, but sold them three a penny last week at a sports-car welly-boot sale.'

'You all right to drive?' I old-joked.

'Mistook the cavalry for Calvary and ended up dyslexic, crucified on a bareback horse going nowhere. And yes, brother Bill, I'm very good to drive, thank you.'

'There's none better.' I lit up, smiling. 'So you've been to America?'

'Both ways and back ways, brother. The beast was four foot high and two thousand miles across. Attacked me with needles, small laws and chainsaws.' Trev spoke fast through slow traffic. 'Godless sun snogged my cheeks through the southlands. Mr Frosty chipped my lips in the North. I found a church in a spotlight, it could've been Blackpool and it could've been me.' Trev punched the steering wheel's padded centre. 'America, America, America!' he cried. 'We have all been there!'

I wasn't really listening. Trev could be worse than me. Or more far gone. I recalled something Martin had said a while back about Trevor being my spiritual father. It'd been late, we'd been fucked, I'd found it funny, almost a compliment, but it struck me different right then. It struck me that if friends thought Trevor was somehow my predecessor, then where the hell did they think I was heading? Did they think this could happen to me? I could probably cope with the schizophrenia, the self-delusion, the non-existent family, the nonsense, even the fucking religion, but sleeping in a second-hand red Cortina, in a fucking car park, I mean, come *on*!

The more I thought, the more occurred.

Trevor had lost his family and friends when he'd been thrown off the racket. Don't think I'd ever heard the story dead straight, but enough bits stuck for me to know that some serious damage had been done. One version was that Trev had headed off around the world, another had him hidden twenty miles up the coast in Fleetwood. Either way, when the lad tried to come back, his gap was gone. He was snookered on the perpetual outside. He was done, his destiny permanently twisted to this. I looked across at Trev, taking me to Chorlton in his mobile motorhome, a traffic light bleeding red over his empty expression. Shit, Trev had been reduced to this. To being a ferry service on the fringes of a world he'd once controlled. The king had returned from exile to find that all that was left was a red Cortina, a very few friends and an insane one-way system.

I deliberately tried to distract myself from more pity shit by looking out the window. What did I care, anyhow? It was all just ancient history mixed with powerful acid. Times had changed, they did that, so what. Whatever had happened to Trevor wasn't about to happen to me. I was fine. I was on my way to Bella's magic bed. Maggie was making me pints. Charlie was from London. I owed him money. I was being forced out. Just like Trev, years before. Fuck. Forced myself to forget about it. Focused hard on early-evening Manchester. I cracked the window as we flashed past a changing traffic light halfway down the 'miracle mile' of Oxford Road.

The miracle fucking mile. The only miraculous thing about this part of town was that it hadn't been firebombed, yet. The miracle mile. It was a miracle that we tolerated it. Fuck, you had to fill out all the right forms, finish your homework, starve in Bangladesh and crawl home crying before you'd even be allowed to squat round here. Fucking students were everywhere. Trevor living in a car, me short a few hundred quid, in real danger and this fat girl was crossing the road with five overstuffed bags of frozen food in her stomach's future. She smiled. I felt disgusted. Pictured a breathless mother halfway up a steep country hill, saw electronic money coming, going, coming, keep going. The only time these people could stand on their own two feet was when someone else was wiping their arse.

'You're quiet, brother Bill.'

'Sorry.'

'You're not the company you used to be.'

'Just thinking,' I muttered.

'Tell me about it,' Trev nudged, changing gear.

'Mothers, fathers, floating waste, the poverty gap, fat people, perversion.'

'Sounds good,' Trev sparked.

'Addictions, ancient history, miracle miles, home-made madness, application forms for drug debts, seaside towns, Bangladesh and all these stupid fucking kids.'

'Well,' Trev levelled. 'Me and the wife try not to waste any time with the kids.'

I wanted to say that Trevor wasted no time at all with the wife or the kids, that he didn't have a wife or kids any more, that he'd been making it up for so long that it was almost finished. Wanted to say that I didn't fucking need this right now, what with the weekend and the debt and the danger and the isolation coming on strong. And I definitely didn't want to remember Martin's joke any more. I didn't want to know that jokes were just the truth hidden in humour. I didn't want to fucking think anything any more. I dug out an irritated cigarette, lit it, grunted my defeat, let Trevor take over.

'We love to read together, as a family unicorn,' he rambled. 'Our favourite pieces of paper exist in magical bobbit land.

I read it aloud every Sunday after a long day at the Edge, Alderly, that is. It's just the right tempter for a good appetite. So, we end the day with a nice sit-down and home-cooked in front of the real fire.'

'You're fucking delusional,' I breathed.

'Corned-beef hash, watch it cunt, and plenty of pickle.'

'Don't forget the peas.'

'Of course,' Trev cheered. 'Fresh-picked peas!'

'One dream world comforts another.'

'You fucking said it,' he snapped.

'Well,' I looked away. 'It all sounds fantastic.'

'You should come along one Sunday, brother.'

'I'll come tomorrow,' I cut back fast.

'What?'

'I said, I'm on for tomorrow.' Sharper, meaner. 'I'll dig out my Tupperware, pick up an orphan penguin and spray "Bilbo was a bobbit" on your personal rock face.'

'Easy now, brother,' Trev wobbled.

'Plus, it'll be great finally to meet your family.'

'No!' Trev's tone went high treble, his grip tightened on the wheel.

'Come on, matey, it'll be brilliant.' Digging deeper, hitting harder. 'I'll make up the numbers in your never-ending game of hide-and-seek.'

I pictured Trevor counting to a million, deep in the forest of loss, while a non-existent wife and unbelievable kids came out of his imagination only to hide from him again.

'So,' I laughed across. 'What's it to be, are we on for tomorrow, or what?'

'No!' Pure white-knuckler. 'No, you can't!'

'Really,' I edged. 'And why's that, then?'

'Well, if you really want to know,' Trev fizzed pure eyebrow mania. 'The littlest is not too well at the moment! The butcher's run out of fresh corned beef! The missus is on the rag! It looks like rain! There's a risk of fire! I'm sick of fucking brambles!'

'I'm kidding!' We were going way too fast. 'I'm just fucking around!'

Trevor's sanity twitched. A crease of awareness travelled from his eye socket to cheekbone, down his neck, into his arms and stretched to his legs. His expression shifted, he razored a grin, slammed on the brakes and leant back. I threw a bit of disbelief at the road ahead, saw we were somehow appropriately paused on the white line of a red light. I started to laugh. Trev slid mellow into his corner of the Cortina; it was where he slept. He looked at me, raised an eyebrow, winked complete clarity across.

'Maybe next week would be better?' he said.

'Yeah,' I grinned. 'We shouldn't rush into it.'

Trevor laughed, span straight up in his seat, put his foot right to the floor. The Cortina roared through the just-changing traffic light. My fantastically unstable driver was back to what he did best. I followed his fine example, snorted a sharp blast straight from the bag, put my numb nose against the wet window and took a look outside.

We'd passed the flyovers of the city and the pushovers of the miracle mile. We were currently crawling along in the heavy Saturday-evening traffic of Rusholme. The curry houses were doing good business down to the no-score draw at Maine Road. Fuck, I'd missed another home game. Tried to remember what I'd been doing at the exact time I should've been heading down to the match, but a cow in a field confused my recall.

Rusholme.

True blue City fans in full battle gear moved in and out of Indian reservations. Curry-house kitchens sacrificed lambs, chickens and unwanted pet dogs in enormous pots of spicy sewage. A mighty Carlsberg stream flowed strong through it all. Grown men dipped their faces into the deluge and sucked deep. Helpless Indians waved on the attack. Welcoming, smiling, nodding, grabbing, counting and cooking. I watched as a boys' brigade charged a single opening in the brick barricade. The curry-house door gave way in the crush. A female Indian fell over, was almost trampled by the fast and fat feet. The scent of various carnage blew through the ill-conditioned air. An entire family of sheep went down in flames of bright red sauce. Chickens screamed, but chickens always screamed. One unsteady blue fell straight through a subcontinental family photo-op. I saw pure shards of hatred in dark, Indian eyes as they protected their ancient, multi-coloured granny. Football, no focus, fucker actually threw up on a toddler's head. Nipper observed a Zen-like silence for a magic moment, then started to suck up the scally vomit. I started to laugh from high up in the trees. I saw the stampede that preceded the crush, that preceded the perfect boy, preceded the final payment of an overdue amount, preceded the murder of a son.

Fuck.

That's what I'd been missing all along. The part of Trev's story my memory had hidden began a slow slide back into the light. The face of a wrinkled-down smackhead from the estates dragged along behind. His mouth moved. Information came back unwanted. That was it. Fuck, that was it. Trevor's eight-year-old son had been killed just after Trev had skipped town. My playful Rusholme visions fell apart. I completely lost my place. The branch I'd used to stay above it all in broke. I lost my balance. Lost my grip. I fell through furious noise.

Falling fast and utterly disoriented, I spotted a red Cortina at a traffic light on the road to Chorlton. The traffic light was intermediate amber and orange at the same time. I focused hard and fell through an opening in the rainroof. Lights changed to green. The road ahead became clearer. Our car made a loud sound and sped up. The man sitting next to me screamed.

'Cecil B. De Mille is a fucking cunt!'

It had to be Trevor.

'I'm not taking Nigel to see any of his fucking films.'

Nigel, fucking hell, that was it, that was the kid's name.

'My boy! My sweet little lad!' High-pitched, incredible pain. 'Nigel, the blessed son of my lamb chop! The apple of my eye-dripper!' Schizo music swelled. 'The Father! The Son! My burnt Holy Toast!'

We were travelling at lunatic speeds on insane acid. The back of a bus blocked our way. Trevor revved right up to its number plate. I made a thousand three-letter words in an instant, stopped breathing, slammed my eyes closed. Trevor was still screaming. He'd become incoherent, but the sentiment was the same. I escaped deep into the darkness of my own head. I finally saw what I'd known all along. The whole story came bleeding back to me. Trevor's son had been sliced headless due to an unpaid drug debt. An unpaid drug debt to a southern racket that had forced Trevor out of his home town. Martin had said I was Trev's son. The connections were getting dangerous. The links were killing me. I pushed my fists into my eyes, went deeper, wanted safer. I imagined a simple blue gate in front of a pretty white house. Put a choke hold on to its small simplicity, waited for the car to stop.

Time passed. The car stopped. I looked left, blue gate, white house.

'Made it,' I said to myself.

'We always do, brother Bill,' Trev edged from close by.

'Yes,' I thinned back. 'But why does it have to be so hard?'

'It just does, brother Bill,' Trev sighed. 'It just is.'

'Fair enough.' I clicked open the door. 'Till next time.'

'There's always a next time,' he smiled.
'Yes,' I said, getting out. 'Yes, there certainly is.'
'Take care, brother man.'

SATURDAY 4.59PM

And there I was.

Bella's nice big house. All painted white with worthwhile windows and fresh blue drainpipes. The brickwork was designed, not thrown. Trees on the street waved gently at their exotic cousins behind the clean double glazing. Ivy crawled her way from bottom to top and all over. The whole affair cut an elegant misshape in times of force-fed conformity. I felt myself breathing good again. It really was a nice house.

One day, I thought, one day I'll turn the key in a good solid double-coated door. I'll feel the resonance of a life's achievement on each and every entry. I'll look around the spacious hallway and hang my coat alongside all my other coats. I'll wander, stress-free, into one particular room at the end of one particular corridor. I'll share a bathroom with six southerners. I'll encounter six strains of overpriced shampoo in one scheduled shower. I'll agree and disagree in equal measure, share pots and wash the pans, watch television in unison, label chemical kippers with my name in permanent marker, discuss the phone bill, learn to talk in public, drink my share of the milk and no more. I'll whisper goodnight and wake up screaming. You can sit down, sit down and roll over, roll over on your comfy fucking carpeting. Sit down, roll over, roll over and beg.

Just visiting.

The gate was this lovely piece of blue latticed metalwork. I booted it a dint, walked towards the front door. I had no idea what time it was, but felt sure I was somehow late. I'd never managed to be on time for Bella. The first time I'd knocked on her door I was already late. She'd asked me round to hers for nine over the sound system of some club, but when I recalled, revived and turned myself up it was at least eleven. I'd stood in the front garden finishing a smoke, heard her voice talking down to a deeper voice. I didn't move for a while. Stood firm and silent till the glow of good police work wore off. Then got well fucking raged. Headed for the front door and kicked the fuck out of it. Kept kicking till some fucking Superman passed me by on his way to a rainy gate and an early bath. I went in furious, ended up in bed with her myself. I've always had an entertaining answer when people ask me how we met.

The day after all that, me and Bella took our hangovers on a Sunday stroll through the local park. Blood flies ate me more than her. We sat on a tree stump facing in opposite directions. Her strong back made it possible for me to lean back. Her soft words made it possible for me to slow down, to listen. Two back-to-back lives met in the middle. When she leant her head, her hair fell down over my shoulders. The smell of her brewed in the Fahrenheit. Bella came into my life smooth and with well-timed singer's lines.

We came close.

I leant on her door, pressed the bell-chime-buzz thing and waited. A light orange blurred on in the long corridor. I threw my still lit spliff into a nearby hydrangea, heard Bella shouting through the door.

'You phoned an hour ago, where've you been?'

I smiled as the door swung soft open, she caught me at it.

'Not funny, Billy.'

My eyes found her face for the first time in a long time.

'I've been waiting for you,' she said.

It looked more like she'd been preparing for me.

'Well?' she pouted, but better.

Well, Bella had levelled a delicate mix of love and neglect into her perfectly balanced features. She'd angled an urban throw-rug over her shoulder and allowed her hair to hang long. She'd blowtorched dark shades of flame into her light brown eyes. She touched the glow of her skin just to know that it still glowed. She knocked me out. This was Bella. This was her. And I would never, ever be ready.

'Billy,' she mouthed. 'Are you going to say something?'

'Hello.'

'Yes, very good.' She moved slightly to one side. 'Hello.'

She indicated with her hand, so I cut past her and into the warm, dry corridor.

'No kiss?' she asked, but I couldn't remember, kept moving.

'Where do you want me to go?' Somewhat overcome by Bella's sudden presence, I stood between the carpeted stairs to her bedroom and the low passage to the shared kitchen.

'Let's have a cup of tea,' she said as her body closed the gap.

'I don't drink tea.' But pushed through to the kitchen all the same.

Once there, I took a fragile chair and a deep breath. Bella started to clink around the clean surfaces. I hated tea. It was the leaping-off point for so many clichés. Any minute now she'd suggest toasted pitta bread with avocado slices, or casually mention the weather, or tell me about a new jazz café round the corner. I nervously dug out a cigarette, didn't light it. Stared hard at a picture of an overweight woman in her knickers playing with a large unlit candlestick. Elsewhere, Picasso grinned superior, Marilyn tried the old game again, a leaf looked like a lung, some large brother fucked a plastic apple and the world got turned self-consciously upside down.

All them postcards varnished to the table top always made me feel a long way from home.

'Billy,' Bella cried. 'Say something!'

'Can I have a drink?' I grimaced. 'Please, that is.'

'You want a drink?'

'Yes, please.' I repeated as the fridge door swung and my spirits rose.

'How about a fruit juice?'

'That would be fine.' FUCK! FUCK! FUCK! I put the cigarette in my mouth, didn't light it, didn't break the ridiculous kitchen rule to do with used cancer, or second-hand smoke, but really badly wanted to.

'There you are,' Bella indicated.

The orange juice smelt disgusting, I closed my eyes.

'You haven't slept, have you?'

'I slept on the train,' I told her.

'What train?' Bella turned to me. 'When were you on a train?'

'Well,' I stammered. There was no way a train could fit into Bella's kitchen. I ducked, moved, lied, fast. 'I took a train to see Luke this morning.'

'You mean a tram,' she laughed.

'A tram?' Awkward fingers dug a box of matches from out of my pocket. 'You could be right, a tram is very like a train, especially when you're sleeping.'

'I don't believe you, Billy.'

The cigarette got snatched from my mouth. The jig was up. I found myself looking down a long corridor called explanation. Couldn't feel my feet, too far away.

'I know,' I said. 'And I'm sorry.'

'You never sleep on trains or trams, in cars or any moving vehicle,' she bopped along. 'You're always gobsmacked out the window, rambling on about the loss of humanity or something equally brilliant.'

I needed to smoke so badly by then that I got up and went for a kiss. Bella watched me rise, leant back against the kitchen counter. The bread bin loomed full of crumbs and one discarded teacake, I closed my eyes, kissed her on the mouth. Just as I was falling in love all over again, Bella pulled away.

'So,' she whispered. 'You haven't slept properly since Thursday?'

'Sshhh!' My eyes stayed closed, I let my head loll on to her shoulder and growled a long snore. 'If you'd just be quiet for a minute I might have a chance.'

'Wake up, you bastard!' Bella laughed.

'So sleepy.' I tightened my grip.

'Stop it!' She was deep in some warm laughter. 'Wake up!'

'Set the alarm, baby,' I slurred. 'I'm done.'

'No!' She struggled to hold me up.

'Be quiet.'

'I can't hold you!' Bella cried.

'Just as well I'm here then, isn't it?' I switched my strength, took hold of myself and her as well. I began to walk us both towards the door, towards the corridor, towards the stairs and her bedroom.

'What about my cup of tea?' she muffled.

'I need clean sheets.' I winked one eye open, moved her up the stairs. 'I need to lie down immediately.' Tried not to fall down first. 'And I need you to lie down with me.'

'It's like that, is it?' Bella tripped from my grip, stuck out her tongue, turned herself the right way up the stairway and smiled. 'Think you can get me in bed that easy?'

'Come on,' I said, climbing. 'Sing me to sleep in clean sheets.'

'You'll be lucky!' she shouted.

'When?' I asked her ascending back.

The wide bed filled the room, I took a crack at filling the bed.

Launched myself backwards, arms outstretched. Sunk grateful and deep into the luxury of Bella's expensive sleeping arrangement. It felt good, reassuringly good. Bella drifted around the room, soundless as a romantic thief. I watched her rustle around her well-stacked clothes rack. Nothing was said. I pictured curtains sitting for an art class. Bella went to and came back from the window. I imagined street lamps on the streets turning themselves on. Bella frowned down to her knees. I rolled on my side to face her. She pressed play on her compact-disc player. Billie Holiday hummed in from faraway Harlem. Bella joined me on the bed.

'You want?' I asked.

'Want what?' Bella eyebrowed back.

I slid a dirty finger down the line of her centre, followed it with my hand, set about trying to undo tricky ties of strandy material. I'd worked out the one-pull system when the challenge switched to clips. I leant back for a little perspective, saw that I'd done enough and buried my head between Bella's breasts. I couldn't see much, but I did see a clenched fist from out of the corner of my eye. Four fingers and a thumb tight closed, but wide open to interpretation. Bella talked something. She said it again, but I couldn't hear her. It all just got muffled. The sound just drowned. I worked my way down to her naked legs and knickers. I didn't like their colour, shape or location.

'Billy!' Bella yelped.

'Not now, love.'

'You're on my leg!' she cried.

'Am I?'

'It hurts, move!'

I focused, sniffed, shook and shifted. Wasn't sure what to do. Knew I didn't want to talk about it, so I bent-necked my head between Bella's legs. Her skin side on the inside was warm where I rested my cheek. She opened up. I licked and licked and licked and coughed a little, so I started to suck instead. Orange light from the electric lamp bounced off my eyes, on to my closed lids, back into my eyes. It made me think of the roads outside. I drank down a little Bella juice, swallowed some, laughed and rose back up her body with a smile.

'What was that?' she growled.

'Well, I'm not entirely sure.'

'About what?' she snapped.

'Come on, Bell.' Light kiss. 'Don't be like that.' More mouth pressure. 'I've been wanting to be in bed with you.' Tongue nudge. 'For fucking days.' Feeling stronger. 'Fucking days.' Wide-mouthed wet kiss. 'And fucking nights.'

Slap!

'Stop swearing!' She hit me again.

'I don't think I can, sweetheart.'

I pinned down her dangerous right and smiled. She still had on her bra, her complicated top-wear had rolled up under her neck. She looked awkward, but saucy.

'This is all so fucking marvellous,' I muttered, trying to unravel Bella's hair from the folds and armpits of her one hundred per cent pretend ethnic attire. It was becoming a touch maddening. I took a breath, leant back and pulled the whacked garment sharp over her head, threw it over my shoulder.

'Be careful!'

'Always,' I replied.

Bella's white bra was synthetic and tight. I loved Bella's bras. Think this one was my favourite, but wasn't far enough away to tell. I could feel her hot, uneven, almost angry breath against my forehead. I deliberately licked the warm skin between her breasts, left a sheen of my shine across her dark skin. I slid the nylon away from her, pushed the flesh full, pressed my lips in. Bella jolted all over.

'Billy!'

'What is it, love?'

'Why don't you just lie down?'

'OK, then.'

I felt the individual feathers of the feather duvet, rested my head on the outline of my neck. I laid back and looked up. Bella's image developed vaguely above me. I reached for a cigarette, she let me light it without a word. She leant back, looked around her room, reached for the discarded top, folded it and placed it carefully to one side. If I could smoke, she could tidy; we had our moments, just like everyone else.

'Undress me,' I muttered from a wave of nicotine euphoria.

'All right,' she replied.

'Really?'

'Have you washed?' She wrinkled a crinkled nose.

'I'm consistently clean.'

'That's not what I've heard,' she said, sharper than necessary.

'Easy now, love.'

'Charlie said you were off your head last night.'

'And he would know,' I tried.

'He said that you were with someone.'

'I was with him.'

'Charlie said—'

'Bella!' Fast defensive action. 'Charlie says whatever you want to hear.'

I spoke my soft bastard's words against the skin that surrounded a recent fall from Bella's bra cup. I found myself seeing some distant time when this might be more than enough. When the debt and the threats had slipped away down streets that I no longer needed to know about. I conjured a far better time, a time when Bella's breasts would be all that there was.

'Was he fucked-up last night?' she asked out of nowhere.

'When isn't he?'

'You can talk.'

'I'd really rather not,' I whispered. 'Not now.'

And Bella could've said almost anything after that. It wouldn't have mattered and I wouldn't have listened. She could've whispered death threats, sang funeral blues, told an anti-Irish joke. She could have told me to stop. It wouldn't have mattered. I'd still have moved to the same place. I'd still have shut it all out and touched her heavy flesh fall with the tip of my tongue. I'd still have run my hand all the way down the valley arch of her back.

I'd still have wanted her more than anything else.

My faraway hand opened soft, heavy cheeks and slid inside her warmth. The room reached for air. My face became cushioned against the whole of her breast, the nipple deep in my mouth. All sound subsided, every part of my attention circulated around a central point. Bella rocked above me like the heavy sky deciding when to storm and when to shine.

SATURDAY 5.47PM

She knelt over me in her well-whitewashed bed.

Closing my eyes, I carelessly cut the distance between her image and bus stops in the non-stop rain. Tried to remember how I ever got near to being here. I pictured nightclubs closing their doors, door bitches being sent home to address their dress sense. I sensed stumbles, fumbles and fall-downs. Plastic charades lining limitless pockets. My regular vanishment to vacant toilets. I spied speeding roads and screaming, bleeding, role models. The dark balanced the light. Pain anchored pleasure. And the colours didn't fade. Details of details became intricate and fascinating.

Bella made a sound, she sounded far away.

Her mouth moved again, I didn't know why. I saw a ceiling, but no cigarettes. I watched Bella bend closer. And I tried to recall what was about to happen. I flicked through potential options on a minute silk screen hidden in the far corner of my head. I saw the word 'SEX', whacked back to the real.

Bella's sarong excused itself. The fabric fell away. She was naked and we were barely apart. Both side-on-side. Some more of her words flew away in a high-pitched and final fashion; I could never catch them back. We were somehow side by side and faced on two fronts. The closest tip of Bella's breast crossed the distance between us. But I couldn't seem to make contact. I looked inside myself, tried to think about for ever. I looked away and back again. I was hardly engrossed, not rich

167

or poor, not rewarded, required, entertained, fascinated, laid open or upon. All me and Bella shared at that moment was the small space between us.

And not much more.

Her hand went down my chest towards the middle. I tried to feel it, but could only fathom the middle of me where crystal particles shifted, toxic fires burnt and tidal waves of whisky flushed through to make room for more, more, more. The middle of me, deep inside the skin, where there was no room for food, no stomach for sex and only a small understanding of affection.

Sex. Unhinging a plastic bag struck me as more rewarding. Who needed an erection when you could get a reaction? The heat in people's eyes could any day outreach the fumbles of their fingers. Power, status, influence, a sense of humour and constant access to free drugs made sex seem just too simple, too static, too stale. It may have gone along well with sweet cider and early-morning mushrooms scattered across teenage fields, but as the wrinkles developed and the shadows darkened it became desperate, not natural; needed, not wanted.

Tastes can change.

And when Bella's hand stroked me lower, I felt three feet from a whipped-cripple fall-down without the chemical taste. Even when it came down to life or more, or death and less, the taste for a taste remained. If and when love occurs people put it down to a chemical reaction. Well, I cut down on the complications, got hold of the chemicals and reacted my head off. For me, drugs had long since overtaken sex in the lifelong struggle against death. And given the choice, I wouldn't have to make one. I wanted drugs. The sharp corner of a big truth cut me straight. I snapped open my eyes to see Bella looking at me. She was somewhere between blank and sad. I felt myself shrug.

'Where are you?' she asked gently.

'Chorlton,' my eyes on the skylight. 'Chorlton-cum-Hardy.'

'Are you feeling all right?'

'I'm trying to stop!' I shouted.

'Stop what?'

'Falling down.'

'But you're not standing up.'

'Then it's too late!' Couldn't help it, panic stations.

'Billy,' her hand on my shoulder. 'Calm down.'

'Yes, please.' I fizzed. 'Two sugars, please.'

'Stop grabbing me!' she cried. 'Just calm down. Put your head on the pillow. Now breathe, just breathe.' Her hand held my hand. I wasn't sure why. 'Breathe, Billy.'

'I am,' I lied.

'Your fucking eyeballs are shaking!' Bella screeched.

'No,' I told her. 'It's only my head.'

'Billy, it's your eyeballs, your head is fine.'

'My head is not fucking fine!'

'Well,' her expression was painful. 'You're probably right. Your head probably isn't fine, but it's definitely not shaking, if that's what you mean. It's your eyes that are shaking, which is actually very disturbing.'

'What did you say?' I asked.

'Billy!' She gripped me tight. 'What the hell have you taken?' She shook me hard. 'When did you last sleep? What the hell is going on with you?'

'No drugs to say no to.'

'Oh, my God!' Bella yelled. 'Stop it, please, stop it!'

'Be nice to me, babe.' My eyes closed. 'Just be kind.'

Her short pause became a silence. Her rough-palmed hand touched my cheek. A half-stroke became a hold. Rare recorded music rolled over on an endless perfect pitch in the all-around air. I felt almost calm enough to hear it. Half the light in the evening room matched days to come and days long gone. Bella's face appeared to me to be every perfect picture strayed from black to white to colour and back. She was so beautiful. She cared about me. She didn't want me to be the way I was, but she still wanted me to be. I closed my eyes, let my head fall into her.

And, I think, that's the closest I would ever come to reform.

It wasn't in the elegant house, the fresh milk, the clean and spacious kitchen, the fresh-smelling flowers, the operational phone, the colour television or the comfy carpets. No, none of that surface shit was ever going to do a fucking thing for me. But the smell of Bella's skin and the silence of her mouth brought me close to fighting off the mania of the back-attached monkey for good. I'd beat the little cunt's fucking brains out if only she helped me. When Bella scratched a finger across my short head of hair, I couldn't help but rumble with the idea of long-term rehabilitation through sex, sleep, fresh fish, love, orange-only sunsets and long, easy nights sniffing her dark skin. When gifted Bella hummed along to her soulful Holiday, I felt ancient magic reach out to me, move above me, teach and utterly disarm me. And, if I stayed absolutely still, didn't say a word, or hear one either, if I shifted down the gears in my brain and breathed only through my nose, it almost began to feel as if I would never need anything else ever again. That's how strong being close to Bella got. And that was as close as it would ever be.

'Billy.'

Before someone said something and ruined it.

'Billy.' Tap-tap, finger on my cheek. 'Billy!'

I opened my eyes.

'Are you crying?'

Didn't think so, but anything's possible.

'Billy,' Bella's tone hardened. 'Will you, please, say something.'

'Hello.' I cracked open half a smile. 'Hello, love.'

'I thought we were going to have sex,' she tutted.

And there it was, the word, out in the open.

'We've been up here a long time,' she continued. 'And I thought we were going to have sex. If you're just going to lie there, I might as well go downstairs and make dinner.'

Dinner, Christ no, not fucking food.

'Well?' she nudged.

'Shall we play the game?'

'To be honest,' she sighed, 'I think anything would be better than this.'

The game is won by stillness and lost in motion. It was invented by a lazy, drug-riddled alcoholic who needed time to focus before being ready to have sex. Bella had never really liked it. Starting positions were, conveniently enough, side by side and facing. The object is to see who moves first. It's sort of like sexual sleeping tigers, but with grown-up prizes. The winner gets 'treated', which can mean anything, but tends to turn out as little more than not being on top. Talking is allowed. Eyes can shift. Involuntary body motion, on my part, is overlooked. We watch, we twitch, I sometimes shake and together we wait.

Bella's breath hummed with more antique music, it made her chest press. I bent my knee and that was it, the game was over, with me beaten as always. Bella almost smiled, but didn't. She rolled slightly away, her chest opened up and the bed sheets slid. Bella was naked beside me and she wanted sex. I wondered, if the outcome had been the other way round, would any of it feel simpler? Stopped thinking. Got on with it.

I moved above her. I kissed her breasts with clenched teeth and worked myself in. I followed her half-open eyes down to a point of forced entry, almost exit, forced entry, almost exit. My own eyes closed, I saw it all happen inside.

It seemed impossible to satisfy her. Satisfy all of her or

any of her. The churning, lunging motion, all hand-presses and breath-pants felt like the most worn-out cliché of them all. So little of what we were was needed. The cock and the cunt. The dick and the fanny. The penis and the fucking marvellous vagina. What earth-shattering inventions! What devices of brilliance! No imagination needed, no sensations 'cept one. Banging and banging and banging with a range of stock sounds. Banging and banging and banging with only one outcome. Banging and banging and banging while the clock ticked in time with as much heart and desire as the man on the job.

Her eyes glared at mine. No meaning was clear. I pumped, she pumped, we pumped. The sweat from my head dripped on to her chest. She didn't like that. So why not wipe it off? Why not reach for a tissue, complain or move? Why not? 'Cos this was sex. We were in the middle of sex and it couldn't be stopped. It had to go on till it had to be stopped. It couldn't be over till it ended. There was no conclusion till the body coughed up.

I bit my lip, scrunched my eyes tight closed. I saw wide-open roads fierce and on fire. I felt afraid and ashamed and destroyed by it all. I couldn't picture a picture. I couldn't call a friend. I didn't have any answers: no lines, no laughs, no sense of release, no feeling of love, or joy, or hope. There was no warm satisfaction at the ultimate commune of the two. Driving and banging and breathing and pushing and banging and breathing and pushing and slipping and driving and falling and crying and stopping. Fucking stopping. The fucking stopping. The fucking stopped.

'Billy!' she cried.

I was wide-eyed for my pants.

'What, the hell, are you doing?'

Couldn't find my fucking pants.

'BILLY!' she screamed.

Still had them on, reached down to the pocket.

'NO!'

Bella pulled my arm away, I fell down on my back, banged my head against the hard wall. I reached up to the pain, but Bella was before me, naked and swaying and avoiding my eyes. She grabbed hard at my cock and pulled me towards her. I pushed my leg out, managed to sit up, but not escape. Her anger flashed, she wrenched me too hard. I banged my head against the wall on purpose, but felt nothing at all.

'FUCK!' I yelped when her whole head went down.

Bella sped and she tightened, her eyes upturned, nose stretched, cheeks hollowed. Her expression fixed, angry and at me. Her free hand rubbed her cunt. Her mouth took me deep. Her tongue and her tits and her dancing on drugs touched me all at once. I strained and I shouted and I felt myself come. Bella pulled her head back, I splashed on her face, she sped up her hand, shouted something insane, lurched into me, all over me, her body shook once.

Her eyes were closed, like she was at war.

SATURDAY 6.16PM

I located and swiftly created a rumpled spliff, straightened it out, lit the fucker up.

I exhaled thick silver smoke into the silent air. Bella watched me from her back, from her bed. I couldn't meet her eyes, but the deeper my lungs dragged, the straighter it all began to feel and soon enough I turned myself round to face her. Her gaze drifted across the ceiling, settled on an antique lampshade. I kept pulling on the smoke till I felt some space open up in my head. Bella's attention caught an ash fall, she made some sound between her teeth, sat up, but turned her face away.

I leant back on the bed, pulled over an empty bedside ornament to use as an ashtray. Rested it on my chest, blew smoke over the top, smiled. Bella heard my sounds, lolled herself around. I wasn't sure how much could be communicated in the essence of eye contact, but I wanted to believe that some sort of brief amnesty of basic understanding might've worked its way between us. That, despite the difficulties of what we'd just been through, getting to the other side had somehow made us stronger, closer, more in love. I conjured an offering of hope laced with good intent and a sweet dose of cheek in one sincere smile.

'Don't look at me like that,' Bella snapped.

'But—'

'That was a complete waste of time.'

'But—' I reached for her.

'Fuck off.'

'Come on, babe.' I attempted to get a grip on my girlfriend and the cracked mood at the same time. 'Come here, love,' I tried. 'Come on, Bell.'

'No!' She pulled free, moved fast above me. 'You're not fucking trying! I haven't seen you properly for an entire week and, now that I do, you're so fucking blasted that it makes no sense.' Her eyes were white-water wild. 'You make no sense!'

'But I've been in a bath.'

'You see!' Right in my face. 'No sense! Non-sense!'

'I have things on my mind.'

'Things! Things!' Bella was well on the front foot.

'Well,' I tried a smile. 'Issues, big issues, you know how it is.'

'You're fucking right I know how it is!'

'Well, then,' I soothed, hoping for safety.

'Don't smile at me, you bastard!' she cried. 'You're out on the town with that fucking spider monkey! That little takeaway tart! That stupid half-pygmy slag!'

'Her name is Nada,' I sighed.

'You bastard!' Bella screamed. 'You complete, fucking, bastard!'

She flexed away from me in a mental and physical rage. I felt Cortinas crash, deals fall apart, dogs die, cloakrooms catch fire, coats burn. Bella's eyes flashed dangerous. Nada danced around my mind in her brand-new designer dress. I think Bella saw my thoughts. I think she reached her own conclusions. I know she went mental.

'Nada!'

Slap.

'Nada!'

Slap.

'Nada!'

Bella swung again with tear traces in her tone.

'Nada!'

She pressed her weight down on my chest.

'FUCKING NADA!'

I slipped to the side of her next slap, held her arm.

'Bella, stop it!' I shouted.

'No,' she screamed back. 'You stop it!'

'Stop what?'

'My arm,' she winced, plaintive. 'You're hurting my arm.'

'But,' I asked, 'is it safe?'

'Yes, Billy, it's safe. Now, let's go.'

I released my hold. Bella's face faded to the side, her shoulder weight shifted, thought she was going to get herself up, start fidgeting about with her clothes rack, but her body span back. Her right fist straight-arm-slammed right into the bridge of my nose.

'FUCK!'

My whole body clicked hard. I caught the motion of her arm pulling back, repositioning. I threw out an arm, toppled Bella off the bed. A thick splash of bright blood spurted from my nose.

'Don't bleed on the sheets!' she blasted.

I fired a quick look across, flicked a hand out at the whitewashed wall to my left. Warm blood sprayed a long, satisfying sweep across its quality finish. A dense bubble of the stuff rolled, ugly, down the wall to the floor. It started to collect on the open page of a well-placed book.

'Billy!' Bella cried, closing the gap.

But when I growled she backed away.

I took a moment to myself, totally to myself. I took my eyes away from her in the corner, closed them tight shut. I doubled up, pressed fingers into throbbing sockets. I travelled deep inside my silent self and arrived somewhere more appropriate, somewhere safer, somewhere far away.

Hard rain fell from the bleak seaside sky. Some Saturday night, years and years before. I could hear a small car engine dribbling along on the promenade behind the bandstand. In the vague distance there was the distinct and repetitive sound of a girl calling my name. One hand held my nose, the other pressed my cheekbone in place. I heard the car door slam and tyres grip the rain-soaked road home.

'Billy, are you all right?'

The fierce sea wind battered the creaky old pier that ranged above me. Human noises gave way to the mad, multi-part symphony of nature. The rain made different sounds as it hit different grounds. The gale bounced off all obstacles available. Something flapped like clapping. I breathed deep, took my hands away from my broken bones, let the weather wash the blood from my face.

'Say something.'

Point is that I started to enjoy lying on that awful beach in the middle of a Morecambe winter, my face broken to bits, my left leg ready for six weeks in plaster. I started to like it. All that brilliant weather coming down from above. The resonant, timeless seaside. The isolation. The tangible but private pain. The growing sense of tragedy. The low-pitched drama. The almost cinematic heroism. The ten to twelve pints of cider I'd necked before did a lot to push the images, kill the pain, keep me warm, but the point is that I faded fast to sleep stranded on that vicious seaside.

And I didn't wake till morning.

'TALK TO ME!'

The point is that it's only the presence of other people that promotes the expression of pain. Of course it fucking hurt, on that beach, but left alone, well lamped, smiling to myself, the pain became a more personal, less publicized affair. It didn't need to be put in its place, didn't need to be dealt with, it just stayed where it was.

'BILLY, PLEASE!'

The fucking bastard fucking point is that it's not so bad to get beaten up in Morecambe by three fellas whose shared girlfriend you might've appealed to, but it's not all right to get beaten up in fucking Chorlton by a woman who occasionally washes your socks.

'YOU'VE BROKEN MY FUCKING NOSE!'

'Have I?'

'YES, YOU HAVE!'

'Really?'

'YES, YOU REALLY FUCKING HAVE!'

I leant up fast, two thick and tasty lines of bright red blood slipped past my mouth, dripped down my chest, pooled on my stomach. I thought it looked good, remembered the acid, began to feel better.

'Lovely,' I smiled.

'Do you need to go to hospital?' Bella asked.

I stayed silent.

'Billy, please.' She came close, knelt down. 'Is there anything I can do?'

'Give Nada a call.'

'What?'

'Ask her to come over and pick me up. Tell her to bring along some hankies and a clean pair of knickers.' I felt airheaded. 'You might have to give her directions.'

'Billy!' Bella cried. 'Don't do this!'

'I've got her number if you need it.'

'Stop it!'

'It's in my pocket.'

'STOP!'

I let the moment walk past in silence, turn the corner and depart in peace. I nodded, Bella exhaled and knee-walked to the side of the bed. She leant across me to reach her 'never know when' supply of handy andies. I tried to inhale her calming scent, but the blood was too thick. My nose made strange drowning sounds as Bella moved slowly, but surely, to be close beside.

Bella's bedside manner was redundant, clumsy, touching. She bunged up both nostrils with pricey tissue. Her fingers took about tracing the bones between my eyes. At one point she whispered 'everything is loose inside of you', but I didn't reply, couldn't compete. I just watched the window waiting in the same place, the light outside becoming noticeably less. Think I might've heard the swelling call on its mates to come over for a swell time.

I smiled at Bella and Bella smiled back.

'How's that?' she asked.

'I think I'll make it.'

'I've got to go for a pee.' She was up and on her way. 'I'll only be a minute.'

'Take your time,' I told her.

Finally alone, I moved as fast as possible to my pants' pocket. Tugged the tissue from out of my preferred nostril. Scrambled through the plastic till I touched the best painkiller known to man. Cut, crushed and hit a massive line through blood and bits of bone. I wiped the wet away along my arm, it made a fine red stripe. I nicked Bella's best pillow, propped myself up, closed my wild eyes and went back to where I was.

I mixed up soft violent memories of splintered bone and seaside towns that lived on the far side of my sight. I welcomed in and grinned at forgotten faces, plastic bottles, half-thrown bricks, empty doors, ghost-town funfairs and young, young girls bouncing back and forth in a mental wind machine on full blast. I saw the strong and pure sea water burst brilliant over distant sea walls and soak itself on the beautiful old scenes. I came in from the cold for a badly burnt burger fried with chip-van ambition. I drowned it all in bright red sauce.

Bella's toilet flushed a level below. My memories whirl-pooled with her piss. I reached for a cigarette, my nose dripped the route. Fuck sake, for fuck's sake, I tried to wipe it away, but only made the mess worse. A flood of frustration made me feel that I'd healed so many times for no reason. Felt like I'd been built up to be torn down. Felt if it wasn't for wasted time, I had no time at all. I felt her eyes arrive on me just as I bundled up the ruined sheet and threw it in the corner. You get away with nothing in Chorlton. But even the worst days have patches of light. The over-privileged girl who'd broken my nose curved towards me with a pint of fine red wine in her silver-ringed hand. I smelt the alcohol, cut my losses, caught perspective, nodded once and reached out.

'Thanks,' I muttered after one long, medicinal swallow.

'Your eyes are red.'

'I put some dye in my tears.'

'You've taken too many drugs.'

'Intermittently,' I said, reaching for a cigarette.

'I mean now, right now,' she sniped. 'You're taking too many drugs, right now!'

'Prove it,' I snapped and spilt wine on the mattress.

'Now look what you've done!'

'No,' I pushed my face at her. 'Look what *you've* fucking done!' I shook blood over booze, lit a cigarette, flicked the still lit match to the carpet, watched it go out, waited.

In the room, we were alone in the room.

'Billy,' she began. 'I said I'm sorry and I am, but I couldn't help it.' Her words were all there was. 'Billy, you're out of control. You're not making sense any more. You've always been difficult, but not like this, not impossible. And I've been talking to people.'

I couldn't help a frown.

'Yes, all right, all right! I've been talking to Charlie, so what! It's not his fault, you owe him money, what do you expect?'

Bella left a space for my answer, more wasted time. 'Look,' she went on. 'I think you're in trouble, serious trouble, and you don't seem to care, you don't even seem to notice.'

'What time is it?' I asked.

'For God's sake!'

'I have to be somewhere.'

'Where?' Her hand banged the bed, broke my nose.

'Not fucking here!'

I pulled my knees sharp to my chest, slid into trousers still safe round my ankles. I picked up and hit back the rest of my pint. I watched Bella's face through the bottom of the glass. And as the red drink went down, down, down, I saw her features more, more, more. Eventually, the glass got empty, Bella looked distant and vague through the thick glass. From my side of the transparent divide, she came through distorted, bloated and cracked. I quite liked the way it looked. I began to revolve the light-bending glass, following the effects. Determined to spoil my fun, Bella tut-tutted and turned away. She rose up, made a sad sound, didn't look back and walked from the room. I wiped a palmful of fresh blood on her cleanest underwear, got about getting myself dressed.

I could hear doors swing, swear words and angry bangs as Bella bounced between rooms one floor below. I heard her call out a fake, friendly 'hello' sound and tensed right up. I didn't want any unannounced visitors to add to the violence. Even Charlie would have a chance if he caught me now. I was fast up at the door crack. Managed to work out that it was only one of the southern cul-de-sacs who shared the soap back from a trip to a place where books were sold. I lit a cigarette, only half heard the heartless back-and-forth between the two team-mates, saw my chance. I banged the door open, banged it shut, jumped the stairs, made it to the bathroom, slid the fantastic lock into its favourite place, flicked the light, saw myself in the mirror.

'Jesus Christ!' I cried.

Twitched back from my reflection cast in such well-lit detail. My face was well fucked. Bloodshot eyes, bent, flat nose, blood lines running dark and ugly around my mouth and chin. Features tense and stretched. I felt like shaking the mirror, so I could see myself standing still, but couldn't be fucked. On the bright side, it occurred to me that my father was forced far away with no chance of featuring in my current face. Thankful for that, but little else, I turned on the taps, lost and beaten in bastard Chorlton.

'You don't look your best, lad.'

'Grandad,' I sighed. 'Of course.'

'Now,' he boomed in the echo. 'Do you recall what I told you?'

'When?'

'Always get the first punch in.'

'Right, right.' I thought for a moment. 'But it was a girl.'

'It was an enemy.'

'It was my girlfriend, for fuck sake!'

'The shame,' growled Joe.

My grandad wasn't immediately visible to me. His voice was coming from behind the crossword shower curtain that I'd long wanted to destroy. My eye caught the clue to five hundred and twenty-three across, 'Life is a bowl of—'. But before I could check the spaces to see if *shit* fit, my grandad's face became clear through the busy curtain. Rivulets and streams of thick blood sprayed down from a hole in his head. It filled up the features of the old fella's face with shifting red. I blinked double-fast, prayed for a trick of light, but the spectre remained. It was inside my eyeball, painted on the membrane. I saw my grandad with his blood flow falling out of control in my girlfriend's shower. I swore silent, stepped hard, swung the shower curtain.

Naked and wrecked, my grandad stood drenched. Thick

blood from the shower head splashed at his feet. I didn't feel frightened, more confused, more unsettled. He was washing away, not noticing me, an old scraggy sponge worked the blood in and out. Details of his face were set sharp and twisted by pain.

'Grandad?'

No answer.

'Grandad, can I do anything?'

Still silent.

'It won't happen again.'

A slight crease of awareness.

'Next time, I'll sort it out, I'll do the business.'

A nod and a slight sound.

'I won't let you down, Joe.'

'Billy,' his voice, my memory. 'You'll only be letting yourself down.'

The noise of water hitting the floor distracted me for an instant. The fucking sink had overflowed. Steaming water dripped over the ceramic sides. It blotched to the floor in ever-bigger pools. I pulled hard on the plug chain, heard the good sound of levels going down. Low gurgling, whirlpooling. I turned back to the shower; my grandad was gone.

'Open this fucking door, Billy!'

'Bella,' spit, lean, unlock. 'Of course.'

She moved to my side, our eyes met, but only in the mirror. Black and white lovers, overexposed in a two-by-four frame. She looked desirable, me, not so. She had on a T-shirt, no bra, and bloodless, square-cut knickers. Basically gorgeous. I winked and gave her an obvious gaze.

She laughed, kissed my cheek. The blood was beginning to dry. I span on the cold tap, worked a cloth over and over the damage. Bella watched me, leant forward, 'oohing' and 'aahing' like a lover might. I half watched her, but kept on washing. Absently made three wishes to pass the time. First, let it be any day, but not Saturday. Two, make it bedtime, not the start of another night-time. And last, I wished that Bella would hold me, make everything feel all right.

'Are you hungry?' she asked.

'Are you joking?'

'No,' her expression huffed, she headed out.

'I've eaten.' But the door slammed. 'Right.'

Fuck it completely, I snapped back, pulled the plug, dropped my face in a towel, destroyed it completely, yanked the door feeling angry, hit sharp turns out and out. I talked to partitions, threw words down dark corridors. My best thoughts found high-wire fences to be battered against. Bella hid as my sounds roared spastic, too sick to find her.

I reached the front door, still raging. My hand flipped the lock action, I heard the wail of a scream and the bang of a pan. Bella came charging down the sophisticated corridor.

'So, that's it, is it?' she shouted.

I handled the door to an angle, swung it to a stop by my boot, stepped half out of the hard-to-leave house, halted, turned my head back and laughed loud.

'Yes, that's it.' I crunched the flash gravel path, shouted over my shoulder. 'This is it! That was it! This will be it and should be it!' I smiled to myself when the southern accent clicked right. 'Do you get it? Can you understand it? Do you see that this is, in fact, all it is?'

The hinge on the pretty blue gate flew off. The entire gate collapsed. Bella screamed and slammed the door. I felt no remorse, not at all; gates should be sturdy, not crap. I hit the street in five easy steps, rehearsed for the next, when the door screamed wide behind. I heard her scurry gravel-path fury. She caught hold of me before I even made the first tree.

'Listen,' Bella held my arm, broke my nose. 'Why don't you stay for dinner?'

I couldn't find the words. I could only feel sick. Span

my head about, sniffed deep on the scent of, what was it, beep-beep-ding, hydrangeas. They were everywhere, definitely hydrangeas. Their purples, blues and pinks soothed me. It started to rain.

'Please get a grip.' Bella shook me hard, it hurt. 'You know what you need?'

I looked around for a book of raffle tickets, some female exchange students and a truck-load of drugs. Didn't see anything close, looked at her instead, shrugged.

'What you need,' Bella rolled on, 'is to come back into the house where it's warm and let me get the dinner going. You could have some more wine, watch telly.'

I smiled, she smiled, we smiled.

'And later we could get a video or go to the local for a quiet drink.'

I nodded, she nodded, we nodded.

'That's right, baby,' she beamed. 'We can have a few drinks, maybe even a smoke. I've got food and wine inside.' Bella's eyes went baby-talk wide. 'And then you could stay the night in my big, comfy bed and keep your girlfriend warm in the night.'

'For a change,' I laughed.

'That's right, for a change,' Bella buzzed. 'And in the morning we can go to the hospital and have them look at your nose. Then we can spend the whole Sunday watching telly, reading papers, making love, whatever you want.'

'For a change.'

'Yes,' Bella smiled. 'A nice change, a change for the better.' She gently tugged at my arm, her prettiest expression on full beam. 'Come on, sugar, let's go inside.'

With equal tenderness of touch, I flexed against her home-made motion. I reached carefully with my face, kissed her temptress mouth shut. And that kiss took me back inside with generous warmth. It fed me fresh fish, poured me pints of fine wine, put me back to bed and kissed me all night and all over. It took me to the doctor in the morning, made the pain fade. It bought me the papers and the golden-age of cinema. It lay me gently down. That one sincere kiss made me feel so much better. It made me feel satisfied and healed. In short, it did all the things that I would never be fucked to do.

I didn't turn till I reached the corner, then I did, left.

Had no idea where I was. Was about to get well lost on the sleepy, pseudo bends of Chorlton, when a hackney cab, what else, nudged the next junction. Legging it along the soggy road, I yelled a clear instruction to the brake pads and, thank fuck, the bastard taxi stopped. Head down, itching my eye, obscuring my face, the door opened easy. Warm, yes, big and warm inside. I pushed into the furthest corner. My temple rested against steamy glass. I sensed that a handbrake was about to let go. That wheels were due to turn. That Steve McQueen and his barbed-wire bike were my best mates. I was even on the verge of saying where to and all that luxury, when my transparent headrest, the window, spasmed a bang, clocked me hard in the head. The rude jolt sent sharp stingers through the front of my fragile face. I scrunched my eyes tight to fight the wobble, whacked them back wide to see Bella's open hand pressed against the wet glass.

'What's all this then?' came from in front.

I ignored the cabbie's question, followed the dark lines splicing Bella's soft palm skin. I didn't know much about the mysteries of the folds, but thought I could spy three kids, a tall, dark handsome man, a holiday in the sun, brand-new bed sheets and a slap in the face for Her fucking Highness if I got thrown out of the cab.

'It's nothing, mate,' softly, softly. 'Just give me a minute.'

'It's your money, son,' he grumbled. 'But watch the windows.'

'Best advice I've had all day.'

My eyes travelled from forwards to sideways. I saw her through the glass again, but this time it touched me deeper. The rain flattened her hair, shined her cheeks, suggested tears, poured on unpleasant. Through the glass she glowed. I pictured Bella's good heart pumping, saw her beauty calling, felt my certainty fading. I reached for the window and a cigarette at the same time.

'Yes?' I said, lowering the glass.

Bella was out of breath, couldn't speak.

'What is it, love?' I tried again.

Still no reply, she finger-wagged 'wait', I loved that.

I looked closer, noticed how cold she appeared. The wind was whipping in, rain swept across, Bella wasn't well dressed, she was overexposed, had to be freezing. I forgot the meter, remembered my manners.

'Bella,' I said. 'You're cold.'

'FUCK OFF, BILLY!' she screamed. 'I CAN HARDLY BREATHE!'

'No, I mean, you must be cold.' I gestured at the general outside.

'Of course I'm fucking cold!'

'Well, all right, that's all I meant.'

'Billy,' she panted. 'I just wanted you to know that I won't see you tonight.'

'OK,' I replied.

'Don't you want to know why I won't see you tonight?'

'It's not important.'

'I won't see you tonight,' she paused. 'I won't see you tonight because I'm going to see Charlie. He's asked me to a club and I'm going to go.'

'Drive!' I shouted.

'I'm going to see Charlie because he isn't a dickless, blasted lightweight who lets me down every five minutes.'

'OI! FUCKHEAD!' I banged on the perspex. 'DRIVE!'

'Watch it, sunshine!' cabbie snapped.

'And you better have his money because if you don't, he's going to kill you.'

I slammed the window closed, leant through the front. Thought I might've fucked it when the cabbie saw my face, but the wanker looked more scared than angry. I poured all the meaning I could muster into a dead man's last request.

'Drive,' I said. 'Please, drive me back to the city.'

The gear finally found first. Bella's hand banged the outside. Cabbie swore a little under his bad breath, but the wheels were in motion and the drama was left behind. After a few smooth turns, I began to recognise roads, began to know where I was, began to unwind. Street lights glowed orange. Rain took the safe colour from the lamps and painted it all over the surfaces of the streets. The tyres touched the tarmac. The circuit completed all the way into me, sat safe inside the cab. I noticed a cigarette in my mouth and a lighter in my hand, did the obvious.

Tried to think of the last thing I was thinking about before Bella had mentioned sex and the whole world went weird. What was it? What, the fuck, was it? Had a vague idea that it had something to do with drugs. Automatically patted my pocket and made out their subtle shapes through the material. The store didn't feel too healthy. A quiet alarm rang inside my mind. If the drugs were running out, time was running out too.

Without pills and powders there was no way I could do what I had to do. It wasn't that they helped me focus, or organise, or be more effective in my minute-to-minute crusade, but they did stop me getting bored. They didn't just make life interesting, they made everything interesting. They turned my immediate world into a non-stop, multidimensional melo-drama. Straightforward situations could not exist. Nothing could be simple. The whole game went back to teenage. Every little detail mattered so much and it took, virtually, no effort to care.

And without them there would be no story. There'd be no point to it. Without the drugs, I wouldn't be in the tricky situation with Charlie, I wouldn't be in Manchester. I'd be on the dole, sucking spam sandwiches in front of my mum's TV, waiting for the next World Cup, or Miss World, or live darts from Preston to come on and save me. Without them I'd be in the perpetual bath, perpetually clean. Without drugs I'd have no sense of humour and, fuck knows, I needed a sense of humour to keep up with all the drugs.

'Where did you buy this cab?' I asked.

'Bolton,' cabbie called back. 'Why do you ask?'

Laughing in the good seats on the smooth drag to the centre.

My room.

Apart from fist holes in the walls, boot marks scattered about the plywood, strewn and abandoned unclean clothes, broken bottles, cigarette boxes, magazines and general mess, the old rectangle looked fairly respectable. I borrowed a light bulb from the bathroom, screwed in some thirty-watt sense. My battered twin tape deck flicked from pause at the touch of a toe and music from two days and twenty years ago drifted into the dull glow. I made and fired a heavy roller, sat back on the bed. A book was beside my pillow, a handwritten note stuck to its cover.

DEAR BILLY.

Blue-blocked at the top. I sniffed my name, cheap, not permanent.

I'M DOING THE DOUBLE!

Good news. Maggie was still behind the bar, surrounded by bottles, thin bikinis under thick sweaters and plenty of waiting-for-me whisky. I'd throw a nod at the nearest big bottle, ask scouse lass how she was doing and get serious with the night. Mags would smile back, quip across some smart chit-chat, lean lovely and ask me about the note. Fuck, I'd better read it.

Clenched, breathed and continued.

YOU DON'T DRINK UNTIL YOU KNOW THE FIRST SPEECH.

'Fuck!'

IT'S ONLY 20 LINES LONG AND AS SIMPLE AS IT GETS.

'What's that supposed to mean?' I spat at silence.

DON'T BE ANGRY! DON'T WASTE TIME! OPEN THE BOOK! LEARN THE SPEECH AND LOADS OF LOVELY FREE DRINKS WILL BE YOURS!

'Devious,' I smiled.

LOVE, MAGGIE.

PS PUT SOME MEANING IN YOUR LIFE, FOR ONCE!!!!

I winced at that final line. Ignorant, offensive and simply uncalled-for. I threw the freshly crumpled note in the corner, glanced at the book. Percy Shelley ponced up at me from the cover. He was depicted among castle ruins, hand on hip, dreamer eyes shining, rouge overdone. Fucking hell, what was this supposed to mean to me? Was this the meaning Maggie thought my life lacked? Not structure, or psychiatric support, or a sixty-digit bank account. No, none of that, not at all. What I needed most was this powder puff's insights into a long-gone, lifeless, irrelevant, academic, convoluted and pointless fucking age. It was exactly the stuff that noticeboards were made for. If Percy was so fantastic, why not let him sort my crap out? Let young Percy put it right. Send Messrs Shelley down to Charlie's gaff in Moss Side. Put some meaning in his sad life for once, for fucking all.

But there was no use complaining: ultimately, alcohol was at stake. To drink or not to drink, that was never the question. I lit a cigarette and reminded myself which part had been forced upon me by checking the play's title. That done, I found the first speech and began to read to the invisible Bond girl curled, silent and naked, at the foot of my bed.

'The third of my possessions, let it go,' I mumbled, clueless. 'I once heard the nephew of the Pope, had sent his architect . . .'

The book must've fallen from my hand when I passed out. It couldn't have been a few minutes, or a week, but when I stirred some strange discomfort dug deep into my forehead. Automatically I reached my hand towards it.

'Oh, for fuck's sake!'

My nose moved, bone jarred bone.

'FUCK!'

I tried to put the pieces back where they'd been.

'FUCK!'

Fresh blood spilt thick down my face. I tried to catch it in my mouth, staunch it with my hands. I couldn't swear, couldn't speak, could hardly fucking breathe. My nose was blocked, my throat choked, bitter-tasting blood filled my pipes with bubbles of vomit and panic. I flipped over fast, spitting, half spewing bile and blood over my Man City pillowcase. I had a flash thought of clean football kits, screw-in-stud boots behind shut shop windows, late-night launderettes and fat old women wearing pink housecoats in the rain. Spat again, wrenched back, spat-spat-spat, saw orange in the black, spat, began to breathe again. Flopped, shoulder-side down, back to the bed.

Blood had splattered across the open pages of the play book. It had blocked out parts of the text. In my delirium, I had a fucking excellent idea, and began to wipe blood from my nose and mouth across the pages. Semi-solid goop sheened the supposedly relevant play lines. I even smiled to myself as my fingers worked a sick Braille over nonsensical verse. From side on, the words looked fairly well obscured, but when I raised my head, I saw that I'd only managed to highlight my lines with dark red shading. Thought for a moment about sad actors who used fluorescent highlighter pens to pick out their inadequate parts. Flicked quick through the whole script, decided I'd be dead if I followed the thought all the way through. Chucked the indestructible book at the wall, managed to sit up, placed my head within a hole of the hardboard.

Seconds split between sleep and not sleep. Shadows shifted. A beach on the west coast of this island called my name in its midnight wind. But the weather didn't reach my room. My room. It came from out of focus into just ugly. My eyes opened purple, winced swollen. My head ached beside, bedside, inside and in front. Lonely life in northern lamplight skinned my cracked heart, strip by strip.

I bit my lip, coughed up more blood, spat it on the bed, sat up. Tracers were cutting deep lines across my vision. My legs didn't want to go to work. I pushed forward on to well-bent knees. Slurred words to and from myself. Different voices worked my mouth, inhabited my brain, spurred me towards the filthy ceiling. I didn't see Joe, or my dad, knew I could if I wanted to, didn't want to. I stuck out a hand, steadied myself upright on the fluctuating mattress floor. I stared down at the random patterns of red around my feet. Picked out a few odd-shaped faces, a large snail, almost a teapot and a complicated dot-dot design that spelt the word 'FUCK'. I spat it all goodbye, headed for the kitchen.

Pushed myself through a door to a door. Paused for a breath, pushed through that 'n' all. Flat street shine slugged from the lounge's far window. I turned away from it and into the unlit kitchen. I didn't need electricity to know which way the fridge was, leant a little, yanked it open. A capped plastic container with an indiscriminate vodka label lay on its side beside an unusual carrot. I pictured a pork-pie exhibition on the top floor of an illustrious museum, paid the entrance price, avoided the vegetables, grabbed up the bottle.

Leant back to glug-glug the approximate half-pint left. Some little light shone on from the still open refrigerator. I focused on a ceiling shadow around an uneven hole where the light fixture used to be. Wasn't entirely sure I wasn't drinking water. Maggie did that sometimes. The shadow above me moved. She'd tap it in to avoid the sad empty. It sort of crawled a little to the left. Swallowing too fast to taste anything. It grew. Didn't feel the familiar throat burn. Weird fucking shadow. I swallowed the last little bit left, still trying to decide. Blinked my eyes, it got bigger. Water, definitely water. I reached up with the pointless plastic mouthpiece of the empty, tapped the dark patch.

'FUCK!'

The shadow swarmed straight at me in flight. My scream sucked what felt like a thousand in. I threw punches at dense patches of the brand-new horror. The hole poured insects out. I was surrounded, puking, eyes wild, spasmed by shock, screaming fury, bloody murder and mad fear. I started to grab instead of punch. Came back with fistfuls of semi-squashed, horrific half-lives. I was catching shadows. I was under the minute attack of a million nightmares all at once.

Checked my hands to be sure the insects were real. Could've been making it all up. Wasn't. Fired by self-belief, I pulled open a nearby cupboard on pure instinct. Cloth, cloth, can of lighter fluid. Fantastic memory in an emergency. I shook the high-pressure container, it was less than half full, like everything else. Checked up to see the shadow was staying high and swirling noiseless above my head. From a crouch, I patted blind across kitchen surfaces. Desperate to discover England's Glory. Mad in search of a life-saving Swan. Come on! Come on! And contact. Yes. Cardboard. Yes. Rattle. Fuck, yes. Huge flow of adrenaline, relief and purpose poured fresh steel into my mood. I rose to my full height, extended my tooled-up arm, fired a match, let the fuckers feel it.

Clumps of flame turned the air all around me into a crashing pyre of insect death. The bright from the burn revealed huge colonies of spineless creatures in the full flow of suicidal panic. The hole in the ceiling poured sacrifice wave after sacrifice wave into the murderous kitchen. I pressed in, up and after every little fucker that dared to come uninvited calling. I kept my mouth shut, kept killing. Got into a rhythm of motion, sweat pouring, flame blasting. I painted sweeps of midget genocide. The lines of fire became beautiful. I began to dance elegant steps of mass murder in the worst place left on earth. I started to laugh, scream, almost sing along. I started to sense that everything could be beaten in time. That virtually every fucking thing could be defeated if the right tools were within reach. That I would, despite it all, be all right in the end.

The lighter fluid ran out.

Without firelight, the kitchen looked dark. Without my maniac movement, the room was still. Without my screaming, it became silent. Without the home-made flame-thrower it was no fun. Most of the insects were dead, anyway. Those that weren't were back in the hole, thinking twice about flight. I sensed achievement, let the can fall from my hand, kicked the fridge door shut, headed back to my bedroom and more important matters.

I needed a chemical reminder.

My hands landed a central role in a high-speed, experimental motion picture. Fresh supplies found their way from pants' pocket to cluttered table top. The emergency stash was looking well stretched. The all-over wrap was showing a thinness that didn't encourage investigation. I quick slipped a speed wrap from the transparent wrapper, unclipped its magazine edges. I read a visible personal ad, didn't fancy Sally, flicked the folds. Rectangle, triangle, square. The pink powder spread out on the quality paper. I sparked up a ciggie, looked across at the tape player, looked back at the speed. Finger dipped, a few grains fell. I followed their tap to the well-placed wrap, started to neck the lot.

Hands cleaned the wrapper, red snapper. Skin tightened, gums fizzed, eyes went from the tape player to the wrap and back twenty times, or more, or less, or exactly twenty, wasn't counting. I swallowed along to the sights, or sounds, of an

African desert, a poster for shandy, Christmas baubles, a teddy phone in Detroit, my last schoolteacher, a soft morning in winter when my dog was still alive, accessories, double-decker buses, Marlon in black and white. Unwrap, unwrap, whack, whack. The worst scenes from the best films, appropriate nudity, a dead blue gate, the rustle of an immortal insect, unwanted photographs, chain letters in silver, my shaking hand. I clenched hard, my face hurt, focused off it. Teacups, general noise, size labels, label sizes. I focused on the most painful point right on the bridge of my broken nose. Thought only of Charlie, only money, only Charlie, only money, only Charlie, only money, only money, only Charlie, only money. Pressed my right thumb hard into the bone between my eyes. Water flowed, blood 'n' all, bone clicked hard. Teeth stayed shut, mouth made no moves, real pain made no sound, stillness developed itself. My eyes fixed, my brain made temporary repairs, my body moved quickly to clothes. The whole performance made me proud. I reached for the lit cigarette, only a third burnt down, sucked the familiar sensation all the way down. Smiled badly, headed for the corridor. The Eastern Bloc skeletons surrounded down at me. A well fucking captive audience if I'd ever seen one.

'A third of my possessions, you can fucking have it!' I screamed.

'Billy.' A voice came from close by. 'Billy, is that you?'

'How do you know my name?' I asked the closest fabric skull.

'Billy, please untie me!'

'You're not tied,' I told the head. 'You're pinned.'

'I'm tied,' the voice came back.

'Are you the nephew of the Pope?' I asked.

'UNTIE ME!'

'Who said that?'

'BILLY, IT'S ME, JIM!'

'Are you the architect?'

'TELL MAGGIE!' came the cry. 'TELL MAGGIE TO LET ME GO!'

'Listen,' I grabbed a floppy arm. 'Maggie knows all about you, she put you up.'

'PLEASE! I HAVE TO GET OUT!'

'Talk to the Arts Council.'

'PLEEEAAASE!'

'It's really not my problem,' I said, slamming the door.

Staying home struck me as unhealthy. Vegetarians, skeletons, insects, dead writers, carrots, pretend vodka, broken bones and pink drugs. It was enough to drive anyone out the door.

And out I went.

'They're all in there,' security guard said as I sped by.

'No, really.'

'Yep,' he indicated. 'All in the bar.'

'I thought they'd be in the bookshop.'

'Oi,' he called. 'Brady!'

'What?' I paused.

'I hope it fucking hurts.' He nodded at my nose.

'Nice one.'

I'd forgotten to bring cigarettes, but retained a sense of perspective. I didn't need distractions, I needed a drink. Stepped sharp into the bar, got a shock, pulled back, peaked.

It looked like I'd shown up at some sort of classless reunion. Around the three-sided bar, rail-rested, feet and inches apart, glasses in various gradients, was a bar full of characters that I wasn't sure I was ready for. I hadn't been noticed. Edged my head a shade further out of my hiding place. I skipped quick eyes across the Saturday-night collection, alive and well, living it up on the skin-side of the cement.

Behind the bar, as always and expected, was Maggie. But the easy ended there. Jabbering in the ear of a two-legged blonde girl was my high-speed hero, Luke. Doubled down and with their backs to me, leant close and confidential, were Martin and Mark. Over on the far, far side stood the singular beauty of soft-toned Nada, tittle-tattling away with two fine lads. There was an old bloke in a bad wig shouting a round in the foreground. I didn't know his name, but knew that he rapidly developed Tourette's whenever he saw me. And there were at least one, two, three, local girls who knew I was a liar and wouldn't hesitate to blast the fact. I took for granted the two doormen who'd happily maim me, one foreign cripple, several softly spoken salesmen, an out-of-work janitor called Mophead and easy over a hundred students, a thousand artists and a million representatives of the indiscriminate ugly population. All filling gaps that would have been better left empty.

I tried to recall the last time I'd shaved, smacked someone in the face, owned up or performed, paid for a round or done anything even close to the right thing. I needed to shake self-doubt off without shaking. I recalled a mirror, remembered blood, looked behind in my mind, feared ahead in my head, turned fast round, read a notice on a noticeboard, 'Billy Brady is The Cenci', screamed my way to the nearest lock.

Lights changed, noises faded straight away. I winked at my luminous reflection in the cracked mirror and checked the various vacancies on all five doors. I slid inside the furthest, favourite, most distant door of them all, struggled with my pants' pockets. Visions of loss, stupidity and regret panicked what little peace was left. Loud screams brewed in a devil's plastic cup. I touched out a half-empty, half-full pure second-day delayed plastic presence. Split the bag wide, rolled the money inside, tried to control myself and couldn't.

Suck, snort, suck, suck, snort, tap, shake, wobble, tap, snap, snort, shake.

Whites went whiter, almost blue. The little bit left looked lonely, so I whacked that back as well. I sat the fuck down when my stomach, my head and everything in between turned absolutely inside out.

'Calm down, Billy.'

The echo distorted deeper, older, different. Wasn't sure

whether it was me or not. I slapped a hand over my mouth, looked fierce at the lock close across. Heard dog scratches, definitely fucking dog scratches, coming in fast from outside.

'No dogs allowed!' I cried.

'Billy lad, are you all right?'

'C'mon Amber!' My voice. 'Come here, girl!'

'Billy, I know you're in there.'

'No, you fucking don't!'

The thin toilet door fluctuated, subsided and shrank. Animated fractions of featured wankers revealed themselves to me. Wiggie adjusted his mistake in a see-through mirror. Charlie was under the sink eating dog food. A naked Girl Guide untied two knots, started on a third. Uncle Jack quit for ever. Trev found reverse. Grandad Joe let out a low growl. My dad adjusted the angle of the light for the last time.

I dropped my drugs.

'FUCK!'

Powder dissolved in shallow piss.

'Look what you've made me do!'

I was down on my knees, getting frantic.

'Come on,' came from the other side. 'You know who it is.'

'NO, I DON'T!'

'It's only me.'

'FUCK OFF!'

'Watch that mouth, lad!'

'FUCK OFF, JOE!'

'Is this really your life, Billy?'

And I fired a wild look up to see Eamonn Andrews's smile spread into a haemorrhage that ate his whole face. The big red book hit the floor. The gold letters on the cover spelt my name. Grandad crawled across the tiles towards me with a pint of Semtex balanced on his head. Underdoor light hit me hard in the face. I pushed what was left of pity back into my pocket, scrambled fast against the bog.

'THAT IS ENOUGH!' I screamed.

My mouth felt well dry. Felt like what I'd just taken was hovering somewhere between my brain and my feet. I started to shake trying to get the shit down. Didn't have what it took to find a cigarette. I heard the noise of the double doors that fronted the toilets, crouched my vibrating head so far down that my ear got wet. A big pair of sneaker feet danced about outside.

'Who's that?'

The silence terrified me.

'Who the fuck is that?' I called, louder.

'Marco Polo,' came back.

'Luke!'

'What're you doing in there, Bilbo?'

Tap swing, flow of water went along.

'What are you doing in there?' Luke asked again.

Door banged, maybe tapped. Luke's feet cut the line, came close enough to kick.

'BILLY!' he shouted.

My shakes went silly bad. I pulled my feet in, held my knees next to my chin.

'Suit yourself,' he said. 'I'll be in the bar.'

Nodded my head, maybe on purpose, maybe not.

'And Billy,' Luke called, 'don't thank me for last night.'

Last night?

I lifted my body with the help of clenched ceramic.

Last night?

I leant against the side divider.

Last night?

I wedged my head stationary in the cross-section corner.

Last night? Luke?

I couldn't fucking focus on any single thing; images spilt

tidal from the overloaded brain bank. The tricks weren't working. I was stumped, lost and stupid.

Think, Billy! Last night? Think!

Clocks ticked, tunnels opened into caves, went back to being tunnels again. Stairs climbed, shifted, changed colour. Cars drove long corners, coat hangers hung coats, the world's greatest cleavage fell from the sky to cover me. And bit by brilliant bit, flash by fucking flash, my shakes began to recede. The cement-cum-hardboard combo that viced my head in place played its part, but the real work was done by my sacrificial mind. Manic head sped ahead of spastic shake. Wobbles worked their way inside, became thoughts.

I recalled the knife, of course I did. I could see Charlie's face. I could probably transcribe the fucker word for word. I saw a green bottle fly through the air and past my face. The details of Luke's rescue looped a thousand times or so before I decided that I'd done enough. Before I found a smile.

Yes, last night.

What a fantastic thing to focus on. I loved those glorious incidentals, believed in the unbelievable options, got off on redundant perceptions. It exercised my mind. The busy brilliance of once-lived life did its job perfectly. And, long story, short story, my bastard shakes were beaten by my busy mind. The shameful tremor went invisible, it went inside.

I whispered thanks to whoever felt they deserved it and pushed off the wall. I confirmed cranial stillness, but couldn't find my cigarettes. A straw split desert humps as it struck me that it was time to move on, move up and move out. I flicked the lock without thinking, saw my perfect haircut in high-speed silver and wandered, gracefully, towards the next disaster.

SATURDAY 9.59PM

I rounded the corner, walked straight into Maggie's eyeliner.

'Speech!' she shouted.

'Shut up,' I angled my fresh wounds at the light. 'Please.'

'Oh, my God!' Maggie's face delayed.

'How does it look?' I asked.

'Not good.'

'Can I have a drink?'

'Yes, yes.' Mags in motion. 'Of course you can.'

Pity worked, bass shifted, hooks came in. I kicked my metal toe against the metal bar rail. I watched Maggie turn, pour and return. I blinked in the blinkers, forgot the little bit of speech I'd ever known. Wanted a drink more than I could say.

'There you are.' She placed a half-pint of whisky before me.

'Here I am.' Necked the lot.

'Breakfast of champions,' Maggie smiled.

'Fucking great stuff.'

'Billy,' Maggie levelled. 'Who was it?'

'Bella.'

'How?'

'In the nose,' I shrugged. 'In bed.'

'She hit you in the bed,' Mags laughed.

'No,' I joined in, couldn't help it. 'She hit me in the nose.'

'Is it broken?'

'Yes,' I told her. 'But I think I've set it fairly well.'

'Christ.'

'Is there any blood?'

'No, not really,' Mags winced. 'But you look terrible.'

And I liked the way she said it. Straight and at me. I never minded Maggie's honesty. It wasn't a quality I normally rated but, with me and her, it helped us become more alone. Right there and then, it helped make the bar pack disappear, the lights fade, the surrounding stage simmer down. Knew that I was getting a fair bit of attention from the crowd around, but me and Maggie managed to hide in what little was left of sincerity. It felt exactly right when our heads came together.

My eyes strayed down her face to her mouth. She followed me. Followed my movement and the meaning. We kissed. Heat blew through open vents. It was brief, but powerful. Even Maggie forgot the speech, I could feel it. I forgot myself. Cool streams of dirty Mersey ran down my scally streets. We kissed again. I sensed more attention in the sound about, reopened my eyes, saw that hers were open too. I smiled, even laughed, looked away, leant back.

'Is it safe?' I asked.

'Billy.'

'What?'

'I hardly ever have any idea what you're talking about.'

'Well.' Something simple. 'How about another drink?'

'Speech first!' she screeched.

Maggie lived on the high wire. Her demands swung at sharp angles to my low life. Her hand touched my arm, gently. She had my attention, my respect, my whisky.

'You got one for the nose,' Mags reminded. 'That was only fair.'

'Very decent of you.'

'Yes,' she replied. 'But you don't get another until I hear that speech.'

Badly didn't want to hurt her. Didn't want to come any-where near to ever hurting her. Would take apart, bone by bone, any fucker who even sniffed close to Maggie's pain. But the subject, the speech, the horror of it all, blasted nasty in my face. I regretted any time I'd spent slaughtering insects, seeing insane girlfriends or doing all sorts of stupid crap instead of learning that speech. I couldn't think of one single way out.

So, I stalled.

'Didn't think much of your note,' I sneered across.

'At least you read it,' she snapped back.

'Of course I read it.'

'Colour?'

'Blue,' I twitched back.

'Paper?'

'Thin, good quality,' I zeroed. 'From the notepad on your desk.'

'Purpose?'

'To put meaning in my life.'

'In your sad life!'

'For once.' I wanted to hold her. 'Right?'

'Yes, very good,' she proclaimed. 'Now, the speech.'

Wanted to hold her, protect her from the pain that thought-less people caused. I wanted to get over on her side of the bar, steal a few drinks, make her laugh. Tickle Maggie purple all the way back to the train ride. The train ride where I should've been stronger and said 'no' to her dramatic suggestions. Deep in dark thought, I watched a black edge appear on the bar between us. Probably just a shadow chucked from a changing traffic light, but it felt somehow more significant. I pulled my focus away from the obvious meaning, placed it on a bottle behind the bar and prayed for some peace.

'A third,' I said slow. 'A third of my possessions.'

Maggie nodded, I felt the brief warmth of a reaction that would never be mine.

'A third of my possessions,' but I cracked, I couldn't even fake it. 'A third of my possessions isn't really worth talking about, is it?' I raised the volume, threw my arms wide. 'The Pope needs a new architect and I need a fucking drink!'

'Billy,' her voice went quiet, eyes fell fast. 'No.'

'Look, I had to deal with an insect invasion.'

'Billy,' strangely quiet, I had to lean close.

'What is it, Mags?'

'FUCK OFF!' she screamed. 'FUCK OFF!'

Pure rage span Maggie away. She hot-headed it across to the side of the bar. She waved on an overweight order, went furiously back to her unhappy servitude. I tried to catch her eye, no chance. I shouted her name, forget about it.

The safe cavern of soft Merseyside had completely kicked me out. I fell back from the bar, walked towards the fire exit, wanted another drink. The storeroom, beyond the emergency exit, was where they kept the barrels, the bottles and the peanuts. Determined and focused, I pushed past some bad-fabric fucker who got in my way. I was all set to kick my way into the corridor that led to the cellar when a girl stopped me. Only a girl, that was all it took, a girl from only a night before.

But she stopped me dead.

Couldn't call it memory, I couldn't call it at all. Her lips moved softly up, then down again. In our lifetime the lights got darker. I rub-a-dub-dubbed the balls of my eyes, looked everywhere that was left. Snap. Clockwork statues disguised as people poured draughts down cracked mouths. Snap. The human chill reached my rag and broken bones. Snap. The fucking queen of hearts went electric. Snap. I saw her standing there. Snap. Magenta Pearl.

SNAP.

She was in the far corner where the light was not so good, darts matches got abandoned and old dogs went to die. There she was, kissing her latest pastime. She didn't see me, I saw her. Bra strap, floral design, on show, only just. The Romeo between us threw back his drink, stamped out his ciggie, blocked my view. I stepped to the left, looked closer, the cellar door would have to survive the night. Magenta Pearl was pressed against the wall. I couldn't face her liquid lips, her drunken lisps, her firm beliefs. All I could do was nothing. I forced myself away from the once-promising corner, back into the mad crowd.

Halfway to the window on a wide, stumbling curve, I caught sight of nobody but Nada. She was beautiful, still. Her sleek black hair shone brighter than jewels ever had. When she back-stepped from the bar, her dress caught a beam of good light from the orange upper deck and all I saw was Nada's body beneath. Delicate shapes of once-promised perfection made me smile, made me feel better. Nada glanced my way, drums hit rolls, blood pumped, sensations woke up. Something somewhere switched itself back on. I felt like a chat.

Tracked Nada's return to a table where two talkative admirers waited. Realised that I wouldn't be able to avoid offence, turned away again, moved towards the bar. Maggie clocked me, looked utterly ticked off and deliberately busy. I glanced over to where Luke was, all across on the other side, surrounded and smiling, out of my reach. That left Martin and Mark. Fuck, I wanted a cigarette so badly and my options were losing weight. Tourettic Wiggie spotted me; he looked geared up for relapse, started frothing my way. There was only one thing for it. I stepped solid in the boys' direction. They were crouched in consultation over fizzy lager at the corner of the marble bar top.

I came alongside.

'All right, lads?' I tried.

Seconds raced by on superbikes, neither spoke.

'Oh, for fuck's sake,' I tried with a smile. 'Come on.'

Martin turned away, looked out, or maybe just at, the light-bouncing window. I changed my tactics to no tactics at all, slapped a hand across the nearest broad shoulder.

'Mark,' I grinned.

He glanced, I took my chance.

'How the heck are you, old boy?' I asked with my arm around.

'No' bad.' Mark was Scottish.

'Well,' I chirped. 'That's good then, isn't it?'

'It's no' bad.'

'Right.' Give me a fucking cigarette! 'Mark, are you still on the B&H?' I over-shouldered frantic around the likely spaces, couldn't see fuck all, nor fags neither. 'Y'see, I'm sort of desperate for a smoke right about now, and I was wondering.'

Mark lifted his hand, showed me the narcotic gold underneath.

'Thanks, mate!'

Grab, miss, grab, grab, fast as I can snap, light, light, slightest shake, deepest fucking breath ever and long, slow, glorious exhalation.

'Fucking hell!' I spouted. 'Did I need that!'

'It's always something, right, Billy?' Martin said with a side smile.

'That was,' I stared at his sharp features in the half-light. 'That was a wonderful remark.' I smiled. 'It really was quite brilliant.'

No reaction, fuck him.

'So, Mark,' I leant in. 'How are the eyes?'

'No' bad.'

'Well, they look fucking awful.'

'Have ye seen yersel' recent, like?'

'Fair point,' nod, nod. 'But seriously, mate, how are they?'

'When I keep 'm clean, they're haf' decent.'

'That's good,' I said.

But it wasn't.

Mark was going blind. He never went into why and all that, just said it was probably to do with the drugs. Well, I've thrown the old windows of the soul out of whack on rain-soaked roads home more than once, and my eyes weren't filled up with nasty yellow shit that needed a surgical swab three fucking times a day. Mark always blamed the drugs, I blamed his eyes. Told him to go and see an eye doctor, but he never would. Said it was inevitable that he'd be blind by forty, said he didn't care, said he'd be dead.

'Maggie won't serve me,' I said, switching subjects.

'Why's that then?' Mark asked.

'Something I did, or something I'm not doing. Fuck, I just pissed her off.'

'You've been doing that a lot lately,' Mark squinted. 'And not only to Maggie.'

All I wanted was a drink, any fucking drink. It didn't even have to be my usual half-pint of Irish. Dry fucking cider would've done right then. Every other fucker in the place was drinking. I wanted to blend in, be average, join the crowd. Not much to ask. I gave Mark a long look that I'd used to give him when we were still friends. It meant something like, 'FOR FUCK SAKE, HELP ME!'

'Tell me about it,' he shrugged.

And whether or not he meant it, he'd said it. I spied a gap in the world's perpetual deafness. My going-blind mate from the good old days, way back before last Saturday, sincere or not, was inviting me to speak. And I didn't mind feeling like the weak one for once. All this shit had begun to gang up on me. And when Mark turned his soft-focus yellows towards me, it didn't matter if he was waiting for me to start, or waiting for me to leave. I was handbraked in fifth gear of the mouth, I had to tell someone.

'You see, it's like this, Mark.' Cigarette reach, nod, smoke, brilliant. 'I've had so much shit banging about in my head since the deal went bad. There's been trouble in the club, close calls with Charlie, he pulled a fucking knife on me. The cunt wants his money back, all of it, tomorrow night. And I want to pay him back, but it's causing me a few problems and it's not good.'

'No' good,' Mark frowned.

'Right! Right! No good!' I cleared my nose, felt the rush. 'I've had a mad train ride, Maggie's been blowing hot and cold on me every five seconds, or less. She wants me to act in her play. She wants me to be the devil. Well, not the devil, but some old Italian child molester who walks around in his underwear drinking goblets of blood and pretending he's the fucking devil. It's ridiculous! Completely unbelievable! Have you seen the posters out there?'

'Aye.'

'Right.' I remembered to smoke, smoked.

'Calm down,' Mark reached out a hand, missed.

'I'd love to, mate, but how the fuck can I?' Mark said nowt, I expanded. 'Bella is turning the screw on me. She broke my nose. I'm finding it almost impossible to breathe. I look like the walking wounded. And I think she's got some sort of sympathetic love thing for Charlie, and there's no way of knowing.' I stepped in fast. 'Do you know, Mark? C'mon, is there something going on with Bella and Charlie? You'd probably, definitely, you *would* know!' I pointed wildly. 'And why does Nada keep looking at me like that?'

'Easy, Billy.'

'Ghosts of my dead grandad and dad show up every time I take a bit. The shakes are winning! My face hurts! I'm running out of money that I didn't have in the first place! I was just in the bathroom and I actually dropped my drugs! Mark! Mark! Me! Billy! I dropped my drugs! I've never dropped my drugs! Never!'

'No, you normally drop other people's.'

'Martin isn't fucking talking to me any more. My oldest friend, not including you, or Maggie, or, fuck, look, he isn't talking to me just because of some drug debt. And Maggie's not talking to me because of some stupid play. Bella whacks me in the head for some reason that I still haven't got.' I flashed panic at the door. 'And Charlie could walk in at any moment, or he could send someone else through that door at any fucking moment, or he could be waiting outside the door, or someone he knows could be round the next corner. The point is, I could be ducking bullets any second and, instead, I'm worrying about some girl in the corner who wants to fuck her reflection and has virtually no tits!' Something broke, new blood didn't surprise me. 'And I can't get a fucking drink! I can't get a fucking drink in the fucking pub that I come to every fucking day of my life! AND ALL I REALLY WANT IS A FUCKING DRINK!'

'Billy!' It was Mark.

'WHAT?'

'Let me get you a drink.'

'FUCK!' Held on, tight, tighter, tightest. 'That would be great, Mark. That would really be something. Thank you! I'll drink anything! Anything will do!'

'Really?' he asked, fishing in his pocket.

'Well, a large of the usual is what I want, but anything'll do.'

'A large of the usual,' he winked. 'On its way.'

Think I might've caught Martin's sly side eye cutting me up as Mark leant away to get the drinks in. And the fucking razor side eye said, 'It's always something and it's always that easy, right Billy?' And the clever bastard might've been right, my whole show could've been contrived to get a drink, but it could also have been true and what was it to him, anyway? Temper rising, I stepped smart and grabbed a thin

Martin-flavoured spindle. Flexing, I pulled him all the way into me.

'The train is speeding,' I hissed. 'The fucker is covered in stickers and I've got no cigarettes. You are a fucking Audi Quatro petrol-gauge poet with a shit girlfriend. Your best lines will never be remembered, they'll just be taken. Women will always want new dresses!' Martin tried to pull away, no chance. 'There's a plant in Chorlton that could take over the world. My bath is better than your bed. Nobody Irish ever actually dies. My dog ran into a parked car.'

'Mark!' Martin flashed.

'TOO LATE, FUCKER!' I pushed him against the bar, raised my fist.

My entire weight was pulled away fast and completely clean. My brain spluttered surprise. I tried to find my raised right hand. Found that I didn't have any right hands available. Wided it wild into the eyes of Martin, but he just looked over my shoulder, even smiled. I span my head, spit ready, but too much strength held me too tight, made me swallow it all back. Mark's smile, as he restrained me, was the final fucking straw. I got ready to completely fucking flip.

'Your drink's getting cold,' Mark grinned.

'WHAT?'

'Leave it,' he growled.

'MY DRINK?'

'No,' Mark managed a laugh. 'Take your drink, leave it!' He nodded back at the beyond. I turned to see Martin walking casually away. I heard a voice come from behind. 'There's half a pint of Jameson's on the bar top, it's all yours.'

'You don't want a third of it?' I muttered.

'What?' came back Mark.

'It doesn't matter, just let me go, please.'

'Enjoy,' he released.

'Cheers, pal.' And I necked the fucking lot.

'Easy,' he cautioned.

'You wouldn't believe how easy that was.'

And, of course, I understood that the drink was a distraction, its purpose to stop me piling into Martin, and it worked. I lit up, looked around a little. The fluids were mixing with the powder and a certain amount of clarity was kicking back in. The world began to look less complicated. I looked across at Mark, couldn't remember what we'd been talking about.

'How are the eyes, then?' I asked with a concerned edge.

'Shut the fuck up about my eyes!'

'What?'

'Save the concern for yourself.'

'What are you on about?'

'Billy, you're blinder than I'll ever be.'

'Harsh.'

'You can't see what's right in front of your face.'

'What the fuck are you on about?' I cried.

'All you need is money.'

'No,' I laughed. 'All I need is love.'

'Be serious,' Mark flexed. 'All this sentimental, self-pitying, amphetamine-induced shit only blurs the picture.' His boiled yellow eyes spat clarity. 'At the centre, at the actual root of all your problems is the money you owe Charlie. If you can sort that out everything else will fall back into place.'

'You're right,' I nodded. 'But isn't that sort of obvious?'

'You need money,' Mark repeated.

'Brilliant!' The blind led the blind. 'I really should've thought of that.'

'Shut up and listen. Money is always close by.' Mark moved his eyes half ahead and slightly across to one side. From the state of his vision, he had to be working close. I followed his stare the short distance to the bar's beer-stained till.

'Fuck,' I blurted. 'You mean . . . ?'

'Desperate times call for desperate measures.'

'That's such a cliché.'

Whack! Mark's face came well close.

'Your life's a cliché,' he snarled. 'Behave accordingly.'

I leant back, my hands held me to the bar. I laughed mad and out loud. Even Maggie turned to look. Soft lass couldn't help a smile, she even stepped a little closer. I was the opposite of, and the same as, a laughing policeman in Blackpool. She took a step towards my inexplicable hilarity. The sharp corners behind the bar fell away. The Ecstasy in the sound system tuned in. The greatest blonde girl in the world smiled my way, I laughed back.

'What's so funny?' she asked.

'Forgive me,' I spluttered through giggles.

'What did you say?' Mags stepped closer. 'You wrecked cunt.'

'Forgive me,' I said, clearer.

'Well,' she paused. 'Let's see.'

'I'll learn the lines,' I giggled.

'You're fucking right you will.' She turned away. 'Close your eyes.'

I closed my eyes tight shut. I growled in my throat, in the complete dark. Bit by bit the sounds around began to break down. I felt myself falling in. Snapped open my eyes in sharp panic to see Maggie's big, bold, scouse smile. Felt myself run utterly and instantly out of breath. Thumped my lung, held it together.

'Surprise!' Maggie squawked.

'Fuck, Mags,' disorientated. 'I mean, thank you, Maggie.'

Big glass of Jimmy was right there. Mags reached out a hand, it occurred to me that I should have done with it and just bite it off at the wrist. It was a gesture I couldn't return. Maggie wanted to make the world a better place, I didn't see the point. As Maggie's features softened and angled in, it all began to feel a bit too much for me to take. Fucking generosity blew my mind every time. I reached awkwardly towards the half-pint on the shifting marble bar top. For no apparent reason, my hand tapped my head a little on the sharp side. I stepped to hit it back. Got slapped with a black and white flicker picture of Maggie throwing herself under the wheels of a fast-coming train that was thundering straight for me.

I fell through the small gap between one life and another.

My flinch snapped back on the reverse angle of a slow-paced attack. Felt pressure on my shoulder. Felt a little older. My head shook west to the bright orange buses turning corners in high arcs of dangerous triumph. I laughed loud, the pressure doubled up. Blood in one part of my body screamed furious revulsion at blood in another part of my body. I staggered, gripped and fucking slipped. Some blockage buzzed from the depths to the surface. My eyes sweat-rolled, knees went bent, whisky glass shattered in my hand. I would've missed my mouth, didn't even try.

Felt familiar female wrap all around, some strong hand was in my back. I tried to flex against the permanent grip of a temporary girl. I recalled mirrors, the way out and rain. I stayed up for a moment, fell fucking down.

Someone shouted near my ear. I looked down, switched it to up. I looked away, lifted my head, looked at Maggie, yes, Maggie, closed my eyes. Silence, contemplation, crazed and dangerous, exhausted, so far on the outside of the orange. Weightless, not warm, once solid, now liquid, bought and completely sold. My head was lifted by her hands, others came in and helped me stand up. I felt a soft flux in the atmosphere, it burst speakers, balloons and my last good eardrum. Swollen enormous, I felt tiny and completely surrounded. I dropped my face to the liquid marble, something hurt. Maggie's features entered the lighting, long shots dragged, body was sound, my mind raved on. Words came in, her words.

'Drink, Billy.'

Saw the drink, saw her face. She hummed, soft, beautiful and somewhere inside my last remaining phone line. She pulled back a hand, hit me. She cleaned me up, kicked me out. No, she didn't. It wasn't even her. It wasn't Bella. Grip. Now. Grip tight and hold on. I started to straighten up. Even managed a step back then a wobble forward, put my hands on the bar, chanced at a cigarette, dropped it. Maggie, definitely Maggie.

'Drink a bit of this, Billy.'

I knew the words, nodded understanding.

'He's all right.' Someone said in Scottish.

'Yes,' I muttered. 'He's all right.'

'What happened?' Maggie was close and gentle.

'I might've overdone it in the bog before.'

'And the bar?'

'Yes, possibly there too.'

'You scared me,' Mags whispered.

'I know the feeling.'

Cans of lilted vocals swung through the Saturday night. I sensed fences falling down, or was it gates? Watched a security guard bury his head between the breasts of a sex-change studio-apartment casualty in the corner. The wind door swung open. The more I saw, the more I missed. Maggie moved a step away from me and the gap grew wider. I reached stupid and drank down more whisky. Spat most of it back with blood and crap. I turned to tell Mark the truth, but he wasn't there. I watched the empty space beside his absence for a while, thought of Martin. Followed the thought over to the far side, the two good old boys twitched me the timing, nodded at the till.

'Forgive me, Mags.'

'Be quiet,' she soothed. 'I already have.'

'No, forgive me.' I stepped up and down a low hill. 'Forgive me for this.'

I was behind the bar. I moved fast past many people's surprised eyes. Bending over the till, I hit the biggest fucking key on the forbidden fucking keyboard. Recognised the synthetic bell-chime thing ding-ding for me. The money tray hit me in the stomach, I knew the best way to hit it back. Maggie was wild at my side, shouted loud enough for everyone, even me, to hear.

'WHAT THE FUCK ARE YOU DOING?'

'Getting the first punch in.'

'DON'T DO THIS!' she screamed.

'MAGGIE!' I clenched. 'FUCK OFF! THIS IS THE ROOT OF MY PROBLEM! THIS IS WHAT I NEED!' She backed away. 'EVERY DOG WILL FALL INTO PLACE!'

I clocked that the security slob had regained interest in the world outside the wet. Put a rush on the job. Got both hands working, dug notes from all the pots. Tens, twenties and minimum wages multiplied in my gripper fists. Didn't have time for change, but who does these days? I grabbed a pack of my favourite-flavoured fags from the tillside, thought fuck it, took two. Turned to see familiar faces widing away at me.

'GET THE FUCK OUT!' Mark yelled.

Martin nodded, my dad and grandad stopped feeding the dogs for a second and actually smiled. Hero Luko, of course, knocked the sad security sack on his flabby back. I watched the never-mind mountain of no muscle bleed like a stuck porky. I retched in a row of pint pots that could do with a clean, waved goodbye to the floating impressions of friendship all round and skipped out the way I'd come in. Had to smack the fat walkie-talkie wanker, from before, in the head. Blew out the door.

Back in the rain, I heard a voice come from behind. Stumbled into the road, fucking traffic couldn't touch me. Fell on the kerb fronting the far side of the road. I shouted from my back, looking up at the non-stop dark.

'MAGGIE!'

I heard the loud girl's seaside voice, tyres gripped tarmac again.

'MAGGIE!'

I crippled to my feet, changed history.

'MAGGIE!'

And there she was, split by the whizz and flash of mad traffic, framed in concrete, backed by drunken, righteous eyes. She was paused on the axis of an Oscar nomination. I spat out blood. She shuffled her feet. I reached for a cigarette. She lifted her head. I cast my vote. My arms went wide.

'I love you, Maggie.'

I said it way too soft for her to hear, almost didn't hear it myself. The truth was hidden within wind and hard water. It was lost in the unbelievable collection of noise sent down to distract us. I watched carefully, saw Maggie raise her head. Then she just held it up, proud and brilliant. For a brief moment we shared something more solid than the same chaotic elements. Peaceful, brief, but pointless. I blinked and it all changed back. Circumstances, addictions and all the bit-part players between returned. I sparked up the obligatory ciggie, clocked a redundant security guard wobbling the same old shit down the same old steps. I made my choices, threw my fag, sniffed the fumes, legged it.

I moved away from the city centre. Money in my pocket and a soft, sensitive, all-conquering payback gaining weight in my mind. I would do the right thing, finally. I would level the playing field and run right across it, fresh, clean and free. I would borrow someone's spare trainers. I would have the right kit, for once. I would turn the problem into a clear solution and be good and done with debt for a lifetime to come. I ran as fast as the awful weather would allow. And knew where I was going.

The Man Alive, Charlie.

It all started with an idea, my fucking idea.

Walking the line. Following the glow all the way to where the fuck. It struck me that I'd been well set up. Didn't take too long to feel the deceit in Mark's loaded advice, the conspiracy in his confidence, the fuck in friendship. I'd been made the fall guy for the sake of a few hundred quid. Times had certainly changed, and fast.

I crossed several streets recalling the optimism, the buzz, the genuine three-way happiness of only a week before. That's what the bath had been all about. Call it disillusion, call it cold and fucking lonely. Call it insane ceramic. Call it love. Call it the slow water treatment working its way through to regret and guilt. I fucked up, right enough, and I was paying for it. I'd let the operation utterly down, and now all I could be was the sacrifice, the compromise, the bad answer to the wrong question. Martin and Mark had set me up to stick that till. They didn't care. It'd become economics. It'd become self-preservation. It'd used to be safe.

I struggled along the road thinking about how close we'd come. Knowing that the final triumph had been wrecked by my failure. Knowing that I was fully responsible. Knowing that I'd started it, finished it and was feeling it. Tried to tell myself that without me and my idea in the first place, there wouldn't have been anything to fuck up.

It didn't help.

The almighty chemical cocktail, the unbeatable Traffic Light, totally my idea. It struck me first one long, wandered-home dawn. I was leant against a cement luxury looking at the flick-flick of the three-stage light control. The beauty of action when nobody was around. The lights went from red to red and orange and then to green with no cars around, no people neither. Stimuli absent, lights still active. The everyday device stood there waiting, they behaved separate and ambivalent for whole half-minutes, then they just changed, for no reason at all. The traffic lights changed purely to entertain themselves. They did it because they could.

Traffic lights, apart from being a permanent fixture of everyone's city street experience, were also associated with irritation and delay. And seeing as though this would be the exact opposite effect of our chemical creation, the name stuck. And it sounded good every time I said it. The Traffic Lights. A lifetime coming. A weekend going. The carnival night had been preceded by a long industrial process. The madness and mania of one weekend had taken months to prepare for.

The three of us had been dealing together for almost two years. Last Saturday was supposed to have been the flag-raising ceremony on the top of a most difficult mountain. I'd been sent out to take the final steps to the summit, to do the selling. But instead, there I was, only a week later, at rock-bottom, right down on the other side, completely isolated and on my own. I'd really fucked it up. Desperate times led to desperate memories. The rain picked up. I scented sentiment in the scenery. I got so tired of living in the present, flashed all the way back to our glorious past.

Only a week.

It had only been one standard set of seven since Martin, Mark and me had sat ourselves down. We cloaked the well-lit kitchen, put the cat out, loaded up on whisky, old jokes, backchat and dreams. We'd sold everything, bought other things. We'd double-locked the door, found our way to the brink of a brand-new world.

Time passed silent. We flipped, lipped and lung-whipped smoke into our bloodstreams. I sat non-stop smiling, contemplating the entire chemical buffet bar emerging before me. Martin and Mark didn't smile, they had no time. They were busy unwrapping and cracking the plentiful pack of orange and green capsules that I'd got from some amateur pharmacist in Cheetham Hill.

The cap colour had been my idea. Orange, the everlasting in-between, the safety shade that sent happy slappers into a squash. Green, picked for the obvious 'go' connotation, but also with an eye out for environmentalists. And I loved the green-orange clash. The only other colour considered had been red, due to the pill's name, but red and orange just wouldn't work, and orange had always been a solid lock from the start.

Mark took care of the green shiners. He rowed them open in a long line before him. Martin placed the oranges lightly in triangles on his side of divide. I just stared, gobsmacked, at the middle ground where the sizeable piles of plasticked ingredients waited. They whispered promises to me.

'How will we know?' I asked.

'Billy,' Martin muttered, not looking up. 'We'll know.'

'But Martin,' I wanted attention. 'I say, Martin.'

He sighed, pulled a perfect backflip in the movement of his eyes.

'How will we know?' I repeated.

'For the last time,' he levelled. 'We will know.'

'Right, got it.'

But I still felt nervous. All the obvious potential made me nervous. I took a mental snapshot of the three of us bathed in harsh, luminous light. From the side it could've been anything, we could've been anyone, well, any three.

But from overhead, what we were was obvious. The green lines and orange triangles bordered piles of white pills, sheets of dotted paper, dragon dabs of pink and white. The complex colour scheme confused me, the trickery of manufacture made me mad nervous.

'Martin!' I burst.

'What is it?'

'They have to be perfect,' I stressed. 'For this to work, I mean really work, the way we want it to. Every one,' I fluttered my fingers over the workspace. 'Every single Traffic Light has to be absolutely perfect.'

'I think we might've discussed that already.' Hard stare, firm tone.

'Yes, yes, yes.' Eyes wide, mind motoring. 'You've said that, Marty, but where was I? I don't recall any such discussion.' My pitch trebled. 'And as a third part of this operation, one whole third, I think it's important that I remember all discussions pertaining to the precise make-up of the Traffic Light. It was my fucking idea, don't forget that!'

Mark lifted his attention from his hands, looked directly at me. I recognised the significance of his steady stare. It wasn't like the first time I'd seen it. Mark was letting me know that something had gone too far and finally reached him. Even Martin's hands stopped for an awkward moment. I gave them my best plaintive shrug and 'what the fuck' face; they both just glared.

'Lads! Lads!' I cried. 'I'm only asking, I'm only curious!'

'Well, now you mention it,' Martin nodded, smiled, I tried. 'We thought the best way to be sure of the quality of twelve hundred pills would be to give all of them to you, one at a time, then sit back and watch your brain explode.'

'Fuck off,' I snapped. 'I didn't mean that.'

'No, you're right.' Smart Marty eyebrow. 'We shouldn't make back the money we've laid out on these until you, Billy

Brady, guarantee complete satisfaction for every customer. Until you, personally, sample every pill.'

'You could be the Irishman in the match factory,' Mark snided.

'Funny,' I frowned.

'Look,' Martin edged across. 'We've discussed it.'

'Right, right, you said,' I sighed.

'Don't sulk, Billy. It's like we said last week, remember, under the bridge, the first Traffic Light will be assembled to exact specifications and be product-tested by the very well-respected third member of our operation,' he grinned. 'And that's you, dickhead!'

'Got it.'

'As we discussed!' Marty fizzed.

'Maybe, I remember, under a bridge, it's possible.'

'Brilliant, now shut the fuck up and let us get on with it!'

It was all I wanted in the first place. It was all I needed to hear. Had some vague recollection of our agreement, but needed to be reassured. It was essential that I was the first to take the taste, the plunge, the biscuit, the drug, the glorious fucking Traffic Light. I had some deep-sown obsession with being the first to try things. No doubt indicated something deep and disturbing about my childhood, but sod that, why should I wait? Second is for stupid people, queues are for cowards, delays are for dawdlers, waiting rooms are designed for the sick. I was about to explain all this to the lads, but they were eyes down on matters in hand and wouldn't appreciate it. I leant back, took a line, tried to relax, took another.

The boys didn't deviate. They walked different lines with psychic links towards a shared outcome. Their regimental lines formed, their battle lines set, their movements were swift. Mark dust-dropped, doubled and redoubled his numbers. Martin shovelled pure portions of MDMA into caps. Twelve hundred separate squads of pink champagne lay patiently in long diagonal lines. Mark nail-scissored Strawberries into blind-man's halves, balanced the bits on crushed white doves and set them down one at a time. Click-clacked-closed my eyes, played inside with the properties of champagne, doves, Strawberries and purity. Arrived at a biblical garden party next to a tennis match. Forced myself to keep quiet.

I felt fairly useless. Private jokes, carpet fluff, flat air, spectator sports, the infinite bind of time, controlled motion, skilled manpower, it all left me cold. The boys got the action, I got to watch. Fantastic. I'd been forbidden from handling the ingredients ever since an unfortunate drink-spilling incident had wiped out an earlier attempt at a cocktail venture. I'd been relegated to the role of stay-out-of-the-way sleeping partner. But only for this stage. I hurried over hurdles in my head, leapt towards my element. Martin and Mark might've had their brand-new toys, but they only got to put the pieces together. I would be the first to fly and I couldn't wait.

'Are we nearly there yet?' I asked.

'Quiet!' Martin snapped.

The devil found work for my idle mind. I leant across to fiddle with the wireless. Our wind-up radio had nine stations on FM, twenty on AM and loads of good noise in between. I followed the red line cutting across the green numbers. Voices, snatches of sound, loud stereo music, weird accents, bad advice, fruit-pie recipes and redundant middle-English warble about the sorry state of the garden. I chanced in on a French woman speaking in soft foreign about something I didn't understand. She paused between sentences for longer than the sentences themselves took to talk. I bloody loved it. Started filling her hissy gaps with my own personal replies. It was like a nice, long-distance, cross-cultural chit-chat, free of charge. Felt let down a little when Fifi put on some horrible jazz record just as I was about to tell her about my holidays, but you can't win 'em all. I flicked carelessly across to the police channel, got halfway through the cut-and-thrust of a pizza order, heard my name.

'Billy!' A hand hit my shoulder.

'What!' I snapped fast, thinking the cops had climbed out of the radio.

'The first one is ready,' Marty smiled.

'Right.' Knew the porky voice had sounded familiar. 'Let me see it.'

Martin opened his magician's hand.

'It's beautiful,' I buzzed. 'The first Traffic Light. Brilliant!'

'I hope you're satisfied.'

'This is too much, I can't believe it,' I pulled up my Oscar speech. 'I'd like to thank my mum, my vacuum cleaner and all the little people that do so much to keep my brain entertained. It's been a long, hard climb, but from up here you can see for miles.'

'Billy,' Martin interrupted. 'Shut up and take the drug!'

'With pleasure.'

Time for capsules. Time capsules. I took the Traffic Light from Martin as Mark looked blindly on. Fucking hell, the first one. I laughed and held it up to the light. Loved the colour clash. The first fucking Traffic Light. Our very own invention, creation, salvation, ambition, wisdom, experience and greed concentrated into one small space. The ultimate and perfect pill for any and all occasions.

'Down in one,' I grinned. And down it went.

The room's intent went back to elsewhere. Martin began to shovel casualty after casualty from division upon division of the little boy's battlefield. Time passed. Foreign music played. Mark's head went down. They combined forces. They dead-mixed. Mixing, the rare tart. Elegant cocktails served in perfect measures with plenty of floating ice. The blimp. The monkey. The backhander in an all-white bathroom attendant's bathroom fantasy. The perfect rug. Wall-to-wall curtains. Soft breezes becoming the hurricane. Forgot to tell my mother where I was going, wasn't sure yet.

My military-minded mates worked from the rear backwards on both sides. Mark set up the supply, Martin perched, paused and poured, perched, paused and poured. The child grew up, made it home, tea was on, buses parked up for the night, comedy stars started to sing-a-ding-ling-long on some palace stage. Retards clapped. But retards always clap.

The circumference of the waiting city outside our walls screamed wide-eyed, slack-jawed, loose-fisted, desire. They knew the supply was being taken care of. They knew what we were up to. They had third-hand knowledge of our thirty-fingered trick. They were dressed up and ready to receive us. They called their friends to double-check the details. One intentional leak had sprung a tidal wave of expectation. A good percentage of the club culture knew what was arriving, when and where it was arriving and with who it would be arriving.

I heard the radio tell the time, wondered if there'd ever be enough.

Watched as two terminals, one orange, one green, came into perfect alignment over and over. Specks of dust, suggestions of nightmares, were blown away from plastic shells by gentle lips. I laughed instantly and smiled at regular intervals. I looked up, fell down a level. Felt the fucker kicking. There was no bamboo shelter, no balanced canopy, no paint over the cracks. There was one bulb in an utterly dull kitchen tomb. The kitchen, I became drawn to the kitchen. Walking gently, trying to keep my feet on the floor, I walked the bumpy three miles to its flavour. I observed a lack of utensils, a yellow fridge magnet, an invisible fry-up, a naked waitress, a spice rack, a solo fly. It all comforted me in the second it took to notice. Martin and Mark were all the way over there. I went over there.

Slow trails animated activity. Mechanisms looped. Hands curved. The bit hit. The drill bit. I tried to hit it back, drifted to the next bit. The bit hit. The drill bit. I got bored, sat down. Sweat-blazed palms made me nervous of naked arms reaching one-finger fists towards plastic elevator buttons. I whacked back a line. A line. A line went invisible inside, stretched up and down stairs. A line. Colour-coded and easy to follow with another line. Someone said something I couldn't hear. I followed my line further down.

Dark stairs. Corridors of cement sweat. Rolling floors, thin walls. From people to people, back to dust. I chased the line all the way back up. Sat on bottle-topped table tops, listened to fat-girl choirs in full flow with fleshy voices. The line turned a corner. I came face to face with excessive orders from party boys, naked girls and a bleeding granny in an electronic wheelchair. There were weekenders, students, schoolteachers, fried curry-sauce sellers, jack-in-a-boxes, tightrope walkers. They lived and died by delivery. My delivery.

To score or not to score, that's the more important question.

The rumour of the Traffic Lights sent mad Manks to the phone and back twenty times in as many minutes. Success, failure, status, quality of life, all measured in an unpredictable moment of contact, all measured by my visit. Unscheduled, unplanned, motor car'd, from somewhere, somewhere, to somewhere, nowhere. My line circulated the city, passed through heads and into hearts. It fired up the mad banging of bodies of Manchester. All on the same substance, in the same place, at the same time.

I grabbed my thoughts, put a nail through their head, laughed at the stillness.

'Fucking hell!' I blinked. 'This drug is brilliant!'

Martin returned, recognisable, to me. Ability to place his face marked the end of the early buzz. I felt the chemical hatches click a little, began to gain control. Martin's sharp smile cut wild. Knife-like snigger noises ak-aked from his thin throat. His sinew-twist hand reached and patted me on the cheek.

'How will we know?' he laughed.

'We know,' I beamed. 'Fuck! We definitely know.'

'I'm glad you think so,' he nodded. 'Now get out there and sell them.'

'Aye, these are not for the likes of us.' A replicant scale fell from the edge of my lip, I felt Nexus seven, at least. 'I best get down the NUS office, set up a stand, I'll need a sign, a solid table, a cash box with a proper lock, maybe even a combination, and a two-hundred-page book of blue raffle tickets.' I gathered up the three bags, four hundred caps in each, loaded up my pockets. 'Look at me!' I cried. 'I'm a walking bag of Traffic Lights!'

'Just take care,' Martin levelled.

'Yeah,' Mark added. 'Keep it safe.'

'Lads,' I laughed. 'Do I tell you how to do your jobs?'

'All right,' Martin shrugged. 'It's all yours.'

'No, Marty,' I grinned, arms wide. 'It's all ours. It's open all hours.'

Martin led me to the corridor, turned the lock in the obvious out. I tapped the false wall with my wired fingertips, flicked a wink at Mark, grabbed a piece of Martin's shoulder blade and said farewell. I took the substance inland.

Martin, Mark and me didn't talk for days. We've hardly talked since.

The three-way operation. The well-worked system of delegation. The responsibility of individual roles. The rain. The unbearable fucking rain. I felt like a bad third of a corrupt fraction. I crossed the road, getting closer to Charlie all the time. I was the weak link in the chain, the gap in the fence, the bubble in the lung, the traitor, the fuck-up. Only a week later and the pockets that had been so full of hopes and dreams were shamed rotten by stolen folds. The carnival night had turned my world inside out, upside down and to shit.

I, supposedly, set out to sell the Traffic Lights. Fifteen quid a go, ten for regulars, the occasional freebie for goodwill or, better still, for favours, but never for free. Never for free ever, all for profit. Not for no profit at all. I'd made a one hundred per cent loss. I'd let almost twelve hundred pills go out, seen no money come back. I'd blown it completely, and my only defence was that we hadn't counted on the effects of the drug. Generosity mixed with God status was laced with a complete lack of perspective or control. And all I wanted was for people to feel the way I felt. I wanted to share the good beans around. I wanted to come down off the miracle mountain and bring a new world to the dark valley below.

My only defence was no defence at all.

I recognised a road ahead that I had to take, recalled something my grandad said. 'The first over the top is usually the first to die.' Lit up, walked on.

A traffic light flicked to red.

RED

SATURDAY 11.32PM

Almost there. Wet, completely whacked, hardly noticed.

I fumbled the stolen money out into the soggy air. Counted it, came to somewhere near three hundred quid. It was payback time. Not Sunday night yet, but forget that, forget Charlie and his precious conditions. I'd be early, for once. Arrive snappy at the feast, smile down the murderous slide, pay Charlie the money and fly.

I paused to light up a ciggie in a rare dry patch. Threw the match in a puddle, sucked back the smoke. Nicotine kicked off a train of thought and I found myself humming down at an odd-number interchange in the black sheen of water at my feet. Three then five then three then five dissolved in and out of focus on the liquid pavement.

I'd blocked my ears, closed my eyes, sunk deeper in the bath the day Maggie had shouted Martin's first message through the door. I'd heard her high-pitched words, 'Charlie', 'owe' and 'money'. I'd swallowed water, spun the tap, shut the sounds out. And, right then, on that wet road, I found it fairly hilarious that, amid the cut and thrust of all this fuss, I didn't even know how much money I owed. Really should know, I giggled. Fell back on my dealer's instinct, mixed with a cynical logic.

'Right then.' I had a little chat with myself. 'Three, I've almost got three, so it can't be that, that'd be easy and it can't be easy. Five, fuck, it's going to be five, I know it is.'

Martin appeared on the damp cement surface.

'Yes,' I cried. 'Of course!'

Recalled a flash frame from before.

'You clever cunt!'

From before in the bar, Martin's four fingers and thumb against his chest.

'I saw you! I fucking saw you!'

His thin lips clipped a 'five' and smiled.

'All right!' I blasted at the pavement. 'All right, it's five!'

'Can I help?'

'What?' I snapped up.

'Are you all right?' Bloke about my age, but younger.

'No, I'm not, actually.'

'What's the matter?' he asked.

'I've got all these big issues,' I cried. 'Big issues! Get your big issues!'

'Yes, well, then,' he looked around my feet. 'Where are they?'

'In there,' I nodded at the puddle.

'Where?' he edged closer. 'I can't see anything.'

'Will it be three or five you're wanting, mate?'

'Look,' nervous step away. 'I don't think you've got any *Big Issues*.'

'They're in there!' Grab, pull, lean, point at the puddle. 'I'm trying to drown them.'

'You're drunk.' And another step away.

'Intermittently.'

'Look, I'm sorry,' he was on his way. 'I was only trying to help. I'd better get going, actually.' Quick wrist check. 'I'm supposed to be having a pint myself.'

'Lend us a tenner,' I asked, catching up, reaching out.

'What are you doing?'

'Just feeling the quality.' I had hold of the toggle on his flashy anorak. He pulled away, but the plastic bit on the other side stuck in the tiny metal hole, jerked his head back.

'Let go!' he yelled.

'Give me a tenner.'

'No!'

'How 'bout a hundred, then?' I yanked the cord.

'No, you're drunk!' Squealer. 'Let me go!'

'Stop repeating yourself!' I grabbed his collar, the sticky stuff split with a nursery-school sound. Got my hand in, felt around. 'Do you have a favourite pocket?'

'Get the hell off me!' he blasted. 'You drunken bastard! Get off!'

Saturday night. The loss, the betrayal, the distance, the money and all this pointless resistance. The target that would never learn to be missed came into focus. I drove my double-ringed right hand through to the back of his loose bob. Bob, if that really was his name, crumpled to the floor. I pulled him up, hit him again. He bumped off the wall, blood from his mouth or nose, spat down his white or yellow, expensive or not, shirt. His eyes rolled. He made a muffled speaking sound. I crouched down beside him, my bad knee cracked.

'Please, leave me alone.' He whimper-whimpered.

'Certainly,' I said, reaching inside his anorak. The fucker was wadded all along. Three fresh tenners came out and went in with the rest. I patted Bob's cheek, felt it move, left him with his dull life.

I growled at a passing vegetarian who'd seen the action. He looked like he might do absolutely nothing at all. I double-checked that the money was safely inside my money pocket and cut across the road. I turned a corner, combination-punched the air at the sight of the 'Man Alive' sign. It was all lit up in electric red in the near-dark. I came to a stop, screamed.

'CHARLIE!'

Charlie, yes, Charlie. I knew he'd be in there. Couldn't hardly believe that all this had come down to something so simple. I focused on the name of the club, 'Man Alive', wasn't sure what it meant, sucked back some smoke and cut past the queue.

SUNDAY 12.49AM

'Is Charlie in tonight?'

'Billy the kid with a sense of humour.'

'Yes, yes,' I snapped. 'Is he in, or isn't he?'

'What do you think?' came back.

Doormen were well on their way to making up a fabulous threesome with cabbies and students, but I didn't have time to get into it. I flashed my thick fold of cash, stepped past the proverbial man mountain, nodded at the cash till.

'Look at you with all the green.' Saucy little ticket seller.

'Not for very much longer,' I frowned.

'You blowing it all tonight?'

'Yeah,' I shrugged. 'Something like that.'

'I love a big spender.'

'I love you, too.'

The raffle ticket clipped across. It was numbered in the high five hundreds, but I didn't see it as significant. A black hand stamped me blue, I left the change. Ruffled a count pre-pocket, three hundred quid, it wasn't nothing, it wasn't enough. But I was there and it was too late to turn round. I trundled down the stained staircase towards another sweat hole and another Saturday night.

And you could fuck the cloakroom.

Downstairs was dark, bumpy, loud, packed popular, care-less, complicated and dangerous. I tried to focus on my topside plan, tried to see it as simple as I'd seen it all before, but I kept bumping bodies, losing my step. The ultra-low, unlit ceiling brushed my hair for me. The walls kept their corners out of sight. I put my head down, pushed through.

'Billy.' Nearly naked, full brown breasts. 'What are you doing here? You never come here! What happened to your face? Why are you wearing your coat? Billy?'

'Charlie,' I muttered.

'Oh, God!' Bella's best friend squawked. 'Look, I'm not sure if he's in tonight.'

'Don't lie, Lisa.'

'Billy,' she hissed. 'Leave it.'

'Lisa,' I hit her with hard eyes. 'You don't understand. I'm going to fix it. Jim's tied to a bed, so it's up to me now. I've got the money. I just need to see Charlie.'

'No!' she fizzed. 'It's you who doesn't understand!'

'And I don't fucking have to.' On my way.

'Billy, please!' Lisa cried. 'Bella's here!'

The name buggered my balance. Of course she was here. This is where she would be. Not only had she warned me, but the Man Alive was where Bella always came on nights after our weekend fights. The music was irrelevant, the location, the name, the price, the crowd, the record pedestal in the purple corner. None of the scenery mattered. Bella came here for him, she came to see Charlie.

And they said we had nothing in common.

So, they were there. The room heated up. I put the bad news to good use. Knew exactly where Bella liked to sit, knew Charlie would be there too. Ducked sharp left, disturbed a bottle-topped table, almost apologised, didn't. I broke through to the relative chill of the chit-chat zone and scanned the far wall. I caught the splinter of a bad picture in the soft part of my eyesight. Over there, in the far corner of the ill-lit lounge, a familiar face flashed. I pushed forward and focused hard. Her hand moved across his chest. Wrong. Her expression was way too warm. Wrong. Her mouth curved less that a second from his lips. WRONG! Ha-ha-ha-ha-ha-their-mouths-met. Christ, that was more than wrong, that fucking hurt.

In the time it took me to light up, Bella destroyed the days, the months, maybe even the years, that could've been ahead of us. Their kiss more than outlived my patience. Cannons loaded, midnights sounded, equators burnt and a whole world turned upside down. I just about managed to hold on. Dragged back on an inverted cigarette, sucked smoke into my involuntary lungs, flicked ashes to ashes, let the cigarette fall to the floor, steamed in.

'Look out!' some spare part screamed.

'What the fuck?'

'Christ, get out! He's going nuts!'

'Out of the way!' I blasted, another table, another round, close enough to fly.

'NO!' she cried, too late.

I was airborne.

Bella whipped herself out of the way on the sliding surface of the wall-length seat. Charlie pushed his chin towards my attack. I stretched full-length, horizontal across a well-placed table, grabbed the fucker by the collar and yanked down hard. Heads came together sharpish. I tried to pull my left round to smack the fucker in the face, but was falling too fast. Readied myself for dirty-carpet contact and a desperate case of cover-up, but it didn't come. My shoulder touched but bounced back. My brain didn't have time to enjoy the brilliant inversion of gravity. A pair of bouncers were speeding me, utterly off the floor, up and out of the club.

'Get the fuck off me!' I blasted.

'Shut it!' bouncer shout.

'FUCK OFF, FATTY!'

BANG! BANG! BANG! Fists came down. Echoes distorted deep inside my head. Sharp pain made me want to grab my cheek. Shook my face instead. Blood spray proved that the cunt wore a ring. Large gaps opened in and around my vision. My feet still couldn't reach the floor. I had a sense of rising and at the same time shrinking. They almost dropped me on the stairs, but a familiar monkey came down from above to minimise the slapstick. The back of my head caught the metal door frame on the way out, but the three fine fellows eventually got me through the gap. They stood me up in the outside and pushed me away. I vaguely clocked that the same people were waiting in the same queue to the same place.

'I've been in and out, you haven't even been in!' I shouted, trying to stay up. 'I wouldn't bother, it's crap, anyway.' Wondered if they remembered me, wondered if they cared. 'Why do you queue up at all? You should all push in, all at once.' Took my hand from my cheek to add a gesture. 'Christ!' The sheer quantity of blood made me aim for a corner. I dropped out of sight into a cobbled alleyway.

I slumped against a wall, didn't feel the rain, pulled my knees up to my chest, closed my eyes. Tried to recall the sequence for sleep. Heard a girl's voice calling, but neither of us could remember my name. I tried to focus on some faraway something, but only felt the immediate stone. Heard the click-clack of bouncers' caps coming round the corner. I shut tighter, scrunched smaller.

'You think he's all right?'

'Fuck him!'

'We don't want another one like last week.'

'He's not dead.'

'What about brain damage?'

'Never did me any harm. Come on, leave him.'

'No, I'm just going to have a quick check.'

'Well, you're wasting your time with that one.'

I winked open one eye and watched as a single pair of black-laced feet came closer, closer still. Opened up the other eye to see that it was the doorman from before. His hand helped me lift my shoulder and he leant my back against the wall. He nodded, I shrugged. I took my hand out from under my armpit, tried to find a cigarette, only managed to tap the pack, but bouncy did the rest. The filter felt good in my mouth, soft fucker even sparked it for me.

'How many fingers?' he asked, hand in my face.

'Two, please, with ice.'

'Still got that sense of humour.'

'Yes,' I smiled. 'Yes, I have.'

'You'll be all right,' he said, on his way to walking off.

'Mate,' I called. 'Did I get the first punch in?'

'Didn't see it, I was on the door.'

'Fuck.'

'Look,' a step towards. 'You know this isn't the place. What were you playing at?'

'Bella.'

'You mean, Charlie's Bella?'

'No.' Smoke tasted bad, I closed my eyes. 'I mean my Bella.'

'Oh, right, right.' Soft laugh. 'That old story.'

'Sounds like.'

'Listen, mate,' he levelled. 'I'll see if I can have a word, you sit tight.'

Kind words in a cold night made warm water edge my eyes. I faced up to the general downpour and all the good it could do. The rain was light enough not to hurt, but wet enough to wash the blood down my neck. I kept my smoke going even after the white paper went damp grey and the inhale tasted like soggy laundry. I heard a dog howling from behind a wall and mixed it with the muffled music coming from inside the club. I tapped my foot to a brand-new tune, wondered what the fuck I was doing.

Guessed I was waiting, waited.

SUNDAY 1.07AM

'Where is he?' Her voice.

'Round the corner.'

'Round the bend, more like it.' She appeared. 'Oh, Christ!'

'How do.'

'Jesus Christ!' Bella quick heeled it over to where I was propped up against the brick back. She leant down close and put a careful hand against my good cheek. Busy brown eyes criss-crossed my face like the stitches I'd be needing. 'My poor baby, my poor, poor baby.'

'Is it too late to consider an abortion?' I asked.

'Don't say that.'

'There's a green field somewhere ahead where I'll be shot in black and white while sleeping in the dark.' I paused to spit, Bella smiled back a tear. 'I don't fear it, there's no need, it'll be peaceful.' Bella had heard it all before. 'I'll be old, warm, full of fish, local beer and late-night music.' How I wanted to die. 'I'll get kissed goodnight by some innocent. I'll burrow down deep. I won't hear the click. I'll just go.'

'My poor Billy,' she muffled. 'It hasn't been your day.'

'Funny.'

'I don't think it's even been your week.'

'I'm sort of hoping that it's not my life.'

'Don't say that.'

'This is not my life,' I razor-pained. 'That was not Eamonn Andrews under the toilet door. That was not my girlfriend kissing a cunt. This is not my fucking life.' Clever Bella sensed a shift in my mood, backed away. 'This is not my movie. That was not my moment. This is not really happening.' She backed away more. 'This is not my blood all over my hands. This is not my head and I'm not shaking like a shell-shocked spastic. This is not fucking funny any more! This is not my life! That's it!' Point-spit-point. 'That's fucking it! This is not my life! I want to swap it back! Can I get a second-hand Scalextric set for the life I haven't lived?'

'Billy!' Bella cried. 'Stop it!'

'It was my turn to see Charlie tonight.'

'Stop!'

'Or was it tomorrow? Did I make a mistake? Have I got my dates mixed up? Is it you tonight and me tomorrow? Is that it?' Wild laughter. 'Does he fuck you tonight and kill me tomorrow? Or is it the other way round?'

'You're killing yourself, Billy.'

'CLICHÉ!'

'Stop!' Her hands hit her ears.

'Is fucking him part of the payment?'

'What?' she yelped.

'Do I get a reduction on the debt?'

'You bastard!'

'A third of my possessions,' the play line came back. 'I let it go.'

Bella thrust up from her crouch. Looked like old Percy Shell-suit had lost another fan. Looked like she was on her way, till she span back sharp, strode to stand above me. Her dramatic change of direction, her furious silence, her big metal-capped boots, her beautiful face, all threw me for a wobble and all at once. I felt my anger scurry out of my system. Some kind of love, maybe the desperate kind, took its place.

I watched Bella rise above me, stand before me, live long

after me and stare down at me. I saw no brighter spark than the fire in her torchlight eyes. Heard no other words than the ones she hadn't said in a while. Taste, smell and touch were pointless senses. I couldn't sense them at all. Only Bella, only her. The wind fell silent, my favourite trick of the light developed. The world became calm and amber. I wallowed in the soft street light and once-in-a-lifetime company. It came in all around, inside me and out.

Orange words rose in my blood-red mouth.

'I love you,' I told her, and waited. 'I said, I love you.'

'WE ARE DONE!' Extremely loud.

'But—'

'You are fucking done, Billy!' Something had burst in her, a tidal wave escaped. 'Everybody is sick of you! Martin's had it with you! Even Maggie won't put up with you much longer! Mark and Luke think you're a fucking joke! Charlie's twice the man you'll ever be! No, Billy! It's just you and Nada! BILLY AND NADA FOR EVER!'

'Baby,' I stammered.

'BILLY BRADY AND CHIP-SHOP NADA FOR EVER!'

'Bella,' I mumbled. 'Have you heard the expression, "kick a man when he's down"?'

'CLICHÉ!'

'Y'see, I can change.'

'No, you can't,' she hissed. 'You are most definitely done.'

'Is that a line from a song?'

'Just fuck off!' She stamped away. 'Fuck off!'

'Sing me to sleep, baby.' I struggled up the wall. 'In clean, clean, sheets.'

I tried to shake off the shakes while following fast-moving Bella round the corner. Fucking hell! A line of skeletons lit against brick. Mean-looking skeletons everywhere.

'Oh, my God!' a death's-head crowed. 'Look at him!'

'Bella!' I cried. 'Wait!'

'What a mess!'

'Is that Billy Brady?'

'BELLA!'

'Who the fuck is Billy Brady?'

'BELLA!'

She was cutting across a lumpy field towards a parked car. I recognised the vehicle, wasn't too surprised to see pizza Lisa waving 'hurry up' from the passenger side. Did some distance mathematics, realised I wasn't going to catch her in time. Imagined the careless car driving south to Chorlton, laughter in the back, passengers safe and warm, Charlie behind the wheel, me out in the cold.

'BELLA!'

'YOU ARE DONE!' she screamed, didn't stop.

And right then I began to feel it. Done. I slowed to a stand-still, tensed, shaking and suspended in the most ridiculous, out-of-place field that the city could come up with. I watched Bella continue to sway away. I badly wanted to follow her to the road, but the weight that held me back felt like power lines running through the hatches of hell, secured deep in the devil's static back. I watched Bella disappear into the smart black car and somebody step out from the driver's side. I wasn't anywhere near in the mood.

'Step off, Brady!'

'Fuck off, Charlie.'

I tried a smile, stood my ground. Charlie came silently strolling from a background of expensive cars, smiling faces, healthy bank accounts, weapons, mobile phones and martial arts. I could see the obvious strength in his movements. I stayed completely still. The lethal bastard kept coming. I would've been frightened if I'd thought of it.

'I told you Sunday,' he levelled.

'I don't give a fuck what you told me.'

'I think you should probably go home,' he said from a long

arm's length away. 'You look like you're messed up enough for one night.'

'Got yourself some tough friends, haven't you?'

'Saved me the bother.'

'Yeah, yeah,' I sighed.

Checked behind his head to where the spoils of the victor hugged soft Lisa in the comfy back seat. If he didn't bring her up, I wouldn't. If he did, I'd kill him where he stood.

'Did you hear what I said?' he growled pointlessly.

The night was growing older, much colder. Friday, Saturday, now Sunday, call it Doomsday, I didn't care. None of it seemed to matter any more. Together, alone, freezing or on fire, what difference did it make? None of this was getting nobody closer to nowhere. It was time to put the blaze out. Time to douse the destructive flames. Time to close the bloody book. It was time to end this typical northern story of drugs, debts and death threats.

'I have your money.'

'I don't want it,' he snapped back.

'What?'

'I don't want it until tomorrow, like I told you.'

'Charlie, don't be fucking ridiculous!' I cried. 'I have your money. I want you to have it. Let's end this now.' I scrambled my hand into my pocket. 'Come on, let's get it over with.' I pulled out the crushed wad. 'Come on, Charlie, just take it!'

'Is that all of it?'

'I think so.'

'What the fuck do you mean, "you think so"?'

'Well, I just fucking think so, all right?' I started to count it, right there and then. Accidentally, cack-handedly, purely coincidentally, dropped a few of the notes on the grass between us.

'Jesus, you really are one messed-up Irish fuckhead.'

'You should meet my grandad,' I smiled.

'Your grandad's dead.'

'The point stands.'

'Look,' Charlie cut fast. 'Do you have the five hundred, or not?'

'Five,' I giggled. 'I knew it was five. I did. I knew all along.'

'Stop wasting my time! Have you got it?'

'Well, let's see, shall we?' I checked the folds in my hand. 'Five hundred quid. Five hundred big ones.' Held the wad up to my ear. 'Five hundred expressions of southern supremacy.' Listened to the money, laughed. 'Well, Charlie my boy, there has to be at least four hundred and fifty here in my hand.' I caught a flash of Bella's face in the distant vehicle. 'And with the fifty I dropped on the floor . . .' Goodbye, love. 'Stupid of me, I know.' Thirty yards to the corner. 'But once we get it all together I'm sure it'll be right.' Thirty yards, maybe less. 'And then you and me can call it quits, right?'

'Right, right!' Charlie hissed. 'Stop being a freak, just sort it out!'

'Yes, of course. You must excuse me, I'm feeling a little disorientated. Loss of blood, bang to the head, I'm sure you understand.' I held up the cash in my hand. 'Now, first things first, let me straighten this out, I want to do this right.' Reverse-origami'd the crumples, counted to myself with an 'um' and an 'aah' thrown in for laughs. 'Almost there, Charles, just be patient.' Still unfolding, pretend-counting. 'Stupid of me to drop some. Hope it didn't blow away, or anything like that.'

'It didn't fucking blow away,' Charlie flexed annoyance. 'It's right there!'

'Good, good.' Lost count, never had it, started again, slower. 'I won't be a minute.'

'For fuck sake! This is insane. I'll get it.'

Charlie leant down, his body bent, his head went low to

reach for his own personal share of fool's gold. My tormentor, practically, knelt before me. It was what you might call a significant moment. And if that moment had been allowed to pass, if that moment had naturally followed on to the next moment, if Charlie had clutched up the cash and opened his hands ready for the rest, if all that had happened, it would all be over. I'd be without money and without any means to make any more money. I'd be without class. I'd be sweeping up the cigarette butts of a bar job that I couldn't bear. I'd be weeping through thick glass at a more satisfied world. I'd be eating my chips with no sauce. I'd be fucked. The game would be up. Or rather, the game would go on, but I'd be stuck on the fringes, forever recalling the moment that my tormentor had, practically, knelt before me.

Plus, Charlie had Bella. All I had was two hundred and seventy quid, my shaky pride and a good pair of kicking boots.

'CHARLIE!'

Of course, Bella would know.

'CHARLIE!' she screamed. 'LOOK OUT!'

I flicked from her back down to him, smiling wide at both. He was turning slightly to see her coming, her running. I laughed at the target, the target that didn't know he was one until it was too late. I took a quick step back with one short swing and WHACK! Contact. I banged the stupid southern fucker hard in the open side of his over-privileged haircut.

'Oh, my God!' Bella screamed. 'Charlie!'

My feet stopped kicking, started running. My hands banged out before me, one-two, one-two, one-two-three-four-five. Counted my losses to keep time. One, Bella! Two, Martin! Three, Mark! Four, that fucking T-shirt! Five, fuck it! Span fast round a drainpipe that marked the corner I'd clocked before. Checked up and down the back alleyway. Stopped sharp to think. It became immediately obvious that I needed a drink, but as I started to regain my running speed, I realised that I actually needed something to go with it. I think it was what Bella had said about everyone being sick of me. I wanted to see Maggie. I needed to ensure that one last safe place was still left. I wanted to be healed and fucking held. I needed a mate.

'YOU ARE DONE!' Bella's scream carried through the still air.

But I'd heard it all before.

SUNDAY 2.41AM

Mad fucking footfalls.

I melted into my own created heat. The cement at my feet sucked up the remaining good left in the drugs. Tried to remember the last time I'd run for anything, but childhood memories were the luxury of those who could remember anything at all. I stayed away from the main roads, skipped across to the edge of the city's bright centre without crossing the path of a solitary soul. Turned on to Oxford Road just above the BBC, encountered clumps of club comers and goers weaving their way across the cracks. Kept my head down, breathed shallow to the pub.

Closed, chained, abandoned, dark and obviously empty. I rested my head on the outside of the fish tank, glared up at the bottle rack behind the bar. Had a brief vision of a flying brick, but knew I'd done enough damage to one establishment for one weekend. Stepping back, I caught sight of my features reflected in the glass. There was an unusual-shaped hole in my right cheek and the skin around it was caked with a dry layer of blood. I pulled a bit off in my hand, practised a smile, badly needed to clean up. Headed for home.

For some reason it hadn't occurred to me that Maggie wouldn't be in the flat. The corridor was dark and the interior spaces made no sound at all. I walked through to the lounge, messy, cold, stained and empty. I tracked back to my room, but found no joy there either. The entire place was so quiet that my impatient search felt almost abusive. Absently touched my forehead, sweat and dirty blood pooled in the hollow of my hand. Flicked it away, watched the spray splatter across a note on my bed.

> BILLY
> THEY WANT THE MONEY BACK.
> I'M WHERE YOU THINK I AM.
> MAGGIE.

But I'd thought she'd be here. Thought again. Some soft-spoken Saturday-night informant whispered in my ear, 'she's in the club, dickhead'. I sighed, feeling tired, battered by drama, close to stupid, but desperate to find Mags at all costs. Needed to sit beside her, lean close into her, straighten out the confusion in my head, find some sympathy, find someone who cared. I wanted Maggie! Maggie! Maggie!

Not thinking clearly, I pushed into her room.

Immediately needed a cigarette.

'Oh, my God!' I blurted. 'Fuck!'

Almost fell over the tiny edge of Maggie's carpet.

Jim didn't look well, not well at all.

'Jim?'

Transparent grey skin.

'Oi, Jim.'

Hollowed body, eyes caked closed, wrist blood and everywhere stench.

'Jimmy, mate, can you hear me?'

Where were my fucking tabs?

'Not my fault,' Jim croaked.

'Fuck! Fuck!' I went down on my knees. 'I know that, honest I do.'

'I just wanted a bit of fun.' Manked mouth. 'Bit of fun, was all.'

'We all need a bit of fun from time to time, there's nowt wrong with that.'

'How did I get like this?' he whimpered.

Jim was a fucking horrible mess. The closer I looked, the less I wanted to see. He was bent out of shape by the restraints. He was utterly fucked stupid down to wanting a bit of fun. Poor lad's eyes split open, looked straight at me.

'What's the matter with you?' he asked.

'Bit of trouble, nothing really, don't you worry about it.'

'You don't look too good, Bill.'

'Funny.' I sucked the cut on my lip.

'Your face is a mess.'

'I'll be fine.' Fucking hell! 'Listen, Jim, do you have any cigarettes?'

'I think I'm going to die on this bed.'

'I think I left them next door.' I got up to go.

'Please, untie me.'

'The thing is, Jim,' I paused, his bloodshot and brown eyes widened. 'I don't think I can let you go, not right now, that is. You see, it's really up to Maggie. You're more her responsibility than mine. If I let you go she might get mad at me, and it's really important that I don't upset Maggie, not right now, anyway.'

'Please!'

'Look,' I explained. 'This will all be over soon, you'll see. We're going to get everything back to normal just as soon as we can. We all have a price to pay for what we want.' Got my hand on the door. 'We all have our debts.'

'No!'

'I think you might deserve this, Jim.'

'BILLY!'

'What is it?' I asked, halfway out the door.

'You've never liked me, have you?'

'No, mate.'

I let the door swing shut behind. Jim's cries bounced throughout the faces of the hanging skeletons. Wondered what the tights and T-shirts had done to deserve their lot as the suspended undead. Stepped into the bathroom, slammed the door and span the taps. The water noise just about drowned Jim's cries. Forget him. All that really mattered was that I got myself cleaned up, got to the club, got to see my Maggie.

Wiped the worst of the mess away. It looked about as bad as it was, but without the dried blood, I appeared more deformed than dangerous. Swilled some colourful antiseptic mouthwash, cold-ragged my swollen eye sockets, mop-mopped the criss-cross cuts. I ignored the busted veins in my eyeballs, decided that my broken nose looked a little less broke. Spat and smiled at myself. Didn't have time to bandage my hands, wait a week for a brain scan, put my feet up till infinity. I'd have to do. I had to find Maggie, and immediately. Buzzing impatient, I pulled the sink's plug and shouted 'see-ya' to the nut roast next door.

SUNDAY 3.40AM

New generations played silly buggers with spray cans of cheap paint.

Some clever little fucker was spraying 'drugees' on the bus stop opposite our entrance. Didn't even occur to me that it was past his bedtime, just wrenched the can from his vandal paw and threw it into the open window of the car park across the way. Heard it bounce off one of the luxury cars that parked in the multi-levels all around me. Started to get into one about ownership, transport and high-speed art, but became lost in an endless loop. Made myself focus on simpler stuff. Checked big painted arrows, bent road signs, slightly lit windows, stationary shadows, pavement cracks and my unsteady footfalls. Significance in the mundane started to mess with my head. I paused and released, lit up, paused and released. The length of Whitworth Street stretched before me.

It was downhill all the way.

I started to play a soft brain game. I had to roll a dice to indicate the number of steps I could take. Rolling, scoring, counting my steps, rolling, scoring, counting. Realised that I didn't actually have a dice and that I was deliberately making the game too easy. Switched the bias the other way, found myself stood waiting for a double six to cross the main road. Fuck sake, sick of this crap, had to make things simple, concentrated hard. The club was ahead of me and I just moved towards it. Got close enough to see that there was no queue outside, walked right past it.

'Is Maggie in?' I asked.

'Maggie who?'

'Why's Trisha not on the door tonight?'

'Trisha?'

'Jesus Christ!' I fizzed.

'He's in.'

'Funny.' I raised my face to show a frown.

'You're looking a bit roughed-up there, Billy.'

'Wedgie!' Big recognisable bouncer face. 'How've you been?'

'Not bad,' he gruffed. 'Had a spot of bother?'

'Yes, a spot.' Stepped a step. 'That's right, a spot.'

'It's almost four.' Wedgie's bulk blocked my way.

'Almost four, really.' I sidestepped, faked a retreat. 'Four-by-four.' Doubled back. 'Late, very late.' Carried on the conversation, halfway inside. 'So, how've you been?'

'Billy, we're not letting any more in.'

'That's good,' I nodded. 'Good thinking, very wise, yes.'

'Oi!' Big hand. 'Where do you think you're going?'

'Listen, Wedge.' I let him look at the mess that'd been made of my face. 'I have to find Maggie. I just got in some nasty trouble down in Moss Side and the fuckers who did this are on their way to burn out our gaff. I have to get the keys off Maggie so I can save the kittens, the vegan cookbook and my beer-bottle collection.' I needed a cliché to cap off the blag. 'It is, believe it or not, a matter of life and death.'

'Looks like it.' Nod-wink-nod.

'Not mine, you silly cunt!'

'Don't be too sure about that, Billy.'

'Look!' Stay close, stay calm. 'I know she's in there. I won't be any trouble.'

'Like last time?'

'I have no idea what you're talking about.' And I didn't.

'Go on then, but don't think that I believe you about the keys and the fire and all that toss.' Bouncer pride. 'And there better be no fucking bother, or it'll be you and me, got it?'

'Right, got it, cheers Wedge!' Fuck him, I was in.

Sniffed deep the dry-ice nostril snort. Passed by the unplugged metal detector. Felt no buzz, but why would I? It was only the same old club. Only a Mancunian dance hall. Only the Haçienda. It was only the most famous club in our Western world on a Saturday night. I felt no buzz, nothing natural occurred, I needed chemicals. Quick picked up a twenty-wrap of whiz from Black Angel just inside the door. Couldn't be bothered with the overcrowded toilets, necked half the business right there and then. As Angel kissed me on the unfucked cheek, I let my head twist away from her grace and take in the bright, bright, multicoloured lights, burning brilliant in the easy distance. Beams of early-morning multiple suns shone on the late-risen children of ruined families. So many hands raised up all at once, spread so beautiful, so high.

I surfed down some short steps that led to more steps. Passed by the hung-over balcony where I'd stopped and stood so many times before, but not this time. This time I rolled through all the noise. Downhill all the way. I aimed myself at a not-too-distant corner where I knew Maggie would be. I ignored obvious openings, went deaf to easy one-liners, still managed to appreciate the plentiful necessities. I still loved spare beauty. Kept moving, all the same. I passed acquaintances, a little blood, might've passed out, but pulled back sharp.

Caught a pretty girl's eye, dropped it.

I knew that Maggie was the only person left for me to find. The simplicity of her features and the predictable tone of all she had to say were the easy answers to all my questions. I pushed angry past people, stepped flustered around loaded tables. Said 'excuse me' and 'get the fuck out of my way' in equal measure, heading for Maggie's favourite spot. Actually, it was my favourite spot, but scouse lass had admitted to liking it the last time I'd asked. Good enough, go on. I got past the last sweating barricade with only one destination left. I clenched tight, felt blood burn, wild eye strain and close to my last gasp. Pushed a handsome, meaningless clone out of the way. Fizzed, stared, swallowed, screamed.

Maggie wasn't where I thought she would be.

SUNDAY 4.32AM

And by the queers in the corner, I sat down and wept.

Right down there in my favourite alcove it all became way too much. Bella's lips opening slightly to meet Charlie's mouth. An attractive couple in a horrific world. The pain the picture of them together caused me was more than enough to overload my system. I dropped my head into my hands. The uneven wounds on my face were only minute indications of the butchery going on within. My girlfriend, my tormentor, my girlfriend, my tormentor. I pushed flat-backed against the velvet swell behind, cracked my fingers, peeked out at the podium where Bella had danced only a night before. Some emaciated teen-dream love affair was thrusting her crotch and flexing away. Fuck her, I thought; realised that was the point.

Imagined there was a weeping wall sign stuck behind me. Sank deeper into the seat, pulled my knees up to my chest. I crumbled against the sweating stone of the heartless architecture. Even said a silent prayer for my distant family. Prayed that I'd never have to face them again. Followed it with a prayer for myself, to myself, about myself, along the same lines. Had to close my eyes mad tight to keep the grief inside.

What I knew was next to nothing. What I was becoming was only a circumstance of other people's actions. I was as close to nothing as I'd ever been in my life. And right next to nothing was a half-empty wrapper of impure loss. Wished

I'd stayed a little longer with the angel upstairs, but it was too late. I'd already fallen, so sod it. I flicked and for ever thumbnail-flipped the two corners of one square. At least a gram, or more, or less, of desperate grains slid this way and that on the sheened piece of plastic paper. I necked the fucking lot. Felt the turn of a chemical tide. My skintight cheeks soaked, throat tightened, a pitiful moaning sound got lost in the noise all around. The shipwreck movement of the beautiful crew made me think of the ultimate disaster at sea. I fumbled for a cigarette, found one among many, opened my eyes, lit up.

One burning spark in the last angle left.

Some passing, pre-pubescent pilgrim on her way to the central altar of disobedient dance banged against my table. I went to steady it with my knee capped, knocked the whole operation over. Frames blurred, the proverbial thin line put on weight, hard focus went soft, bad music became less bearable, company was definitely required. Felt absolutely no surprise when my father sat down beside me. He nodded my attention towards my grandad, waltzing in the good old-fashioned way with a topless teenager trapped between him and history. Me and my dad actually smiled at the same time; cheered me up no end, that did. Took another deep drag as Joe kicked the little bleeder into touch and dropped in beside us.

'Where've you two been?' I asked.

'Upstairs,' Dad grinned back.

'He's a crackin' DJ on that top floor,' came Grandad.

'Not bad at all, Joe.' I passed the stolen fags around.

'Nice job, well done, son.'

'Cheers, Dad.'

'You did us proud there.'

'First punch, right Joe?'

'Exactly.' Grandad ripped the filter off his smoke, sparked

up with his service-issue Ronson. 'You're definitely getting the hang of it.'

'It felt easy,' I smiled.

'That's the way it should feel when you catch it right.'

We sipped invisible whiskies. Grunted and groaned different internal complaints. Farted in two-out-of-three unison. Leant back, took a look at the skirt sliding by. Nodded the occasional wink at one another. And finally, fucking finally, we were all together on the same level at the same time. We weren't fighting in the far backs of snooker halls, we weren't at odds under toilet doors, we weren't pretending that we felt far apart. We were finally in it together. And what a rare and fucking fantastic collection of family we were. Six strong, sharp and well-dangerous elbows came together around a cheap purple table top. We leant in, we went back.

'Feels like the first time we shouted you a drink,' came my dad.

'It does that,' I smiled.

'Who'd have thought it.'

'Thought what?'

'That you'd come to this.'

'Now, hang about.'

'All these drugs you're taking,' he edged. 'It strikes me as a sad waste.'

'Not this again.'

'Listen to your father,' Grandad cut in. 'He's got a point.'

'But—'

'No, you should listen. We've been watching you. All this time we've been there, watching you.' Grandad growled judgemental. 'And it's getting a bit obvious that every time you don't know what to do you just take more of those drugs of yours.'

The nasty turn in their ancestral tone made my visions buckle and slide.

'What is it you're on now?' My dad's teeth dripped slime, his words started to distort. 'Smack, speed, acid?' His tongue started to slip from his mouth. 'Dope, pills, weed, powder?' He spat, blood smeared the table top. 'Don't know why you can't stick to beer and fags like any normal individual.' Cough, cough, cough, his teeth fell out.

'Fucking brilliant,' I sighed.

'Watch that swearing!' Joe went to thump my shoulder, missed.

Dad was flashing panic, grabbing at his sunken chest. Joe started to gargle. Deeper and deeper still. Grandad's head went slap on the table top, blood splashed my shirt, the back of Joe's bald head went open and ugly. Dad was way back in his chair, pale as fuck, choking to death. Looking back and forth between them, I began to laugh, laugh really fucking loud.

My dad's lungs fizzed through his chest. Grandad epied, his brains flew everywhere. Well-washed white cubicles sprayed red. Dad's frame crumpled, his intestines came out of his gob. Joe stood up, fell down. Skin split. Floods returned. My ancestors were deteriorating before my eyes. I stood up, shaking like shit. Box Car, the family undertaker, pulled up sharp.

'Need any help?' he asked.

'FUCK OFF!'

The evil bastard skipped on the last tear-soaked train out of town. He looked over his shoulder one, two, three times. My attention was snapped up by a naked fat girl on the familiar slide between black and white. She hurried past the cameras towards the stairs. Wide-boy on the bottom lay on his back and looked up through the ladder effect at her revealing steps.

'BUT SHE'S NAKED!' I screamed.

Thought I saw my dad's face in a crowd, spat at it. He spat back and smiled. My tears were really flowing now. Blood curled through all my inherited curves. The crawling frame fell down. Walls bounced their sounds to where I struggled. Huge reverberation broke strong backs, a sick chorus of singalong swingers crowded in, faces multiplied in my mind. I wanted to scream 'one at a time, please!' I wanted to tell the world 'not now!'.

Different features double-split on upper decks. They left the flyovers in pieces. The roller coaster turned into the holy leveller between above-ground sounds and below-ground moans. The world crashed into concrete, killed everyone on board. Old walls came tumbling down. The incorporated drug dealers, Jerry & Co., took their drugs from behind reed curtains and skipped town. I searched the floor for a weapon, found my father and grandfather face down, completely fucked. Lifted them both on my back, took the weight, the responsibility, the fucking blame, again and again. Pushed a passer-by into the busy traffic, heard the brakes scream, cut wild on to the open floor.

'MAGGIE! MAGGIE! PLEASE! MAGGIE!'

'Billy!'

'MAGGIE?'

'No, my name is Lucy.'

'FUCK OFF!'

'Maggie's over here.'

'Where?' Stopped flipping, shaking and screaming, opened my eyes.

'Over here, it's not far, I'll show you.'

'I can't see you.' I grabbed around, someone stopped my fall.

'Hold my arm.' Strong words, stronger than me.

'Shall I come with you?'

'Yes, you should.'

I touched my face with my forearm. Soaked the entire length of the thin shirt. Hand cupped lukewarm red water. I put it to my mouth, swallowed and spat. Unknown Lucy took a step forward, led me ahead. My eyes focused slow and careful on an electric centre of a scarlet light. It replaced my world. It became my new world. I forgot how to breathe.

'Are we almost there yet?' I asked.

'Yes,' she replied.

'Is Maggie close?'

'Yes.'

'Will we make it on time?'

'Yes.'

'What the fuck do you keep saying "yes" for?'

'Calm down,' she soothed.

'Sorry.'

I glanced sideways at the strange, faithful beagle that pressed against my arm. Lucy led me along. Night and day glowed in her sweet fruit pie. She pulled me towards the eleventh hour of an epic journey. Vague tables and lights, slow halls and faces, bodies and brickwork framed the way. Someone stumbled, someone stopped the fall.

'Here we are,' she said.

'But where are we?'

'You'll be fine, Billy.' Lucy let go of my arm.

The Samaritan story became another memory on my short-term memory shelf. I pushed one last bastard out of the way, recognised the familiar approach to my favourite table. Swore I'd been there before, but wasn't sure when, didn't care. I simply stepped through the last in a million tricks of the light, saw Maggie holding court straight ahead.

Her scouse majesty majestic.

And all the postmen re-routed to Crosby. Red-faced gasmen muttered their meters aloud. Gold-trimmed blood shirts crowded the box. The corner dipped under stands. The piss ran over cement and into my nose. Ringo Starr tapped a teddy bear. Big Ted tapped back. The boys in the band got called in for tea. Rita got educated. Yosser drowned in the first jobcentre flood for a thousand years. Bill Shankly, in a four o'clock silhouette, read aloud from his own tombstone. Liverpool rose from the valley, sounded its vowel sounds loud.

I'd found her.

'How do,' I said, sliding in.

'For fuck sake!' she cried. 'Here we go again!'

SUNDAY 5.57AM

'For the last time, I don't know anyone called Lucy!'

'Forget it, just forget it!'

'Is that your new mantra?' Maggie sniped. 'You want me to forget everything?'

'Come on, it's not as if it was your money.'

'It's my job!' she cried.

'But it's not your fault.'

'No, it's yours! That's my fucking point!'

I'd been so desperate to see Maggie that I'd forgotten I had some flak coming. I'd charged into another tricky situation. The faces changed, the song did not. I began to think that Billy Brady was not Billy Brady's best friend any more. Isolation was getting new mates, I was losing mine. Had to stop fucking around. Had to hang on to what was left. Didn't want to end up any more like Trevor than I already was. Had to tighten the bolts on my friendship with Maggie. Had to stop being a three-day nightmare, start being a pal. No more expectations, pure and simple, good intentions.

'Come on,' I sniffed. 'Give me a chance.'

'Another fucking chance, you mean!'

'Yes, all right! Another fucking chance!' Too harsh. 'Please.'

'Let me tell you a story.'

'Would you?'

'Are you sitting comfortably?' Her arm moved.

'Hang about.' Lowered, slid, adjusted. 'Yes.'

'Once upon a time,' Mags toned.

'In a land far away.'

'There lived a patient washer-woman who cleaned crap off fortunate people's clothes. Day and night she worked and worked, washing clothes. The patient washerwoman who worked in an awful wash shop. All manner of folk would come calling with dirty clothes for her to clean. And she cleaned them without a word of complaint or a thought for her own lot in life.'

Echoes of meaning mixed in Maggie's underground voice.

'Now, one night, just before Christmas, the heavy door to the wash shop swung open and in stumbled the dirtiest bugger the washerwoman had ever had the misfortune to lay her sad eyes upon.'

Felt Maggie's hand on my head, closed my eyes.

'Now, rather than turn that dirty bugger back out on to the cold street, dressed only in his filthy rags, the patient washerwoman turned up the heat on the broken fan heater and told the dirty bugger to sit down.'

Leant closer, she spoke softer.

'The washerwoman put aside the enormous pile of clothes that still wanted washing before morning and told the bugger to undress. And, as he fumbled out of his pitiful clothes, the washerwoman began to sing to the dirty bugger.'

Maggie sang to me.

'There is a deeper river, flowing under all this hurt and pain. There is a deeper river that'll bring you home again.' Good voice, nice choice, the story went on. 'Now that the washerwoman had the bugger's clothes she was able to take a closer look at the extent of the dirt. And in all her time working at the wash shop she had never seen such filthy dirty clothes. They were sprayed with blood and vomit, nose stuff and even more unnamable substances. The original colours were impossible to see. They were the filthiest rags the washerwoman had ever had to clean.'

'She didn't have to do it,' I muttered.

'No, Billy, that's right. She didn't have to do it and she knew that. The washerwoman knew that the dirty bugger had no money for the work. She knew it would take her the best part of the night to clean his clothes and that she'd have to work Christmas Day to make up for her kindness, but she started to wash the clothes anyway.'

'Why?'

'Because, Billy, she was a patient washerwoman.' The hand stopped stroking my head. 'And because she was lonely and unhappy. She was lonely and unhappy and she didn't think she'd ever seen anyone who looked more lonely and unhappy than her. But there was this look in the dirty bugger's eyes that made her think of herself, her life. And on that almost Christmas night, she decided that if she couldn't help herself, she would help someone else instead.'

'So, she washed his clothes.'

'Yes, she washed his clothes.' Maggie sighed. 'She gave them the full and expensive treatment. She used every lotion, every powder, every piece of washerwoman magic she'd learnt in her long years of being a patient washerwoman. She scrubbed and dipped, span and scrubbed. She worked on the clothes for hours. At one point, in the middle of the night, she looked up from her work to see that the dirty bugger was asleep, curled in the warm air of the fan heater. Looking at him, all peaceful and at rest, she knew she was doing the right thing.'

'Happily ever after, the end.'

'No,' Mags breathed. 'There's more.'

'I knew it.'

'The washerwoman worked on the dirty bugger's clothes until almost daybreak. The last wash had really done the trick and now that the clothes were pressed and clean the washerwoman could see that they were actually very fine. Underneath the unbelievable dirt that she'd struggled against for the entire night, the material shone quality and the colours were happy and bright.'

'Orange,' I smiled.

'Yes, if you like,' Maggie smoothed. 'The clothes were the most beautiful orange.'

'I like.'

'But, after all her hard work, the washerwoman was exhausted. She knew that she was far too tired to start in on the enormous pile of stains and spills that she'd put aside. The dirty bugger was still asleep in the comfy chair, so the washerwoman just put her patient head down on the workbench and promptly fell asleep.'

'Bad move.'

'Yes, it was a bad move, Billy,' Mags sighed. 'And I'm sure you know why.'

'He nicked off.'

'When she woke up, the dirty bugger and his clothes were gone.'

'Of course.'

'And, of course, the washerwoman felt awfully abandoned. She felt used and taken for granted. She felt that she might never do a good turn for another person as long as she lived. She felt, at that moment, that she had instantly grown old.'

'Why can't these stories ever have a happy ending?'

'No, this story does have a happy ending.' Mags sat up; I was forced to adjust, sit up too. 'You see, it was after Christmas and New Year. It was late January, the weather was even worse than it'd been before, the washerwoman was walking to work through the early-morning rain, when she noticed a curled figure sleeping behind the big industrial bins right beside the wash shop. Straight away she knew it was the dirty bugger, and she could see that the dirty bugger's clothes were dirtier than they'd ever been. The fine orange clothes she'd washed so carefully were filthier than anything the washerwoman had ever seen. Filled with an unusual rage, the washerwoman went over to where the dirty bugger lay and tapped his head with the pointed toe of her shoe. The dirty bugger woke and looked up at this washerwoman with bloodshot, vacant eyes. It was obvious he had no idea who this woman was, kicking him in the head. And in that moment, the washerwoman realised that she wasn't the most unhappy or the loneliest person in the world and, more importantly, she knew that she wasn't ever going to be patient with anyone ever again. Least of all with herself. That day she quit her job at the wash shop, bought a ticket to Paris with her savings and became a top fashion designer and a millionaire. Thank you very much,' Mags flourished. 'The end!'

'She lived happily ever after?'

'Of course.'

'Selfish cow.'

'That's what you would say,' Mags angled.

The old storytelling scenario had slowed me down somewhat. Even though the ending was weak, the characters stereotypes and the deeper meaning shallow, the simple familiarity of Maggie's voice had talked me back down to earth. The long exhalation from my first deep drag drifted above our heads. Shades of grey, blue, green, orange and, finally, red smoke transformed into scenery of the air. I laughed at my well-soft observation, took another drag, spat on the floor. Leant across and stole somebody's badly cared-for booze. Took a deep swill of slightly stale Guinness.

Raising my eyes slowly above the lip of the glass, I took in happy smiling faces moving in and out of other happy smiling faces. Recognised where I was for the first time in a long time. Clocked the world around me very well. Felt comfortable in it, calm, even, and satisfied – fuck it, I felt at home. And on top of all that, I clicked that I had a fresh load of cash burning a fierce hole in my favourite pocket. The familiar throat tickle returned and told me that life wasn't so bad. Good sense whispered the word whisky in my ear. I leant over to Maggie and kissed her on the cheek.

'Drinks?' I suggested.

'I quite fancy drugs, actually.'

'What's the occasion?'

'Losing my job.'

'Fucking hell!' I pulled her up from the table. 'You've got the whole situation the wrong way round!' Hooked hands, moved her towards the toilets. 'They've been wanting to bar me for years, they'll probably give you a medal.'

'I'd rather have an attractive brooch,' she giggled.

'Funny.' I lost her hand. 'Where are you going?'

'Girls!'

'No, boys.'

'Ladies!'

'And gentlemen.' Grabbed her arm. 'I give you the boys' toilets.'

'There's no way I'm going in there.' Mags planted her feet. 'Please don't make me.'

'Slag patrol it is, then!' I shouted, heading in the adjacent door.

'Wait!'

'What the fuck are you doing in here?' Some local colour crowed.

'SLAG PATROL!'

'Be quiet!' Mags cut in between. 'Sorry, he's with me.'

I was bundled into the far cubicle. Couldn't help my giggles: suggestive door rattles, moaning sounds, couple of horsy grunts and more giggles. Ruby redhead from outside banged some abuse on the door. Maggie had to slap my face to stop me completely wigging out. I smiled to show she couldn't hurt me. Cracked up stupid at a fart from next door, couldn't stop laughing even when I realised that I hadn't got any drugs.

'No wonder you're cracking up,' Mags edged.

'Don't worry,' I dribbled. 'I've got more at home.'

'Have you?' Maggie pulled three wraps from her bra.

'Thief!'

'It must be catching.'

'I'm glad to hear it.' I grabbed happy, unclipped a wrap.

'You should take it easy,' Mags warned.

'Quiet!' Fizzed up my gums. 'I'm only just beginning to enjoy myself.'

'All I'm saying is that we should go home soon. We have things to do tomorrow.'

I placed my crystal-covered finger to her mouth.

'Well, if you put it like that.' She grinned, took the speed from off my skin.

'More! More! More!' Maggie cried.

I gave her what she wanted.

'Maybe you're right!' she buzzed.

I cleaned off the wrapper, fed her the last.

'Fucking hell, Billy! I haven't had a good night out in ages!'

'Too much patient washerwoman,' I smiled.

'You could be right!' Watched her features widen. 'Come on, let's go nuts!'

'Exactly my point.'

'Let's have the best time ever!'

'You're getting it!'

Our heads laughed close together, the door bang-banged.

'FUCK OFF!' we yelled in unison.

'There's a man in there! Melanie! There's a man in there!'

'He's mine!' Maggie scoused back. 'Find your own!'

'Fuck this!' I hissed at Mags. 'Let's get upstairs and kick off!'

'Run for it!' she screamed and whacked the lock.

Skin-flicks sniped themselves back into my eyes. Melanie was gorgeous, but her friend was insane. I flipped the empty speed wrap into the sink, pegged it out of the girls' toilet and into the fire. I looked around a bit, my lids slipped across underground celebrities. I saw the short skirt of sweet 'Nutter' Nancy, leant in a cake display by the bar. Shaved DJ knew my name, knew hers 'n' all. I grinned my best crocodile. She flicked back a mad, well-made-up, almost tree-frog smile. A hoard of the 'we like to dance, but never on the dance floor' brigade shuffled in the spaces. A fat lad dribbled down his chin. It was all happening.

'Drink?' Maggie mouthed.

'Right behind you.'

Mags sped ahead. She mingled her fresh stardust grins with a thong throng in the foreground. She'd stopped to speed-waffle, but I still hadn't moved. I happened to be at a point exactly equidistant between old friend Maggie and even older friend stairs. It became a bit of a countdown conundrum. Tic-toc-tic-toc-tic-toc. Downstairs or up. Tic-toc-tic-toc-tic. Maggie or Me. Tic-toc-tic-toc. The unbearable underground, or overground, wombling free. Tic-toc-tic. Mags or myself. Tic-toc. Go to sleep, or go fucking nuts. Tic. The big finish music came in, but I'd known the answer all along.

Quick step, hand hit the metal rail, held my weight. I looked down and across just as Maggie turned to see where I'd got to. She saw where I'd got to. Mad flash, angry scouse, her eyes went full of conflict and a rare, defeated expression. But I knew all about the last straw and the camel's back and I knew she would follow me. I shrugged, she shouted.

'What the fuck are you doing?'

'Upstairs!'

'Wait for me!'

'Come on, then!'

I kept moving, coordinated spastic, up the stairs. Rising up from the flatulent, faked-out bottom, escaping the sick-animal chit-chat. I was beginning to feel much better. I was heading straight for the mouth of the club's pulsing throat. Come on. I wanted its wide-open spaces and glorious high ceilings. Throw me up. Turn me into a rubber-panted big space invader. Project me out. Blast me from the familiar into only the imagined.

I span round the connecting staircase, heading fast for the highest vantage point imaginable. Checked quick behind to see that, yes, Maggie was in tow. Accidentally clipped the top edge of the very last stair, didn't fucking care. Rolled along to a perfect gap in the high gallery rail. Took hold with both hands, breathed in massive and looked out.

SUNDAY 6.34AM

Sound and fury bled in through my eyes and my ears.

I bled right back at them. Opened my arms wide, arched my broken back. The dark gravity of the weekend's threatening events evaporated straight away. I began to rise above it all. Floating, wide-eyed, staring at the entire sick kingdom opening up all around me. Felt like a special guest of Jesus Christ on the old hilltop. The devil asked him if he wanted everything he could see. Holy fucker said 'no', I slapped him down, screamed back 'YES!'

The glorious repetition of a single sensation never felt so good.

I pushed my body out over the rail. It all just burnt crazy. Lights flashing, chests expanding, rolling thunder, bass noise, arms all raised, shock absorbers switched off, one thousand senses turned full on. The chaos flow, the rambling eyes lost in human woods. I snapped at chance expressions on sweat-drenched faces. Hundreds of locals enjoying their particular brand of imported-water torture. We were sweat-gland communicators. We couldn't lie. A nod and a wink, but no fucking blinks. Huge electronic heartbeats, synthetic eardrums, lifetime guarantees.

I beamed out brilliant. My focus was thrown all around. I took in each working part of the whacked-out man machine hitting overdrive beneath me. It steamed on, night after night, through the most unlikely landscape on earth. Fifty-way feelers, fuckers, eaters, snorters, sweaters and shitters, all travelling at way over full speed. Smiling tears, shielding light, grabbing, smoking and cruising for ever on autopilot. I clocked that all of the girls were wearing none of the clothes, that double negatives always made a positive, decided that I wanted a drink and immediately.

'S'cuse me, love!' Small upstairs bar. 'Oi!' I tried again. 'S'cuse me!'

'Yes, what do you want?' Long-haired barman.

'Whisky, please.'

'No chance.' Head shake, his, not mine.

'Fuck.'

'So, what will it be?'

'Whisky, please.'

'No,' he frowned across. 'You don't understand. We don't serve alcohol this late. It's a dry bar. Soft drinks or chewing gum or water, you know, that sort of thing.'

'I'll have a water, please.'

'Which kind?'

'Tap, please,' I smiled. 'Make it a double, with plenty of ice.' Slapped down a tenner on the pretend marble and watched the good lad make it a large one straight from the tap. He added a ton of ice and even a fine sliver of brown lemon.

'It's free,' he said, pushing my money back.

'No, that's for you.'

'You what?'

'Take it!' I hissed.

'Shit,' he took it. 'Thanks, mate.'

'Now, come here.' Gestured him close, held his shoulder. 'What is it?'

'Y'see that pigswill-size bottle of Jameson's right there?'

'Yes,' he edged.

'I'll give you a hundred quid for it.'

'Fucking hell!' He was very excited. 'A hundred quid!'

'Look, lad.' I clenched his delicate shoulder. 'Calm down, take it easy, just unclip the bottle, like you would an empty, and put it on the bar. I'll have it away fast, you just bang a full one in its place and pocket the hundred.'

'What's to stop you running off?' he bubbled.

'Bad knees, overcrowding and you get the money up front.'

Poor little fella knee-jerked a throat noise at the sight of five twenties half obscured by my hand. I'd picked him as a student, but his reaction to three figures suggested otherwise.

'Do it, now!' I snapped.

Penny Pincher held back a soft scream. He checked here, there but not everywhere, I'd covered that. He fumbled the cash off the bar top, clearly didn't know what to do with it. Daft blowtorch almost clicked open the till, but saved himself at the last possible moment, slipped the cash inside his pants' pocket. After checking back and forth at my smiling face three or four thousand fucking times, he unclipped the big bottle and nerved it to the bar. When he finally grew the guts to hand over the half-full, two-litre bottle, he almost put the prize on its side.

'Watch out,' I snarled. 'You'll spill it.'

'Fuck, fuck, sorry!' Close call. 'Here you go.'

And there I went, moving fast to anywhere, elsewhere. Liquid whisky splashed my thumb, wedged tight in the bottle-neck. A pretty girl got in my way, she started to yap-yap, she made me wish my thumb had a throat. She took a breath, I took my chance, scrambled for the hardly used corridor behind the DJ booth. I checked the angles for eyes, whistled the all-clear, popped my thumb, took a deep breath, submerged.

One, two, three, four, can I have a little more. I lost count, kept swallowing.

Great fires filtered in. The excess of dry, dangerous powder in my chemical system went damp and safe. Intoxicated by the poison, almost on my knees to its wet chaos. Eyes clenched tight to take a bubble, time to take a break. I forced the significantly less-than-half-full bottle away from my sucking mouth. Throat burnt, ducts spilled, legs had a fight on their hands, but, bit by bit, the spinning world returned, corrected and in better shape than before. The same girl from before caught me up and said something sweet. My back bounced off the thin DJ wall when she pushed me for a kiss. I had a strong sense of sudden and unwanted attention. The muscle cover for the vinyl spinner had stepped out of the booth. I took my well-sauced lips from the mouth of a most dangerous girl, checked the bouncer, watched him step off, breathed out, went on my Mancunian way.

Obviously, said 'see ya' or something equally brilliant to the wet-mouthed girl, but my words were lost in properties of fire, powder and smoke. I almost fell down the only partially visible stairs, but got the hang of their comedown and wound up with my feet firmly on the main dance floor. One entire circuit of the club complete. Checked my watch, didn't have one, didn't mind.

'Y'see! Y'see!' I screamed. 'A third of my possessions! I LET IT GO!'

Don't think the glorious plastic doll on the outside edge of the mad dance floor got my meaning, but, yeah, yeah, yeah, who cared? Deeper meanings, please. If it's not on the surface, then who has the time to search? Stories, anecdotes, double meanings, wise eyes and sharp tongues, yeah, yeah, yeah. You might be well observed, sometimes brilliant, but what do you do for entertainment? I just wanted to come together with my demo and have a dance.

Kicked over and off the unbelievable edge.

Arms and legs went nuts. Bass boomed the steps. My hands went up just like the rest. Me! Me! Pick me! I need the toilet more than anyone else! ME! ME! ME! I looked around to see all the excellent fuckers who'd made it out of their childhood. We were still in one piece. Still in time with loads to spare. The natural fury of release rose from me. Pent-up irritation and tension sparked its mad way out. I felt far beyond fine. Might've lost track a little, started to swing the loaded whisky bottle above my head. It was a feel-good chorus and I couldn't fucking resist. Side-clocked this fat, too-familiar bouncer boy push himself through the crowd. This game was getting predictable. It was time to go, again.

Didn't fancy being outside, but fucking Bungle and his furry mates were closing in fast. Hit the drink, once for luck, once for nerves and a couple of times purely out of habit. Kissed goodbye to the plastic girl by my side. Headed fast for the fire exit. The door happened to be one of my favourite metal-barred, kick-from-the-inside variety. I was choreographing a Bruce Lee leg lift when I clocked that Bungle had somehow managed to block my way.

Funny thing, at that exact moment, snapping around for an alternative exit, I saw Maggie. Just as Bungle and the beef brigade began to close the gap, I saw her. Scouse lass was half dancing with a slim vegetarian type who kept leaning close and playing with her clever curls. I had a twisted vision of some company for Jim; had to laugh at that. Started to pogo up and down in the sweaty air, screaming Maggie's name, pointing wildly at the invisible outside. Wasn't sure if I got my point across, but knew it'd have to do, had to get out before I was thrown out. Cut fast through the undefended centre of the dance floor, aiming for the main entrance, the early exit.

I could tell the rented suits were coming after me down to the fizz in my wake. Clocked a big, fucking, mad-dancing hard man start slapping the happy crap out of an offending black and white. Call it telekinesis, call it shared demons, call it very fucking useful. I gave him the thumbs-up, skipped up the one, two, three stairs leading to the main door. Thanked Christ I hadn't left my coat. Would hardly've aided my speedy escape. 'Hang about, lads, don't murder me, I just need to find my soggy ticket, it's in here somewhere, hang about!' Couldn't resist tapping Wedgie on the back of his bonce as I flew out the door.

'That's it, Brady!' Wedge yelled.

'Don't even try and come back here!' Second bouncer backed up.

'Shut up, Fatty!' I crowed.

'YOU LITTLE! FUCKING! FUCKHEAD!'

It wasn't like I needed to run, or anything. I just stood on the far side of the road and had a good cackle. The big brave boys over the way couldn't even cross the road without a court order to hold their hand. The boundaries to their dumb battery finished with the fresh air. I was well beyond safe, I was protected by paper.

'That's it!' Wedgie blasted. 'NO MORE! NEVER AGAIN!'

Fat fucker could spout all he liked. It didn't matter and he didn't matter, at all. I took a big mouthful of the good strong stuff, breathed the pure outside. Giggled and spat, bloody or otherwise, and sat the fuck down. Found myself reposed on an unusually placed, southern-style park bench, by the side of a dirty northern road.

There I was, outside the all-nightclub, not getting back in. The cheap Brylcreem boys shuffled their feet on the kerb across the way. Watched them pretend that something was going on inside without me. Not likely, but the fuckers head-checked and waddled into the dark, all the same. My eyes rested on the warm gap in the wall. The coast was clear. A sharp gust of wind travelled through space, picked me out, alone on the street, dug under my skin. The sun's rare light rose for its brief morning appointment with the north. The sky became true blue and clear. I guessed it was sometime before eight, and no way near nine. Leant back against the wooden bench, looked up.

A daft, out of place aeroplane shat a glamorous smudge from its distant tail. In birdy world, a seagull cut a sharp diagonal line across my sight. An early cloud was thrown out of the cloud club and floated by to give me a bit of fluffy company. None of the sights made a sound. I liked that: flying, flapping and floating didn't need any noise to be noticed. Thought I might've gone deaf, but leant my shaky neck back far enough to hear the crack. I laughed out loud, heard that 'n' all, stubbed out and reached for a cigarette.

My ears buzz-fucked on the inside. Eyes skipped from nowt to nowt. Cigarette and bloodstained hand, tight on the bottle. Liquid and inherited magic sloshed close to the inevitable bottom. Fumbled in my pocket for a box of matches. Found the cardboard, but the baby-mouse house was empty and I threw it in the road. Spat anger, tried pure air inhalation, it didn't come close. Had to shut tight my mad, speeding eyes.

Light echoes of the gathering wind sang around the cement. Grim, terraced thoughts cluttered my cranial landscape. Shaky peace of mind balanced on the handlebars of a dodgy second-hand bike. A loud dog barked in the distance. My nostrils isolated the distinct scents of morning. I washed out my lungs in three deep takes of fresh, and wondered what it would be like to be clean on the inside, or out, or either. Gradually the black in my eyes began to brighten up. I kept my breathing steady and opened wide.

After all the interior darkness, the morning glared in painful. I squinted across at a girl and her brand-new boyfriend pressed up against the facing wall. Pushed my sight past them and through the bricks and into the club. Knew it would still be shifting. The bomb raids of bass muffled in the open. I badly wanted to be back inside. Was in exactly the right frame of mindlessness for another hour or so. I still had the properties of fire, powder and smoke in my person. Still had something to say to somebody, anybody. Still had one long day to live through.

The bottle was on its last wobbly legs by the time she came out. She was shouting shit to someone out of sight. Probably the vegetable from before. I was surprised she'd spared him, but she did have a space problem. Her body was bustled up under fake, warm fur. Her blue face flashed my way then ducked into the wind and set off up the road.

'Oi! Mags!' I rushed myself to standing.

'Fuck off!'

'Hang about!' Running.

'Go away!'

'Mags!' Misjudged speed and distance, couldn't stop, slammed into the wall.

Lights from a far-off pier span back inside my head. Memories of fists that flashed, cold blows that landed bombs in soft butter faces. Memories of being grievously bodily battered. Some lad who didn't deserve it, got it, I screamed give it to me and they did. I dug my hands inside my head, pressed pointless memories down and out. Pain just moved places. Remembered a bottle I'd had in my hand, opened an eye, got an extreme close-up of Maggie's yellow trainers.

'Can you hear me?' she scoused down.

'I don't think so.'

'Stop fucking around,' Maggie toe-poked. 'I want to go home.'

'Just leave me.' Had second thoughts. 'Can you see a bottle?'

'You broke it when you hit the wall.'

'No.'

Pushed my face into the pavement, got a bit of glass in my chin.

'Christ!'

Pulled it out, licked at the faint trace of whisky, cut my tongue.

'Get up,' Mags said, a little softer. 'Let's get home.'

'Can't do it,' I mumbled misery.

'GET UP! I'M FUCKING FREEZING!'

Banged forced motion into my body. Sped through a complex process of coordination, took a brave step towards standing. The wall helped me, and so it should've, what had I ever done to it? I stood up and grinned at the good face of delicate Margaret, pleased at how unlike me she looked. She didn't return my smile, but reached up to wipe some crap off my face. Kind of her, I thought. Maggie's face came closer, her lipstick cracked.

'Where are you?' she asked.

'On a cold road in Manchester, North of England.'

'That's right, keep going, you're doing ever so well.'

'Funny.'

'Is it?' Her heated breath burnt a hole in my memory.

'I don't know.'

'You find this funny?' Exhalation like she was crying, but no tears.

The rain finally began to fall just in time for another new day. Didn't need to look up to know it was there and everywhere. Remembered blue skies, but couldn't be sure from where. I knew it was morning. Knew what was coming more clearly than what'd gone before. I shuddered deep, harsh and spastic all at once. Pulled my attention into place, looked directly into Maggie's eyes.

'It's Sunday,' I said.

SUNDAY 7.42AM

'Will it be all right?' I asked quietly.

'What else is there?' she murmured, face turned away.

'Fair point.' Felt ice begin to form over my open cuts. 'Let's get going.'

And we took our first step together.

The numerous steps home. Didn't know exactly how many there were, but felt each one distinct and clear. Forced my eyes to stay away from the slow business of Sunday morning. Focused on the unchanged overcast of the looming sky. Imagined the clear, spacious blue hidden above, behind and by it. Too much. Started to conjure all the details of concrete and countryside beneath it instead. Wanted to ask the clouds if they could see anywhere safe for me to hide. Pictured my bath with the bathroom ceiling gone, with the flat, the entire building, blown away. Caught sight of the bath in an evening graveyard. Me and Amber curled together in the ceramic coffin. I felt my tremors begin to work in. The gusting wind crackled all around. Absently prayed that Sunday night might somehow save me. For the want of something better, I turned my attention to my shifting legs. Sensed the pavement's flat hunger, it ate remaining strength through the soles of my feet. I wanted to separate myself from its surface. Wanted to float gently off and away.

The sky got a half-shade lighter as expectations dimmed.

I began to slow down. Life didn't feel like a long time. I

stopped, leant against a wall, closed my eyes, tried to sleep. Without saying a word, Maggie touched my arm. I shifted my weight away from the wall, went back to walking, eyes still closed.

'You know what you have to do today,' Mags nudged.

'Yes.'

'Good, I thought you'd forgotten.'

'How could I?'

'Well,' she slanted across. 'You have every other time.'

'What other times?' I asked.

'We've been rehearsing for two weeks.'

'Rehearsing?'

'The play!' she snapped. 'Rehearsing! *The Cenci*! Today! Open your eyes!'

'The money!' I blasted. 'Charlie! The debt! Today! Open yours!'

And off she stormed, racing ahead. Without her company, I felt forced to see the world for myself, opened my eyes. Had made it to the traffic island, only halfway home. My pace faltered, then quit. I triple-checked the complete absence of car engines either way for miles upon miles. The city looked like it had stopped, faded into photograph. Wouldn't mind fading myself. Even the traffic lights didn't change. I didn't move. Maggie reached the other side of the three-lane lifeline, span fierce to face back. I sensed that her pure frustration was building bricks on the white lines between us.

'Will you be there or not?' she cried.

'Where?'

'At the church, at the rehearsal, at three o'fucking clock!'

Sheer volume blasted the pretend bricks away. The odd insertion of a swear word into the day-to-day utterance warmed me up. I smiled down at the kerb, so Maggie wouldn't see, stepped off the low concrete coast of my private island.

Human carrots, ultimatums, hard rain, crossed roads.

'Of course I'll be there,' I nodded.

'Really!' Maggie double-eye-scrunched. 'Oh, Billy, thank you!' Her body bounced up. 'I knew you wouldn't let me down.' And her body bounced in.

I just about managed to hold her.

'I knew you wouldn't!' Nose in my neck, feet off the floor.

Got the hang of it, held her up high.

'Everything will be fine,' she squealed. 'You'll see!'

'I won't let you down,' I grinned.

'You better not!'

'In fact,' I laughed, 'I'm not going to let you down at all.'

'Billy!' Giggle, struggle. 'Let me down!'

'But you said.'

'Let me down!'

'So, you actually want me to let you down?'

'Billy!'

I let Maggie go. She dropped the foot and a half to the pavement, bounced back smiling, patting and playfully pushing me around. It felt odd to be thanked. The burning sensation of gratitude. Warming to a point, but potentially unpleasant. It did make the walk home go by faster. Distance that would have taken a billion brain tricks under duress passed by pedestrian. And, before I thought about it too much, we were turning the corner up our steps. The magnetic door opened ordinary, the repaired security cameras caught my face, could keep it. I glowed grateful in the key turn, Maggie pressed herself happy into my back. We passed the skeletons, kicked through to the filthy, ill-lit lounge.

'Cup of tea?' I shocked myself with the mundane question.

'No, I'll do it.'

'Probably best,' I sighed.

'You go and clean yourself up.'

'Do I have to?'

'Yes,' Mags firmed. 'Go on, you'll feel better if you have a good wash.'

'Cleanliness is next to emptiness.'

'Just do it, Billy,' she directed. 'And thanks.'

Let the door whine shut behind me. Stood for a moment, leaning against its dark side. Breathed invisible corridor air, tried to calm down. Been such a long time since anyone had thanked me for anything, and now it had happened twice in the space of one memory. Granted, it was the same person and both times for basically the same reason, but still it struck me. It had been a busy chorus of 'thank yous', 'ta, mates' and 'cheers' the night I'd handed out the Traffic Lights. I'd been every bastard's best benefactor one week before, and look where that'd got me. Stuck in a bath, pushed far from any familiar shore. Clocked the sensation that had me stopped against the door, nervous, pure nervous. Nasty bladed edges of anxiety worked down my throat and into my guts. 'Thank yous' made me certain that something was going to go wrong and soon. Sighing trauma, I pushed through to the bathroom.

Hit the electric, banged the door, sat myself down on the outer edge of the bath, looked at the lock, tried to remember what I was supposed to be doing. Noticed everything meaning nothing in a long sequence of single seconds. There was a mirror in the door, a door in my eyes, a lock on the door that unlocked my mind. Fuck, back in my head again. Tried to work the connections out, not in. Saw a dripping tap, a plughole, cold water to invisible black, a pipe to the sewers, the devil drinking diluted shit at a student party round the corner. Fuck! I booted the plastic bath. I would've broken it, if it wasn't already.

All this crap running around my dug-down skull. Wanted to know what I was doing in the bathroom. Almost got up to get out, but my eye caught a small tile in the middle of a big wall of small tiles. It had a tiny, almost too small, number one biro'd on it. I remembered the bathroom-tile game, got stuck in.

Starting with tile one, I mentally numbered the tiles around in ever-increasing laps. The trick was not to go off line and unintentionally count a tile on the row above, or, worse still, a tile you'd already counted. After three tries, I still hadn't beaten my record of eight straight. Breathed out as the for ever insignificant poured back in. U-bend, blocked. Hole in the corner where that big mouse lived. Shameful finger muck on the bath base. Sunburst soap that I'd never seen before.

And I got it the moment she banged. I was supposed to be cleaning up. If Maggie had squeezed the tea bags for half a second longer, I would've been up and at it. Just as Bright Lass outside banged the cheap hardboard divider, I didn't need her to.

Pushed up, flicked the lock, Maggie burst in.

'Right,' she snapped. 'I knew you'd lose it.'

'You should've told me.'

'Come on,' she encouraged. 'Let's get you washed.'

'Look.' Made a move to the sink. 'I can do this myself.'

'Of course you can,' she smiled.

Mags cut in front of me, plugged and filled the sink in record time. I tried to step away, but her hand was in my back.

'Now sit down,' she coaxed.

But where was the chair?

'Sit on the edge of the bath.'

I would've got it, given time.

'Now try to relax,' she soothed.

Breathed oxygen only as the hot water flowed. Maggie used a green facecloth and the orange soap. She wiped firm lines across my face with the luxury items, previously reserved for her use. I tried to look into Maggie's eyes, but they were too busy working. The flannel repeatedly made contact with a particular part of my cheek. I recalled a battered reflection, imagined pain, made myself flinch.

'Hurts,' I mumbled.

'Does it really,' she edged.

'Sarcasm is the lowest form of shit.'

'You're brightening up,' she smiled. 'The patient washer-woman strikes again.'

'Dirty Bugger never did change,' I reminded her.

'That was just a story.' Unnecessary pressure.

'Fuck!' I pulled back sharp. 'You did that on purpose!'

'You could be right.' Maggie breathed out, leant back. 'I'm sorry, but I can't help thinking you might've deserved it.'

'No, I'm sorry.' Head went down. 'You're probably right.'

'No, I'm sorry.' She mocked my tone. 'I'm fairly sure you deserved it.'

'No, I'm sorry.' I began to smile. 'I definitely deserved it.'

We came gently together in the sharp, harsh light of the bathroom. I felt life laughing at us, was glad to have Maggie to laugh back at it with. Familiar reality returned when a tear crawled down my cheek. I didn't know where it'd come from. Wiped it back with my arm, pulled straight, held Maggie's shoulders in my clean and steady hands.

And even though she scrunched her gaze, I knew I didn't look that bad. 'Had worse', 'you should see the other bloke', 'save the steak for the dog's dinner!' and all that nonsense. I shrugged at Maggie's nursey head shake. She took a breath and reached out to pat my cheek with the 'brave boy' expression that I'd seen a million times in a thousand faces. Decided that Mags was the most beautiful, most recent and easiest to remember of them all. Realised I was making reasonably clear connections, a positive sign, began to cheer up.

'How about that cuppa?' I chirped.

'How about it?' She giggled, pirouetting up.

'I'll just brush my teeth.'

'Don't make me have to come and fetch you,' she warned.

'Don't be daft.' I span the cold. 'Now, get the tea!'

She left, false-fuming, giggling and swearing a bit. I watched my father's face drip dry before me, but I knew it was my face too, towelled it dry. I wondered if these were the moments that put Dad and Joe out of my reach. That when I was clean and cared-for they were truly dead and gone. I looked at his face, increasingly destroyed by my life, felt a little sorry.

Flicked the lock.

Sorry that they weren't around to give me a hard time. Sorry that they only saw me at my worst. Sorry that I took too many drugs and drank like a job lot of tuna fish. Going into my pockets for a cigarette, I found the wraps from Maggie before. Cigarettes and speed. Worth thinking about. One helped with my hypertension, the other made me want a cigarette. I absently unclipped the wrap, missed my dad and Joe, necked the lot.

'COME OUT, NOW!'

Had just begun to hear ancestral footsteps when Maggie's mad bangs turned the atmosphere too dangerous. I caught sight of a broken head striking cheap wood, rattled my toothbrush, looked at the door.

'Not so patient these days,' I said, trying to muffle the desperation out of my voice.

Heard Mags head back to the lounge. I felt, simultaneously, closer and further away from those who'd gone before. Part of me wanted to stay in the bathroom and follow them all the way down. I wanted to get back in that bath.

'BILLY!' Mags banged the joining wall.

I flicked the lock, went blind through the corridor, stepped through into our horrific lounge. It was like Sunday morning stepping out of Saturday night, into the insane.

SUNDAY 9.18AM

'I gave you the bigger mug.'

'What a treat.' I took a swallow without looking. 'This is soup!'

'Thought you could use the nourishment.'

'I hate soup!' Jolted my mug to make the point. Hot, ugly stuff scalded my arm.

'Don't spill it!' Mags shouted.

'Fucking soup!' Tried to throw the cup, splashed my face. 'FUCK!'

'Oh, dear,' Maggie giggled. 'What are we going to do with you?'

'WE?' Dripping, burning, fuming.

'Yes,' Mags walked through. 'We, me and you.'

'Well, maybe we could stop bothering me with threats of amateur dramatics.'

'My play is not amateur.'

'So, pay me,' I muttered.

'Pay you?' A flicker of heat sparked Maggie's eyes.

'Well, I could certainly use the money.'

'You think that's funny,' Maggie's edge split through the morning shadows. 'Do you know that I've borrowed money from almost everyone I know just to do this play? The rest has come from me working seventy hours a week at that shithole.' She dropped into the broken armchair, looked tired. 'And now I'm going to lose my job because of you.'

'They won't fire you,' I soothed. 'You're the best they've got.'

'I'm all they've got,' she sighed, hand in her hair. 'I hate that job, Billy.' Mags looked hollow. 'I hate it so much, but without that job there'd be no more "amateur" dramatics, that you think so little of.'

'Mags, I didn't mean—'

'They're the only chance I have of getting out of here.' She pulled some straw from a split in the grandpa seat. 'I haven't told you this, but there's a London agent coming up to see the first night.'

'London, of course.'

'Yes, London.' She stared me down. 'You know I want to go.'

'Not now,' I flinched. 'Please, not this, not now.'

'Stop saying that, I hate it.' Maggie's voice was quiet, measured, sad. 'It can't always be not now. It isn't not now for me, Billy. It's ten days. Ten days to the first night of my last chance, and the lead actor and my best friend hasn't shown up for a single rehearsal.'

'That's terrible, what's the fucker's problem?'

'Billy,' Mags went low. 'Where are you?'

'Here.' I shrugged at the grim room.

'Funny,' Mags looked at me blank. 'You're a genius of comedy. You've got it all worked out. You're right on top of your game.' She didn't mean it. 'You're so brilliant that you can't even do the smallest thing like learn a few lines.'

'Too many distractions,' I murmured.

'It seems to me that distractions are all you have left.'

My head clouded over, Maggie's rain fell in.

'This is your chance, too, Billy. A chance to do something that might go somewhere. You've had it with the drugs, you know that. It's time you did something worthwhile with your life. And I can't believe how much you don't seem to care.'

'I care.'

'Of course you do.' Insincere, but subtle. 'You care about Martin and you. You care about Charlie and you. You care about Bella and you. Mark, Luke, Nada and you. Drugs and you. Money, alcohol, snooker and you.' The rhythm levelled me. 'Well, you are throwing your life away on a world that doesn't need or want you any more.'

Turned away, looked at the window.

'But it could be so different,' Maggie eased. 'This play is a chance for both of us. It's a great part, Billy. You could do really well. I know what you think about acting, but you do it all the time and you're good at it.' She breathed. 'And you know what it means to me.'

Dirty windows appeared further away. I knew what it meant to her. The light outside looked less light. I stopped breathing. Looked across at the car park. It meant she would go to live in London. I imagined an orange convertible on the top level, parked and waiting. Not me, though, never me. Saw a dog in the back seat. I wished that London agent could've seen Maggie's morning performance and have done. The orange sports car didn't exist. Maggie did.

'The rehearsal's at three o'clock?' I said, turning.

'Yes, at the church down the road.'

'I'll be there.'

'And the lines?' She looked around. 'Where's your book?'

'In my room,' I told her.

Honesty and simplicity, strange bedfellows.

I struggled myself to standing. Found myself far above Maggie. She looked suddenly tiny. Guessed that I'd grown, but maybe just older. Maggie's face was balanced in her cracker-ringed hand. The orange one on her thumb had been a present from me, a long time ago. I reached down, touched it, she nodded, I smiled. Poor girl looked done. I reached for my smokes, the box was empty.

A delicate chainsaw buzzed crazy in my brain.

'You should have a lie-down,' I smoothed. 'Take my bed.'

'What about you?'

'I'm going to the shop, then I'll get on with those lines.'

'It's going to be all right, you're going to be fine.'

'I'm going to be fine.' Found a smile.

'I want you to be,' she breathed soft. 'You know that, don't you?'

'Yes,' scratched my eye. 'I do know that. And I know that you're right about a lot of things. I'm just having a bit of trouble focusing at the moment. I'm going to get some cigarettes, then get my head into that Italian bastard you love so much.' Hand on the handle.

'Please, take care,' she said.

'I'll take it where I find it.' Corridor, door, corridor, door, door.

SUNDAY 10.41AM

Whitworth Street was practically deserted.

Stepping along its pointless three-lane pavement, I pictured the roads, the avenues and the cement tributaries that spread throughout the mundanity of Sunday morning.

A double-decker bus pulled empty in the opposite direction. It lurched heavy and loud when the driver touched his brakes at the sight of me. I smiled at his knee-jerk enthusiasm for the job, shook my head, almost waved, but didn't. His attention shifted back to the road, foot on the go-faster pedal. The overweight engine dragged him on, towards nobody, for nobody.

If I was him, I'd fuck the route. I'd take a trip to the country. I'd visit my girlfriend. I'd speed the shitheap up and slam face first into the nearest bit of brick. I'd put an end to the misery, paint my uniform in blood, plough the powerful orange into a stationary high-street bank, get wadded up and head straight for the airport. Probably why I wasn't a bus driver.

The wind waited for me round the corner. It didn't matter.

The bloke with the *Big Issues*, bright red Scottish hair and bad legs had dropped off in the doorway to the pub. His dog was pulling on the lead. Thought about letting Mutty off, waking Jocko up, or maybe a bit of both. Sharped that I was still way up there and that I'd better just get my fags and head home. Pulled Mutty's ear, easily avoided her solitary tooth, crossed the road to Ravi's Newsagent.

'Morning, Rav, you bald immigrant cunt.'

'Good morning, Billy, you ignorant, no-good, pale-faced hedgehog.'

'Hedgehog?' I grinned.

'You surprised me,' he cried. 'It was the best I could flipping do.'

'Not good, mate.'

'I know,' he nodded. 'I'm well fucking sorry, mate.'

Ravi had this well heavy accent, a shiny brown head and a rare sense of humour. He was a psychotic cigarette salesman with a touch of job-induced Tourette's. I'd been feeding him a rich vein of English clichés, catchphrases and various blue stuff for a while now. His big favourite was Bob's Full House. I'd set him up for the big blast once every five or six visits. Approached the counter, nodded up at the miniature Silk Cut clock above and behind him.

'What's the bleeding time?' I asked.

'It's fifteen minutes to eleven o'clock. No,' he corrected. 'Quarter to eleven o'clock.'

'Just eleven will do.'

'That's right, Billy boy.'

'Time flies,' I winked.

'Time flies,' Ravi fizzed. 'Time flies when you're having fun!'

Despite all the fun, this was usually about the time I'd had enough of the counter-culture crossover. Ordinarily, I'd ask for my fags and get the fuck out of there. But somehow it felt safe and warm in Ravi's Newsagent. Wide awake, friendly and funny on this most awkward of days. Good enough for me to go on. Plus, there was a vast and eclectic collection of magazines, greetings cards and novelty items for public consumption, and I had about two hundred quid playing the flame game in my pocket. It was all I ever needed. Give me unoriginal remarks, bendy literature and fan heaters, forget the freezing outside. And, to top it off, there was nobody around to bother me.

Sometimes, not much is more than enough.

I dawdled in thought. Found myself in the gap between shelves. Breathed out, took a look about. But what about all these fucking magazines? Mad, impossible to explain, completely over the top. I mean, it's bad enough that people wank over naked women, but to get it going for cars, motor-bikes, telly times, cycles, cooking, stamp collections, gardens, foreign countries and knitting patterns was just plain sick. I reached the end of Ravi's complicated but well-organised racks of mags, had a quick pause and looked back along the full shining length of vicarious life. I let out a silent whistle at the order of it all, started back in for a bit of a mess.

Top shelf hit my natural eyeline the hardest. Soft cell after softer sell. Rows of stapled, chopped, glossy, plastic examples of outgoing women smiled down from the balcony of the naughtiest maisonette in town. And so many more promised themselves inside. Keys cost less than three quid a go. One particularly uncovered cover girl snapped me to a standstill halfway down the row. She floated below the ceiling, upside down on a park bench, naked, bristling and huge. Her eyes were soporific hophead. Her mouth, far too wide. Tits, silly-big. Cunt, badly out of focus, or maybe just smudged. Enforced modesty mixed with animal cruelty had me laughing. I reached up to feel her spine.

'No touching the girls,' Ravi pimped.

'I'm having this one.'

'You're a dirty bugger!' he blasted.

'Good.'

'Dirty bugger! Wanker! Wanker! Wanker!'

'Also good.'

'Lazy, pale-skinned, no-good fucking cunt of a HEDGE-HOG!'

But what a life. Don't touch rules. Fucking five am alarm bells. Three kids and an unhappy wife in Burnage. Idiots like me and maybe worse. All sorts of unnecessary pornography, pork pies, strains of Vimto, cigarettes, edible baby toys, tampons, flavoured condoms, crisps, mixed nuts, occasional cards, chuddy and tots. What a mess. What crap. To top it off, Ravi didn't even own Ravi's Newsagent. He had it on a monthly lease from some mean fucker like Smiths or Menzies. Come on, monthly for eight years. What crap.

Glanced at an Asian landscape stapled to a B&H promotion, reached the counter.

'Cigarettes,' I nodded.

'You mean the "usual",' Rav grinned across.

'Go on then,' I smiled. 'Sixty of the usual.'

'These things will fucking kill you!' he said, passing the packs.

'Not if I kill myself first.'

'Touché!'

'Have a good Christmas,' I said, putting a twenty in his paw and setting off.

'Fuck Christmas!' he blasted. 'Billy, wait, your change!'

'Put it towards the grief.'

Back on the road, I felt some glow of good humour, almost optimism. Warm thoughts mixed with the cold of morning and tasted pure northern. I lit up, lingered by the Palace corner for a while, wondering if there was any fun to be had. Skenned various surfaces. Watched a double-decker turning a sharp corner purely for my entertainment. Glanced at the upper deck, no one on board, but my elevated eyeline spotted Dopey Wendy cleaning the café above the pub.

Wendy was bent over a table. I watched her scratch her nail and look closer. She scratched again, shook her head. Tutting and scratching, scratching and tutting. I guessed that Wendy was picking at a bit of shit some fucking student had mayonnaised to the table's silver surface. I stood still and waited for Wendy to look out and see me. Knew she would, eventually. Knew that Dopey Wendy loved her windows. She said that they gave her a perspective on life. She said that if she was near a window, she could always see somewhere she'd rather be. Interesting comment. Maybe Dopey Wendy wasn't that dopey, after all. But we'd called her that for years. Think I even came up with the moniker. Fuck sake, 'Dopey' wasn't a nice name. I caught the movement of Wendy turning to look out the window, ducked my face fast and ran round the corner.

Safe and out of sight, went back to walking. New cigarettes filled me with fresh adventure. Knew I wasn't heading back to the flat just yet. Something in my memory told me it was a complicated place to be. I turned left, kept going, turned left again and couldn't miss it. And what better day than a Sunday for taking a bit of air by the convenient canal? Its steady flow suggested depth, while remaining shallow. And I badly wanted to get away from the street, however quiet. Needed to freeze even the suggestion of hustle and bustle out of my thoughts.

Silence the roar of ugly traffic, watch the river flow.

I shook a happy, passer-by wave at the lonely dwarf who provided questionable security at the canal car park. He was propped up, cosy, warm and wireless'd in the twenty-four-hour pay booth. My friendly hand flutter was meant to say, 'We're all waiting for something, hoping for nothing.' I think he got the first part, second went right over his head.

SUNDAY 11.11AM

The Manchester Shit Canal.

It ran stagnant history through the city. It was a good place to put new pubs. It had smart bridges. There was a mud path where folks walked their dogs. Someone told me it was connected to the ocean, but I was sceptical. I liked the enormous locks and the sometimes quiet.

Tossed my still-lit ciggy into the polluted shallow. It landed on a plastic bag. My head sped through the possibilities of toxic fire, fish slaughter and council reprisals. Distracted myself by wondering what time it was. It'd been a quarter to eleven o'clock back at the shop, must've been half past by then, maybe later. That left only three and a half hours before the church doors were set to swing expectant open and the real theatrics would kick off. I tried to work out how long it was until Charlie might come calling for his cash, got to six sets of sixty and stopped caring.

Turned another left and walked towards the nearest bench. It reclined opposite a flashy southern-style bar for puffs and the friends of puffs. By Sunday morning it'd probably seen enough abuse, but I wanted a sit-down. On my way to the love seat, I happened to pass under the particular canal bridge where my shakes had first taken hold. Honoured the passing with a vague wobble, almost stopped to count ripples, but was eager to have a beaver at my brand new magazine.

Moved out from underneath potential tremors and the

echoes of dangerous nostalgia. My boots sank in the mud, but the bench eased closer. I was thankful for its wooden simplicity, its regulation angle, its inability to speak. I finally made it to the public seat, sat down and shuffled myself comfortable. Checked to see that the world wasn't near enough to watch, opened my morning literature.

I'd got used to inspecting these glossies in the dim of a twenty-watt, but sitting there, unpeeling the pages in the bright wide open, I had something of a late revelation. Felt a mixture of disgust and fascination at the pictures I saw and the picture I must've made. Lighting up, looking around, I saw a bus brow the bridge, upper deck sparsely occupied. I stood up, pulled the centre spread open, raised it above my head. The bus stopped at a light. Two kids and a halfway granny looked down, out and across. I screamed, wide-eyed, cutting up dribbly. The three empty expressions didn't change. The bus moved on.

I stepped out on to the path, the concrete square was dry so I sat down. Page-turning was annoying me, I needed it all and all at once. I set about unhinging the staples of the magazine and laying down the double spreads in ever-increasing circles around myself. Each exhibit, each example of exhibition, was placed with distinct and focused care. The overlaps were no coincidence. The only words visible were made-up names. I kept working on my creation until the surrounding circle was four double pages deep in every direction.

What a display. Blowtorched features. Soft-focus sex. A circle of random sleaze. Light rain was falling. For want of something better, I used the weather's random drops to guide my eyes. Drop. Colour-enhanced red pants. Drop. Nipple, but in the wrong place. Drop. Lower loop of a fancy 'F' for Sofia. Drop. Contorted thigh of an emaciated curly. Drop. Lycra-hidden stomach. Drop. Flagstone. Leant forward, made an adjustment. The rain was coming harder. I was having a job keeping up. Started to turn myself round, still seated, clocking the drops at ever-increasing speed. Blonde. Plastic. Hoover. Gob. Swell. Cunt. Fruit bowl. Claw. Bra. Choker. Bedspread. Tit. Tit. Tit. Began to think that I was being selective with which drops to watch, needed to take a break. Leant back for a ciggy. A little blond-haired lad was standing six feet away with a rocket lolly in his hand.

'What are you doing, mister?' he asked.

'Nothing,' I snapped.

'Those are mucky pictures.' Kid must've been about six.

'Yes.' Fucking hell.

'Why are you sitting on the floor?'

'Look, I don't know.'

'Why are you looking at all those pictures?'

'I don't know, all right!'

Kid was definitely freaking me out. Felt utterly trapped by his attention. His eyes flicked from me to the pictures, the pictures to me. I caught a glimpse of a wide-open woman, wanted to run, couldn't move. I put my head in my hands. What the fuck was I doing? This was worse than ridiculous, it was pathetic. A raindrop ran down the back of my neck. I looked up to see the kid had moved closer. He was stood on the outer edge of my sick circle. His eyes moved over the images.

'What's your name?' I asked.

'Conny,' he mumbled back, without looking at me.

'How old are you?'

'Almost nine.'

Tried to go back to when I was a similar age. Couldn't remember for sure, but the set-up didn't seem appropriate. I was straightening out fast enough to know that I was an active participant in a well-sussed situation. Needed to distract the kid. Had to escape. Wanted to scream, but knew it wouldn't help. I snapped sight of the lolly, just before it slipped. The tricoloured spaceship melted off the stick, splattered across a whole segment of the circle. Kid started to cry. Clocked a potential parent come round the bend. Brain spasmed a way out. I snapped up quick, began to use pornography to wrap the dropped ice.

Bundled up all the pages and hurled them into the still water. The dodgy nature of the material was by no means obscured, but it was moving downstream. I considered the Irish Sea and almost believed, but snapped out of it to see a mother closing, a child screaming. I did the distance to the flat in a fraction of any time before. Didn't look back, around, or inside. Almost got knocked over, but steamed up the stairs, panted through the locks. I sweated down the corridor to the open space of the lounge.

The long room had been left alone, but I knew where she'd be. Pushed soft open the door to my room. Maggie was snoozing, curled under covers, peaceful breathing. Lying beside her closed eyes was the thick, ugly book. I sensed all those tired words sealed inside, but the unusual vision of Maggie's silent dreaming had me eager to please her. Leaning gently, not breathing, I lifted the book from her reach. Took a last look at her open lips, caught a movement, made a bad connection, closed the door quietly and went back to the hollow lounge to learn the devil's lines.

And somehow the walls bordered something called space.

The room looked the same, but the book in my hand brought changes. The light was familiar to the way I felt. Neither hither nor thither, overcast and ambivalent, shifting vaguely towards darkness. The silent sky marked dangerous time with its unstoppable and descendant shades. I didn't even want to think about it. Turned away from the window, pulled the old armchair to the centre of the stained room.

Looking down at the book in my hand, I felt irresponsible violence struggling with a guilty conscience on the battlefield within. I wanted to rip the book's binder to bits, destroy the dead words, flush the whole sad affair down the toilet. I bent the spine over on itself, tested the breaking point, remembered Maggie's slumbering features, her recent words. 'London', 'agent', 'leave Manchester'. I breathed deep but held on, let the book bend back from the brink. Flicked quick through the stale pages from back to front. Caught one familiar name, my name, my new name. Mister 'Cenci', an Italian in italics. Caught sight of the squiggle, writ at the top of an enormous speech. Couldn't believe that anybody could talk so much, for so long and in verse. I watched the smoke winding from the cigarette, jealous of its simplicity, its single dimension, its lack of complicated life. Considered that I was having enough trouble keeping a grip on my God-given character without having to get to know a new one. Plus, the Cenci happened to be a demonic, child-molesting pensioner, and, as far as I was concerned, that was a bit of a leap for me. I raised the book, ready to throw, but Maggie's face flashed back, full of meaning. Come on, do it. I propped the horrific paperback open, blew smoke and fresh traces of red spit over the highlighted page. Began to read, aloud.

'That if she ever have a child and thou, Quick Nature! I adjure thee by God. That thou be fruitful in her.'

It all sounded a bit *Carry On*. I looked back at the first three lines, crinkle-creased my brow. Spoke the words again, slow and careful. Thought of Maggie's wise eyes. Her hope. Made it to the word 'adjure' for a second time, scanned down the remaining twenty lines, dropped the book flat on the floor. I wanted a fucking drink, but there wasn't any to be had.

I couldn't see any easy way to proceed. The struggle between loyalty, sanity and feeling utterly empty sucked up my energy. I recalled a canal encounter. That little lad hadn't been bad company. Wondered if he was still around. Mister Cenci, dirty old head case, would probably enjoy a little private time with the blond innocent. Pictures I didn't want to see formed in my mind and sent any attempt at imaginative characterisation into filthy water. I couldn't do it. It wasn't working. I lamped the book at the wall, checked about for something easier to grasp.

My ancient cassette player sat stalled and dusty in the corner. It was one of those handlebar jobbies with the plastic flip top and a single inbuilt speaker. No radio, no CD, but it did have an exciting three-spooled tape counter. I crawled over to it, wondering if the relic would still turn. Hit the 'play' button, put my tongue on the rotating cog. The turn felt a little slow, but good enough to go on. Bag of tapes from another lifetime were jammed inside an adjacent bin bag. I reached blind inside the big rustler.

Picked out the cassette tapes one by one. All sorts of once-essential sounds found new love after a long time. I read down and across songs, biro'd with care on the cards, slotted in the boxes. Fast associations of people, places and past times ran along with my reading. One colourful tape had the classic cut-up-postcard approach to its cover. The artwork depicted a skull-head, felt-penned red, with magazine letters individually cut out to spell 'deViL MuSiC'. A bubble of memory popped in my brain, sent a warming, but slightly painful fluid straight to my stomach. I flipped the lid, fucking knew it, not my handwriting. The delicate curved letters of long-gone French Isabelle listed the tunes. I couldn't read the calligraphic car wreck, but old life snagged me back.

Wasted seconds contemplating international time zones, weight loss, thick lipstick, anal sex, frozen yogurt, seedless kiwi fruits, cold showers and awful cooking. Started to get confused by the subtleties of selective memory, slammed the tape in the slot, whacked 'play'.

Nothing. Well, a hiss and clicking, but basically nothing. Got down on eye level with the wheels and reels, nudged fast-forward. The spools were set dead level when I hit 'play' for the second time, but, again, nothing. Began to remember that this was a good tape and that I really wanted to hear it. Shook, rattled, tap-tapped and inspected the entire device. The fucking volume roller was stuck on zero, smiled at myself, span it up. Got the fantastic hiss gap, banged the box on a shelf, stepped back. 'Live And Let Die' (Full Orchestra Version) schemed in.

Dance worked its way through the bass numbers of my back. Arms reached out, head went back. Wailed a northern vocal over the tack of southern strings. A mad, probably bald, clarinet player took the melody all the way to the chorus, then the whole bizarre show stormed in. I was drumming the bass on the walls, figure-skating, shadow-boxing, swan-diving, close to fucking raving. I remembered Isabelle flying back to France when her bras didn't fit any more, but she'd left the tape and that was more than enough for my memory. Beauty slid back from the Continent and into my sweating arms. Cigarette ash fell down our chests, eyes beamed Nexus love. We swung together through the fantastic scenery of nostalgia.

My levels were definitely lifting. Second time the clarinet tweaker climbed towards the chorus, it took me well high. Empty landscape views came on for no apparent reason. Trains of solid thought soared up the steepest tracks. They headed in a frenzy towards the end of sense. Music was waiting for me behind the darkest mountain. And I wasn't afraid any more. And I had nothing to be afraid of. And, when the track finished, I snatched up my abandoned play book, riffled for a page, let my eyes hit a line.

'I do not feel as if I were a man!' Better, much fucking better! 'But like a fiend appointed to chastise the offences of some unremembered world!' I swung a perfect actor point and a furious glare at the world outside the window. Fat girl on the upper deck looked like she was going to one-and-two it. Poor bleeder managed a smile, but her body wasn't into it. As the bus moved off, she slid to hide under her seat. Flabby face got funnier the further down it went, but fuck, what a fantastic reaction. If I could only do that to the posh wankers, white-wined in theatre seats, we might have something on, Maggie might be right.

Double-checked back to the book, sped-read. This shit got better. I needed to know if the upper-deck disappearing act had been a fluke. I wanted to test this play's power, and my acting, on another guinea pig. Where was Maggie when I needed her? Typical. Young Conny probably wouldn't get it. Titch, at the car park, would, eventually, call the police. I laughed out loud at a sudden conspiracy of circumstances.

For the first time in my life, I was pleased to know Jim. The vegetarian chef, whether he knew it or not, had just become the last word in captive audiences.

Moved myself consistently faster, faster, faster through the necessary motions. Mouthed cigarettes, hooked the book, employed the fabulous gripper on the tape deck, checked my pocket, good enough, go on. The door turned into the corridor, wrap was open before the bathroom light flicked on. Dropped the book, but not the drugs. Dab-lick-dab-dab-fizz. Came across cardboard soaked in acid. Smiled at the Strawberry icons, popped back two tabs. Brains short-waved bye-bye to the bathroom. Span back to retrieve the book. Coming up from catching its cover, my eyes met other eyes, many other eyes. Laughed mad as the for ever stuck-up skeletons came falling down, one by one. Their long limbs unstuck easy. Their bodies creased, silent and grateful, into my waiting arms. I dropped one. It hit the floor weightless. Didn't make a sound, good skeleton. Flipped it back up with my foot, threw the suicidal fucker over my shoulder. The lifeless clan of fabric skeletons twined in and out of each other. They soaked up my sweat. I kissed the closest sock head on the mouth. Took a deep sniff to clear the airways, banged through Maggie's door.

And there he was, passed out on the bed.

Chef Boy was ugly, contorted, off-colour. I dropped the book beside the bed, got to rehanging the skeletons in their brand-new home. Their material limbs arched and stretched and split and leant over and stared down and looked fucking brilliant. I had five up, was working on the upside-down sixth when Jim began to stir. Must've been my boots stepping around his head. I pushed in the last hook, spliced a skeletal hand, crucified the fucker directly above Jim's face. Jumped down to be within breathing distance of the cabbage's waking head. Picked up the book, found the appropriate page, blew smoke into Jim's unscrunching eyes. Hit the 'play' button on 'deViL MuSiC'.

'I do not feel as if I were a man.'

'FUCKING HELL!' Jim screamed, mad tugs on his four-limbed bondage.

'But like a fiend appointed to chastise.'

'PLEASE!' Eyes wide awake, flashing at the ghouls above.

'The offences of some unremembered world.'

'OH, MY GOD!' Jim's eyes epied.

'My blood is running up and down my veins.'

'JESUS!' His eyes leapt from skeleton to skeleton to me and back again.

'I feel a giddy sickness of strange awe.'

'GET ME OUT OF HERE!'

'My heart is beating with the expectation.'

This time Jim just screamed, well loud. Blood runners in his body pumped visible. Eyes skated along the precarious edge of a breakdown. The smell became suddenly worse.

'OF HORRID JOY!'

'HELP ME! OH, GOD! PLEASE HELP ME!'

Would've gone on, maybe for ever. But the fucking speech ended. Thanks a bundle, Percy. Knew that soft fucker had no idea when it came to real drama. Just as I was beginning almost to appreciate his art, the ponce ran out of steam. Flicked quick through the pages, but Percy went back to whimsy. It didn't matter, Jim was screaming too much to hear anything at all.

Loud double bang whacked the wall from the other side. What was through there? Knew this one. That was it. My room was through there. But who was in there? Maggie, of course. Something must've woken her up. I wanted to see her. It was always my best intention. She'd be blown away by my progress. I left the tape for Jim and the skeletons. Had to admit, his screams were beginning to get on my nerves.

SUNDAY 2.01PM

Bang! Bang! Bang! on my bedroom door.

'Let me in,' I called.

'I'm getting dressed,' Maggie shouted through. 'You'd better be ready to leave!'

I fell silent, almost over. Mad rush of reactions charged my head all at once. My damaged world processor, upstairs, began to break into splintered pieces. Broken bits of brain span crazy, out of control. I winced distinct pain when fractures touched my thoughts. Put my hands up to hold my mind in place, missed.

'I'm not ready for this,' I muttered.

'I want to be early,' Mags fizzed. 'What are you doing out there?'

'Not sure.' I found myself completely lost. 'No, nothing.'

'Do you have your boots on?'

'Yes, but,' I stammered. 'I'm not ready.'

The door swung open. Mags was fully clothed, perfect make-up, ready to go.

'Good lad,' she grinned. 'Let's go.'

I looked at my feet, banged my head against the wall.

'Stop mucking about, it's time to go.' Perpetual-motion Maggie, door-to-door, fast.

Jim and the skeletons, the speech, the safety of home, Isabelle and her music, little Conny, mad Ravi, the fat girl hiding beneath the bus seat, none of it seemed to matter any more. All fascinating at the time, useless to me now. Faced by the outside world once again, I began to get a sense of the inevitable. Forever dragged towards danger, none of the details mattered. All the images, ideas, insights and abstract experiences meant nothing. I was half a day away from taking my place on heaven's noticeboard. My life was missing the point, repeatedly.

Knew I could've delayed Maggie with a mix of details, or force, but a sense of the inevitable stopped me. I'd turned all the corners to come back to the same place. It was time to fall in with the heavy flow. Time, finally, to join the crowd. To be led by the blind all the way to the end. To shut up and take my punishment, like a good meat-eater should. Of course, I still had plenty to say, but no one wanted to listen. I'd come to be in this busy world alone, and I felt more than ready to leave it the same way. The streets were as safe as the houses. It was time to leave.

I grabbed up a blue padded jacket, dropped it, picked it up, put it on.

The door slammed loud from my furious swing. The relief of accepting my no-win situation had spurred some final energy. Felt lighter, brighter and, above all, determined to dismiss the details. Smoke sucked up, foyer passed by and the double doors did what double doors do. Maggie was waiting on the street with an expression I didn't need to see.

'Did you learn the lines?' she asked.

'Yes, all of them.'

'I don't believe you.'

'Why don't you wait and see?'

'Whatever.' She didn't offer her arm, I didn't want it.

'You should let Jim go.'

'I thought you'd already done it.'

'Maggie,' I levelled. 'It's not my purpose in life to clean up your mess.'

'I think that's the stupidest thing you've ever said.'

In the hard silence, I spied an old bat dragging a screaming child through matinée traffic. The kid stumbled and fell face down. I took a knife out of my memory, slit the brat down the centre of his sobbing back. I pulled my costume-department cloak around the bloody scene, buried myself in the child's warm guts. I chewed on his sweet neck. I halved and quartered him, fed him to the pack of hounds that perpetually followed me around. Clocked a reflective surface coming up on the right, put on a smile, wasn't surprised to see myself screaming. I spat an accurate gob of saved vomit all over my ugly face.

'You should've saved that for the rape scene,' Maggie edged.

'Rape scene?'

'You could've used it for lubricant.'

Puked all over the pavement. The colour-matched spit and face fluid from before. It appeared that I was vomiting blood. Of course, there was other stuff, but blood appeared the most obvious, most red, ingredient. The mix within me was coming out. My insides and outsides were merging as the division between them fell apart. Who I was, was slipping. What I was, was cracking up. My hands went to my knees. I watched, detached, as powerful, fluid crap poured out of me. I saw a blonde girl, slightly overdressed, standing off to one side.

Began to understand what was happening as I reached my bile. Could taste who I was becoming. Knew that the Cenci had crawled inside me. I pictured my dad and grandad having to move over to make room for him. Joe went to stare the Italian devil down, but Mister Pizza-eater didn't budge. He just sat himself down in the armchair of my soul. He laughed out loud in my shipwrecked vessel. He occupied my energy. Put a sick humour in my smile.

'So,' I rose up. 'Who did I get to rape?'

'Your daughter.'

'Is she pretty?'

'It's me!' Maggie squawked. 'I'm your daughter! You rape me!'

Saw a blonde girl with partially visible breasts. Considered raping her against the bus shelter. I pictured a pair of priests stood either side of the scene with holy whisky ever ready to serve. An inner voice whispered that I wasn't allowed in churches. Told the mutterer to spare me. Told silence to, please, return. But nobody was listening, at least, not to me. It was more than a mood bubbling in my brain. Splintered voices, furious colours, occasional visions, had to snap about to remember where I was.

A midway traffic island. Caught sight of a red light, strong and alive, above my head. Pointed at it, opened my mouth. All the monsters inside me made different noises all at once. I flashed around for someone to understand me, but it was pointless, even the blonde girl was gone. Caught the eye of a wrinkled flat cap across the road. He gave me a mean and angled look. I recognised the spirit of disastrous Dunkirk revving up in his bitter engines. I span away from the war-torn eyes to a dog stood by his side.

It was my dog, it was Amber.

Almost knew it wasn't, but felt certain that it was. Cross-breed, low to the ground, vacant eyes and a slight tick where the haemorrhage would've kicked. The dog's mouth hung open, sweating pleasure in the presence of its true owner, me. A car horn blasted. I looked down and across to see that the rude sound had come from a parked car. I fisted a punch, needed a target. Waiting at traffic lights, my dog across the road, a car parked beside me.

Call it coincidence, call it loud.

The excitement of association pumped fresh blood to my

brain. The brightened-up circuit box snapped back that this wasn't Amber. That this was not my dog. That this was an old soldier's dog. Not my dog. His dog. Not mine. My signals fizzed old information in new packaging. Amber had run into a parked car. Not this parked car. This car was not parked. It was idle at a light. This dog was on a nice lead. His dog. Not mine. I watched the crinkled poppy-dodger take slow steps across the road. Dog wobbled along by his side. I set out from my side of three-laned auto-vein. And I tried to avoid them, but was not sure, not at all. The injured bark of the orange hound turned me absolutely inside out. I lifted my guilty foot from off its paw. Canine eyes met half human eyes. The dog wasn't blind, wasn't Amber.

Dark red fluid burst my gut, sprayed out of my power-less mouth.

'You dirty, good-for-nothing bastard!'

'My dog ran into a parked car!' I screamed at his wrinkles.

'Get out of the road!'

'It wasn't my fault!'

'Get out of the road!'

Saw that the old fella's face was splattered by my blood. He was trying to push past, but couldn't work out a way round. Dog was pulling him off balance, its tongue eager to lap. Little Shep wanted some road sauce. Disgusting animal sucked at my sickness. Definitely not my dog. Switched back my attention to catch distorted fury drivelling from the decrepit veteran's gob. My leg caught in the lead. The little man pushed me. My grandad pushed him back. The dog bared its teeth.

The Cenci bared his.

Lights changed. The inevitable became aware of itself. I caught a spasm of pointless action when the old git went to throw his body between, but a greater weight was already above the pretend dog's head. Saw the flash of dumb dog fear in its accurate eyes. I understood better, cared less. Swing, hit, whine. Felt a brittle hand grab at my shoulder, but the damage was ready to be done. I scooped the dog from his cement floor. The lead snapped free from the old fella's weak grasp. Teenage car-borrower assumed the crash position as an orange dog took a short float at his windscreen.

The stand-off was rapidly over. Posh windscreen bounced. Dog bounced back. Horns blared everywhere. People definitely shouted. Dog pelted in a frenzy up Whitworth Street. Old man hobbled off after it. He turned to scream something, didn't have the gas, went crooked after his spooked dog. Designated driver for the day checked his sanity, felt the full blast of Oxford Road's impatience come from behind. He checked my eyes, slammed his escape vehicle into gear and left the scene.

Bus driver's opinion. Dull daylight. Old people's pauses. Blood pumping. Sickness passing. Student cackle. Reflections and sounds, pure mixing. In all sorts of confusion, I saw the girl from before gesturing for me to come closer. Didn't know another way out. Went further in and across. Managed the kerb. Recognised a pub that I'd have to forget. Caught sight of a flailing, almost falling, figure that looked so much like me. Was about to wave when a blonde blur hit the dark shape. The wall hit my back. Maggie was foaming in front.

'What the hell do you think you're doing?' she screamed.

'Getting into character,' I shrugged back.

'What?'

'If I can rape my daughter, I can puke on the street. If I can puke on the street, I can throw a dog. If I can throw a dog, I can win a raffle. If I can win a raffle, I'll get my good coat back. If I get my good coat back, I won't be cold. If I'm not cold, I'll be able to play the devil. If I play the devil, you can go to London.' I pushed her aside. 'And that's all that matters!'

'You're scaring me!'

'I do not feel as if I were a man!'

'I don't like this.'

'But like a fiend appointed to chastise the offences!'

'Stop it,' she tried to hold me. 'Please, stop!'

'Of some.' Flexed away, arms wide. 'Unremembered world!'

'I can't cope!'

'And I need a drink,' I grinned, nodding at the nearby pub.

'But we're late!' She span, furious.

'If we're late, it must be after three o'clock. If it's after three o'clock then the pubs are serving. If the pubs are serving, I want a drink. If I want a drink, I want a fucking drink!'

'NO!' she screamed.

Maggie said 'no' to me, to my drinking. It didn't suit her. Her face went old and cabbaged with future years of worry and regret. The down-turn on her mouth made her chin fall off. Pensioner's disapproval creased her face. Her eyes shrank small and mean. Her enthusiasm became pathetic. Her ambitions irrelevant. Her play a mistake. I ripped my arm away from her smaller arm, headed for the pub's familiar steps.

Blinked my eyes, saw a million fat fuckers tuck their shirts into one pair of dirty underpants. These were the men. These were the swallowers of the only answer left. This was where my ambition lived. I buzzed vision through the fish tank, saw glasses behind glass, pumps loaded with glory and bottles of endless fluid ready to drown in. The proximity of desire, the powerful pull, the glorious pint, the quadruple short. My mind passed through the window. It slipped inside. It got beneath the whisky flow. I had one hand on the optic when a face dragged me back. Maggie pushed hard into me.

'I'm the director!' Maggie looked strong, started to cry.

'No,' I corrected. 'You're my daughter.'

Flashed back to see the skivvy manager come out of the storeroom. The storeroom. I'd been in there. No, I hadn't, but I'd wanted to. Last night. That was it, I'd wanted to rob the storeroom. I paused, a movie played. I watched it till the end. Realised that I needed to find another pub to drink in. Turned fast and walked the twenty feet to the next hole in the wall.

'NO!'

'The lights are red.'

'BILLY!'

'I can't stop.'

The potent current from the Subway Bar's stairs had me snatched. Mags reached out to grab me, but I wasn't for saving. Unexpected hot air, alcohol's stale aroma and the predictable law of gravity had me slip and fall. Covered up, got bumped about a bit, grabbed for the banister, missed. In mid-laughter and one piece, I landed at the foot of Subway Bar's, name appropriate, staircase. The inner door was propped open and the Sunday fumes had me rising.

I needed that drink. Had no idea how long it'd been, but knew I'd been through enough to deserve it. The door whined behind, I clocked a corner, bit my tongue, made it. The barmaid behind the bar let memory get one right for once. It was Debbie from Saturday morning in Neptune's. She was leant on the business side, biting her nails. The wrap I'd palmed her was visible in a welcoming smile. I laughed out loud, approaching the bar. Debbie's beam got brighter the closer I came.

The whole world was in debt to someone.

And southern-style bomb raids could've blasted above my head. They could've flattened the entire overground town. They could've had the city and everyone in it. I wouldn't have noticed, couldn't have cared less. And if they hit Moss Side by mistake and flattened Charlie's house, I would've pinned a medal on them myself.

I leant to giggle against the good wood of the bar top. And after all that had been said, and all that had been done, Debbie just smiled across and asked me one simple question.

'What'll it be?'

'Two and one, please.'

'These are on me,' she flourished.

'Cheers, Debs.'

I avoided her eyes. Only more details, not necessary. Knew Debbie was scoping my scar tissue. Pressed a thumb into my cheek, it came back pale red, caused pain. Arm hurt from a fall sometime before. Double whisky wobbled on the local brewery towel. I didn't think twice, got it down, headed for the toilets.

A mirror came my way, it stopped me in mid-memory lapse. I looked at myself. The soft light and smoked surface let me stay awhile. Circumstances didn't force me from my reflection, for once. And, yes, it was still me. Saw that Joe was present in the broad forehead and boxer's eyes. My dad smiled at me from the crooked mouth, and his splayed wrinkles fanned out around my eyes. Good old Amber remained in the colouring. Ancient Cenci was beginning to look comfortable with a shaved head, scarred cheek and bent nose. They might've possessed many features, but I possessed the rest. The palest blue in the eyes, the bottle-broken brows, the intentional burns and the forgotten whiskers. Yes, it was definitely me. Physical evidence fought back spiritual doubt. A vandal scrawl on the wall behind me bounced back the wrong way round. It was as unreadable as my expression. I almost tried to Braille it, but recalled my greater purpose. Free beer waited just around the corner. I was determined not to get distracted. Snapped on the nearest tap.

Pure cold hit my grateful features over and over. Hard in the face. Brutal and honest. Innocent and consistently effective. It woke me up, calmed me down. Could clearly see Debbie getting my measures around three easy corners. My mind wandered to Maggie striding towards her so-called 'last chance'. She'd be triple-checking her notes, not looking where she was going. I watched her pass by faked-out restaurants, deviant travel agents, popular takeaways and slow-motion people. I took a step further into my imagination, put myself in Maggie's head, just to see how things stood.

Fuck.

I snapped back. Well, she could feel like that if she wanted. It wouldn't get her anywhere. I, on the other hand, was only a spit away from a swallow. I wiped my face on the rotating towel and adjusted my pants. Wrap in my pocket! Where was my head! Been in the bathroom for ages, hadn't even thought of it. I might've dropped my drugs a few times in the past, but I couldn't remember forgetting them once.

It was the last wrap. Maybe that had something to do with it. Maybe my subconscious was trying to save the last buzz for a special occasion. Well, I'd just have to take the drugs and make it special. Physical need overpowered common sense every time. My hands did the flip-flip tricks. The pile of crystal looked promising. I didn't quite polish it off. Left a little for emergencies, certain they'd come. And I would be ready. I clenched my fists and hid behind them as the mirror began to look less friendly. Threw a flurry of punches at my evasive self. Took a set of powerful breaths, sniffed, shook, stopped it dead and headed back to the bar.

And you can't tell me that I didn't feel like screaming.

Debbie was bent double in the corner, fiddling with the

cardboard crisp boxes. The lurid pink of prawn cocktail packets made me ponder the barmaid's skin. She was body-wrapped like an underground, night-dwelling creature, but what I could see of her surfaces looked grey. Heavy make-up, multiple piercings and a viscous red slash of mouth all added to the overall ratty effect. Debbie looked like the sort of specimen that the Cenci might be attracted to. My eyes roved the pressure pipes, the gas pump and Debbie's visible bones. A speed rush had me splitting her in half, sucking on the middle. I felt thirsty, reached for my pint.

And the drink hit me as hard as I hit it. Which was always hard. Despite appearances, I've never been much use in the cut and thrust of local battery. I've lost more toe-to-toe fist affairs than I've won. But when it comes to the bottle, I've always put on a good show. I've gone long rounds, won consistently, always lived in the heavyweight division and never forgotten how to laugh. Thing is, with the booze, it comes in the front door. It's never subtle, always visible. All the alcohol pissed out, had to be poured in. No fucker has ever made me do it. Potent bottles didn't sneak round corners to surprise me in conveniently open-mouthed brain lapse. I've poured all that liquid in by myself. I've encouraged its effects. I'm the landlord of its liquid possession of the premises. Drink is the kind of fight I understand. And win or lose, it's only booze.

But you can't tell me that I didn't feel like screaming when I checked the Sunday-afternoon company. The last Cub Scout had popped all his spots and was playing pinball to my immediate left. The noise from the loser's machine made me want to eat children. Elsewhere, a coupon dribbler sat on the back bench and wet himself, precisely as I watched. Over in the far corner, a raucous, infected gobful of students told each other toss stories between fizzy sips. The company almost picked up when a tough-looking lass tripped round the corner. She skated across my icy eyes, tutted to herself, turned away.

I thought about following her, but not often.

Drinks applied themselves to all my vacancies. Slow time cruised. Walls merged with other walls. The sound from the pinball sounded like a twenty-pence future and I had no interest. When Debbie put them down, I picked them up. She put them down, I picked them up. And I really couldn't feel myself. The bar propped up my numb body. I, intermittently, muttered 'cheers', or 'ta love', but it wasn't required. Debbie Rat took my glasses, brought them back, but better. Structures fructured. I focused on the part-time-barmaid-beauty-queen-come-rodent. After a while, she started to stare back at me. Debbie didn't say a word. It was up to me.

'Have you seen my grandad?' I asked.

'I don't think so,' she frowned. 'What does he look like?'

'He likes it in here, I'm meeting him tonight.'

'That's nice.'

'I've a busy night on,' I smiled. 'All in all.'

'It's good to be busy,' Debbie said without conviction, drifted into pause.

'It was my fault,' I broke the silence. 'All my fault.'

'What was?'

'Letting Amber off the lead.'

'Amber?'

'Rolling the ball too far.'

'You've lost me,' Debs shrugged.

'I know the feeling,' I frowned. 'Probably best for me to be on my way.'

'You're leaving?'

'Well,' I faltered. 'Pour me a couple for the journey.'

'The journey?' Eyebrow arch. 'Aren't you waiting for your grandad?'

'He'll be there.'

'Where?' she asked.

'Church.'

'Church!' Giddy rodent. 'Why the fuck are you going to church?'

'I have an appointment,' I smiled.

'With your grandad?'

'No, with the devil.'

'Oh, Lord,' Debbie cracked, hilarious. 'You are drunk!'

I nodded, picking up the smaller first in the fourth round of the two. Click-clicked my glass with my other glass. Threw back the whisky, took a look at the pint. In the solid black curve of the surface I saw Sunday nights. All of them. Not all the way back to childhood, but as far back as my brain went. And they all looked the same. Thin. Ready to be wrecked. Weak. Unsure of themselves. Sunday nights were the last throw in an already dead game. They were the time that anything would do. When even the last little bit left looked like a lot. When any pub, any company, any rodent death, would do. I turned the pint in my hand. The dark side went back to childhood. And a church came into view. A fucking church! I started to laugh, lifted the glass off the bar top, looked into the white top. From my new perspective, I couldn't see the dark beneath. From above it all, it looked clean. Brought the top to my lips. Knew the dark was still there, but could forget about it for a bit. Decided that everything was in the angles. Like goalkeepers and lamps, it was in the way you looked at them. Realised I was laughing, stopped, smiled across at dark-eyed Debbie.

'Down in one.' And down it went.

Of course, I knew that I was in proper bother. There was no way out. Charlie had probably labelled me dead even before Friday, and I'd only made it worse since then. Wasn't up to kidding myself any more. There was no doubt what Charlie's intentions were. He hadn't got his money. I'd whacked him twice for his trouble. He'd reputedly done the violent death thing before. So, I'd pretty much set myself up for the ultimate fall.

But I'd seen a church in a pint of Guinness, so I would go to Maggie's church first. You never know, maybe I'd be saved at the last possible moment. Maybe there was still some way to stop it all. Not that I was expecting Maggie to rescue me; it'd gone beyond that. But it would be good to see her, all the same. So, that was it, the church and Maggie. Maybe even a bit of acting, for a change, for a laugh. Then I'd just take it from there, see where I fell.

Scrabbled up spilt matches, the few loose fags, some of the money, stepped back leaving a bundle of notes on the bar. Debbie, not a shy rat, pocketed most of it, clipped some into the antique till behind. Spinning back to face me, she made a gesture that either meant 'wait' or 'crouch down'. I waited. Was about to tilt the pinball machine intentionally and mash Spotty's face to an even worse pulp, when Debs turned to face me with a half-pint of whisky in her hand.

'I've heard this is your usual.'

'You heard right,' I replied.

'For the road.' She passed the glass.

'It'll be my last.'

Significance shifted, went back to its place. I slammed the drink down without feeling anything. Debs found something funny in my expression, clasped her hands to her chest, squeezed her eyes into a smile. I shrugged half a mouth-move back, turned to leave. Did a quick check on the distance to the stairs and set off after them. A mad, rodent barmaid from before snapped in hard on my blind side. Her arms went around me.

'What the fuck?' I jolted.

'You're so insane, I want to kiss you, just once.'

Debbie's hands grabbed either side of my battered head. Her pint-pulling arms flexed me in. Bit of a wobble had me bang against the bar, but Debbie closed in on her target, fast and with full force. Her mouth hit me like an uppercut. Lips forced mine open, then further apart, her eyes shut tight, I closed mine. We kissed. Not for long, but we definitely kissed. It was that simple. It was unbelievably brilliant. Her arms went down my back, her mouth drew away. She beamed up at me, looking happy.

And that kiss contained everything I always missed. The spontaneity of action. The ability to care less. The fucking frivolity of unlikely contact. And Debbie's vermin laugh, as we looked at each other, was the purest sound I'd heard in days. There was no hidden meaning. No threat. No need. No fucking details. It had been a kiss and then it was over. I'd remember that kiss. It had bled significance back into my bile. It had occurred all by itself. It stood alone with nothing to obscure it. And I'd endeared myself to someone, if only by apparent insanity, I'd appealed to someone. Someone new. Someone irrelevant and peripheral. Someone who wouldn't mind my drinking. Someone who would share my drugs. Maybe someone who'd provide me with a new place to hide. I leant close to kiss her again.

'Fuck off, you bastard!' Debs squealed. 'That's all you're getting!'

'But—' I had no idea what to say.

'Go on!' She released. 'Go on, get out!' Pushed me. 'Go and meet your devil!'

I struggled to get away from her gutter sight, her rat world, my confusion. The stairs swayed fun-house-style. I grabbed the banister, hauled myself up, little by little. Orange light from the street lamps crescented through the reinforced glass door. I paused inside, looked back down at the mountain I'd climbed, laughed quietly to myself, but not for long. I swung the wood divide and sped into the rain.

Didn't want to be late for church, now did I?

SUNDAY 4.08PM

It was well on the way past brutal outside.

I put my face into the wind. The fierce element made me feel that I could be anywhere. 'Youcouldbeanyfuckingwhere-youfuckingcunt!' banged in my head. I could be anywhere, any beaten-down body struggling along any old road. Anger helped me reach the first corner, then forward momentum and warming whisky kicked in. Brief heat had me realise that this wasn't just anywhere, that I wasn't just anyone.

This was all there was and I was this.

I clocked a batch of terrifically young, typically male students coming round the corner. The wind was at their backs and they closed on me fast. I paused on the pavement, tried to keep my balance. The self-satisfied, Sunday-night swillers grinned up the street towards me. Their strange, giggling, spluttering, nonsensical acne noise cut through the boisterous wind. I began to feel irritated. When the wankers came alongside, I tapped the nearest on his shoulder.

'Oi!' I snapped. 'Where's the church from here?'

'Which church would that be?' Southern Tone asked back.

Knew I'd forgotten something.

'The church of the poisoned mind?' he quipped.

Had I ever even known?

'The church of the damned?' another offered.

Why did I never know the details?

'He's drunk, leave him.' Loud, fizzy, lager laughter.

'Are they giving away free blood of Christ?' A third voice trebled.

I couldn't even find places I didn't want to go.

'Good luck finding your church!' Moving away, laughter.

'Yourself!' Laughter.

'Your brain!' Laughter, laughter.

One smart step, a grab and a smack, no laughter.

The largest of the student froth pushed himself forward. His chest was in my chin, or the other way round. I looked up at his horrific acne'd face. The chorus behind him played cold, wrong, rumba as they tried to get their fallen study mate off the deck. It might've looked one-sided, but the streets that'd thrown me up, would hold me up. Whisky boiled, Grandad smiled and, right on time, the Cenci strode from out of my soul and into my movie.

'COME ON THEN!' I blasted.

On my own in good company. I quick-stepped away, created a new angle and rammed the fucker with the top of my high-speed head. His fist simultaneously un-set my nose bone, but the fucker was on his way down. Halfway through his fall, my boot caught several descending ribs and bone snaps sounded. With his face against the floor, the big lad looked like he'd found a new friend. I stamped his knee to remind him of the negative effects of concrete when combined with cheek. The breaking sound made my point, satisfied my need and pulled the plug on student morale. I stepped over the casualty, addressed his retreating mates.

'Lads,' I levelled. 'All I want to know is where the church is from here. I'm fairly sure it's walking distance. Maybe you passed it on your way up Oxford.'

'There's a church opposite our halls.' Small, diplomatic sound.

'Is it a large church?' Hands wide, nice smile.

'Yes,' he said. 'Fairly large.'

'And it's this way?'

'That's right,' he nodded. 'About a mile.'

'No,' Helpful Type added. 'It's more than that.'

'Don't worry, mate.' I started off. 'Thanks for your help.'

Of course, it had all been a big mistake on my part. I was totally in the wrong. Not writing the name of the church down had been typically vague and plain irresponsible. Didn't think it was very nice of those boys to make me feel foolish just because I lacked a little information. But I'd made my point well enough, and lessons were there to be learnt.

Stumbling along, I saw what had to be a granny. It struck me that students probably weren't the best people to ask about churches. But the bend-over ahead, with the backwards trolley, looked well religious. She glanced up to see me and I decided that she was perfect. Well, not perfect, more ancient, decrepit, close to the call and nervous, but she did look like she'd know a bundle about places of desperate grace.

'Excuse me.' What to call a granny? 'Excuse me, miss.'

'Yes?' She eased to a barely noticeable stop. 'What is it, son?'

'I was wondering if you knew of a church round here.'

'Is it mass you're wanting?'

The day-to-day flow from brain to mouth was derailed as my eyes and ears clogged the circuitry with unwanted senses. I slipped inside her bloodshot eyes. Caught myself stomach-turning at the sight of two tons of low-grade ham piled high in her trolley. Her granny coat was thin in the wind. The body inside it hardly a body at all. Standard sentimental, I didn't really give a toss about old folks in bad weather, but her voice had sent me reeling. Her rhythm, accent and razor-blade lilt were the double of my grandad's.

'Is it mass you're wanting?' she asked. 'Or a simple confession?'

The smack in my face from the battle before started to hurt.

I looked back up the street to see how long ago it'd been. There was a fella still on the floor, so it could've been hours. Reached up to my nose for clues. My hand traced a bone that had gone somewhere it shouldn't have. I automatically braced the affair with my thumb and pressed hard. Looked back to where I'd left the granny, tried to talk. Gooey bitter liquid filled my mouth. I watched the frail ancient reach out an arm in an attempt to support me, had to laugh, hit the ground hard.

Death pulled a heavy bag along desperate streets. It brushed me softly on its way.

'Son.'

'What is it, Grandad?'

'She could never have stopped your fall.'

'I know what you're going to say, Grandad.'

'Only you can stop your fall.'

'Maybe I should've hit her?'

'Billy,' he blasted. 'Get yourself up, get down that church and pray to Christ that you remember who you are and what you are capable of, before it's too late.'

'It's early yet.'

'Don't be lippy,' he growled. 'Now, watch yourself and know your place.'

And my place appeared to be slumped on the shifting cement of something called the civilised world. The subtle aroma of dog shit did the most to inspire movement. Pictures from the past faded. The sound of Joe drowned in the shriek of wind flying dangerously close to the ground. I struggled against gravity. Perspective began to change, heat hit my knees, there was a hand on my rising shoulder.

'Come on, son,' she encouraged. 'Get yourself up.'

'I'm all right now.' Shaky smile. 'Thanks.'

'Well, if you say so.' Her buckled wheel squeaked. 'It strikes me that you should take more care of yourself. You've no idea how long life can hold on.' She started to move away at no speed. 'If you still want to know about a church, St Peter's is that way. Nice priest.' She crossed herself. 'Catholic.'

The further we went, the closer we got.

Whisky dripped into the dying fire of my physical fuel. Flames crawled up the inside walls. Parts of my body proved themselves to be operational. The wind didn't strike so cold. I felt a rhythm, footstep percussion. I needed a melody for my new tune. Grandad's words were close enough to be recalled. 'Pray to Christ'. Sunday, a church ahead, my life alongside, if not behind. Well, it'd been a long time, but I had nothing left to lose.

'Oi, Lord!' I blasted.

And if anyone heard, he was the only one.

'Oi! Are you listening?'

No response.

'Well, if you can find the time, would you remove this cup from my lips? I don't want it. I didn't ask for blood, whisky would be better. You of all people should know better. I want my usual.' Laughter, probably me. 'And while you're at it, make my matches light in strong wind. Better still, cancel the wind entirely. And do something about the weather, or maybe just stop it altogether. And shorten roads, or put your churches nearer city centres. It'll be better for business. Better for you, better for me.'

A big bastard bus noise just missed me. Span around, arms out, looking for a law enforcer to enforce the not-getting-knocked-down law. The offensive mobile pulled to a stop at a traffic light immediately ahead. I inspected the failed assassin from behind. Double-decker, no doubt, orange-backed, many-headed, too large to attack unaided. Standing half in the road and half insane, I found myself simply lost and in terrible shape. Struggled not to fall, get knocked down or run over. Made it back to the pavement, began to feel desperate.

Didn't want to face my fast-growing fears. Knew that some

master clock was winding down on me. There was only a little left on the big tic-toc. I'd travelled beyond the synthetic boost of a stock-up sniff, pep pills or gummy powders. I was coming down on a street that I'd known backhanded my entire life. I was lost, increasingly alone and searching for something that I had no good reason to find.

And just as I was about to give the whole shit parade up. Just as a particular slab of cement looked like a last hope. Just as a bullet struck me as probably kinder than the wind, my heroic attention climbed to the pinnacle of a towering steeple. It might've been officially classed as spire. It might've been a fucking spaceship, for all I cared. But I was calling it a steeple and I was walking towards it, thanking students and ham suckers every step of the way.

Not one, but two, holy steeples pointed the way all good people thought they went. From my ever-decreasing distance, the church didn't appear to be open. Struck me as strange for a Sunday, but then, if it was open, it probably wouldn't be for a play rehearsal. Closing in, I saw a sign. A bolt of lightning rent the bastard steeples in twain. Pitiful actors ran from the belly of the beast, mad screaming, badly burning, scripts and careful hair ablaze. An enormous shaky finger parted the clouds, pointed at a Greek chip shop across the road. It exploded. Showers of mushy peas and kebab garbage rained down on the dirty northern road.

It wasn't really that kind of a sign.

It was more a piece of white paper, stuck with Sellotape to the church door. It said 'Actors this way', with an arrow pointing off to the right. I looked in the suggested direction, expecting to see a line of snivelling freaks clutching soggy pages to sunken breasts. Not the case. Not surprised. Not warm. Not here. Not finding this shit funny any more, I headed round the dark corner towards a half-open door.

Got close enough to feel piped heat coming from inside.

Shuffled towards the warmth's source. The surface beneath my feet went from modern cement to old stone. I was half inside, half out, saw lights coming from up by the altar. I moved my head, body shuffled along behind, arrived at a better view. People, not priests, busied themselves back and forth on the raised platform. As I watched they boomed senseless, flailed stupid, picked noses, tweaked clothing. They looked uncomfortable and completely out of place.

Actors.

Men, women and no visible children. The breed apart. Burgundy, grey, plenty of brown, blonde and blue hair. Elbows at angles. A reading class without chairs, or personality. In the distance a twenty-two-stone porridge sucker with too much cleavage and lank curls waddled about in an aimless manner. In the full knowledge that I'd just encountered my stage wife, I stubbed my cigarette on a statue and started to approach.

I passed through the entrance-hall-atrium affair. The air was heavy with empty blessings. The atmosphere was still, with a faint scent of wax. I sensed an excess of broken promises and false hopes. I stepped warily into the body of the church itself. Felt some invisible spirit detector pass over my soul and come back negative. Medieval architecture imposed from on high. Tricks of changing light tried to fool me into thinking of a better place, but it was too late. I closed in on a stone bowl, shallow with holy water, sucking the blood off my finger. I dipped it in, pulled it out, saw no smoke, put a cross on my head and my heart.

I smiled and placed the still-damp finger in my mouth. Had a small drink of Jesus to keep me going. Flicked a mischievous eye at an adjacent table top. Stacks of blue newsletters beside a wicker bowl. The crafty piece was piled full of pennies. I stepped and bent slightly, read the instruction 'GIVE'. Buried my hand in the copper guilt, wondered what

I could get for almost fifty pence, stuffed the haul into my pocket.

The pretend devil had arrived.

Red candlelight flickered on God's dining table.

Actors mingled, temporarily listless, under instruction. I beaded into the source of the solitary familiar voice, stepped around a stone column, saw Maggie straight ahead. She had one palm on a pew, the other held an open play book. She scratched her head, tilted her hips, pursued ambition, wasted her time.

'All right,' Mags snapped. 'Not bad, not bad at all. One thing though, Melissa!' Stray waif picking spots in shadow.

'Please try not to giggle when the Cardinal speaks Latin.'

'I was crying!' Melissa exclaimed.

'Crying?' Maggie faltered. 'Why were you crying?'

'I was crying because that bastard ate my baby!'

'OK, two points on that.' Maggie's finger clawed pew wood. 'One, it's the Cenci, not the Cardinal, that eats your baby. And two,' deep breath. 'It hasn't actually happened yet.'

'Whoops!' Melissa giggled. 'Sorry, Mags.'

'That's all right, Mel.' She flicked pages. 'Let's skip the next, one, two, three scenes and move on to the banquet scene. Everybody, positions for the banquet scene, please!'

The actors mumbled some private grievance. I sighed understanding that it had to be something to do with my absence, shifted closer to cold stone. My initial excitement at finding the place had worn off. I started to feel a little lost. The space around me was enormous. Silent light beamed in all directions above my head. I squinted eyes at an unbelievably complex arrangement of tiles on the rippling floor. Elsewhere, wood and stone carvings were ornate and off-putting. On top of that, it was impossible to judge sound. The hollow acoustics placed spirits and ghouls even where there weren't any. Details confused my focus. Shapes of benches were nostalgic and reminiscent. Purple drapery reminded me of my lifelong least favourite colour. Fake silver and gold made me itchy. Statues of martyrs, guilty. Pictures of pilgrims, bored. Stained-glass windows, almost violent. My eyes buzzed at busy candles, righteous brickwork, impossible ceilings, mysterious nooks, invisible crannies and the vast red carpet that covered much of the floor. It all made me extremely anxious. I scrambled three hundred and fifty-nine degrees, my hand reached, my foot banged a bench.

Maggie span round, saw me, screamed.

Action on the altar halted. The spastic interchange of the banquet scene spluttered to a stop. Various actors' attention shifted from pretend mealtime to me. Their clipped gaggle, their mumbled snide, their pointed eyebrowing all registered, all annoyed. Maggie frenzied through her notes. The actors muttered, the actors turned, the actors waited to be told how to act. I tried to imagine them in the throws of an actual performance, but could only see dumb animals, dying on their backs, whining for help.

'Right!' Maggie called out. 'Act three, scene one, off the book and with energy.'

'Maggie.' Young Prince Type. 'Is that him?'

'Look!' Maggie snapped edgy. 'Just do the scene! Positions! And go!'

Nothing happened on stage, but Maggie span sharp on her squeaky heel, aimed herself at me. That rubber-soul noise matched the edge of anger and upset in her eyes. She was steaming down the aisles towards me. I knew her show of fury was as much for her cast as it was for me. But it worked on both. The actors had found their places and were struggling through the first lines of their latest attempt. Maggie sliced into my anxious world.

'You're drunk!' Gripping hand, hissing mouth. 'Admit it.'

'Well,' I squinted. 'You're an actress.'

'Hilarious,' Mags snapped. 'Anyway, where is your script?'

'I think I might've left it in the pub.'

Started to reflect vaguely on naked Debbie turning pages. Rodent barmaid frowned thoughtfully over a particularly obtuse couplet, sipped the top off a sweet cider and sprayed fizzy spit all over the Old English nonsense.

'Stop grinning,' Maggie razored.

'I think,' paused to prove it. 'I think that I have to sit down.'

'What about the rehearsal?'

'In a minute,' I wobbled. 'Just need to get my bearings.'

Wind sound sweeps angry outside. One sharp, brave gust cracked through a flaw in the holy vacuum and bounced a high-pitched shriek around the building. The supporting cast sucked up a breath, perfect in time, possessed with beautiful unison. Maybe they weren't that bad, after all. I flexed my arm, still burdened by Maggie's restraining claw. Her authoritative stare, her clenched jaw, her hold on me, all released, all at the same time.

Maggie hid her face, but I'd seen a tear.

I staggered away. Making for one side, or perhaps the other. I found it difficult to walk in churches, drunk, straight, young, old, or otherwise. I beaded in on endless rows of empty seats, a prophetic omen, wove my way towards them. When my hand touched bench wood and my knee collided with ornate carving, it could almost have been a proper Sunday from all the way back. I might've drifted into memory, but for a huge 'bang' sound from up on the altar. I snapped up to see that my oversized wife had knocked the little Jesus box off the altar, probably with one of her tits. The tabernacle had broken open, but Jesus wasn't in there. Maybe he'd found it too cramped. I let out a bad-husband laugh, lit up, sat down.

'All right, Billy, you sit there.' Mags's tone suggested I was a retarded attack dog. 'Just sit there and try to calm down. I'll just have a word with the cast, then we'll need you.'

'Billy' sat there. 'Billy' tried to calm down. 'Billy' started to tap the wood on a hand-carved curve. 'Billy's little head shook like it might drop off and go for a funny little 'Billy' roll across the floor. Think I missed calm by about one million miles. My ticks flicked full on. Midget shepherd in the far corner didn't even try to look real. The wanker on the cross was made of wood. Ceramic saints were frozen solid like victims in science fiction. The nativity was worse than a garden gnome display on a council estate. The plastic characters glowed orange, but even their grace couldn't save me. Decided I'd found a new home for the skeletons, wished I'd brought them. Checked up at the actors on the altar, wasn't sure for a second, but decided that they were real. Maggie was halfway up the steps, addressing her dumbshow.

'Everything is fine,' she chirped. 'Let's rerun that scene, it still lacks something.'

'The lead character.' Princey Boy smile, close to the wind.

'Now, Jeremy!' Maggie snapped. 'That isn't helpful. The Cenci only provides monologues. Be aware of where he is.' All attention turned to me. 'No! Be aware of where he will be on the stage, as we rehearsed, and, please, concentrate. Now, positions. And go, Brenda!'

Scuffles of mundanity broke out on the altar. Brenda, my fat wife, did her best to 'go', but her voice wobbled high with panic and echoed off into nowhere. I noticed that she was continually banging the top of the wooden altar while shouting at her various servants. She must've been wearing a ring, because bits of sacred wood were chipping off, falling to the floor. I began to laugh. Maggie leant, full frame, across my view. She was much closer than I'd realised. Her hand touched my arm, the air smelt bad, her face stretched weary.

'Get your act together,' she levelled. 'You've made it to the church and that's good. Now, let's get to work on this character of yours. See how it goes, little by little, all right?'

'I have recently become the devil.' Slurred nonsense.

'I can't believe it,' Maggie shook her head. 'You are so incredibly drunk.'

'I shouldn't be in a church at all.'

'You promised.' Eyes fierce and full.

And Maggie's blues could've done so much to me right then. The power and the fury in them. The belief and acceptance. The brilliance and stupidity of her patience. The inexhaustible tolerance taken to a ridiculous degree. Her ambitious eyes could've roped me in. They could have dusted me off and polished me up for a stab at the big time. But it'd all gone too far. I'd borrowed too much light from them already. The last three days had seen me sacrifice action for thoughts. Friends for threats. Progress for details. And it wasn't going to be in the details any more. Nobody was going to give me another three-minute reprieve from the inevitable. It was in the action, not the acting.

I smiled as it all made sense, thought I'd say goodbye in style.

'I do not feel as if I were a man!' Rising up.

'No!' Maggie grabbed, was shrugged away.

'But like a fiend.' I moved fast, kept pace with the ever-changing architecture. Aimed myself at the altar steps. 'Appointed to chastise!'

Overweight wifey leant her bulk against a delicate statue. 'THE OFFENCES!' Made it smart up the steps.

Brenda stopped leaning, started crying. I span round to see an old bugger fiddling with the white cloth that covered the sacristy. I stumbled and laughed at the easy flow of good theatre, approached the cunt. This specimen looked like he only cried alone and in bed.

'Of some unremembered world!'

Old Timer took his hands off the cloth, I turned away. Young Pretender Prince made some sort of disapproving noise in his throat. I hunched towards him. It clicked that my character wouldn't like this lad. It wasn't method, it was convenient. I stretched out of my hunch into six foot two. Spoke down on him.

'My blood is running up and down my veins.' I hissed a step forward.

He didn't take one back. Something in his face reminded me of me. There was a minuscule trace of something in his eyes. I stepped in, breathed closer, hard at his face, wanting to see it, wanting to know what we had in common. And there it was. Fear. We shared a state, but for utterly disproportionate reasons. Knew I had the chicken fucker. Stepped in, grabbed his arm, shot an unscripted aside.

'Now, you listen to me.' He pulled, I held. 'Find some community centre, go round a friend's house, sit in the back of a bar with a white-wine spritzer and wish you had more lines. You look at me like that. You talk back to me. You fuck with anybody I care about. You threaten me. You want your money back. Too late, fuckhead. You're not going to get your money back. Not tonight. Not ever.' Pulled his blurred features right into me, roared a bite that became a light kiss. 'I know you're not Charlie, but you might as well be, you might as well be anyone, or no one.' Pushed him sprawling. 'Fearful pleasure makes me prick and tingle!'

Found myself stood alone at the centre-front of the altar. The entire platform had cleared. The silent, untroubled, holy space was mine. I faced myself out at the waiting faces. My eyes went over their heads to the mighty church firing massive before me. The seat shine. The natural light. The big-space buzz. The golden cross. The peaceful organ. The huge and distant door. The entire combination of detail and meaning. My spirit, empty for so long, fed itself on the ancient reverb of worship. I breathed in for almost for ever, let it out loud.

'My heart is beating with the expectation of horrid joy!' Almost hit my knees, but didn't need the melodrama. Looked around at the empty silence, the perfect setting. The completion of my first dramatic speech made room for the start of my final prayer.

'In the name of my grandfather, my father and myself.' Brought my eyes down, down, further down. Crossed myself. Took a lungful fit for failure and acceptance of such. Stared around at my final sanctuary. Saw a woman take a seat and an old man put his hand on her shoulder. The rest imitated statues, frozen, lifeless.

'Look, I'm sorry.' Soft shrug. 'I'm sorry about your play. I'm sorry for all your wasted effort. But don't get me wrong, that's not what this is all about, that's not why I'm up here. And anyway, I'm not really that sorry. Noticeboards are bad enough as it is, you've all got lives to go to, London is not the only answer.' Caught my train of thought as it left the station. 'What I'm sorry about has to do with much more than you.'

Looked across at a cold saint, he fixed a needle, smiled at me.

'Martin, is that you?' Vision blurred, statues stirred. 'I never meant to give away all the Traffic Lights. It was a mistake, that's all. Happiness, excitement, the pump in the blood, please understand. And I pray you have the patience to build yourself another empire.'

Heard murmurs, watched an orange dog lead a blind man up the aisle.

'Mark.' Statues looked like people again, began to make sounds. 'Mark, I'm sorry for all the trouble. I know you've lost money and your eyes are on the way out. Listen, my friend, I hope you see brighter days.'

And I knew it was Amber this time.

'Good girl, that's a good girl.' Dog wagged by the blind man's side. 'Listen, Amber, I'm sorry about the ball and letting you off the lead and leaving you on the road and all that. You've always been my favourite dead legend. So, stick to open spaces and take care of Mark.'

Large figure on the outskirts, grinned at my obvious show.

'Luke!' I cheered. 'Hero Luke! Thanks for everything. How many fucking times have you pulled me out of trouble? I'm sorry it wasn't worth it. I won't be needing your help any more. I'll see you on the other side.'

'This is pathetic!' The Prince located his missing voice.

I beamed hard at the Virgin Mary, ringed by candles, made her into naked Nada.

'Nada! This is a church! Where are your fucking clothes? Go home! Go home to your mother and father. Let them dress you in expensive chains. Let them hide you for ever!'

My voice was breaking apart. My audience was restless. I pushed closer to the edge.

'Jim!' Couldn't see him. 'Where are you, Jim? I thought you'd be here!'

'Lucky Jim!' Prince shouted.

'I just wanted someone to suffer more than me.'

'Don't worry, we are.'

'Someone will help you. Not long now, it's Sunday, it's all coming to an end.'

'Well,' Young Pretender shrugged. 'You're right about that, I'm leaving.'

'Jeremy,' Maggie's voice. 'Please, don't.'

My blurring eyes skated high ornate walls to orange windows and the outside world. Knew that the scene was falling apart, that I hadn't sustained the drama, that this meant more to me than it ever could to anyone else. Saw one, then two, then my wife, turn to leave.

'Bella!' Fierce and angry. 'I won't stay in bed all day! I prefer baths! I don't drink tea! Shopping is not my greatest thrill! Your friends are not my friends! Charlie might be right about me, but he's wrong for you. And I hope we can all move on!'

'Don't worry, pal.' The Prince led a leaving party. 'We are.'

'No!' Maggie cried.

'Go on! Fuck off!' I shouted. 'I hear London's nice this time of year!'

From bone to bone to being increasingly alone.

The walls began to blur. The holy altar was becoming too small to balance on. I felt the destructive storm shake the rock outside, the spirits within. Everything inside me shifted, last remembrances came to mind. The world dipped. My head went down. My eyes closed. Speech was the only sense that worked.

'In the name of my grandfather, my father and myself.'

'Billy,' Maggie's voice. 'Please, stop.'

'Where the hell are we? How far have we come? What are we even doing here?' My questions echoed back without answers. 'Come on, where are you? Talk to me!'

Silence opened my eyes.

'Dad! Joe!' I called. 'Where the fuck are you?'

Statues might've looked like them, but weren't.

'I need you now. All those other times you were there, but not now, is that it?'

Nothing.

'Don't be dead, you bastards! Come on, that's not fair! Don't be dead!'

Nothing.

'All right, then.' Pushed forward. 'Be like that, I'll see you tonight.'

Gathered figures, real or otherwise, created a gap. The cast, if that's what they still were, had definitely thinned down. I took one step at a time, made it to the platform's edge, caught sight of an expression that could only be called pity. Tried to shrug at the old lady responsible, missed my step, got the red carpet treatment sooner than planned. Scrambled fast to my feet, focused on wooden doors, ajar in the fluctuating distance.

Talked myself towards it.

'Take me to a club and pay for me to get in. Give that girl in the cupboard my coat. Put a raffle ticket in my hand. Seal my grip with fresh stitches. Give me scissors. I'll cut myself open when it suits. I'll have my coat when I need my coat. Come on, carry me to the balcony. Leave my soft friends alone. Take me to the top of the world. Prop me up, buy me a drink, don't play any more songs for me or about me. Keep that chemistry set coming. Make the test tubes hum. Don't tell Mum where I've been.'

The door grew, it had to be closer.

'Let that girl with no clothes on get through the crowd. Ask her to come to me. Have her mop my bleeding brow. Pick up my sticks. Throw the fuckers away. Let me unravel. Shine lights in my eyes. Any colour you like. Darkness is winning. Tight T-shirts rule the world.'

The door, I'd made it to the door.

'Keep all the doors locked till Monday. Let nobody out and no more me back in. Save the room for anyone left to be saved. Let the bathrooms breathe. Pump the lungs of first-timers. And let us live alone. Leave us all alone.'

Cold air blew in, a hand reached out of nowhere to hold me.

'Leave me alone!' I screamed. 'LEAVE ME ALONE!'

I stretched towards a five-pence piece that was getting wet in the slicing rain. My body lurched, head span, arms flailed, legs failed. I took another tumble, didn't feel a thing. Went to lift myself up, but everything inside me stayed down. Only for a moment, though, then it all came up, too much, too young and far too fast. The delay between body, blood and all that beer caught me completely off guard. Harsh, fast spew exploded from deep down in my revolted system. It sprayed far and wide. It splashed upon the furthest stone of the cold church steps. I still tried to stand up, but the expulsion threw me down. I reached out a hand for someone to help me, but I'd obviously missed my chance.

Dirty fluid splattered meaning between me and nobody being there to help me. And for the first time, in no time, my eyes were wet with tears. The stench of myself rotting inside poured fluid down my face. I cupped up a free hand to try to halt the vomit flow, to try to force it back down, to try to keep what was mine, but the surfaces slipped and my hand filled with failure. Fresh spurts of nasty strong stuff blasted its way out of me. On my side, on the deck, I tried to curl away from the vomit source. My body contorted in self-revulsion. The sick kept coming thick, rising fast. I caught sight of my clothes, they were covered in blood.

The sight had me shaking hard. The familiar spastic sensation gave me the nervous strength to stand up. Ascending slowly, I locked my hands to my knees, spat fierce swear words and puke at the vicious ground. I clenched my fists, let go of my legs, stood up straight. A bus was stopped at a nearby bus stop. I tried to smile for the bent heads on the lower deck. The bus driver appeared to be waiting to see if I was a passenger or a pop star.

SUNDAY 7.00PM

The bus rolled on.

It was dark. Manchester dark. Northern cold and Manchester dark. Forever threats of heavy rain. No lights. Long tunnels. Trains speeding. Wrong tracks. No class. The last man standing would be the first to fall. Almost Christmas. The last to fall. Almost free. All the same. Tricoloured lights interchanged. Highly nostalgic. I swayed in bitter engine sound. Knees unlocked. Left foot hit a crack. Body utterly unprotected. Wanted for warmth. Right foot left the ground. Architecture twisted. Dogs chewed fresh bones. Special offers sold across busy streets. Fingers splayed for hands that were never there. Two peas for one price. Never balanced. Never likely. I hit the street. My paid-for material suffered more abuse. I rolled over. Only the sky stayed where it was, where it was meant to be.

Stars, bars, second-hand cars. Everything enjoyed a good laugh. A single diamond in the astral darkness giggled down at me. The sound took a thousand years to reach my cement bed. Faces, fluids and a fucking awful cackle sound came in all around. I didn't recognise individuals. I didn't know names. I spotted a falling bottle that did not break. Started to laugh to myself, at myself. Features in moving windows stretched wide. Stars, bars and second-hand cars were all that made sense.

'Do you fancy some chips?' Maggie's voice.

'Funny.'

'You're telling me.' She crouched. 'That speech was good, the first half, anyway.'

'Don't do this any more.'

'I'm not doing anything,' she chirped. 'The Arts Council is kindly buying the entire cast a bag of chips to stop a walkout, and I wondered if you'd like some.'

'Mushy peas are on special,' I said, sitting up. 'Two for the price of one.'

'Well,' she pouted. 'Don't tell anyone, but I think I can stretch to buying my lead actor the works. Fish, chips and two twenty-five-pence pots of mushy peas, it's definitely about time you ate something.'

'I can't do it, Mags.'

'Don't be daft,' she nudged. 'All you need is a good feed and we'll be laughing.'

'I said, I can't do it.'

'Just fish, then. You love fish.'

'Shut up, you insane bitch!' I roared. 'I mean, I can't do your fucking play!'

Tensed myself for a fierce, hot-blonde, scouse reaction. Turned my head away, waited. Turned it back, waited. Left it where it was, waited. Looking across, I saw that Maggie's face had closed its double doors. A heavy chain secured her expression.

My world began to spin once more. Brief clarity, church step chit-chat, special offers on mushy peas, all belonged to another era. Maggie stared at me with a Braille expression on her face. I wanted to reach out and read her, but my hands were too fucked. Began to wish that I really was blind when her blank eyes sank deeper into me. Needing a distraction, I squinted a cigarette from out of my crushed pack. Checked back at Maggie's face while lighting up, no change. Knew that the sour taste of her silence would ruin my fag.

'I'm sorry,' I soothed. 'I just think that it's better if I don't do the play.'

No sign, not a hint, no suggestion of a reaction, no choice but to go on.

'I don't even think I can go in that church again.'

'Is that right?' she said, so quiet.

'Yes,' I breathed. 'Yes, I think it is.'

'You're afraid of the church?'

'Yes,' I nodded. 'That's it, exactly.'

Maggie's empty eyes went right past me. I turned to see what she was looking at, planning to comment on it, whatever it was. I wanted to make a clever turn in a hazardous conversation, steer the subject away from silence and into easy speech. Felt that I could spin the jabber-jabber on any subject, but not on no subject at all, not on absolutely nothing. Maggie was staring hard directly at absolutely nothing. It might've been a small bird pecking at the edges of my vomit, but, when the sick creature flew off, Maggie's eyes didn't budge.

'You should have a go at finding someone else,' I offered.

Her blank eyes did a delicate roll and flicked to an over-loaded student service disembarking at the immediate bus stop. I followed her gaze. Her attention flicked and followed descent after descent until all the gaggles had gathered and got on their way. One fat old woman, possibly not a student, maybe a cleaner, or an exotic dancer, struggled with a hand cart in the heavy rain.

'Wonder if she'd do it,' Maggie smiled.

'Do you want me to ask her?'

'If you leave me,' Mags breathed slow and turned. 'You will become nothing.'

Her eyes bled with pure belief in the powerfully stated truth. Her words hit me hard. Her expression did the rest. My empty belly turned inside up. I felt myself sinking, dead-weighted, all the way down to the bottom of her opinion. She sneered at my battered features. She glared, motor car, into my rabbit eyes. She crinkled her perfect nose at my stinking clothes. Maggie looked at me, all of me and through me.

I felt her scornful wind blow my insides to pieces.

I stared around at the unforgiving Sunday street, dark under the ominous steeple. I took the raindropped, wind-blown, fucked-up setting all the way in. I understood the weather, the architecture and the way it had to end. And despite the pain, the hours, the years, despite everything that ever mattered to me and Maggie, Maggie and me, I knew what had to be done.

Looked hard into her eyes, killed her hope.

'I can't do it.' Made myself speak slow. 'Not now and not tomorrow. Not after fish and chips. Not with more time. Not if I'm sober, or drunk, or fucked-up. Not in the safety of my own home and not on the battered altar of some sacred church. I can't do it and I won't do it. Not now. Not ever. I know what I promised you. I remember the exact time and place of every time we've ever talked about it. But I'm not doing it, Maggie. I will never escape this city. I may not even escape this day. Ambition is irrelevant. Yours, or anybody's. London is not a place that I would ever help someone to go to. You are the last person that I ever wanted to let down, which is good, because you are the last person I will ever let down.'

'Why the last?'

'I'm meeting Charlie tonight.'

'So?'

'So.' Hilarious. 'You're not actually the last person I'll be letting down, sorry.'

'What?'

'I haven't got his money.'

Maggie exhaled for as long as I thought possible. I felt the last cord trembling to be cut. Her face hid itself away for a moment, then double-backed, dramatically darker. Her eyes hurled a frenzy of stillness at me. They contorted as if searching for words. She knew there were no more maybes. I'd made it as clear as someone like me ever could, or would. Realised I was matching her heavyweight stare, but without good reason, so I looked away. Maggie hurled herself at me, blazing, raging, right into me.

'YOU SOFT! DRUNKEN! USELESS! FUCKER!'

'Fair.'

'You haven't got the money! You useless fucking waste of time!' Her sitting-down swings were easy to see, easy to take. 'You're fucking right I'll find someone else!' Maggie hit me hard, my hands went up. 'I'll find someone who doesn't have a list of excuses for every possible occasion! I'll find someone who isn't scared of his own fucking shadow! And even more terrified of everything else!' Hard plastic edge of her orange cracker ring. 'Go on, let the whole world down. It's you that it'll fall on. You know you've destroyed this play. You know it won't happen, now. And all you can talk about is Charlie and the fucking money. You think you're living in a movie! Well, it's a shit movie and there's no one left who hasn't seen it. Go on!' She pushed me over, I staggered to my feet. 'Go on! Hurry up, Billy! You don't want to be late for your next disaster. The disaster you've made up just so you can leave your last disaster behind.'

'I'm not making this up!'

'Who cares?' she blasted. 'Who cares whether it's true or not? What do you want me to do? Rob a pub? Take up a collection? Start a fucking Billy Brady charity shop? Write a letter to the Arts Council outlining your predicament?' Her tone dropped, she turned away. 'Go on, Billy. Get lost. Fuck off. Take the last train to Blackpool for all I care. And don't send me a postcard, I've got enough crap to remember you by.'

'You don't fucking get it, do you?' Step and grab. 'This is not one of your plays.'

'You total cunt!' She spat in my face.

I said nothing, set off walking. Sped up when she started shouting abuse in the rain. Her high-pitched screams were lost to the interference of the elements. Whatever she said would've had the same effect on me even if I'd heard it. None. None at all. I didn't care. It was only details, and I had no time for meaning any more. The drama had been stuck in the mundanity of making sense for far too long; it was well past time for some simple and entertaining action to kick in. I stepped into the road without bothering to look. A tyre squealed. Angry horns blasted. A man yelled obscenities and an out-of-work actress screamed the whole world down.

It was music to my ears.

SUNDAY 7.49PM

Felt in my pocket, felt nothing. Tried another pocket, felt
something. Swung open the high-pitched door of a brand-
new phone booth with a twenty-pence piece in my hand.
Knew what had to be done. Didn't need to know a single
thing more.

Pressed my head against the horizontal Etch-a-Sketch of
red and blue figures dancing. Tried to recall the six digits that
might lead to death. The number. Charlie's number. I'd used
it before. Times of withdrawn pain. Times when he was the
easiest dealer to reach. Times made harder to remember by the
need involved. But, despite the details, drug numbers tended
to stick. I sank down to the bottom of my busy self in search
of the six digits. Sucked my finger, made red shapes on the
clear pane. Bloody numbers formed, combined, changed and
slowly made sense. My hand departed the artwork and went
for the phone.

Dialling tone, six touches.

'Yep.'

'Charlie?'

'Who wants to know?'

'Billy.'

And there was silence. Anyone who still had breath left
took a deep one. I tap-tapped my head against the window,
spat on the red and blue ballerinas, waited for Charlie's reply.
Thick red gob slid down the mass-produced commercial art;

it was my considered opinion. I lit up, wanted to smile, but hatred, fear and exhaustion all got in the way. I exhaled away from the receiver. The tense quality of silence made the wait stretch longer.

'What do you want, Brady?' Charlie eventually growled.

'It's Sunday night.'

'So?' he snapped.

'We should get together.'

'And why would we want to do that?'

'To finish this,' I levelled.

'Right.' Heard him smile. 'So, you have it?'

'Always have.'

'Why don't I believe you?' he snarled.

'Problems in your childhood.'

'What the fuck?'

'Look, Charlie.' Keep it simple. 'I have your money. Are you coming or not?'

'Coming where?'

'I'll be walking towards town on the left side of Oxford Road.'

'You'd better be, Brady.'

And the phone went dead. It had suffered a major stroke on the Moss Side end. The receiver's last breath buzzed and farted at me. Another partially used twenty pence clicked into Telecom's bent coffers. Some pre-recorded hairdresser told me to replace the receiver. I fought my natural instinct for vandalism, carefully placed the black plastic back on its metal shelf. The time had come to conserve my energy. I abandoned another public place for the privacy of one more walk to town.

Wind and rain blew in and out of the cracks on my face. Dark shapes of night-time intercut with synthetic lights. Some moving, some changing, some plain and just stationary. I started to cross from the right to the left side of Oxford

Road. My eyes travelled up the thin slip of a street lamp straight ahead. I paused on the relative safety of Oxford Road's dividing line. Cars flashed by on either side while I sure-footed on the untouchable white. My life rested in the hands of the Highway Code. My hope shone in the burning orange bulb of a road-service-orientated sculpture.

Shining orange light, raindrops in my eyes and a cigarette I'd been sucking on for a while, all had me thinking about what I was doing. Advertising my position, waiting for my tormentor to open a car door and switch off my lights. A reasonable panic began to speed through my head, looking for a way out. I forced my eyes from the well-loved street light and looked back over my shoulder at the shrunken steeple. Didn't see anything worthwhile, but thought about tracking back, all the same. Thought about throwing myself on middle-class mercy, falling asleep in ever-safe churches, having chips for my tea. It all began to sound convincing. I even took a step in the backward direction. But a double-decker, of course, came close to saving Charlie the trouble and wiping me out. As the enormous road monster growled by, my orange light was obscured and my hopes lost focus. By the time the bus had passed, the optimistic spell had broken and my last-minute delusions were left shattered. I quick checked the oncoming traffic and legged it through their dull white lights, their meaningless noise. I stepped up the pavement's edge and found myself, finally, on the left side of Oxford Road.

Fuck it.

One way or another the money was gone. I had to face it. Didn't feel so bad when I accepted it. No doubt I'd had my fun. I'd made my drunk lion's share of mistakes, but I wasn't anywhere near to being ashamed. Sorry, maybe. Ashamed, no chance. Taking a fresh breath, I skipped a few detailed thought traps and decided that I really should be heading for the slaughterhouse unhindered by worldly possessions. It struck me that I should take the high path and face up to Charlie without money, without trying, without even an attempt at playing my part. I knew exactly what had to be done. Hunched myself down in the cold pizza air. Started to empty the property of my pockets on to a dry patch of the ancient road.

Tissue paper, used, thrown. Coppers and silvers, carefully piled. Two fivers, folded under the weight of one penny. Powder, final rub, finally done. Crumbled tablet and half an orange capsule, combined and taken. Keys, kept keys. Battered Strawberry tab, licked and sucked back. Three phone numbers, forgotten. Cigarettes, half a pack, placed next to the money. Box of matches, chucked. Cheap plastic lighter, beside the cigarettes.

I leant low and scanned my vast collection of nowt. About thirteen quid, total. Cigarettes and a lighter. Apart from that, nothing else required much thought. Pulled the cigarettes out one at a time, propped them up against the nearby wall. Left three inside the foil for emergencies. Turned my attention to the money. I couldn't throw it away, that'd be too easy. Checked my surroundings for the possibility of expense. Didn't fancy a pizza, couldn't afford a holiday. Looked around for charity cases, but it was the wrong part of town, no one local was in need. Forced to palm the money, I took a last look at the line of ciggies, a painful farewell. Separation anxiety made me spark one of my remaining three. I inhaled and sighed goodbye.

Moved myself up the road.

The money in my hand was interfering with my late-in-the-day quest for purity. A deep blast on my fag clicked an old saying from somewhere. There are no nights that don't last all night, and no solution except drink. That was it. It was all I'd wanted all along. I spotted the green light shine from this shithole plastic Paddy pub, straight ahead. Did a little space-and-time equation in my head. Concluded that Charlie would just about be finding first, at least fifteen minutes away. Realised I had nothing if I didn't have the time for one last drink. Sped up, ducked myself inside the random watering hole.

The place was well packed. Sunday-night quiz leaguers, cider swillers, bottled anarchy, bad lighting, obvious music, uniform fashion, loads of shit chit-chat and no sense of violence. Simply put, students were everywhere. I pushed through an immediate crowd, caught a high-pitched grumble, didn't deviate, didn't need distractions. I made a space at the bar, caught sight of myself in the mirror.

My face was well lamped. Nose had been bleeding again. Caked crap around my swollen snout and cracked mouth. The hole in my cheek was scarred and ugly. Eyes were as red as they'd ever been blue, or yellow. Thick wipes of dried muck went down both cheeks. My neck was an embarrassment. The wobbles were winning. Crazed expression bounced and bounced right back. Hair was somehow wrong. Clothes, a state. Had to make the best of a bad do, so I flicked up my collar and smiled.

Shakin' Stevens, back in town.

'What'll it be, lad.' Old Irish fella tippled across.

'You'll serve me?'

'C'mon, lad,' he gruffed. 'What do you want?'

'Fucking hell,' I laughed. 'This place is worse than I thought.'

'Less lip,' he snapped. 'I don't need it. Now, what do you want?'

'To get the first punch.'

'We'll have no trouble in here!' Old soldier, steamed as his specs.

'Right you are,' I smoothed. 'How about a take-out of Jameson's?'

'No problem,' he swayed. 'We've got the litre for twenty-five quid, or there's the miniatures at four pound a pop.'

'You've been around students too long, pal.'

'What was that?' he twitched.

'Let's have three pops, Grandad,' I winked.

'Give me a minute,' he slurred, stepping off.

I'd give you everything I had, Grandad. I'd give you it all. Almost nipped back outside to gather up my streetside altar and hand over the goodies. Couldn't be bothered, felt sentimental, looked fucked, stayed put. Let my loose-fisted bits of money rest on the nearest beer towel. Covered it with my three-ringed hand long enough to feel the last tug of attachment. Stubbed out the first of my three cigarettes, breathed slow, careful and calm. Saw the old fella paining his way back towards me. Whispered another 'goodbye' and lifted my hand.

'Keep the change,' I nodded.

Pushed past the same people on the way out as on the way in. Saw a wrong expression, heard an unnecessary mumble. Shouldered the stupid extra out of my way. What the hell was I supposed to do? How could any of these people ever hope to reach me? When had any of them ever really mattered? Even a Spanish-type girl with long hair and a red-wine smile meant fuck all to me. The world was running out of people to love. People to lie to. People to believe in, or grieve for. What the hell had happened to all the artful chit-chatters, the graceful butchers, the girls that ruled the worlds? Where were the intelligent forgetful, the responsible dealers, the skilled betrayers, the stylish believers? What was this world coming to? A severe shortage of chemicals in student quarters was the only explanation I could come up with. But then, what did I care? Fuck them! Fuck them all! I pushed past the same people on the way out as on the way in.

And that was all.

Back on the street, bottle top twisted, head back and glug-glug-suck. I dropped the first empty to the floor. It

355

didn't break, I stamped, it broke. Walked my way towards the town I'd never reach. Somehow felt myself returning to the legwork of all my longest walks home. My breathing became balanced. The hum in my head, flat and familiar. The cause was obvious and easy to follow. And, even though my grandad and my dad were dead and gone, I knew where I'd come from, knew what I'd come for, could guess what I was coming to. My head began to fly, free and nostalgic, through vague thoughts of the last walk home.

It kept me going for a while.

Bored and in danger of becoming self-absorbed, I switched my mind back to the mundane. I conjured a vision of the parking space where Charlie kept his flash car. My movie worked the route with him. I argued turns, criticised bad driving, stabbed the fucker in the neck when he wasn't looking. Parts of me got lost and parts of me just stayed where they were. It all felt magnificently final. It was clear and true, completely without detail. And, though nothing ever truly ends, I realised that it was possible to turn the volume down, at least once in a while.

It was possible, sooner or later, to fall asleep.

Forever cars chugged past me on the right. I was waiting for that particular engine sound that meant slowing down. Laughed to myself, the speed these Sundays were going at, it'd be almost impossible to tell the difference. Kept my ears tuned, all the same. Felt for the keys in my pocket, jingle-jangle, was glad that I'd kept them. Absently conjured all the locks that had ever been made. The multi-makers, the frame workers, the myriad shapes in a million doors. Doors that opened and, even better, doors that closed. And, finally, ultimately, I imagined the lock on the door of the last way out. Jingle-jangle, I moved towards it.

And, of course, I knew that escape was always an option. I knew the films. I understood the function of stations. I carried a local's passport to a million cups of tea. I could borrow bedspreads, inhabit spare rooms. Temporary breasts and fridge access had always been a speciality of mine. Knew, full well, that I could cover the country in streets where I would be safe. I could make it to Scotland by closing time, Leeds for last orders, London for daybreak, Fleetwood by the fucking sea, Dublin by Christmas, New York by Christ. I could outrun Charlie with both legs sawn to stumps and nothing more than a bus ticket in my hand.

But where was the fun in that?

I'd learnt my lesson from the book of Trevor, and I wasn't about to leave this town without a fight. It'd never really mattered where, or how numerous, the ways out were. I wasn't interested. I always ended back in, anyway. And this outcome had long since been decided by my own actions. Fallen friends, three sleepless days and a family-size supply of drugs had put me where I was and I wasn't about to question or complain.

It was much too late and there wasn't far to go.

I popped the top on my second of the three miniature whiskys, put off smoking my penultimate cigarette and kept moving past the inevitable lights. Knowing, full well, that I was being tracked with every step.

SUNDAY 8.08PM

Heard the pure bass first.

Then the horn section blasted in. Some high-pitched, obnoxious diva sentiment repeated and repeated itself. Whatever you'd call it, you'd call it loud. Sensed well-oiled, soft-compressed foreign brakes being carefully applied. Lit my second-to-last cigarette. Heard a car door click open. Didn't need to look.

'Oi, Brady!' came the shout.

Turned to see an empty seat on the inside. Took a quick look at what was left of the outside. Beautiful, wet and orange, all around. I whispered goodbye and bent my head into Charlie's car. A woman I'd never heard before screamed about something I never wanted to hear again. I slammed the door, didn't even hear it close.

'DO YOU WANT TO TURN THAT DOWN?' I yelled.

His mouth moved, pointless. I gestured at the stereo, wided my eyes and shrugged, all at once. Charlie leant forward and flicked the tape out. Hardcore Moss Side dub reggae radio came in even louder. I slammed my hands over my ears. Was about to start screaming, but Charlie flicked a switch and it all went quiet. Thought I might recommend a Bonnie Tyler purchase, but Charlie had other things on his mind.

'No smoking in the car,' he snarled.

'You smoke.'

'Not in the car.'

'Look,' I reached. 'I'll open the window.'

'Just put the fucking cigarette out!'

'All right,' I breathed. 'Where's the ashtray?'

'Not in the car.'

'Brilliant.' Flicked my fresh-sparked ciggy out the window.

Control-freak tendencies satisfied, Charlie shifted the car into low gear. He snapped the handbrake free and cut out in front of a bus. I pretended to yawn, turned slightly to see the side of my chauffeur's face. There was a heavy swelling all around his left eye. Was going to ask how he got it, stopped myself just in time. Last night's mugging considered, I had to be fairly grateful that he hadn't done me in already. A kick in the head was no laughing matter. Still, I had to suppress the giggles. Almost wished the music was still on, so I could have a good howl. Felt a warm, giddy glow inhabit me. Recalled all the recent drugs and booze I'd just quaffed. Couldn't hold it, had a laugh.

'What's so funny?' Charlie growled.

'You've got a black eye.'

'And you look worse than anyone I've ever seen.'

'Fair point.' I smiled, reaching for a ciggy. 'Do you need directions?'

'Directions?'

'To Castlefield NCP.'

'Where?' he snapped.

'The multi-storey down by the canal.'

'Why?'

'If you want your money we have to go to Castlefield NCP. That's it, it's that simple.' Flicked my lighter, inhaled. 'Your money is there.'

'NO FUCKING SMOKING!'

'Shit! Sorry! I completely forgot!' Went to flick the filter outside. 'Fuck!' It was the last of my lucky three. Had to tap the burning cherry off on the window edge. Sparks flew all over me. 'Bastard!' Dabbed the hot tip against my tongue. 'Jesus Christ!' Burnt my lip. Needed a drink, knew where to get one. 'Brilliant!' Whipped out the last miniature, cracked it open, had a good pull. 'Fuck, I needed that!' Leant back and laughed.

'Shit!' Charlie stared across. 'You ain't pretending. You really are messed up.'

'All I need is a bath,' I shrugged.

'A brain transplant, more like it.'

'Funny.' I swilled the bottle, deadpan. 'Brain transplant, that's hilarious.'

'What did Bella ever see in you?' Charlie sneered.

'It's red,' I muttered at the fast-approaching traffic light.

'It'll change,' Charlie accelerated. 'You'll see.'

'To orange, to green, to orange and red again.'

'There!' The light changed. 'I fucking told you!'

'Charlie,' I levelled.

'What?'

'One, grow up. Two, don't mention Bella again.'

I had the miniature palmed, empty, ready. Charlie shifted in his seat, glanced across at me, smiled. He made this cool sucking noise between his teeth, changed gear, swung hard left. I didn't need to look to know we were close.

'So,' Charlie cut across. 'Why is the money in a car park?'

'I put it there so as not to spend it.'

'Sounds like you,' he laughed.

'And you would know.'

'Where did you hide it?' he razored.

'Glove compartment, red Cortina, level three.'

'Whose car is it?'

'My dog's.'

'Your what?'

'It's my friend's car,' I told him. 'We both have a set of keys.'

'Where's he?'

'For fuck's sake, Charlie!' Q & A gone nuts. 'He's out at Alderley Edge for the weekend. He's taken his family for a picnic. Come to think of it, he asked if you were free.'

'Shut it!' Charlie snapped. 'Why didn't he take the car?'

Struck me that people didn't get any better at it with practice. The more questions they asked, the stupider they got. Of course, I understood that Charlie was trying to check me out, but what did he expect? Did he think that my story would crack under the pressure of relentless monotony? His pursuit of details only served to show him up for the misguided idiot he was.

'Well?' he insisted.

'Well, what?' I sighed.

'Why didn't he take the car?'

'He's lost his licence.'

'What for?'

'Charlie!' I finally snapped. 'Are you going to keep this quiz-show shit up much longer? 'Cos if you are, it'd be easier for me to print up a leaflet and circulate it around town.'

'Fuck you, Brady!' With another smart tooth-suck.

'Could you teach me to do that?' I asked.

'Shut up!' He banged the wheel. 'You just better not be messing me about.'

'When have I ever messed you about, Charlie?' I smiled.

'Just shut up!'

'You should trust me, mate.'

'SHUT UP! NOW!'

Car almost crashed into a bus idling along ahead of us. A tense silence came in thick between us. Shame, I was just beginning to enjoy myself. Just getting to grips with asking my own set of stupid questions. Maybe there was something in it, after all.

Settled for gazing out the window instead. Lost myself in

the distortion of raindrops. We were pulling away from the pretend civilisation of the centre. Closed shops were giving way to closed-down shops. We sped past the arches of the railway bridge, the occasional flash of the canal, anonymous pubs I'd never been in, never wanted to be in. The road hissed wet. Smart heater worked even with the window down. Charlie took a sharp turn down a dark alley. I sat up in my seat. The journey was almost over.

And, despite all my fancy talk of details, meaning and truth, I had no idea what I was doing. Didn't have a clue why I'd picked the NCP when Charlie'd asked where to go. Wasn't even sure why I was bringing all this trouble down on Trevor. Knew it had something to do with tradition, but probably more to do with cement. Its cold familiarity would be a comfort, plus the mess would be easy to clean. Perhaps I wanted Trevor to see that I wasn't going to run, like he had. That I was going to stand my ground, on our ground. That I'd take a bullet before I'd take a train. Perhaps.

We pulled up to the last set of lights. I focused on them, ferocious. I bled into the red. Loved the slow orange. Didn't have time to see the green. Tyres squealed and we hit the entry ramp of the car park at high speed. Engine roar echoed around the entrance. I enjoyed the symmetrical balance of the structure, loved the arrows that pointed the way. For a brief moment, the atmosphere reminded me of a church.

Knew I'd picked the right place.

'Level three?'

I didn't answer, just flinched a nod.

We turned harsh corners. Other cars bounced at angles in my ever-changing perspective. Snaps of exterior orange made the dark inside look darker. I took in the interior, the low roof, triangle ramps, the absence of watchmen, the mad bouncing noise. I sat, smiling, ascending, nodding, winking, my brain quietly exploding. The car sped through a vacant stillness, Charlie turned the final corner.

'Is that it?' he asked.

I tried to suck through my teeth, couldn't do it.

'I'll park opposite,' he said, swinging to face the Cortina, killing the engine.

'Perfect.' My mind went blank.

'Are you going to get it?'

I ignored him, clipped the door, swung it open, stepped out. Quickly crossed the gap between the two cars. From behind me, I heard Charlie's electric window wind down, didn't look back. I stepped sharp along the Cortina's driver side. Trevor was hunkered down, asleep behind the wheel. I had to wake him up, but how? Needed to come up with some subtle waking-up sound. Fuck it, I banged hard on the window.

'Is there a problem?' Charlie leant out.

'Fuck off,' I muttered, the window-tap had worked, Trev was awake.

'What did you say?' Charlie's door clicked.

'I said stay in your car, everything is fine.'

'You better not mess this up, Brady.'

'Already have,' I muttered.

'What was that?'

'Look,' I pointed. 'My friend is asleep in the car, I don't know what he's doing here. If you'd just be patient and show a little style for once, I will get you your money.'

Trev's questioning eyes beamed up at me through the window. I quick clipped my cold hand under his door handle. Yanked open the door.

'What's going on?' Trev blurted out.

'Fuck,' I stepped back. 'You take a shit in your car?'

'I get bad gas when I'm nodding.'

'No kidding.'

'What's going on?' Trev yawned. 'Do you want to go somewhere?'

'Nowhere left to go,' I shrugged.

'Is this going to take long?' Charlie shouted across.

Questions coming from all sides. The good, the bad and the well smelly. Pointless questions deserved questionable answers, so on and on it went. I checked round to see Charlie stepping out of his car. Clocked his arm reaching back beneath the dashboard. No time to think, time to act. Trev was spluttering out of a smackhead's sleep. He wiped tattooed fingers across his wrinkled face.

'It's time for you to move house,' I told Trev.

'What this all about?' he frowned.

Trev's voice was starting to show traces of fear. I could tell that my battered appearance was tripping him out somewhat. My focus flashed back to Charlie. He was moving up, out and determined. The dangerous-looking fucker rose to his fighting height. He leant back, slammed his driver's door shut. The hard metal contact echoed off the walls, chiselled a sharp point to the extreme of my attention. I could see that Charlie had something in his hand, hidden behind his back.

'That's Charlie!' Trev's hands grabbed me.

'Easy, Trev.'

'That's Charlie fucking Charles!' Trev spazed.

'Calm down,' I hissed.

'What the fuck is happening?' Trev almost pulled me through the window.

'Shut up and let go of me!'

'What the fuck have you done, Billy?'

'Let go of me!' I cried, Charlie was closing.

'This is bad!' Trev raved.

'For fuck sake! Shut up and let me go!' Finally snapped my arm free.

In full control of my limbs, I reached down and bent

my head inside the Cortina. Forced the ever-ready ignition keys to rotate. Trev's leg auto-extended, pump-pumped the gas. The cracked old engine roared loyal and loud. Revs peaked panic-high. Trev's hand hit the handbrake. His wild eyes hit me.

'Get in!' he cried. 'Just get in, and we'll get out of here!'

'Alderley Edge?' I smiled.

'Fuck Alderley Edge!' Trev blasted. 'Just get in the car!'

'One dream world comforts another,' I said stepping away.

'There must be somewhere you want to go!' Trev cried.

He was probably right, I took a moment.

The end of a pier. The sick liquid. The edge of hard rain. The end of powder. The high point in a club spark. The broken bones and pointless dust. The inside of Maggie's shoulder. The waste, the waste of it all. The plastic clip on the first plastic bag of Traffic Lights. The fear, the intimidation, the hate. The empty seats of a smoking InterCity. The motor stuck in permanent reverse. The land where lights changed every mile. The edible sewage. The cigarette machine. The open-heart buggery. The space between the face and the fist. The empty platform. The top of the bottle. The freak accident in the portable toilet. The edge of the bath. The no-win situation. The snooker hall. The strong breeze blowing terror through pebble-dashed houses. The last place worth saving. The only exit left. The piled-high table. The fallen street light. The hot sink. The traffic island. The lips of Magenta Pearl. The lock. The frozen ocean. The funfair camel ride. The bus station, no, not the bus station, the peanut carousel.

Too many to choose, chose death.

'Trev,' I levelled. 'Go now.'

'All right,' he flat-toned, understanding. 'See ya, Billy.'

'Take care, Trevor.'

I did a kiddy-wave and smiled, Trev shook his head. Halfway through the away swing his eyes stuck absolutely still, they fixed dead ahead. His thin brows went berserk. Trev's fist hit the stick. The Cortina roared in reverse and swung a perfect arc into great open space. A squeal and a shift saw the battered red Cortina bombing from the car park at incredible speed.

I turned to see for myself what Trevor had seen.

Fuck.

Forty feet away, Charlie stood bolt solid, his arm thrust out.

And at the end of his arm was his hand. And in his hand was a gun. He was a difficult distance away, but it appeared that the weapon was pointed directly at my face.

My brain damaged.

'I want my money, Brady!'

The silence after he spoke passed in between and all around us. It spilled out the exit ramp and down, down, down into the Sunday-night streets. The whole city grew quiet in my cinematic mind. If it'd been allowed to last, it might never have ended.

Do something, I screamed at myself.

'I said,' Charlie bellowed across, 'I want my money right now!'

I took a step towards my tormentor with a friendly face. His loud loop echoed big in the cement world. I took another step. Saw that the corners of Charlie's angry mouth turned down at the edges. Took a step. My speechless approach was clearly working wonders on Charlie's enjoyment of the situation. Step. He didn't seem to believe my silent advance. Step. His gun hand tremored ever so slightly. Step. I sympathised with his condition. Step. Poor fella looked unsure. Step. And stupid. Three quick steps.

'You better have the money!' he snarled.

'I didn't know you had a gun.' From twenty feet away.

'You must be the only one.'

'Must I?' And step.

'Yes, you fucking must!'

'Well, to be honest.' Step. 'I did know, I was just winding you up.' Another step.

'Shut up!' he blasted. 'And stay where you are!'

'Where am I?' I laughed, spinning three-sixty, wasting a step.

'SHUT UP! SHUT UP!' Charlie was cracking.

'Would you like me to put my hands up?'

'Yes, you clever cunt!' he fizzed. 'Put your hands where I can see them.'

'There you go.' Lofted my palms, ten feet and closing.

I finally pulled to a stop within a three-stride range. Checked Charlie from close up. His eyes fidgeted. His arm still tremored. His hand gripped tight. His gun was real. Vaguely wondered if the bullet would pass right through me, or would I be able to stop it where I stood? Decided that my face wouldn't do the job, pushed up on my toes, lined up my chest with the small black hole. Taking the bullet felt like some final challenge. It was action, not detail.

It was something tangible to think about.

'Nice of you to shut up, for once,' Charlie edged. 'Bet you think I won't do it.'

'I've no money to bet with, Charlie.' Small step.

'What did you say?' His face convulsed with rage.

'Maybe you could lend me some, then we could have a bet.'

'You're a fucking idiot, Brady!'

I was one step away when I started laughing. I clenched my fists and laughed mad out loud. My head went back. My eyes dug escape hatches in the cement ceiling. Cackle sound bounced loud all around. I laughed longest, loudest and last. Caught sight of Charlie raising the gun above his head. Didn't let it spoil my fun.

WHACK! FUCK! FLOOR!

Grabbed a hand to the top of my head. Nasty goo had spilt red on my fast-checked fingers. Pushed up on an elbow. Fell back on my face. Felt the old seaside sensation. Brain buzz-buzz-buzzed. Eyes rolled. Head shake. Better. Elbow thrust. Blood spit. Checked up.

GUN!GUN!GUN!

'You stupid little cunt,' Charlie snarled. 'Where's my five hundred quid?'

GUN!GUN!GUN!

'You couldn't even find five hundred quid to save your life!'

GUN!GUN!GUN!

'I hope your habit's worth dying for!'

GUN!CLICHÉ!GUN!

'I wish Bella could see you now.'

BELLA!CLICHÉ!GUN!GUN!

'You disgusting fucking excuse for life! It's time you paid!'

CLICHÉ!CLICHÉ!GUN!

'And this is where you pay!'

CLICHÉ! CLICHÉ!

'With your life!'

CLICHÉ! CLICK!

Click was the safety coming off. Fucking clichés and that unnecessary mention of Bella had changed my mind. Absolute terror and the imminent prospect of being shot in the head definitely played their part, but Charlie had sparked my survival instinct with his complete lack of style. My life was not going to be wiped out by a quiz-show product. Charlie had ruined the real drama with television lines. His mundanity made him unworthy. This was not the tormentor I'd imagined.

This was a fucking stupid southerner with a satellite dish and a little boy's toy in his wobbly hand.

I switched to automatic and whipped my legs round. My steel-capped boot broke his shin bone. Charlie's left leg collapsed. He came down fast, almost on top of me. Felt hard metal against my shoulder. Twisted round.

GUN!GUN!GUN!

There was a pause. Our minds stalled. Our eyes met. I could see that Charlie was shocked and unsure. But I had the answer.

'Get the first punch in.'

My fisted rings pummel-punched the soft front of Charlie's face. Warrior screams echoed and merged. Sensed him struggling to free his hand, but too fucking late, mate. My face was close enough for love. I rammed my forehead through the bridge of Charlie's nose. Blood sprayed. His head lolled back. The front of his face had changed shape. I slapped the firearm out and away, butted the fucker in the head a second, third, fourth time. Charlie didn't react to the last impact. He was out cold. It made no difference. I got above him and dragged his unconscious weight by the shoulder of his expensive jacket. A smudge of blood painted the cement red. I gripped tight, mumbled madness, kept pulling.

Vaguely surprised to see that Charlie's car had a metal bumper, not moulded plastic. Cheap crap dressed up flash. Figures, I thought, focusing on the sharp steel edge. Check, check, check. Nobody nowhere. I screamed a wild-animal sound, imagined the devil's dogs baying back. I grunted pure grandad and lifted Charlie by his head. I held his life in my hands for a moment. It was heavy. Knew I couldn't hold him for long.

Do something, I screamed at myself.

Slammed Charlie's head against the bumper's edge. Slammed Charlie's head against the bumper's edge. Missed the bumper's edge. Dinted the bonnet. Adjusted the angle while looking at a blood splash that had covered a 'stop' sign ten feet away. Too late. I slammed Charlie's useless fucking head against the sharp metal edge of his own parked car.

Charlie was utterly fucked.

His head was sliced and battered to bits. He had no face. His body was still. Blood spill had taken him away. The top of his head had almost come off. I looked at where his eye had once been, but Charlie wasn't there any more. The poor bastard was dinted, broke up, well done. He looked a lot like my dead dog. Almost wanted to pat his head.

Didn't.

Memories of my dog, my grandad and the devil trickled through the bits and pieces of Charlie's skull. I closed my eyes. The three distant forces came together, trinity strong. I breathed down deepest, exhaled to myself. Felt the mad heat within begin to melt the man about. Slowly drew myself, line by line, back to the surface world. I sniffed in the silence. The faint pitch of past chaos rang numbers in my ears. I didn't look down, afraid I might fall.

Somewhere to my south, movement blurred through a glassless gap. Rapidly returning senses tuned my heart strings tight. The door slams, the backchat, the battle-cries and all the related sounds were bound to bring the old boys torching. It seemed safe for the moment, but self-defence had definitely gone too far and I wanted away.

I wanted to be outside, stay outside.

Something said 'security cameras' soft inside my head. I checked the corners of the closest combinations, saw none, sighed. I turned away from the obvious exits, headed down two internal levels, crossed to the hidden canal side. Fresh air swung in through the absence of concrete. I rested my hands on the pebble-dash parapet, looked down. One level, twenty feet, it looked possible. I didn't look back. I lifted up on the first-level ledge and jumped. Hit the ground hard, but with good form. Slipped, fell, fell well, got to my feet. I wiped a grass stain from my blood-caked trousers and departed the scene without so much as a funny line or another thought.

Looped round the back of the car park at a safe distance and moving fast. I slowed to cross a narrow cobbled yard. Popped over an eye-height wall and slid down the bank bordering the canal. The cool flow of water would take me all the way home. Looked down at my boots in the light of a tourist distraction from across the way. Thick blood was red and guilty all over my soles. Heel-slid both boots off, kicked them into the middle of the water. They splashed and sank. I turned and walked barefoot along the deserted path.

The night was a peaceful night. The cold wind was as honest as anything left in the city. It was Sunday, late now. Late for Sunday, anyway. Passed underneath the first of five bridges. Felt no tremor, no shakes, little else. Like fugitive tunnels ploughed through the peakless mountains of Manchester, the canal bridges hid my progress. I walked on over dirt tramped down years before.

The second bridge became the third. I passed slow and sure beneath them both. The next bridge came along soon enough. My naked feet found the ground softer and simpler each time they touched. The scaled-down fourth bridge passed impassively away. A sharp gust of wind was the strongest thing I felt.

The last bridge wasn't too far. I passed under it just as the four before. Just as I'd passed under bridges all my life. My name echoed off the underside of the brickwork. It came back to me sounding soft and peaceful. I was finally ready to rest.

In time, I reached the gate that led to one major road and my front door. I stopped for a moment and leant against a railing that just happened to be there.

No one came to me. No thoughts occurred only to be overtaken by no more thoughts. The view wasn't worth the word. I pushed off and turned towards the building's steps, less than a hundred of mine away. Some light tension flirted, was worked out with motion. I crossed the road, nothing happened. I watched a big orange bus turn the far corner, heading away. A traffic light flicked to red. I didn't stop. I went up the steps, through the doors.

The flat front door unlocked and opened. Silence passed out. I passed it going in. Knew I wasn't alone, knew I soon would be. Went into Maggie's room. Woke Jim up. Untied the ties one at a time. Told him to go. I imagine he went.

I leant into the dark bathroom, locked the door and turned on the light. I reached over the bath and turned on the taps. The water sound came in common with what I'd expected. I undressed. Saw the mirror. It was working, but somewhere else. I waited, patiently, for the water to rise, then slipped, one foot, two feet, into the bath and sat down.

And the dreams erupted, exhaustion won. The dog was gone and the ancestors loved their son. And so on and for ever on and on. The silver before me looked like two taps. I leant away from all the pictures. I watched my body submerge. I closed my eyes. And as the neutral light shone, I felt all my tightness fall apart. The walls between me and the world came down. And on the very edge of my final fall, I realised that Charlie had deserved what he'd got about as much as Amber had. Not that much, really. But they'd both ended up the same, killed by a car they didn't see, dead, at my feet.

This is a dangerous world for dogs and men.